I0741416

# THE ART PLANET CHRONICLES

## The Making of the Fifth Ring

by José Argüelles

The Art Planet Chronicles: The Making of the Fifth Ring
ISBN 978-0-9862005-0-2

Written in 1981 by José Argüelles • Published in 2014
Copyright © Law of Time Press • www.lawoftime.org


Cover Design by Jacob Wyatt from original artwork by José Argüelles

FOR HEIDI

*Whose secret knowing
transcends the speed of light*

# CONTENT LOG

# PART III: THE ENCHANTED TRIANGLE



# PART IV: TO DISCIPLINE THE DEVIL'S COUNTRY

# PROLOGUE: FROM THE ANNALS
# OF THE ARCTURIAN ARCHIVES

Once upon a space-time vector, so it has been told, far beyond the fair Arcturian skies, in the distant galactic cloud, called by the wise, Velatropa, there was a stellar unit, Velatropa 24, which produced a planet, Velatropa 24.3. Now renown for its brilliant system of rings, trans-galactic travelers often ask: "how did Velatropa 24.3 get its rings?"

Naturally, as the keepers of the chromo-cellular archives of Arcturus 108x, having long-pioneered in extra-galactic communication, such queries are almost always directed toward our radiant orb. In the interest of putting to rest such well intentioned curiosity concerning Velatropa 24.3, we, the aging though not yet totally senile Archivists of the Arcturian Annals have compiled a definitive answer in the form of a story or, more precisely an interplanetary fable.

Culled from a larger record, THE ART PLANET CHRONICLES, our story, THE MAKING OF THE FIFTH RING, like any gem or fine stone, must have a proper setting in order to be fully appreciated. For this reason, we must first set forth our own tale, telling in as simple a manner as possible how it was that we of the Arcturian chromo-cellular brigades first discovered and established contact with our sister sphere, the harmonic-hued and distant, Velatropa 24.3.

As is well-known, and in accord with the Arcturian Articles of Unification, we of Arcturus 108x, have, by tradition as old as the Speaking Rocks of O-Mo-Lung-Ring, taken it upon ourselves by the Vows of Universal Liberation, to establish direct communication with intelligence, not only beyond our own stellar unit, but beyond the confines of the Arcturian Galaxy itself.

Well, it was during one of the earliest of the extra-galactic expeditions, the first one to utilize synchrotronic communication beams, that we penetrated the milky galactic cloud, the wondrous Velatropa. That celebrated expedition had been led by none other than AhKa IV. Intrepid cosmic voyeur, commandante extraordinaire, seer, knower and weaver of the beginnings and endings of time and space itself—yes, it was the, nimble-witted space clown, AhKa IV who first narrowed the synchrotronic radiation beam on Velatropa 24.3.

> *"How blue and fair this globe;*
> *how breathful fine she be;*
> *if only she possessed the mind*
> *to know Arcturian camaraderie"*

Such was the first communication received from AhKa IV following his preliminary orbiting of Velatropa 24.3.

In his wisdom, AhKa IV knew not to intervene, at least not directly. "Honor the intelligence." Guided by this slogan which comprises the pith-essence of the oath taken by all Arcturian Extra-Galactic Scouting Parties, AhKa IV checked his enthusiasm for this precious cosmic pearl, Velatropa 24.3. Though we were careful not to intervene immediately or directly, we also knew from prior experience that the entire universe resonates and is submissive to the law of mutual reciprocity. Thus, even though the mind of Velatropa 24.3 had no direct knowledge that it was now under surveillance by a chromo-cellular intelligence unit from Arcturus 108x, in what it later came to call its "unconscious," it knew—"we are not alone."

But back to AhKa IV. So enraptured had he become by what he encountered on the blue-green pearl, Velatropa 24.3, so akin did he feel to its polar energy tides, and so urgently did he wish it to become a galactic twin with Arcturus 108x, that he began to scheme and develop the following plan.

First of all, he requested of Hierarch Central an opinion on the feasibility of sacrificing himself and transmuting as a native Velatropa 24.3 life-form. While Hierarch Central went about the arduous task of correlating information fed back to it in the luminous corridors of Arcturus 108x, AhKa diligently continued his own reconnaissance, optimistic that a decision would be made favorable to his plan.

In brief, what AhKa IV himself observed about Velatropa 24.3 was this:

Oscillating delicately between two snowy magnetic poles was a fine, multi-leveled atmospheric sheathe. Diffusing itself out from the two poles in the manner of a constantly rotating electromagnetic ring, it was the richly pulsing foundation of this atmospheric sheathe that most attracted the highly sensitized light spores of the old galactic explorer. Swirling, gauzy blue, white, and green spirals of pulsating energy forms completely intoxicated AhKa IV' s cosmically weathered sense-spores. Love, that's what AhKa IV felt for the teeming network of activity that formed the immediate surface of Velatropa 24.3; love—seasoned and spiced with a high risk dash of compassionate curiosity.

Though the texture of the planetary surface was a dense and profuse soup of countless symbiotically interwoven life-forms, the advanced sense-spores of AhKa IV picked out one genre in particular upon which to focus all of his keen-witted attention. These were the two-legged ones—the spirit-chasers, the seekers of enchantment, the dancers and the builders. Dispersing themselves from pole to pole throughout the capriciously changing land masses of the delicately pulsing planet, these highly mobile life-forms had created a fine invisible membrane completely enclosing Velatropa 24.3.

Skimming through rain-forests and over grassy plains in his rapidly vibrating space-cocoon, AhKa IV observed that whereas the majority of these two-leggeds found nourishment while roaming in simple patterns close to the ground, a few small groups, no more than half a dozen, cultivated the soil and erected in stone what the others only dreamed of in their dances. The former group AhKa IV called "the dancers," the latter, "the builders."

Though things had developed somewhat differently on Arcturus 108x, AhKa IV recognized that the over-all pattern on Velatropa 24.3 represented a much earlier horizon of intelligence than that now current on his home planet. Nevertheless, it was this fact alone which most instilled in the old galactic warrior a nostalgic yearning tempered by a sense of worrisome caution.

But finally, what most magnetized the curiosity of AhKa IV was this: no matter how simply they lived, no matter how monumental their aspirations in stone, the two-legged Velatropans endeavored to accomplish everything with a sense of proportion, maintaining a harmonic relationship between themselves and their temperamentally precipitous environment. It was this magnificent tendency, proof no less of a genuine intelligence, that moved the primal adventurer, AhKa IV to such rapturous heights of incantatory contemplation:

> *"In Velatropa far away*
> *though devoid of mind's full sway*
> *in measured form with rhythmic heart*
> *all that's done is done as art!"*

For this reason AhKa IV dubbed Velatropa 24.3 "the Art Planet," while naming its two-legged pioneers of intelligence, "artiers." It was Velatropa 24.3's prophesy to art that gave AhKa IV the ultimate incentive to abandon his highly evolved spore-frame and assume a much lower level of incarnation. In the mind of AhKa IV, it was this artistic Velatropan tendency that augured at some distant point down the evolutionary road the appearance of that full bloomed mind that would take total delight in the galactic sports so treasured by the likes of planets such as Arcturus 108x. Naturally such luminous presentiments only filled AhKa IV with the greatest maternal anxiety—oh, how he wanted to intervene and speed up the process!

"No! No! Not so fast!'" came the reply from Hierarch Central. "The Gyroscopic wobble on that sphere's too touchy. You'd be committing suicide. Don't do it—at least not yet!"

Hierarch Central's Voice jolted AhKa IV out of his extra-terrestrial reverie. Setting his perky little frame on total alert, blinking his lavender ocular lids in rapid succession, AhKa IV set his determination at a pitch of octave registration 9.9. Such resolve shook the very coils of the Arcturian Central receiving station. Immediately, reconsiderations began:

"After all, AhKa IV has pulled off a number of other transmutations which we felt to be totally out of order..."

"Yes, there was, for instance, that terrible time in the magnetic drift just outside of Arcturus 108x, when AhKa IV engendered the anti-negatron wave-bank..."

"Hmmm. And, too, there was the dreadful encounter with the Slogdian force-field. As much as it aged AhKa IV, he did manage to tame it..."

So went the murmur of voices at Hierarch Central and as the train of thought recounted the various triumphs of the old Chromo-cellular veteran, the station's receiving coils slowly ceased their trembling. Then, as if he were sliding down the central coil itself, so sudden and close did his voice sound, AhKa IV spelled out his plan.

"Oh, all right," he began, "I understand your concern. That gyroscopic wobble you've picked up is evident in the atmosphere of this place: unpredictable, moody, volcanic even. Weather bimbos running wild. But listen. Things are moving along here, though with a schizoid twist. So when I put down, I'm going to split up and head for two different places. That's right, two... One will go to the large Southern Island. Extremely stable pattern there. Probably because it's so isolated, but so much the better. For certain, the two-leggeds there are dancers. The other one I'm directing toward a river valley running through desert land, due north from the equatorial band. Cultivators and star-gazers they are, and even though they're builders, they're obviously going to be more unstable than the Southern Island dancers. The river valley one, that's going to be my mover; as the pattern shifts he'll become a shape-shifter himself. But don't worry. I'll be discrete. The point in my taking two incarnations simultaneously is this: the Southern Island Dancer will keep me stable, close to the ground… and simple. The other one will have me hopping. This way I won't lose touch. As the schizoid pattern develops… I may go schizzie with it… but believe me, I won't lose touch."

AhKa IV paused triumphantly. Indeed, he seemed to have sized this situation up with his customary daring. Candace Helicia, Commander of Extra-Galactic Monitors, took her turn to respond. "Beloved chromo-cellular voyager, AhKa IV, you of venerable lineage and wisdom, your words are received with single hearted care! The sacrifice you propose is awesome. To incarnate on a strange planet with no precise knowledge of how many thousands of years you may have to endure before equivalent enlightenment is established is one thing. But to do what you have proposed, to split yourself up into a double incarnation at two widely separate points on an alien planet, that transgresses the bounds of Arcturian Outrage! AhKa, you are an utter fool! A cosmic dolt! An extra galactic idiot! Come to your senses!'"

Though Candace Helicia sputtered on, AhKa IV remained unmoved. Or rather, determination to carry out his plan was not in the least affected. Sensing this, Candace Helicia changed her tone. "Oh, AhKa," her light-and-honey voice conceded, "You're the one out in the field. You call the shots. Do what you must. But may I be correct in assuming that for our purposes the Southern Island incarnation will be our grounding monitor on Velatropa 24.3?"

Candace Helicia waited for a reply, but none came. "AhKa…," she called out once, twice, then a third time, "AhKa…;" but the only sound she received in return was the grainy whoosh' of light-years of unmediated silence.

Then, just as she was about to dampen the control coil with the familiar amber fluid, a coarse burst of laughter crackled through the ruby crystal receiving coil, sending a lightning arc right up to Candace Helicia's flabbergasted spore-fronts. "…Wandjina Poontutjarpa riding the rainbow serpent to the Ubi-Ubi mountain cave of dreaming! We are here; we are both here. Poontutjarpa in the Southern Island; Rennutet, the sky-walking serpent in the Black Land of the Upper Nile…We are both here…"

As she dampened the receiving coil, Candace Helicia chuckled to herself, "Well, AhKa as you sing the stanzas of Velatropa's rhythmic blend, may we continue to learn of them as well?"

For well over six thousand Velatropa 24.3 years we monitored the heroic AhKa IV's double manifestations. That of the Great Southern Island remained as AhKa himself had predicted: stable to the point of boredom, yet because of that, an excellent transmitter. From this one we learned of such strange things as kangaroos and boomerangs, kundelas and kadaitja's. In one incarnation after another, AhKa, now known as Poontutjarpa, proved himself to be an obedient keeper of tribal lore and initiatory secrets.

The instrument AhKa used for contacting us was the Tjuringa stone, a tactile maze-like device for placing its users in a trance, transporting them to what they called the dreamtime. We all appreciated AhKa's wisdom in choosing these highly conservative two-leggeds of the Great Southern Island for maintaining communication with us at Arcturian Hierarch Central. Nevertheless, it was not at all apparent to us how, after so many thousands of years in this simple, but desolate and highly isolated outpost, he was going to reunite himself with what he had come to call his "civilized double."

Ah! That civilized double! Rennutet the Egyptian, as he was first known, proved to be as sly and clever as Poontutjarpa was tenaciously steadfast in the "old ways". Incarnating for close to two thousand years in the Black Land of the Nile, AhKa's other half learned well the craft and wisdom of the builders. Then, exemplifying the mysterious lore of death and rebirth which constituted the deepest wisdom of these Builders of the Black Land, the old Galactic Scout jumped track.

We next picked up transmissions from a certain Ennu-Gil of Babylonia, an organizer of weaving guilds, scribe and tax collector. Allowing himself to be slain in battle some twelve incarnations later, the extra-galactic gnome was next heard from as a Master of Ceremonies in the Imperial Court of the Great Central Land called China. Anahuac, Tihuantisuyu, Magadha and Macedonia—anywhere on Velatropa 24.3 where the builders established their guilds came to be home for the ocean-skimming, continent hopping AhKa IV!

Indeed, as the years wore on, AhKa IV's facility in attaining transmutation after transmutation on Velatropa 24.3 ("Earth" as he had become fond of calling it) almost came to be his undoing. It was after he had pressed himself into the service of a certain king of Central Asia that the Keepers of the Arcturian Archives ceased to personally supervise the activities of both of AhKa IV's Velatropan manifestations. The reasoning behind this decision was simple: AhKa IV clearly must have known what he was up to. Such marvelous ability had he realized, even by his own admission, that the Arcturians of 108x placed his monitoring on synthomatic remote. Besides, other of the Arcturian chromo-cellular brigades, emboldened by the example of AhKa IV, now needed more attention than the foolhardy AhKa now deserved…or demanded.

It was none other than Candace Helicia herself who idly sauntered into the Synthomatic Monitoring Unit one day, some four hundred years later, only to discover the rupture in communications that had occurred between Velatropa 24.3 and Arcturus 108x. "AhKa the blessed, the primal galactic wonder, warrior of star-fields most remote—GONE! All systems registering sub-vital, "AhKa IV, gone!"

Candace Helicia's broadcast aroused the Energy Banks of the first eight quadrants of Arcturus 108x' Red City into a condition of high alert. Following a swiftly organized council meeting of unit heads, a major squadron was dispatched immediately to Velatropa 24.3. Never before had the ejection of so many space cocoons on a single synchrotronic transmission beam been so reverentially attended, for great and far had the fame of AhKa IV spread throughout the bright expanse of the Arcturian galaxy.

Though a significant number of years had passed since Ahka IV himself had first commanded a small squad to survey Velatropa 24.3, the change in the atmosphere, nevertheless, took us all by surprise. Ahka's initial reports of a polar ice-capped "art planet" possessed of capriciously changing, yet ultimately harmonic weather patterns, no longer held true. What we beheld instead was something far more grim.

Obscuring what once had been verdant meadows, starkly tranquil desert terrain, ice mountain crags and seemingly infinite seas rolling from shore to distant shore was an atmospheric warp, a displacement of the spheric rings fueled by burnt-off carbon monoxide, radioactivity and other noxious particles. The cause of this disturbing, anti-biotropic displacement we found to be in the dense network of combusturies that darkened the Velatropan landscape, particularly of its Northern hemisphere.

Worse than this bio-chemical plague, however, was the intensely random electromagnetic bombardment, the cacophony of sounds and attempted communications that assaulted our brigade. This activity seemed to be most intense at the fourth, or outermost atmospheric ring of Velatropa 24.3. Though we deigned from time to time to lower our frequency of vibration and hence risk becoming visible to the odiously noisome Velatropans, we found that such exercises made us vulnerable to high flying military observations in the form of "spy planes" and "satellites." We also learned that our existence, whenever it was perceived, was almost unanimously interpreted as a threat to the planetary system. "Flying Saucers" and "UFOs—Unidentified Flying Objects" were the most common and childishly derogatory terms applied to our mission.

Despite such hostile reception, while brushing aside the ghastly thought that AhKa IV had erred in describing Velatropa 24 as an "art planet," we avoided as much as possible any direct contact with the Velatropans. Single minded in our purpose, we did manage to establish contact with AhKa IV, at least one half of him. This was the manifestation that had been recently dislocated from his ancient Southern Island abode. He was now a "case-worker" in an alcoholic treatment center in one of the large urban centers of that land, Sydney.

"Can't say much now," the inveterate Poontutjarpa/AhKa warned us," things have gotten very tight around here. But hang in there. As soon as I've emerged from this damnable war-zone, I know I'll get in touch with my double. Until then, you should go into hyper-tranquility. Don't worry though: when the old AhKa meets the old AhKa—won't that be the day? This old earth, Velatropa 24.3, according to you Arcturian straight-liners, this old earth will see its roundness ringed with chromo-cellular light…"

Setting our fleet in high vibration hyper-tranque, we followed the orders of the venerable Commandante. The war-zone to which he had alluded broke out with unrestrained vigor not too long after. As much as some of us felt like intervening, we held back, though great pity and sorrow shook us to see Velatropa 24.3 enveloped in such a cataclysmic fever: volcanic eruptions, radioactive clouds, columns of fire rising from the center of the sea, and the massive electromagnetic storms breaking from on high. Monitoring all of this activity over a period of some 25 Velatropan years, it was with great relief that we observed the subsidence of the tumult. All the while we wondered at the heroic endurance of AhKa IV to have undertaken the taming of such a turbulent planet.

Even so, it was another hundred years of spotty contact with AhKa IV before it became evident to us that his original, optimistic perception of Velatropa 24.3 as an "art planet" might be valid after all. Finally, from a site called Angkor, the Poontutjarpa manifestation of AhKa IV signaled us to be on intervention stand-by.

It is here that our interplanetary fable, THE MAKING OF THE FIFTH RING be best left to unfold on its own. Fortunately, we have a series of taped transmissions which tell that story better than we ever could. So now listen to this tale, recounting in fine form how Velatropa 24.3 got its rings.

"Beamed by lovers on that blue and gleaming orb, too many star-meters distant to be measured, we, the ancient ones of the Arcturian Archives, followers of the galactic warrior-lord, AhKa IV, have only preceded, allowing others far more poignant and keen of their own hearts to tell the bold and daring acts trident-sprung from listless war to spring to art that eerie, twinkled sphere, three orbits out from Velatropa 24. Called by them "Earth," its human passage had gyred four rings, yet lacked a fifth; and lacking such, lacked all unity, stellar visibility and galactic accountability."

And so this tale unfolds by two hearts interwoven…

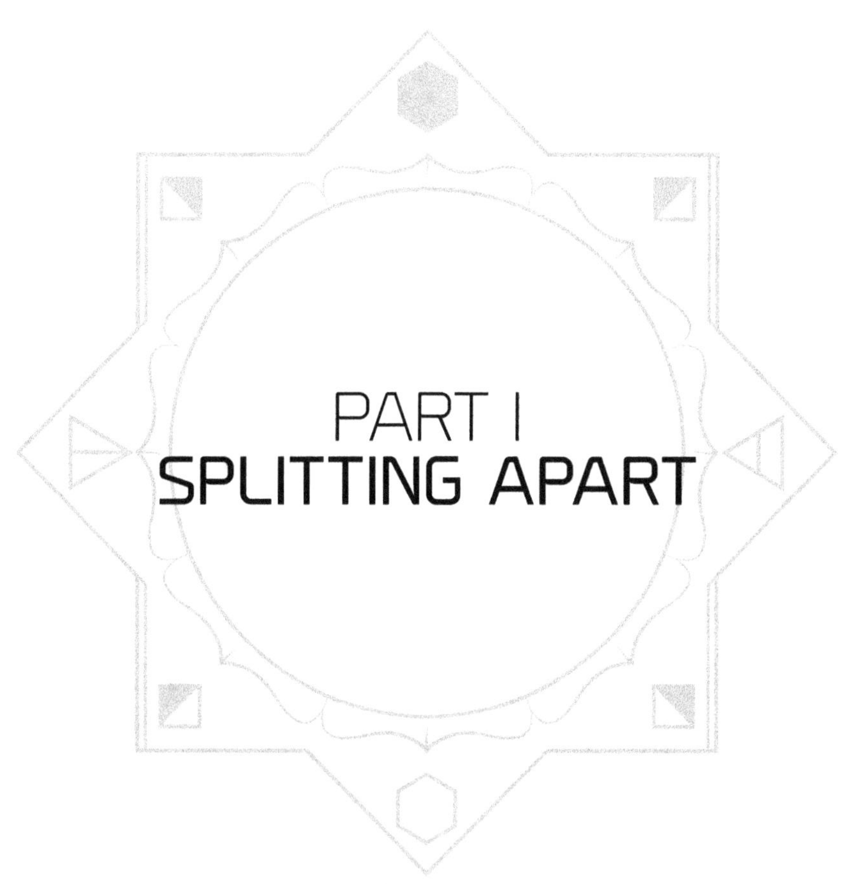
PART I
SPLITTING APART

# PROSPERO'S TAPE LOG:
# THE EL DORADO STATION

### Entry Number 24.36, El Dorado Monitoring Station, Rocky Mountain Sector 240 AH

For some time now I've been alone in this monitoring station. I guess the Caribbean War has escalated to a major degree. Our network has been jammed for three months now. The last report I got was from the Tikal Mission in Guatemala. They were monitoring bulletins from the Egyptian Mission, headed by Abdul-Rumi Hassan and Chandrasekhar Das. From that last report I was able to place three more coordinates on the radiosonic beam that operates from El Dorado Mountain just south of here. The harmonics still aren't complete, though the broadcast has been helpful in keeping some sense of order up here.

Three times a week I make that broadcast. The initial electromagnetic screen-ray oscillates for just over an hour. But that's enough time for the biopsychic receptors to receive a charge that stimulates the harmonic network of the neural infrastructure for at least 48 hours.

Gruber, the old man who runs the Eco-squad supply station in El Dorado came up last week and told me that the Gulf Coast had been swept by heavy laser bombardments. That means that all three coasts have now been ravaged by laser attacks. Refugees have been trickling into Denver for at least two months. If this turns out to be anything like the Atlantic Siege, then we can expect another half year of black-outs. I don't know how long I'll be able to hold out here. I'm not even sure right now where I would go if I did get out of here.

Whatever the case may be, the Caribbean War marks the end of a ten-year lull. That was a good period. Ten years ago, that was 230 AH. I was 27, just a few years out of training which I did at the Angkor Wat terminal. Though the effects of the Atlantic Siege were still being cleaned up, things in the Pacific-Asian Sector were calm. Not that anyone was fooled by that calm. That's how the polar rhythm has worked for the last one hundred years. First it's the Eastern Hemisphere, then the West, then the Southern Hemisphere, followed by blow-outs in the North. The Syndicate manages it pretty well that way. A simultaneous polar blow-out would put them out of business too.

But back to Angkor Wat Terminal. Those were great days. My mother, who had been a field-worker in the East Pacific Psycho-Aesthetic Service Corps was able to use her influence to get me registered in Angkor, despite the fact that it was totally out of her sector. I was just fifteen when she first accompanied me there. The ancient landing strip awaited us, a sooty white band waiting to be devoured by lush jungle. The refurbished golden towers of Angkor gleamed in the distance. A smoky violet haze stretched in a thin bank across the horizon—effects of the thermochemical anti-mutation experiments conducted there for almost a century.

My mother, Tara Andromeda Jones, must have been about 40 at the time. I was at just the age to appreciate that she was a stunningly beautiful woman, and that she was probably more woman than she was mother. African-styled hair framed her flat-boned face with an aura of luxuriant dark curls highlighted by brief streaks of red. She ceased being mother and became Woman when she greeted my first tutor, Poontutjarpa Jayavarman. Coming off the landing craft, she stopped dead in her tracks. Her face became calm, then profoundly pensive. A slight tic pulled at her face just beneath her full sensuous peach-blossom colored lips. I knew that tic. It happened to her whenever anything important was about to occur. I felt her energy narrowing down to a thin, highly concentrated beam. Following that beam from her eyes I saw that it led directly to the eyes of Poontutjarpa Jayavarman. I remember thinking to myself, very clearly, precisely: "This Jayavarman and my mother, they have a pure connection. This can only be good for me."

Poontutjarpa Jayavarman was older than my mother, though it was hard to tell how much older. Maybe he was 45 then. He never really did tell me his age. Too sly. His head was topped by a full head of bushy, curly hair, much of it now steel gray. His face was quite dark, glistening in the tropic sun. His typically Australian nostrils radiated a massive sensitivity. They seemed to quiver and flare to an extraordinarily subtle rhythm. His clean-shaven face rested like a reassuring weight atop a brilliantly colored but etherically textured gold tunic. His whole appearance was nothing less than dazzling. "Gold," Poontutjarpa later told me, "the map of history is inscribed by the search for gold. Puny little grains sparkling in a stream—why should people kill each other for that? No, that's not it. Our nature itself is gold. When neurosis happens, the inner gold becomes invisible, and we greedily search for it outside. But it is true: our nature is pure gold!"

For my mother, my education in Angkor Wat was the instrument of her destiny. Poontutjarpa was the man, the romance she had been waiting for. During the days, as my chief tutor, Poontutjarpa regaled me with the key points of Global Psychodynamics, from the beginnings of the Holocene era to Hiroshima. Once I understood these points, we would go on to a study of the intricate relations between the Planet Art Network and the Syndicate for Material Evolution from their inception some 100 years after Hiroshima to the present.

But I saw just as much of Poontutjarpa in the evenings as during the day. My mother had but a six-month leave in Angkor, and upon meeting this golden descendant of Australia, she was going to savor every moment of her stay.

I don't know why I'm putting all of this personal material down. Perhaps because of the total uncertainty with which I'm faced. Though I must add that reading some of the previous reports from this Monitoring Station have encouraged me to wax on in such a personal vein. There is something totally heartening in those earlier reports.

I mean, take this excerpt from Tape log Entry Number 17.17 from the El Dorado Station. It's dated 144 AH and reads… "Completed 96th coordinate of Radiosonic Beam, correlation of architectural structure of the Sun Temple of Konarak and Bach 'Partita for Violin Number 5.' Filled the valley with tremendous light. Nadja stayed up with me all night during first transmission. Lying on the deck overlooking the streambed we made love. Our rhythms perfectly synchronized with the Beam. After orgasm we lay silently in each other's arms; the harmonic tremors did not subside for several hours. As the sunlight replaced the oscillating light of the Beam, Nadja looked at me, weeping. 'Now I can go,' she said. At noon we arrived at the Rocky Flats departure strip. Picked up by an x-12 type hovercraft, she was gone. This evening the valley is still tender with the effects of last night's beam. A deer even came into the Station. I cannot go to sleep, so I'll let the new moon entertain me, the new moon and thoughts which I can't articulate. Is it passion or the lack of it that mocks us?"

That was one of my predecessors at this Station. Miguel Chrysostemo von Meier-Becker. He was number seventeen to take charge of this station. And I'm number 24. We've all gazed at the same moon rising above the canyon, steeped in our solitude. They never leave either, the other agents. Oh, physically of course, they're all gone, just as I'll be gone. But their thoughts, their feelings, their moods--they cling to the air. They seep into your dreams. They don't let you go. And to this continuum, I add myself: Prospero Edmund Jones, planet citizen and Aesthetic Monitor, rank three. Child of hazard, I was born 37 years ago in Mozambique. At the age of three, my father, Nkwame Lao-Tsu Jones, a Network technician, was killed in a Syndic ambush during the Zimbabwe Reconstruction. My mother's grief was matched only by her determination to persevere. Through her diplomatic skills she was transferred to the East Pacific Sector, and I completed my childhood at Shasta Abbey, on the east slope of that magnificent peak.

My mother was in charge of Geomantic Surveillance, and traveled often. Sometimes I accompanied her. Once to Macchu Picchu and Tihuanaco, and again to Teotihuacan. I'll never forget the dismal sight of Mexico City: miles of shattered concrete and lava formations, swamps and a giant ring of tumbledown shacks and Relief Stations. But Teotihuacan was thriving. It had been some two hundred years since the great Mexico City disaster and the vapors arising from the site were still thick with foreboding and pain. In Teotihuacan they had an expression describing what had once been Mexico City: Mictlan Nahui Ollin, Cemetery of the Fifth Sun. For the Teotihuacanos, Mictlan Nahui Ollin symbolized everything that had gone wrong with the Age of the Machine. It was a lesson.

I was ten when we stayed in Teotihuacan. We had simple but beautiful quarters in the Palacio Octavio Paz, a kilometer or so north of the Pyramid of the Sun. It was there that I was introduced to the notion of the Kingdom. Our hostess was Sherab Gyatso Sanchez. Her high-cheekboned face was a perfect blend of Mexican and Tibetan features. Dressed in flowing turquoise caftans she would speak animatedly with my mother about the progress of the Campaign of the Kingdom. Against my mother's hesitant protestations, Sherab insisted that it was perfectly proper that I should start learning about the Kingdom. What I heard at that time intrigued me. More than that it corresponded to something I had felt in my heart ever since I could remember: a feeling of truth, of home, of real home; that there was such a place as a real home that others knew of and could share with each other, even if it did not yet fully exist on the planet.

From listening to those conversations I pieced together the fact that the Planet Art Network was but the visible work-front of an intelligence that did not presume to assert itself openly in the world. This secret intelligence operation, the Kingdom, I further deduced, was the central organizing force coordinating all activities aimed at the final overthrow of the Syndicate.

Though my mother spoke to me little about it for the next five years, I now knew that she was deeply involved in the Kingdom. Between my studies and my play, I gave much thought to it. It was an obsession.

The next important link-up came in my association with Poontutjarpa Jayavarman. It was the inevitable outcome of the study of Global Psychodynamics and the subsequent history of the Syndicate for Materialist Evolution and the Planet Art Network.

One hot afternoon seated at the side of a pool in the Angkor Learning Complex, I popped that question to Poontutjarpa point blank: "What can you tell me about the Kingdom?" The question did not seem to affect my mentor in the least. He was lying on his back, floating, motionless like a water-bug.

"First, you tell me what you know about it," was his languid reply.

I didn't know where to begin. Nervously I brushed a fly away from my face. "It doesn't make sense any other way. The purpose of PAN is to restore, maintain and enhance harmony, which the Syndicate also claims to do. But why then is there such antagonism? Because we claim the primacy of the biopsychic energy field, is that it? That's just a piece of logic. I mean, it may be effective, and we may have the means to make it operable, but still, from my understanding of the dialectic, there's still a synthesis or something beyond those arguments. Even if we win the rest of the world over with our techniques, where does that leave us? What will happen next?

PAN is just the technical arm of a more purposive intelligence, isn't it? And that purposive intelligence, that's the Kingdom, right? It's not power we're seeking, is it? If it were, how would we be any different from the Syndicate?" I felt my questions come out in a barrage.

But my anxiety had no effect on Poontutjarpa. He lay there with his eyes closed, a slight smile on his face. Irritated by his silence, I jumped into the pool, landing almost on top of him. Before I knew it, he catapulted over me, and though he now sat by the side of the pool, I felt a force pushing me, keeping me under the water. It was his Ki. Just as my lungs were about to burst, the force let up. Without the resistance, the momentum of my energy thrust me up from the water. Like a jelly-fish, my limbs going every which way, I found myself clutching to the pool-side drain trough. Coughing and spluttering, I shouted at him: "You miserable aboriginal son-of-a-bitch, you're using your powers like a coward!" Needless to say, Poontutjarpa had a good laugh.

That evening, two days before my mother's departure, Poontutjarpa arrived at the customary hour. Dinner passed in unusual quiet. Spiced beef-strips and curried rice with vegetables. It was especially tasty. Despite the quiet, the air was charged. I felt an excitement all over me, and soon I began chattering away. As I talked about my studies and progress at the game of Go, I suddenly experienced another conversation occurring simultaneously within me. Immediately I understood that it was Poontutjarpa's Ki energy from the afternoon that was transforming itself in my hara. My lower abdomen felt warm and solid. I heard a voice within, quite distinctly, even as my own voice continued babbling away. I flashed on the mind-tracking practice and despite the disassociation, I maintained my control.

"…And insofar as the ability to join Heaven and Earth has always existed, the Kingdom, too, has always existed. Long before the Great Disorder began, the Kingdom had become secret and was hidden from all. It had become the Invisible Kingdom. In scattered parts of the Globe, its memory was cherished by a few. But the effects of psychosensory elaboration forced even the memory of it to be regarded as a childish dream. It was only after the Great Global Awakening at the beginning of the present era, that the necessity of the Kingdom emerged as a means of salvaging that planet from nuclear waste, chemical pollution, and social degradation. The Kingdom is to be found only by those who are pure of heart. To purge body, mind and heart of the stains of psuedo-sophisticated psychosensory habit patterns, this is why it is important to practice mind-tracking, this is how to arrive at a purified heart…"

At this point, my ability to keep control broke off. Everything stopped.

My mother looked at me tenderly. "Prospero, Prospero," she called me softly, sweetly. Her face was radiant. Its deep ochre hues seemed like silk illumined from behind. Her coffee brown eyes flashed with knowing. She took my hand. "It's all right. We know what's happening."

"You do?" I looked at her with astonishment. I wondered if they were playing a trick on me.

"Hey, hey! The boy's been seized by the Primordium!" Poontutjarpa jumped from his seat and started doing a little dance.

> *"When Dante was in Purgatory,*
> *and Blake, he sang in Hell,*
> *Amitabha shone with Joy,*
> *Knowing for both that all was well!"*

Singing this little song, Poontutjarpa took me by my hands and began dancing with me, until I too was singing with him. Afterwards, Poontutjarpa said to me: "So you see, boy, your questions about the Kingdom will be answered as it becomes necessary. No need to do mental wandering. It'll all come to you, boy. It'll all come to you.

---

Two days later, my mother left. It was a very sad parting, for all of us, even Poontutjarpa, in whose trust I was now placed. I did not realize it would be ten years before

I saw her again. I had never seen her so happy as while she was with Poontutjarpa. All the usual things about me that irritated her simply didn't happen during that time.

Later, she was to tell me that what had happened between her and Poontutjarpa was as complete a love as she had ever known. "Everyone should find that kind of love at least once in their life. Do you know why? Because everyone should experience what it's like to break the physical sound barrier through making love."

She spoke like this when I had returned to Mt. Shasta. I could tell that she obviously knew I was no virgin. Rain was falling softly and we sat on the covered verandah. To the east of us the valley floor rose imperceptibly into pine covered hills. Through the drizzle you could make out the three luminous radar dishes gyrating slowly, each at a different rhythm, yet all in synch.

My mother continued in her warmly philosophical way. "But it takes time, and you never know who it will be or when it will happen. That's why it's so important to approach everyone and everything wholeheartedly. Because you never know when it will happen. And, I hope I'm not boring you, Prospero, but allow yourself lots of relationships. There's nothing worse than an erotic miser!"

I spent two years with my mother before receiving the orders to take on the El Dorado Monitoring Station. Most of that time she was on leave from her geomantic surveillance duties. It was a good period for her. In addition to a number of retreats, she practiced brush painting in the manner of Sesshuand Mu Ch'i. For myself, I was busy in the Advanced Synaesthesia Lab, putting to the test much that I had learned from another of my tutors at Angkor Wat, Nagarjuna Holmes.

Regarded as one of PAN's top adepts in the practice of synaesthetic radiation, it was Holmes who initiated me into the subtle art of linking biopsychic and electromagnetic energy in order to project a three-dimensional field-vision. Here again, the mind-tracking which Poontutjarpa was so keen on my developing proved to be of immense use. One stray thought form, and the whole projection could backfire either causing severe pain in the projector, or transmit a distorted image, resulting in harmful psychic after-effects on the receiver. Of course, it was this kind of training that was so essential in order for me to take on the El Dorado Station.

This training also had its benefits. For all the arduous hours put into the Advance Synaesthesia Lab, there were the peak moments of ecstasy and insight. "You must dismiss dwelling on these experiences," my supervisor, Wolfgang Shlovski repeatedly admonished me. His words went to the heart of one of PAN's most basic principles: "transmute energy only for others; power for oneself is power abused."

Nevertheless, those two years were nothing short of euphoric for me. "Prospero, with that kind of energy, you should find a proper outlet. Aren't there any women at the Lab? I mean of course, women to your taste?" My mother would raise her head above the rice paper, holding the brush firmly in her right hand. Around the house she wore a simple black tunic with butterfly-wing sleeves. I must say she was little short of stunning. She loved mocking me, yet she did it so gently. Ripples of resentment on my part, quickly gave way to the realization that she was actually sharing with me her experience and wisdom of the world.

"Where will I ever find anyone to equal you?" I would return the banter. "You won't!" she would snap back, touching her tongue to her upper lip, looking ridiculously seductive and charming. It took everything I had in me to keep from taking her seriously. If she saw me hesitating, after such a response on her part, she would stop what she was doing and look me in the eyes. It was wonderful, that look of hers. It said everything, and I would remember who we were and what we were all about. Hugging each other, we would laugh until nothing really mattered anymore.

One evening towards the end of my work at the Lab, I arrived home only to be greeted by a small party. I had never seen any of the people before, three men and a woman. They were a troupe of musicians. The spokesman was a gaunt, highly energetic fellow. Almost bald on the top of his head, what hair he did have still managed to hang down to his shoulders. There was something wild about him, wild and generous.

"So this is Prospero," he said coming toward me, "I've always wanted to meet one of these Synaesthesia Lab Rads. Radiate for me!" Chuckling madly, more to himself than to anyone else, he took my hand and shook it until it was ready to fall off.

This wild man was none other than Diamond Wave Ionelli, one of the leading practitioners of the music known as Global Riff. My mother had told me about him, and I had heard some of the performances of his group, 'Wandering Diamond,' on tape. It wasn't too long, however, before my attention focused itself on the woman of the group, Francesca Della Francesca. While Diamond Wave and I were exchanging greetings she had been standing several feet way, her head cocked to the left, eying me with an impish grin. Her eyes were green like the Pacific on a cloudless day. You could almost see sunken coral reefs in their depths. Honey blond hair came down past her shoulders. She wore large circular silver earrings inlaid with turquoise, and her dress was a simple white tunic belted with a narrow gold chain. She stood barefoot. The next thing I noticed about her was her nose. It had obviously been broken once; its highlight was a marked thrust to the right in the middle of the bridge. That gave her otherwise innocent, oval, rosy-cheeked face a real touch of class. I fell in love with her immediately.

"So you think Gauguin, the Primitive, was a Synaesthete, do you?"

"Well, yes," I answered Francesca somewhat on the defensive, "but obviously primitive. I mean, you have to take into account his awareness of the color theorems of Zunbul-Zade and his tremendous interest in Borobadur."

"I think he was a neurotic bore." Did she think I was boring?

"Have you been to Borobadur?"

"Yeah. Like I've been to the far side of the moon. Do you laugh?" I gave her a nervous example.

"You can do better than that," she replied, sticking her tongue out at me. I burst out laughing.

"That's much better. Shall I take your temperature next?"

"I can tell you it's rising."

"That and what else?"

"I think it would be impolite to say. You see," I said going to a whisper, "that's my mother across the table."

"Hmmmm. And she wouldn't approve? In that case how did she have you? Don't tell me. It was by psychic osmosis; that's how you Synaesthetes multiply, isn't it? Come on, tell me the truth."

"The truth is, I never met anyone like you."

"Your food's getting cold, Prospero. Eat!"

I was totally captivated by her. She could have eaten asparagus with her feet and it would have been charming and graceful. After dinner, the group performed. Diamond Wave manned the percussion with all the zest of a man pulling gold coins from the sky. On the amplified harmonium was a little gnat of a fellow, Itzack Pearlstein. On wind instruments was a tall, grinning athletic Nigerian, Oscar Roadman Ife. Francesca sang. Following a rhythmic tour of outer space entitled "Pythagoras in Africa," they did a number which showcased Francesca. She used her voice like a terrestrial probe, exploring the limits of sound and passion. I don't remember the title of that piece, but I do remember some of the lines:

*"...and when your eyes have seen the end*
*of what never did begin*
*begin again to see the end*
*of all your cares and fears*
*don't you see: it's just me*
*you've been waiting for all these years..."*

After the performance Francesca said to me, "It's not often I really get to sing for someone. Did you like it?"

To be continued...

# FRANCESCA'S TAPE LOG:
# SHASTA ABBEY 231 AH

He's gone. A speck of time we had together, and now he's gone. So it's the taste of my loneliness I'll write about. But then, who's not familiar with that taste? The texture of night, of stars whose names you wished you knew, of muffled sounds and crickets singing, and the sea breaking somewhere, crashing on a thin white strip of beach. What shall we call that beach? Beach-where-the-heart-tastes-itself; it's hardly visible, a narrowband curving sinuously down the coastline of passion. It's mostly hidden by all the things we choose to think about in order to forget. I mean, is it really possible to live with your heart painfully open all the time? Is that what the War is about, to keep it covered, to say: "no, it's impossible, you must hide it and never talk about it?" Is the heart so obscene?

There was a point in the performance tonight when the whole group was suddenly involved in one of those oceans of crescendos and decrescendos, with the ampliphone bleeping away someplace close to Pluto, and Diamondskin himself sculpting sound from the cymbals like he was modulating some itinerate cosmic wave, coaxing it to fit into human ears—it was in the midst of all that carefully controlled chaos that you suddenly came descending into my vision, slipping swiftly but discretely into my heart. You landed very softly, but then you're like that. It wasn't so soft I didn't feel it, that ever-so-gentle tug, just strong enough so that it registered as pain, about a frequency-and-a-half above the normal threshold. But it was the kind of pain that you could nurture for a moment, going into its slight, vibratory tunnel, letting its bittersweet resonance palpitate on the clear, contour-line of memory, the memory in this case being that of your face, sweet and startled as I crouched over you, dressed only in a black slip, just a few nights ago. That pain, that memory, that experience was as clear as it was elusive, when—pssshoop!—the whole thing flew right out the window of perception. And then there was just a woman standing there, running her fingers through her hair, feeling another gust of wind rush up against her face, waiting for her cue, listening to the rhythmic changes of a group called "Wandering Diamond."

And Prospero, what I learned in loving you was this: that so often—no, most often—we hold on to the body for fear of losing it, but in making love we use the body to let go of it and go beyond it. We even go beyond love itself, into the Big Pool where nothing has any boundaries, and we swim without name or memory.

The last time we made love, Prospero took me down, lay on top of me. But that wasn't enough; I couldn't give enough in that way, and I wanted to give until there was nothing left to give, and my body itself was transformed into the simple purity of the verb: to love. He had already penetrated, and we were sinking into each other, when I heard what seemed to be the voice of the Original Amazon Mother. She urged me, firmly, gracefully, she urged me to summon my strength and share with him the true beauty and power of my womanhood.

To really show Prospero my love, I realized that was what I had to do. Gently but with utter conviction in my actions, I eased my hands onto his buttocks and began turning him over on his left side. As we slowly changed positions, his hands clutched at my shoulders like a child. I could feel the apprehensions mixed with wonder coursing through his fingers into my flesh. Then with a final push, like placing a new plant into fresh soil, I lay on top of him. His eyes moved about, seeing everything and nothing, blank and full at the same time. Half-sitting, half-crouching over him, I felt myself opening as wide as I had ever been, as wide as all the skies between Asia and America, and as clear. Yes, totally as clear. To probe me and feel me as deeply as he could, he began arching his back, lifting me as well. As I felt my control leaving me, I took his shoulders in my hands and pressed myself to him, holding him as hard as I could. Then the energy began to take us. It began in slow tremors, shaking us in slow unison. It rose and it fell, only to rise higher, piercing us, until we were nothing, not even rags of flesh drenched with sweat and come. Every muscle, every emotion, every nerve in both of our bodies was shredded by the same vibration. After the first orgasm, there were one, two, three, four more. And then I understood that making love is art itself. There are no rules, only the guts and the logic of the body to pursue fully and completely what began as only a simple feeling or intuition.

———————————

Long talk today with Prospero's mother, Tara. Some impulse drove me to go see her. It was the first time I had seen her since Prospero left two weeks ago. I guess I've been hiding out. Diamondskin's been spending most of his time in the Abbey. It's his way of cooling out. I suppose I should spend time there too. It actually looks inviting, all constructed of wood, painted red and gold. It reminds me of a toy house, a doll house, but real, set in the woods, among the firs and the junipers.

Anyway, when I arrived at her quarters on the north slope behind the Abbey, she was out in the garden cutting back morning glories. She looked lovely, her graying hair and that splendid African face, the color of burnished ochre. She wasn't the least surprised to see me. In fact I asked her: "Have you been waiting for me?" "Hardly," she replied. The casualness of her answer was actually seductive, especially since it was followed by a smile that could have lit up the night.

We sat down on the terrace. The garden was ablaze with marigolds, morning glories, chrysanthemums and daisies. Butterflies and bees, too, and lots of them.

"So?" she fixed me with her gaze, her eyebrows arched. She wore a simple white body length tunic. Her arms slender, sleek and almost powerful were adorned with two matching silver bracelets. Quite ornate, they slowly revealed themselves to be two sets of intertwined dragons. Her bare feet were crossed, moving in a slow circular motion against each other.

"I don't really know why I came here this morning. It's just that I had to talk to someone." Voice trailing off, body feeling like an ember thrown on the hot sand. Why was I there?

"You don't have to say anything if you don't want to," was Tara's relaxed reply. She let her head fall back exposing her throat to the sun. Looking at it, I was again struck by the combination of sensuality and power. One of the veins throbbed every so slightly as if to prove the vulnerability of her otherwise powerful presence.

Tuning into the vulnerability revealed by that throbbing vein, I began to gush out. Words, incomplete sentences splattered the silence. What I realized I was trying to tell her was that I was more fascinated with the experience of making love than with her son, the person with whom I shared the experience. That's exactly what had been bothering me the past two weeks. One voice inside of me had been telling me that I should really be diverting my attention toward Prospero, not that I didn't think fondly of him. But the lead voice in my dialogue had been saying: "No! Prospero's all right, but thinking about him isn't what's important right now. What's important is understanding what your energy is up to and where it's going to take you." Even though Tara was Prospero's mother, I still felt she was the only person who would understand this conflict I had been going through. Yet, because of that, I didn't want to hurt her feelings.

"You poor thing!" Tara chuckled, nodding her head. "You've been going through feminine guilt syndrome."

"Listen," she continued, leaning her head close to mine, "Prospero's going to be all right. He's a thousand miles away. Big deal. And here you are all alone, refusing to face up to your own energy. Tell me about yourself. I mean, tell me something besides the fact that you're a singer in a global riff sound-group. How old are you?"

"Twenty-five," I answered. I think I must have sounded contrite. I don't know why.

"So where have you been all these years?"

"Oh, someplace between a sheltered art commune and being a vagrant singer." It all seemed so matter of fact. "Father was a Network technician," I continued, "worked the sound circuits in a small beam near Salt Lake. That was before the Syndiclone blackout. That had us moving about. Mother, well she held us all together, until she had a schizophrenic break. But that's also when she started to sing. I was ten at the time. We were in Phoenix. There was a healer who came to see my mother. He did acupuncture for awhile, but no results. He liked her singing though. And then he put her on somadrome. Her singing changed. She really began working at it, gave it rhythm and texture. I was very frightened, because she spent all of her time singing. But I also liked it. She would sing. Maybe singing's not the right word. Using her voice, that would be better. Anyway, she had a different sound for each hour of the day, and it was actually quite lovely. I was at a Network Educenter and decided to apply myself to Audio-harmonics. It was then I discovered my voice. Nothing else interested me too much. Oh, maybe a little of the synaesthetic history. I liked the light shows. But mother died two years later. Father had kind of held back during that time, but now he had to do something. He told me that we'd continue living in the Phoenix commune another two years, and then he was going to enter an Abbey. Retire, finish his Search. Those were a touching two years. He spent a lot of time with us, just doing small things, talking to me, guiding me in my vocal studies, exposing me to what he knew about audio-neural patterning. He also explained to me a little bit about the Search. That seemed so pure. I guess I knew that I'd be involved in the Search someday too. I still know that. Maybe that's why I'm here. What do you think, Tara?"

"Could be, Francesca. Could be." She paused. "What do you know about the Search?"

"Well, the way I got it from father, it's like a large Gameplan. And the Syndiclones don't follow it. Or maybe, their not following it might also be part of the Gameplan. I don't know. But anyway, those of us in the Network, if we're really of the Network, we get told about it and if we can hear it, something wakes up in us. And each person has her own thing to work out and understand to plug into the Search. Sometimes it's what you choose to do. But sometimes, what you choose to do is only a lead-in. It's something that gets you connected with someone or some experience that triggers…", I stopped because something lit up in me. Even though I looked to her for some response, Tara didn't say anything.

"You know," I talked excitedly now, "I think that's what's been happening to me the past two weeks. It's been sorting itself out, this inner dialogue about Prospero and the love-making experience—I think that's been my lead into the Search."

"Let's go inside. It's getting too hot out here," Tara spoke, getting up from her chair. It was then that I became a student of Tara's. Tomorrow we begin on a formal basis. Sexual Tectonics and Matrihistory.

––––––––––

Today at Tara's, met Dr. Hassan. Abdul-Rumi Hassan. Immediate connection. He's 42, tall, lean. Intense brown eyes. Serious and nervous, but nervous like a cat, and just as watchful. His mind is like his body, fast, lean and sleek. No fat to his thoughts. Just quick arrows that he beams out, urgent yet gentle. And each one finds its target.

Tara and I had been discussing psychosexual energy transference, when Abdul-Rumi was announced. It couldn't have been better timed. Immediately upon his entering the room, you could feel the energy magnify and shift. Tara drew hers in. I could feel her readjusting. With me, she had been expansive, fluid. The energy poured out of her in an evenly diffused arc, surrounding me with a warmth that was bright but not intense. I had been like a receiver, bell-shaped and open. Even down to my pores, I could feel information coming in. When Abdul-Rumi appeared, Tara gathered her energy in and drew it upward. It was like a burning sword, the hilt of it held tightly between her legs. I shifted my position, still completely open.

Abdul-Rumi sized Tara up in a glance, smiled and said, "Hello," then quickly turned to me. No sooner did that happen, then I burst into a quiet, easy-going laugh. I couldn't separate my laughter from Abdul-Rumi's gaze. They were one and the same, and it felt good, really good. I had heard Dr. Hassan's name before, mostly in connection with the Radiosonic Beams. I had understood that he was a major figure in the development of the refined frequency beam, and that it was his staff that had worked out the formula for synthesizing visual harmonic patterns with subliminal audio frequencies.

Seating himself on a cushion, the three of us formed a perfect triangle. Tara's energy now poured like a fountain from the top of her head. Abdul-Rumi seemed to absorb it and then send it out towards me, or rather towards my heart. At least, that was how I was picking it up. During the conversation, Tara cast a few glances at me as if to say: "Don't worry about a thing, just take it as it comes." It was interesting to observe the different levels of communication that occurred. They were distinct, yet not unrelated. Though I knew this is how things often are, I had never experienced this so clearly.

"So Tara, this is your protegé?" The way Abdul-Rumi asked the question it was difficult to tell whether he was amused, surprised or impressed. He spoke with a smile, and that was reassuring. At the same time, I felt something dangerous, as if there was some subtle plot behind his being here.

"A protegé," Tara replied, "well, that literally means someone whom you protect. Am I protecting you, Francesca, and if so, from what?" I wasn't prepared for this conversation. I felt stupid. I looked at Hassan. The expression on his face was intense, but somehow compassionate. I knew he read my dumbfoundedness. He spoke for me.

"Anyone involved in the Search needs protection. But it's not as heavy-handed as it sounds. To protect also means to be hidden, and what we do must remain hidden, at least the heart of it must. The Syndicate is never sure of our motives. At a surface level we are psychotechnic competitors, much in the same way as the capitalists and the communists were once materialist competitors. Do you know what I mean?" He stopped with this question, his eyebrows raised emphasizing the aura of expectancy his words had created. At another level his question penetrated me deeply. A surge of excitement spread quickly through my nervous system, so that I felt flushed and warm in the face.

"But it seems so old, this combat—empire against empire, man against woman, capitalist against communist, and now the Network against the Syndicate? Is it really necessary? I mean: will it really ever end?" As I responded I could feel the naive urgency in my question, yet I also felt detached from my words, like I was looking at this woman leaning forward, saying something, but the words, the questions were really only a way of building a bridge, of making an offering to this other being, a man seated across from me. How would he accept the offering, and what would he do with it? The game was on. My heart beat faster for the excitement of it.

"It goes back to the heart." Abdul-Rumi's choice of words told me he had accepted my offering. "We know all impulses flow from the heart, the potential for ignorance as well as for wisdom. Who knows when it all began. It just did. The texture of ignorance, so devious, so clever, is the cornerstone of history. The Syndicate is the embodiment of history, which is like an elaborate game of hide-and-seek. To the Syndicate it looks like we are participants in this game. And that is good. It appears as though the Network sustains them by giving them something to oppose. But in the Network, we see it differently. In some ways, things are much simpler now, because there are only two forces working. Or at least it is clear that there are only two forces, the Syndicate and the Network. And we know, don't we, Tara?"

"My, you certainly are confident today, Abdul-Rumi," Tara's reply was characteristically mocking, but kind. "Well, if we know anything, it's that it is a game of hide-and-seek. But while the Syndicate thinks that the goal is the conquest of the Network, at which point the seekers would be hidden completely, we suppose that the force of the heart is supreme. It is destiny, itself." When Tara finished, it was as if she had thrown down the gauntlet. But since we were in agreement, there was no one to pick it up. The white walls of the room shimmered with light reflected from the pools outside. A fern nodded gently in the breeze.

It was my turn. "And the destiny of the heart is its own fulfillment?" Though I phrased my words as a question, I knew I had spoken a declaration. I looked at Abdul-Rumi. His eyes, deep and dark, soft, yet sharp, caressed me with their light. I continued, very quietly I said, "And so biding our time, we play with the Syndicate, while within we develop what—the destiny of the heart?"

"Yes," Abdul-Rumi completed my thoughts, "and who knows: one day we shall witness the Dynasty of the Heart."

We all sat silently for a few moments. It was as if we were locked into a common wave-pattern. Abdul-Rumi broke the silence.

"Francesca, the Protegé, what have you learned about love?"

I looked at him, probably with some sense of astonishment, for he then said, "Come now, one doesn't become a pupil or intimate of Tara's without learning about love."

I looked at Tara. She sat on her cushion like a cat, totally relaxed.

"That learning to love we go beyond love." Finally answering the question, I'm sure I must have sounded like a school girl.

"How dull," Abdul-Rumi laughed and leaned closer to me. "You can be more specific than that. Love is also poetry. No one as lovely as you and in the fullness of her womanhood can be without poetry, so recite for me the song of love."

Feelings of intimidation flashed through me. But, no, he was not here to intimidate me. What I had learned from Tara, if anything, was confidence in the purity and strength of my womanhood. Something clicked. I leaned closer to Abdul-Rumi, and, fixing him with my eyes, I spoke:

"Son of the Pharaohs with your worldly eyes, I know that inside you're quivering and trembling with anticipation. Of what? Of the gesture I, as a woman will make toward you. And in that anticipation you are like a little boy. But that's sweet, Abdul-Rumi, that's sweet and quite all right. Because you have passion as well as I, and you have daring as do I, and our daring is like a surfboard riding the wave of passion. And all that matters is knowing how to make it to the beach, on our feet, hand-in-hand…"

"Tara," Abdul-Rumi spoke softly, but with distinct emphasis on each word, "This Francesca, she is indeed your protegé."

"Won't you play us something on the violin, Abdul-Rumi?" Tara always has such a way of absorbing and deflecting the current of energy. I admire that so much in her. It's so graceful.

While Abdul-Rumi went out of the room to fetch his violin, Tara came over to me and spoke with the greatest affection. "You're absolutely lovely. Guts and charm, it's a great combination. See now what you can learn from Abdul-Rumi. He's rare."

Pronouncing the word "rare" in a most exaggerated manner, Tara finished by placing her tongue on her upper lip, winked at me, and returned to her cushion.

Abdul Rumi performed Bach's Second Partita for Violin. It was breathtaking. His command, his composure were impeccable. And the music—I can't add anything to it.

Afterwards, Abdul-Rumi talked at length about sound and healing. He glowed, really glowed, and I could feel all of his manhood rippling beneath his black and white checkered caftan. He's so beautiful. I wanted to kiss him right then and there. But I restrained myself. In so doing, I could feel my own energy building up inside of me. It was good and rich. I knew the build-up was sweet, for when the outlet comes, it will be as full as anything I have given. And to give is all.

To be continued…

Gruber came up again today. "Hee! Hee! Hee! Orchids in the Rockies, big as your mother's tit when she was nursin' you!" Gruber's choice of metaphors was peculiar, but then you didn't expect anything different from him. Big, wide-toothed grin. Always two days growth of silvery brown stubble on his chin. The magenta and green badge of the Eco-Squad hanging loosely from a sweaty denim shirt that fairly rippled with dirty old man perversity. Gruber was going on about his spare-time gene-splicing experiments.

"Oh, 'n' by the way, Prosp'," he paused in the midst of his genetic diatribe, "Fella came by. Little darky type. Told me to giv' ya this. Said you'd know all about it. All 'bout it heavy on the "all," like he was looking into a telescope and seeing something that shook him to the core.

Though my heart leaped with the knowledge that it was undoubtedly Poontutjarpa, I tried to hide my excitement. "Uh-huh. And I suppose he was riding a kangaroo?"

"Aw c'mon, Prosp. Wun't no kangaroo he was ridin'; ridin' a jackass, he was. Weirdest li'l guy. Don't see many o' them 'round here, tell you that much, Prosp. But seemed like he knew you right well."

"How was he dressed, Grube?"

"Like a miner. Kinda reminded me of a gold miner, like you see on those old video relays."

No one else but Poontutjarpa. I knew that. "So what was it he gave you to give me?"

"If'n you ask, here 'tis." Gruber reached inside of his shirt and drew out a small silver case, about the size of an old fashioned vacuum tube. Westinghouse. Maybe 5 AH. On it, embossed in gold was a kind of serpent, the kind any Mesoamerican archeologist knows about. The kind associated with the Great Lord Quetzalcoatl. I remembered my days at Teotihuacan in a flash. Especially the face of Sherab Gyatso Sanchez: High Aztec-Tibetan cheekbones, copper-colored skin blazing against electric turquoise caftans. . . and the bittersweet taste of peyote tea.

"Hey, Prosp, you still here? Hee! Hee! Hee! Looks like that silver cigar stung yer brains right smart! Hee! Hee! Hee!" Snorting, laughing and coughing all at once, in a manner as obscene as it was disgusting, Gruber spat sharply into the earth outside the radiosonic dome.

"Uh, yeah. Just reminded me of something I saw once when I was a kid, that's all."

"Childhood mem'ries, huh? Well, look sharp, Prosp, ya' ain't no kid no more. Word's got it ther's lottsa Syndiclone Agents movin' into Denver. More'n we seen inna generation. Yep, more'n a gen-ee-ration." The way Gruber pronounced generation the second time gave me a start. I looked at him closely. Just then the wind came up and started tossing his mangy gray hair every which way.

"Hee! Hee! Hee!" Slapping his crazy old thighs I brushed away the thought that the syndicate had cloned and reprogrammed him. But then…

After Gruber left I went back into the Rad-Dome, where I fell into one of my typical post-Gruber reveries. As usual, paranoia gave way to irritation, which dissolved into admiring curiosity. Damn that bastard! He had the most cunning way of being stupid. So cunning, I always felt he was a Syndic Decode. Hmmmph. But reliable guy. After all, if this platinum-plated, deoxysilicon psycho-transistor tube were actually from Poontutjarpa, and if Gruber were a Syndic Decode, and a smart one, playing real dumb at that, why was it he who was giving me the tube? And then there was the easy way he insinuated my name: "Prosp." Hell, no one ever came that close to me, only my mother. To everyone else I was just RadLab Agent 24, or, at best, RadLab Agent 24 Jones. So where'd he get the balls to come up with this Prosp-crap?

Let it go. Breath out and let it go. Let it fade into all the other conceptual lint hovering about a few badly programmed neurons.

I took the tube to the deck, the one facing the canyon. It was nice, a late September afternoon. A few flies, dragonflies and moths flitting about, their wings burning silver in the early autumn light. Sitting down at the deck table, an old-fashioned laminated cable-drum, I took my right index finger and ran the nail gently down the slightly depressed groove that distinguished the otherwise smooth surface. I opened it carefully. Yeah. Inside was a little synthe-deoxybonucleic coated silicon psychotransistor chip. Small little devil. Nothing else in the tube, except the psylicibo-phosphate tape by which the chip adhered to the tube's inner wall.

Licking the tape, then rolling it into a little ball which I then placed most carefully on the table, I took the chip between thumb and index finger feeling for the intricate pattern engraved in ever so low relief on its minute surface. There it was. Pressing gently so that the pattern on both sides of the chip left its imprint in reverse symmetry on the top of my thumb and index finger, I eased myself back into the deck chair and relaxed, but not so much that I would release the gentle grip I held on the chip. It was important to keep the hold steady so that the psylicibo-phosphate secreted itself through my digestive system, the synthe-deoxrybonucleic coating of the chip dissolved into my skin in precisely the form of the pattern on the chip.

You never knew which code word they were using. There's only 64, but they always transmit different. It usually took about half an hour for the electric activity at the pulse points of the fingertips to be ignited by the coating of the chip. But that was also the amount of time needed for the psylicibo-phosphate to get through the digestive walls and into the circulatory system.

This time it seemed to take longer. That must have been because my system had been mildly inhibited by thoughts about Gruber. Good Old Gruber. I shouldn't be so hard on him. It's just as easy to think of him as a PAN-liaison as a Syndic Decode. And if he were a PAN-liaison who knew what his real position was in the Network. As this thought was occurring, I simultaneously remarked on the positive nature of my state of mind, positive at least in contrast to what it had been just after Gruber left. And then I knew the program was about to begin.

The tingling at my fingertips as biopsychic fusion occurred swiftly coursed through my body. Synaesthesia time. I closed my eyes. The photomenes always triggered first. I recognized Code Word 24. The coincidence of the number of the code word and my RadLab Agent number could hardly have been less unnoticed. I felt something blue-violet and deep in the pit of my stomach. It was the signal for a memory-release. I was in a cemetery, or at least what seemed like a cemetery.

Poontutjarpa was hunkering. His voice came on, one part high Anglo-Australian, one part lilting Cambodian, and yet another part disarmingly obsequious Hindi all fused together in a mock-metallic cyborg intonation. Half wailing, half chanting, the words coursed through my nervous system like an ethereal pneumatic drill.

> *"In the Dreamtime when the Primal Helix*
> *In the Dreamtime when the Primal Helix unfolded*
> *diamond-backed and pure*
> *when the primal helix unfolded . . ."*

As Poontutjarpa chanted, he drew a figure in the earth. It was the same pattern as that which was engraved on the chip. Code Word 24. My mind snapped with the phrase, Project Quetzalcoatl. The psychoaesthetic enzyme coiled and uncoiled. The photomenes formed and then dissolved repeatedly in the same pattern, like a snake shedding, growing, and re-shedding the same skin a million times a second. In synchronistic counterpoint the audiomenes flashing the triplet figures of Code Word 24 put me into auto-samadhi real fast.

All the while, Poontutjarpa is swaying slightly on his haunches, one snake running down each arm, spiraling around each arm.

> *"...when the primal helix unfolded,*
> *first the gold,*
> *then the silver,*
> *then the bronze,*
> *then the iron,*
> *the blacksmith's brow burnt bright*
> *when the primal helix first unfolded . . ."*

"Nezahualpilli! Nezahualpilli!" A woman's voice calling. Early morning light. Brightness, an aching for even more brightness. Mingling with the gentle clatter of clay wind chimes, the voice called once again: "Nezahualpilli! Nezahualpilli!"

Opening my eyes from a dream which faded without want of further recall, I gazed upon Maxtlalxochitl—High Poetess Five Flower, Our Lady of Tula, the butterfly-throated singer of Texcoco. Delicately carved white shell combs shaped her obsidian black hair into two massive spirals moving in opposite directions from each other on either side of a part that ran like a ray of light across the top of her head.

"Nezahualpilli, it's late. The others are already waiting. The moment bidden by the stars has landed on your brow." Maxtlalxochitl. The brilliance of her way with flowers and song was present in everything she touched. With her everything became as red coral and white shell, obsidian and turquoise. As Maxtlalxochitl spoke, the memory of the day took form in my heart. Yes, it was almost a full round of the Tonalamatl since I had wagered with Montezuma, played against him in the series of five ballgames, and won. Five games, one for each Sun. Almost one complete round since It-lil-po-tan-cuah, Her Servant Feathered with Black Plumes, announced to me:

"Nezahualpilli, Lord of Texcoco, Holder of the Lineage of the Toltecs, Emissary of the Lord of Dawn, I, It-lil-po-tan-cuah, Keeper of the Shrine of Toci, Our Grandmother Heart-of-the-Earth, Chief Diviner to the Invincible Lord of Anahuac, Montezuma, address you.

"What has occurred today on the Royal Ball-Court is a feat of great moment. With reckless daring you wagered your entire Kingdom against three female turkeys as proof of the superiority of your astrologers and diviners who have prophesied the imminent destruction of Anahuac, Turquoise Navel of the Fifth Sun. That you have won should be no great joy to you. If your vaunted astrologers are correct, they have also sealed your fate as well.

"Nezahualpilli, Lord of Texcoco, take heed. If what you have displayed for us today is mere arrogance, the jealous stupidity of a petty vassal wagering his witless self against the Invincible Lord of Lord's, Montezuma himself, then a worse destiny awaits you than that prophesied by your seers for the whole of Anahuac."

It-lil-po-tan-cuah's black-feathered headdress rippled in the torchlight. His face was like a deep pool you come across on a moonless night, its presence becoming apparent only after intense concentration upon its waveless surface. And what that surface finally revealed was a writhing nest of scorpions.

"It-lil-po-tan-cuah," I replied, measuring the featureless depths of his face, relieved only by the slight raising of his nostrils which emerged like a frog barely showing its eyes above the water. "It-lil-po-tan-cuah, your title is a mockery. Toci, Grandmother Heart-of-the-Earth, could only be a stranger to you. But then, Anahuac today is a mockery. My father, Nezahualcoyotl, greater than any man in the depths of his wisdom than any other in Anahuac, bided his time with you Aztecs. Yet he told me when I was but a child that it would come to this, and he begged me to summon the courage for this moment. That I have done. Betrayers of the Oath of Quetzalcoatl, you have only sealed your own destiny and doom. What I take with me today are not only three turkey hens, but the goodness of the Toltecs. Never shall it shine upon you again."

And now the time had come. Departure to the North. Nearly a complete round of the Tonalamatl I had kept in fasting and penance, seeing no one but Maxtlalxochitl. Today we would leave and those of Texcoco would learn of my "death" by nightfall. Departure for the North. And with us would go the wisdom of the Toltecs, the wisdom of the Red and the Black ink, the wisdom of the flute.

"Maxtlalxochitl, come to me." Embracing the full womanliness of her body, I whispered into her ear, "Love, my only love, today, if only for one day, let us be as great as the ancients…"

By the time the sun had pierced the midpoint of the sky, dressed as merchants, we were already some leagues north of Texcoco, making our way through dry creek beds where only the lizards came to say good-bye.

The image faded. In front of me, Poontutjarpa, holographically pure, motionless, crouching like a tiger, continued his chant:

*"Fork diamond back voice*
*tracing the trail of all voices*
*twining and untwining*
*dust of dust, stellar dust*
*blowing like jewels across the thousand-tongued goddess*
*earth, never cease to speak as long as your children*
*suffer and die without knowing,*
*earth, never cease to speak..."*

Then Poontutjarpa himself faded.

———————————————————

Darkness was rushing down from the mountains. I took the chip and deposited it once again in the silver tube. A great wave of exhaustion swept across me. I took myself to the decoding room. There I placed the electrodes on my head and fell into a deep, dreamless sleep.

What I like most about the psycho-transistor chips is the morning after. It's like every cell in the body has been nourished on pure bliss, a steady diet of reality void of any concern, like the clear blue sky on an October day. Removing the electrodes from my head I did about an hour of "wall-gazing," to use the phrase I picked up at the Shasta Abbey, then with controlled eagerness, I sat myself down before the Decode Monitor screen. Punching the Code Word 24 key as well as the date, I proceeded to read the Instructions for Project Quetzalcoatl.

Real basic, this one was. It explained the enzyme code manifesting as snake worship and its relation to the psychotechnical dialectic. The reincarnation flashback about Nezahualpilli fit in nicely with the decode. The karmic link between Montezuma and the Syndicate was undeniable. Then came the good part. I was to seek out a certain Syndiclone, Natasha Eisenhammer, and divert her drive for control of the Central Rockies Geomantic Surveillance Zone. The only clue as to how this was to be done was "Quetzalcoatl." That didn't seem like much of a clue, except for the fact that Natasha Eisenhammer seemed to have a definite karmic link with It-lil-po-tan-cuah.

After the Decode, I went for a walk up the Canyon. Sitting down beneath a clump of junipers on an overlook that gave a stunning view of the high range, I was able to digest the information bit that instructed me to destroy the El Dorado Station. That was one to wrestle with. It brought up the old paranoia: was the psycho-transistor chip another Syndicate plant? How could you know? The level of combat had gotten so sophisticated with each side using the other's techniques, while operating from the same psycho-genetic information pool, how could you know?

It was getting hot. I took off my shirt and lay down on a large flat rock, closed my eyes and listened to the hum, buzz, drone and chatter of the foothill forest, junipers and scrub pine taking the place of the yucca, thistle and purple and yellow wild flowers that characterized the arid heath where the station was located. Why was I scared? I had been at the station for nearly ten years. I was the twenty-fourth to man the station. And now I was to put it out of commission, destroy it. Right, wreck it and move on. I fought the feeling of frustration and anger that prickled my skin as it passed over me in fiery waves.

Then I thought about Poontutjarpa, the crazy tjuringa-yogi, the mad mahayanistas odd as a duck-billed platypus. As I turned him over in my mind, I realized that my fear and anger had nothing to do with destroying the Station. It had to do with the fact that I had never been given an assignment of the nature of the Quetzalcoatl Project. It was so obvious. When I saw this a feeling of freshness passed through me. High adventure! Reinvigorated I returned to the Dome.

Return. That was the key to Code Word 24. Back at the Dome I hit the Master Program Monitor. Hooking up the Master to the Decode monitor I punched a few select keys: Genotypes, Meso-American; Hierarchical Structures; Late Urban Metamorphs; Psycho-Genetic Defects, Statistical Probabilities of; and then set the Program for Decode Analysis.

Leaving the Program Monitor, I stepped out to the deck again. Twenty-four hours had passed since Gruber had given me the silver tube. If indeed that had been Poontutjarpa—riding a jackass no less—then he was still quite likely in the area. But where? As I pondered this question I let my eyes loosely fall on the jagged horizon of the Flatirons. Crazy country. A few old-type cowboys. The Deserted Rocky Flats Plutonium mill on a high mesa to the South. And Denver. In all my years at the Station, except for the missions to Hopi Mesa and Yellowstone that I made for periodic triangulation checks, I had left it most infrequently. Denver three times. PAN agents weren't known as the roving kind, and I certainly was no exception, until now at least. And besides, Denver was boring. It was a typical postindustrial urban site. Fleets of hovercraft flying over the freeway beds, blocks and blocks of air conditioned electronic arcades, and overcrowded psycho-treatment complexes. You never knew who was in control, so best stay out.

As my memory casually jogged through my years at El Dorado Station, I was startled by the sound of glass breaking. Bolting up I rushed toward the Dome. There in the Recreation area was Gruber. Not good old gene-splicing, spitting over his left shoulder, "Hee, Hee, Hee!" Gruber, but wild-eyed wielding a sledgehammer into the Psycho Art Index Carrousels' Gruber. Reels of magnetic tape were flying like leaves in an autumn gale. My heart sank. That tape had given me more sensorial pleasure and insight than anything else at the station…

"Gruber, you fucking mutant, stop it!" I shouted as I rushed him. Like a grizzly bear, he casually took his left arm—I could have sworn it was a paw at that moment—and sent me flying like another spool of electromagnetic tape. As I careened into the styrofoam padding outside the Recording Booth, I remember my self thinking in a wry manner, that it was true, in all actuality, I was nothing but an electromagnetic tape spool, each of my senses being a genetically sensitized record or replay device. Sprawling in a pile of tape, I began laughing to myself. "What the hell Gruber. You got a sledge hammer for me?"

The last thing we destroyed was the Master Program Monitor. I took out the last program indexed on a number of extra-photo sensitive silicon chips and placed them in the silver tube which Gruber had handed me the day before. I didn't have any enzyme-coating substance, so I would have to get to a radiosonic mixer to get maximum use from the chips. That meant Hopi Mesa. Would Poontutjarpa be there too?

"An' who'd ya think I was, Prosp. Some mutant? Hee! Hee! Hee! You know mutants ain't like that. They's too sing-song polite. You know, servin' others 'n all that. Now do I seem like a servant to you. Jes' cuz I wuz bustin' up all that fine psychotechnical machinery. Shit, don't mean nothin' to me. Now you take gene-splicing. Gene-splicing tubers 'n seeds I mean…"

The next morning, Gruber, myself and two horses named Dragon-Power and Morning-Glory were headed for Vail Pass.

To be continued…

# FRANCESCA'S TAPE LOG:
# THE ABDUL-RUMI HASSAN AFFAIR

Now that it's over, I can talk about it. Not that it's easy. It's not the love part, but everything else that went with it. I'm scared now, but at least I'm alive. Still I don't know who or what will turn up next.

The seduction between Abdul-Rumi and myself had been mutual. How much Tara Andromeda had to do with this, I may never know. Nor if ever I shall see her son, Prospero, again. Who knows. He was a sweet guy. But that was ten years ago, and now here I am at the Hopi Mesa DeCode Encampment.

It's been two months since I got here. The training has been excellent. If anything snapped me out of my despair it was the snake handling exercises. For that I'll always be thankful to Karuna Monongye, her kind grandmother face, the brown skin lined with arroyos of age, accompanied by the soft rustling of her Morning Star skirts as she let herself down the ladder into the darkness of the kiva.

But Abdul-Rumi. Abdul-Rumi Hassan, you wise, clever, mean son-of-a-bitch. When I think about the whole thing now it's like taking a spiraling timetrip back through a randomly arranged sequence of time warps.

After an idyll of two years we left Shasta Abbey. I thought of Abdul-Rumi as the wisest, most sensitive of men, a god even. This is hardly to mention how good a lover he was. The trip to Egypt was uneventful enough. A solar-propelled hovercraft cruise from the Bahamas Station across the Saragasso Sea to the Azores. There we stayed on for a period time. A languid idyll among the Atlantean Psycho-Archeologists, an ingrown and tedious lot. A few trips into the Bathysphere among the darting fish, wildly growing seaweed and the blocks of stone, grooved and spiraled with ancient designs; then through the strait of Gibralter, skimming across the north coast of Africa to Giza.

By the time we reached Giza, I began to question the whole affair. I don't know exactly what triggered it. Abdul-Rumi's coolness seemed to have been set off by an encounter on the Azores. Some mix-up happened at the Inn where we were staying. The desk-clerk referred to him once as Agent Shiraz or something like that. Abdul-Rumi didn't say anything for what seemed a painfully long time. Then he hissed through his teeth, "You must not have slept well last night. Perhaps you should take the afternoon off and relax in the baths." I thought it an odd comment, but dismissed it as an example of Abdul-Rumi's sometimes bizarre sense of humor. Yet it did linger in my mind, set itself up as a minor landmark in our relationship.

I was hardly prepared for the situation at Giza. Though Abdul-Rumi had told me a lot about the Radiosonic Transmission Stations and the PAN Triangulation Project, in no way did I anticipate the spectacle that the Giza Station presented. Abdul-Rumi's chief working quarters were in one of the ancient boat pits alongside the Great Pyramid. Using the pit as base and foundation, the structure of magnificently hewn cedar and gold-leaf took the form of a great fish or dolphin. Where the eyes of the sea-creature would have been were two bubble-dome light apertures.

Entering through the Sea-creature's mouth, we descended a set of stone steps. What awaited below was a wonder-world of lightbeams and synthesized harmonic chords. Getting accustomed to the marvelous ever-changing interior, I observed the banks of Terminals and Program Monitors on either side of the concave walls. Taking my hand, Abdul-Rumi led me to the "fish-tail" of the RadLab. Parting the curtains I found myself in a cozy, womb-like chamber.

"Francesca, now we can practice what the ancients taught, and I, the son of Unas, the Star-Walker, shall fill your mouth with the sweet nectar of oblivion." The way Abdul-Rumi spoke took me off guard. Half humorous, half heart-felt, yet laced with mockery, I paused to look at him. Before I knew it we were embracing, falling on a set of cushions, embracing, falling, and making love. I had never felt so ethereal as I lay on my back in this womb-paradise far away from time. Abdul-Rumi played with my gold chain necklaces, kissed my breasts, ran his fingers up and down the inside of my thighs, talking all the while of Unas, of the voyages of Unas, of Unas' conversations with the stars . . . that was how it began.

For two years or so, Abdul-Rumi let me be and do as I wished. Hours, days, weeks, I spent in the elaborate gardens, shaded from the afternoon sun by the Great Pyramid. There I slowly came to know some of the other members of Abdul-Rumi's "Palace," as his sprawling living and working quarters were referred to. Shakti Livingston, a psycho-choreographer whose thin, bony nose and cheeks were set off by streams of burnished bronze hair; Socrates Escalantes, or the Gnome, as we called him. Born in Macchu Picchu, no one knew how long ago, Socrates was a real pro at fooling you. One moment, he was a doddering, hump-backed dwarf droning on and on about the effects of stellar magnetism in its relation to the psychogenetic decode process, and just as you were ready to say, "Shove it, you crazy little elf, you lost me," he would jump into the air, do a couple of double backflips, land flat on his feet, and without losing his train of thought continue to explain the biopsychic equation for formulating karmic flashback experiences as derived from the numeric sequences of extra-stellar radio impulses.

Shakti really loved old Socrates. One evening on the Pavilion of the Quest, the Garden's centerpiece, a sunken mini-garden bi-sected by waterways and lush with the perfume of hybrid Flowers of Paradise, she performed a dance in Socrates' honor. She was perfect. Never did I see a human, especially one with Shakti's lean, angular frame, possessed of the magical ability to transform itself into every shape conceivable. In one half-hour performance, accompanied by the sometimes lyrical and sometimes frenzied sound of a single Oud, she completely recreated the psychic as well as the physical world of Socrates. I was convulsed with joy when Shakti finished. But Socrates' comment was the best. "The high point for me, mind you, but perhaps for no one else but me, on the other hand, one never knows, nevertheless, was the delicate handling of Shakti's insight into my emotional state as I perceived the correspondence between the chromosomic separation and the harmonic interval of radio impulses from CGN 5127. Yes, very fine. I wonder if she could perform that part again?"

But the one to whom I grew closest, and who ultimately saved my life was Fa-Tsang Wronski. Quiet and shy, Mongolian moon-faced, Fa-Tsang had been working on the Mirror Room. His main feat had been to suspend an auto-luminous sphere in the center of the room without resorting to strings or wire. This he achieved by sending out psychomagnetic impulses. It was all right. I liked sitting beneath the auto-luminous sphere in the midst of the infinite reflections of myself.

Yes, the reflections of myself.

Things changed dramatically after the second year. Abdul-Rumi had been most busy, and had made a number of long visits to the Zimbabwe Station. The last time he returned he was in a remotely euphoric mood. This was just before the Islamic Uprisings and the Great Ramadan Massacre in the Sinai. Several days after his return there were large announcements around the Giza Complex:

**NIGHT OF THE WIZARD**
**SYNAESTHETE THEATER PRESENTS**
**NATASHA EISENHAMMER**
**REVELATION**EXPANSION**RE-CREATION**

The evening before the performance, Abdul-Rumi called me from the Synch-Booth where I was mixing voice patterns with synthesizer. I had been thinking alot about Fa-Tsang Wronski, my talks with him, the work he was doing. We had begun sleeping together during Abdul-Rumi's last trip to Zimbabwe. Because of this liaison with Fa-Tsang Wronski, I had realized how distant Abdul-Rumi had become from me. It had happened so imperceptibly. Yet it also had a feeling of inevitability about it. Abdul-Rumi was so smooth. That's what it was. That's why I felt such god-like adoration for him by the time we left Shasta Abbey. Now here I was entering an altogether different world, a world of mirrors, empty calm, and infinite reflection. So when Abdul-Rumi called for me, what I felt was an intrusion of my space. The irritation I felt surprised me. At that moment I had a very precise recollection of the Search, of my father setting off, of mountains and canyons…somewhere.

"Francesca, that was a beautiful, beautiful song. It's a pity more isn't being done with you," Natasha Eisenhammer glanced sharply at Abdul-Rumi as she spoke.

"Are you suggesting, Natasha, that I am keeping Francesca in bondage? I think we could take a somewhat more enlightened attitude than that," Abdul-Rumi replied, squashing out a cigarette deliberately in the large marble ashtray sculpted in the form of a soul-boat. The ambiguous irony of his reply ignited a moment of intense calm.

"Well, perhaps, if you don't mind, Abdul, Francesca could come with me to the war-zone. That is, after my performance. All in the interest of enlightenment, of course." Natasha's manner of speaking was puzzling in a way I couldn't put my finger on.

"As you please, Natasha. 'No owners and nothing to own,' if I may quote the Mullah, Answar-Din. Besides, there is the material from Zimbabwa to be synthesized. That shall take me a bit of time. But do bring her back…glowing." Abdul-Rumi answered with a pleasurable comfort.

"Is there some possibility I might have something to say about all this?" I interjected.

"But Francesca, my dear, by all means. I mean, you know, we are all equals in this…ah…endeavor." As Abdul-Rumi pronounced the word, "endeavor" he winked at me, as if there were some great joke occurring. Whatever the joke was, the wink disarmed me.

"It was nothing really, I guess. It was just…," I couldn't say it, couldn't say that I felt like a pawn. Something stopped me. "Of course, I'd love to go with you Natasha. Will it be dangerous?"

"Francesca, come now, life is dangerous," and Natasha laughed, a deep, low laugh that trailed into a spasm of coughing. "Please Abdul," she choked out the words, smiling nevertheless, "another glass of Raki."

We left for the Sinai, the day after Natasha's performance. We left early, before the sun had risen. We moved out in a hovercraft steered by Natasha. Feigning sleep, I closed my eyes so I could try to piece together what I had experienced the night before.

On a dias set in the center of the Great Garden, Natasha had stood motionless, her arms perpendicular to her body, itself clad in an ancient Greek *chiton*. Her slightly slanted green eyes set deep above high Slavic cheekbones glittered like stars. Lush black hair, gathered together by simple gold clasps which matched the luminous sparkle of her eyes, framed her face like a nocturnal halo. As she began to chant, her arms moved slowly upward, finally forming a diamond pattern with her head in the center. The palms of her hands faced outward, fingers splayed like sprays of moon-lit winter branches. The tips of each index finger and thumb were joined to form a smaller diamond above the larger diamond of her arms.

> *"There is one race of men*
> *One race of gods;*
> *Both have breath of life*
> *From a single mother.*
> *But sundered power holds us both divided."*

The magnetism of her voice, the haunting elegance of the words she chanted, the diamond-armed pose which she took, all synchronized in an unadorned beauty which completely captivated me. Night of the Wizard it was, from the opening invocation of Pindar to the closing incantation of Isis,

> *"Osiris! Osiris!*
> *When the Ra-disc glides onward in the Sun-boat*
> *flame spurts spew off the prow*
> *O may I catch thy spurts O Brother*
> *as the shrieking human*
> *catches the Sun!"*

In between had been a rapid succession of psycho-impressions, some familiar to me, other totally foreign and grotesque. What I got it from was a dramatization of the psychic underpinnings of the five-ringed female/male dialectic: the alternation of power beginning with the female, and after three major back-and-forth shifts, expanding to female once again. I remembered the days with Tara, sunny Tara Andromeda, in the pine-bowered pavilions of Mt. Shasta. But still, the whole performance left me numb, shocked, exhausted. It was almost as if Natasha had thrown an invisible web around me. As I went to sleep that night, I wondered if others had also felt that invisible web. Abdul-Rumi, taking me in his arms, whispered, "If it is a web, let it be a web of light. Unas, the sky-walker weaves only webs of stars…"

"So how do you like gliding in my Sun-boat? Have you noticed the flame spurts spewing off the brow, sister?" Natasha's voice startled me. Yet her arched brows completely entranced me. All around us was a barrenness that recalled the Nevada highlands. To our right in the distance was an awesomely massive crater. "Momentos of the great Post-Hiroshima disaster, Francesca," Natasha's voice was matter of fact. The Wizard of the Night before was hidden, but where? I wanted to find it, know all about it.

Throwing my arms about Natasha's neck, fondling her hair, even I was taken by surprise as I blurted out, "Natasha, I love you. Please let me stay with you!"

And stay I did. Though Natasha was only a few years older than me, she was 33 when I met her, she possessed a power equaled in other women only by Tara Andromeda. I became her accomplice. We performed together, created a great act. Expanding from her original performance-piece, we put together a dramatization in which we exchanged male and female roles, chanted, sang, made music and acted in a counterpoint harmony that made us one of the best-received psycho-historic mime acts in the network.

So in love was I with Natasha, that I ignored the patronizing manner with which Abdul-Rumi received me whenever we touched base with him at Giza.

So in love was I with Natasha, that I was oblivious to Fa-Tsang Wronski's warnings. "Francesca," he would say to me, taking me aside when he could, "Francesca, this woman, Natasha, do you really see her? Do you really understand what she is doing?"

Brushing aside Fa-Tsang's words, I would rationalize them to mean: "You sweet darling little imbecile, do you really think you have the creative ability of Natasha?" Thinking in this way, I could place Fa-Tsang out of my mind, label him, and cast him away as a jealous fool. So in love was I with Natasha, that I ignored her drinking, saying to myself, "It is what she needs, it is her Dionysian medicine, her elixir." And so in love with her was I that I ignored the fact that I had begun to drink"…to keep up with her," to enter the self-same primal space from which I believed she drew her energy and inspiration.

Our performances took place mostly in war-zones. It was to comfort the laser-burned, the bereaved, the outcast. It was to uplift their vision, so Natasha told me. And

I believed her. And Abdul-Rumi, he always agreed, pouring us each another glass of Raki. He always agreed.

It was almost two years ago at the Avebury Outpost that it occurred. We had spent the afternoon, Natasha and I, circumambulating the main cairn. It was October, the weather had been crisp and unusually dry. Ten weeks, ten hard weeks at the Liverpool force field had exhausted us, and we needed this break.

"Tashy," I spoke tenderly taking her hand, "do you really think you can go on tonight?"

We were to do a performance for the Avebury Psychoarcheological Batallion.

Natasha had been concerned with a new psychocharacterization, It-lil-po-tan-cuah. She had been terribly distracted. The night before she and I had spent the whole evening drinking, talking, making love. Bizarre incoherent bits of information began to emerge. When I awoke that day it was already high noon. It dawned on me that our use of alcohol had passed beyond the cathartic Dionysian border-line. I was worried. When Natasha awoke, she immediately began to drink. That's when I asked her to take a walk with me.

"Bitch! Stupid, naive, witless bitch!" Natasha spat out her words glaring at me, "Don't you know what's going on?"

"I really don't know what you're talking about," I replied, fighting off the mixture of nausea and fear growing like a spontaneously generated time-bomb in the pit of my stomach.

"Just think where we've been the past four years, and think of what we've been do-ing...just think about it! Do you think this has been some kind of lark? As far as I'm concerned, this is worse than bad theater. And the worst thing is, I'm just as bad off as you are."

I was stung. I could have died right then and there, but I was too confused. Suddenly nothing made sense. What had I been doing? In an instant, what had been a dream, a blissful intoxication, became a nightmare.

"Neither of us are going on tonight, Francesca. Neither of us." Fatigue, degradation, confusion. That's all I felt. I thought I should have felt rage, anger. But no, just fatigue, degradation, confusion. Our Amazon Sisters act had been just that—an act.

Within a few hours we were in the hovercraft. Avebury never happened. Had Giza happened? Or Mount Shasta? Dozing, I dreamed that I was back at the Liverpool force field. Swarms of mutants were crawling all over me, biting me, pulling at my breasts, poking at me, sticking their filthy boots in my vagina. I awoke crying, sobbing. Still manning the hovercraft, Natasha looked at me with a mixture of irritation and help-lessness.

We landed some place to the far north, the north coast of Scotland, I imagined. Abdul-Rumi was waiting at the landing strip.

"We understand you've not been well, Francesca?" The smile on Abdul-Rumi's face caused a wave of anger to come over me that more than counter-balanced the intense paranoia I experienced when I saw him waiting for us. A Syndicate Psycho-Treatment Complex, that's where I had ended up. But why me? I was too sick, too exhausted to care or to fight it. The only question I could ask was: why me and why in this manner?

The next two years were spent at the Cape Wrath Sedentary Rehabilitation Unit. Natasha and I were immediately separated out. Where she went I do not know. Initially, I struggled to maintain myself. I would remember Tara Andromeda, our talks about the Search and the nature of feminine energy. Finally a combination of disgrace and the sophistication of the Syndics treatment procedures, not to mention the generally dismal Cape Wrath weather, undermined me completely. My feelings of betrayal, hurt, and bitter chagrin slowly evaporated.

Within six months, and following a series of psychogenetic decode experiments performed on me by none other than Abdul-Rumi—Agent Dr. Shiraz—himself, I gladly took my position among the Cape Wrath Staff. My main duties consisted in monitoring a small psychoradar system. Being at Cape Wrath, this didn't amount to much excitement, and I understood it to be more a training activity than anything else. The psychoradar unit was programmed to pick out Network transmissions, scramble them, and send them with a contrary code-bit to their original destiny. During this time, I rarely, if ever thought about my life before Cape Wrath. As I later found out, even my dreams were scanned by psychoradar and re-programmed.

Abdul-Rumi, Doctor Shiraz, as he was known at the Cape Wrath Rehab unit, disappeared after the initial six-month treatment. Before he left, however, he had a long "chat" with me.

"Please don't ask again, 'why me?' That will become clear to you in time, my dear Francesca. But we must be agreed on one thing before my departure, and that is this, my dearest Francesca, that is this: The Syndicate is only here to help you. Our goals for you are no different from our goals for the Planet. Individual Prosperity, Collective Happiness, a Globally Functional Brotherhood. Maintain yourself. If things go well we can work together. There is much that you know already. We can be very useful to each other. Very useful."

The attack on Cape Wrath came toward the end of winter, late March, shortly after the Equinox. For several weeks prior I had been picking up unusual bursts of activity on the psychoradar monitor. My Squad Leader, Julius 21x, a veteran of the notorious Skinner Batallion skirmishes in Zimbabwe, dismissed them as the harmless radioactivity of a band of Psychoarcheological hold-outs on the Hebrides.

It came just after midnight. I had been asleep for several hours in my cabin at the north end of Out-Patient Residency. Two explosions shattered the windows. Searing vapor lights and laser tracers lit up the darkness, diffused by the light fog. I threw a shawl over my shoulders and went to the door. Who was attacking? Was it a mutant raid? Great bursts of flame shot up from the central complex. There was a lot of screaming, choking, and crying, slightly muffled by the fog. I began running. Where I was going or why, I didn't have the slightest idea. Just run. I felt an eerie sensation, as if I had been shot through a vacuum gate.

There, standing in front of me, wearing a Network helmet and dressed in lead-lined battle fatigues was Fa-Tsang Wronski. "Are you still interested in mirrors?" he asked, as if it were a conversation at high tea.

"Mirrors?" I replied, feeling like I had been shaken awake. "I think it's been years since I really looked into one."

To be continued…

"Ya see, Prosp'," Gruber said, tossing another stick on the campfire, "we ain't so different after all. All's I'm tryin' to do is make a little beauty with them orchids o' mine. Just a little beauty."

"I believe you, Gruber, but why don't you lay down this crazy old Eco-Squad self-image and tell me what you really know. I mean about this whole weird thing we're involved in."

Gruber sat there, cross-legged, the fire lighting up the grizzled crags on his face like they were aerial photographs of mountainsides.

"OK Prosp, what yer sayin' is you want me to shoot it to you straight, is that it?"

"You got it, Gruber."

"Well, it's like this. I've stayed alive by actin' like this—crazy old Eco-Squad self-image as you call it. But like you y'urself see, there's'lot more to me 'n that I seen a lot, and I been to a lot o' places. But I'm a watcher. I learned early how tricky it is, 'n' how everyone's trying to get everyone else, and how hard it is to tell who's who, 'n' who their workin' for, much less what they want from you. Back in the old days, even after Hiroshima, it was easier. There was governments, all kinds of 'em, and they each had their little territory staked out, even the smallest of 'em. And they fought and killed each other according to what each government believed. An' all that fightin' and killin', it didn't have nothin' to do with the earth. It was all in people's heads. Not that they weren't messin' with the earth, they certainly was. That's how we're in so much trouble today."

Though I was slightly impatient with Gruber's stating the obvious, I knew there was a point he was getting at, but when? Out of deference to his experience, if not his age, I continued quietly listening.

"After the Post-Hiroshima Disasters, people wised up some. They saw killin' in the old style wasn't gonna work no more, but as you know it was long time before things got to workin' again, and when they did, wuz two voices talkin'. Wuz they the same old voice or somethin' new? Wasn't politics they were talkin'. It was geotechnics and geomantics, Geotechs and Geomants, that's what they wuz. You PAN-liaisons, you wuz operatin' under the wing o' the geomants, you know that, o' course, hee, hee, hee, ain't no dummy, you, huh Prosp? You probly know all about that synaesthetic history bit, don't you?

"Anyway, as I sees it, you're probably on the right side, but I don't know your side's that much difren' than the other, with all your sophisticated equipment, radiosonic beams 'n all that. I mean why'nt you get down to the beans of it. If it's all biopsychic, why'nt you do it that way straight?

"Now lookee what's happened. The Geomants got the North Pole, and the Geotechs the South Pole. An' you both know theys some relation 'tween geomagnetic energy currents and biopsychic energy. That's what y'ur both workin' with, right, Prosp? An' every refinement one of you makes in understandin' this relationship—it's a subtle one, huh Prosp—your helpin' the other side. You both locked in, actually helpin' each other, maybe even helpin' the world, in the long run, that is. But you're paranoid. Now it ain't exactly like the old days when the commies and the cappies they was doin' it with nuclear energy, but it's kinda like so, huh? Hee, hee, hee! we sure are dumb ain't we? Hee, hee, hee!

"But don't get me wrong now, Prosp, I'm on your side. 'N you know why? Cuz I know you're right. Not good 'n bad right, but cosmic right. Now you take the Syndics. They're smart, they're tough. No goofin' with that bunch. And they might outsmart you yet. But why're they doin' what they're doin? They say all they's workin' for is 'prosperity and happiness.' But who's prosperity and who's happiness and fer what end? But 'fore I answer that one, Prosp, you tell me who you workin' for, and for what end?"

Gruber got me on the paranoia. Right when he stuck that question to me, I immediately wondered how safe it was to tell him anything. "Hey Prosp, c'mon. Your wriggling like an angleworm on a hook. What you afraid of?"

"Well, do it," I thought to myself. "What's the worst that can happen, anyway? Gruber turns out to be a Syndiclone, and I end up in a Syndic Rehab Settlement, where I get deprogrammed, become a Decode, and maybe end up running some remote psychoradar installation for the Syndicate? That's it, but would that really be the end?"

"I know what your thinkin' Prosp, an' I'll tell you; no, that wouldn't be the end. It might be a long time 'fore you got your wits back together, but it wouldn't be the end."

"That's pretty good Gruber, pretty good." Gruber was tracking me with one-pointed accuracy. "Surrender, my boy. Surrender," I thought to myself not wanting Gruber to relish saying that to me.

"Surrender m' boy. Surrender. I'll say it anyway, Prosp'. Now do you want me to continue, or do you wanna just sit there with your paranoia?" Gruber eyed me with a sly smirk.

"No, no, go on Gruber. You got a captive audience," I replied, actually feeling comfortable.

"So, Prosp' you're a well-trained PAN-liaison, working for the Geomants. That's OK. Hee, hee, hee! Just hope them fellers in Geomant Hierarch Central get a load o' this one. Hee, hee, hee! Well everyone's on the right track, especially that one you been workin' on lately, Stellar emissions 'n DNA Transfer Tracks. I like that one, that's sharp, mighty sharp. But what's the big deal? Tell ya, Prosp, it's this: during the Great Resettlement, the Syndics missed a basic point. Like they was so busy concentratin' their camps, relocatin' their power stations, they missed a wave, they got onto lottsa waves but they missed this one. The Pre-syndics, the Fusion boys, they looked at matter as power. The Syndics inherited that one, like they got a transmission, ya know? Nowadays you both talk 'matter is energy,' big synthesized blasts goin', 'matter is energy, energy is matter.' But cuz o' their fusion transmission, the Syndics still see it the same way: matter is energy is power. That's the word in the Syndic Hierarch Central: matter is energy is power. That's fatal, ain't it Prosp' but you probly know that too, huh, Prosp? Hee, hee, hee, ain't no synaesthete for nothin', hee, hee, hee!

"Now what's wrong with power? Huh, Prosp'? What is power, anyway? Power's just not wantin' to let go. Hee, hee, hee. Who ever heard o' holdin' onto a sunbeam, not to mention cosmic rays, huh Prosp? 'N how d'ya know when to let go? By stayin' right there in biopsyche central. Long's you guys got that one happnin' for ya, ain't no way ya gonna lose it, cuz ain't nothin' to lose, right Prosp'? Hee, hee, hee! Haw! Hee, hee, hee!"

Gruber was rolling on the ground, cackling like a fool. "So damned simple," he was muttering whenever he got his breath.

"Hey, Grube, don't choke to death. I don't even know where we are, I need you." When I said "I need you," a funny feeling came over me. It was the first time I had acknowledged how I felt about Gruber. The crazy fucker, he was as close to me as my father. And that made sense since my father, Nkwame Lao Tzu Jones, was hardly even a name to me, dangling like a gold necklace from an unreachable precipice of my memories.

"Helluva lot bigger 'n the Grand Canyon, that's how big 'tis, difference' tween brain 'n mind, yep, helluva lot bigger 'n the Grand Canyon…"Gruber's monologue accompanied me into sleep.

The next day we arrived at Chaco Canyon. We were greeted by a small surveillance crew headed by Ixchel O'Shaughnessy, the daughter of a Lacandon Curandera and of the famous PAN-liaison explorer, Finn "Moon-Man" O'Shaughnessy. "Moon-Man" would always be remembered for his work on the relation between lunation cycles and RNA transfer enzymes. He became lost in the Orinoco Basin about fifteen years ago, but his last transmission was a classic that was beamed radiosonically at the close of many broadcasts:

*"Man to moon! moon to man!*
*Moon man moves what moon began!"*

Ixchel was quietly stunning. Her blue Irish eyes were about all that she got from Moon-Man. The rest was pure Mayan, Lacandon, right up to the long black hair that trailed off just beneath her buttocks, and just above the hemline of her multi-colored tunic. She had just completed a mid-day prayer observation in the Casa Rinconada Kiva.

"Mr. Gruber," she spoke, with a strong emphasis on the word 'mister,' "your arrival couldn't have been better timed." She took his hand and shook it warmly. Then she paused, eyeing me very carefully. "This is Agent 24?" she asked, her voice betraying a mixture of amusement and disbelief which had me manning my anti-paranoia gun stations.

"Something the matter?" I asked, screwing up my face, then letting my tongue lollygag about my lower lip.

"Prosp, yer catchin' on, hee heee heeee," Gruber's laugh trailed off into the pale October light. Ixchel just stood there, her right hand at her hip, looking at me with a quizzical familiarity.

"Prospero Edmund Jones, am I correct?" Ixchel's bemused smile turned to triumph.

"I'm sure that wasn't difficult for you to figure out. But anyway how'd you know?" I replied.

"Let's just say a little Australian told me to be kind to any Semi-Afros who crossed my path," Ixchel answered, narrowing her eyes in a manner that let me know that she knew. At that moment, I became completely enchanted by her.

After lunch, Ixchel took us up to the Sun-shrine just below Penasco Blanco. She sat with her back to the cliff wall. Above her were the ancient petroglyphs, star, moon, hand and sun. Crosslegged with hands on her knees, Ixchel sat motionless for some time. Gruber and I sat in the same manner, facing her.

*"Cuchulain! Kukulkan! Cuchulain! Kukulkan!" she chanted softly.*
*"On each foot seven toes, seven fingers on each hand*
*Each eye bright with seven pupils*
*Serpent body, feathered crown*
*Come where man has kissed the ground!"*

Ixchel bowed to each of us, then arching her body forward, bestowed a fragile kiss to the dusty earth on which we sat. A wind had come up. Strong gusts blew her hair in fine black wisps against the canyon wall.

"Gruber," she finally spoke, "Before you go to Hopi Mesa, you've got to get down to Jornado del Muerto. The Syndics have gained control of the Caribbean. Tikal has fallen. Teotihuacan was abandoned before they got there. We're headed for a major re-group. But it's all right. There's a major planetary line-up coming in about eight months. We're letting the Syndics take the Carib Zone as far up as the East Coast Wastelands. The PAN Polar Monitor Station at Thule will be completely synched in during the planetary line-up. A sub-tectonic radio wave will be generated, a Urantian megawave. It'll travel down the Mid-Atlantic Ridge to a point just West of the Azores, where the African, Eurasian and North American Plates meet. At that spot we've placed an Atlantean transformer. The Urantian megawave will be diffused into biopsychic bombardment units streaming eastward through the Eurasian and African plates. But heading due southwest the shock wave from the Atlantean transformation of the Urantian megawave will be directed precisely to the Bahamas Surveillance and Psychoarcheological Outpost. It will reverse all energy fields throughout the Carib Basin.

"Following that, we'll send another electromagnetic condensation in the Muhlig Hoffman mountains in Antaractica, due east of the Mt. Rex Syndic Polar Monitor Station. The wave patterns will be programmed so that Syndic thinks we've launched a two-part bombardment, one in the Carib and the other near their Polar Monitor Station. We anticipate they'll send detach units to the Mühlig Hoffman Mountains. When their units get there and begin to do radio scans, the electromagnetic condensation will take the form of a space vessel, the kind reported in Geotech South Atlantic surveys. As they approach it, it'll take off in the direction of Mt. Rex, scrambling all the patterns at the Syndic Polar Monitor. We'll have it tuned to ultramax harmonic. That'll initiate a major PAN decode operation at Mt. Rex. Decode Units from Tihuanaco are already moving down the Cordillera toward Tierra Del Fuego. We don't know if it'll work, but we think it should be our most sophisticated geobiopsychic operation yet."

"Ya mean," said Gruber, "all that fancy wave stuff and electromagnetic mind-games, just to take their Polar Station? All's I hope is that wave does somethin' right decent to the rest of us, like sharpen our wits a little hee hee hee!"

"Don't worry, Mr. Gruber, Geomant Hierarch Central has seen to that. Even if the strategic operation fails, the biopsychic bombardment released from the Urantian Megawave will intensify harmonic field patterns so that we receive maximum reception of the planetary line-up. It will be a biopsychic field-day, Mr. Gruber, a biopsychic field-day."

"So whud you need to waste our time, 'n yers o' course, too, to tell us all this, Miss Ixcheli O'Shaughnessy?" Gruber piped up, almost wistfully.

"I mean, to me it sounds like a typical Geomant fun 'n games set-up, playin' war-games all the while they sendin' subtle geostellar patterns into folks' gene-banks. Hee, hee, hee, that's what I always liked about Geomant operations, hee, hee, hee."

I had to agree with Gruber. As far as I could tell Geomant Hierarch Central had always played a good game. Acting like the enemy, they did a good job of teasing the Geotechs into ever more sophisticated levels of feedback counter-strategems, which Geomant Hierarch Central would program into the Planet Master Plan.

"What Gruber says is correct, Ixchel. I know you've got something else up your tunic, so what is it?" I asked my question with enough sexual double-entendre that Ixchel shifted her position to accommodate my double-coding. She stretched her left leg straight out toward me, and drew her right leg up so that she could rest her chin upon it for a moment as she gazed into my eyes.

To call that gaze penetrating is as insufficient as saying the sun is bright. In that one moment she communicated to me all that I needed to know about her intentions with both Gruber and myself. But the immediacy of the biopsychic contact was embellished with all of the haunting beauty and lore of her genetic programming.

The vision in which the information was framed consisted of this: an Irish wizard, snow-white beard and hair falling in luxuriant folds over shoulders and chest, perched atop the Temple of the Inscriptions at Palenque looking into a duodecahedron crystal. Two Mayan astronomers stood at either side of him, holding baskets of copal incense in their folded arms. While the incense gave off great plumes of richly intoxicating smoke, the Irish wizard, the crystal held aloft in his right hand, a gnarled walking staff in his left, spoke in words that were at once like water rushing over stones and great sprays of stellar sound coming from a radiotelescope audio transmitter:

"Though this was so then, eight brief years before Hiroshima, it is not so now. There at the Jornado del Muerto, where the god Vishnu proclaimed, 'Now I am become death, destroyer of worlds,' 23 days before Hiroshima, there is now a rod, a technetium-plated rod lodged in earth's jeweled crust. As long as that rod remains, there is no way the earthlings can receive the beneficent vibrations of the stellar program. Those who do not fear the journey of death can take the journey of death."

Upon finishing his exhortation, the Celtic wizard tapped his staff three times upon the top step of the Temple of the Inscriptions.

Ixchel's foot was tapping at my right knee. "So Prospero, be a dear, and communicate to Gruber what is needed of both of you." Ixchel's disarmingly seductive smile disappeared as if a cloud had suddenly ambushed the sun. In its place were a pair of motionless, sensuous lips, the chief adornment of the lower part of a face that had turned to stone.

Slowly withdrawing her leg and resuming the original cross-legged posture, Ixchel pointed to the petroglyphs above her head. "For a long time now we have known the secret of crossing stars with earthlings, for a longtime now we have known this secret. It is nothing difficult, yet trees weep and the deer become lost on the barren mesa."

*"Cuchulain, Kukulkan, Cuchulain, Kukulkan"*
*"On each foot seven toes, seven fingers on each hand*
*Each eye bright with seven pupils*
*Seven wheels roll down the ley line straight*
*May destiny claim Kukulkan as her mate."*

When Ixchel completed her chant, she drew a circle on the ground with her left index finger. With her right hand she took a blue powder and made a small circle at the center of this circle. Then, taking red powder, she made a circle around that one, and finally with white powder she colored the original enclosing circle.

*"On the Journey of Death must you go*
*On the Journey of Death must you go*
*White for your body, red for your speech*
*Blue for your mind*
*keep well the secret*
*that no force can unbind."*

On our foreheads she placed a dash of the white powder, on our throats the red, and upon our hearts, the blue.

Leaving Penasco Blanco I felt a strange sadness. The hills were lit up by the evening sun so that they appeared to have been soaked in blood. Randomly scattered mesas cast large purple shadows on the ancient earth. Ixchel placed an arm around me. "Prospero, tonight, go to the Great Kiva at the Casa Rinconada. Be there at midnight. Don't ask me anything, just be there at midnight…"

---

"So what yer tellin' me Prosp, is that we gotta go to Jornado del Muerto 'n pull that rod outta the ground huh? Sounds worse 'ngettin' a mutant to look in a mirror, if'n you know what I mean. Hee, hee, hee!"

"Yeah, Grube, that's it. It also seems to me," I went on, following a hunch, "that the Syndics are still messing with nuclear fusion. If I got the picture right, that rod is fixed so it points a beam right to a timer that's programmed by the Syndic Polar Monitor. The right signal sent from the timer would trigger the rod. The shock waves from the rod going off would hit the timer causing it to set off a polar reversal charge at the South Pole. If the Syndics got wind of the Urantian megawave plan, they'd do that, and that would stop us in our tracks."

"That's a lotta trouble to stop us 'n lotsa other people as well. Would they be that stupid, Prosp'? Huh? Would they set off somethin' that would get us right into an axis tilt? Sounds like Atlantis to me, Prosp' play it one more time, Atlantis roulette. Hee, hee, hee."

---

Using my light beam, I picked my way to the Great Kiva at Casa Rinconada. Circular ancient stone walls. As I clambered up them, I could hear lizards scrambling among the rocks. I made my way to what felt to be the center of the kiva. Turning off the light beam, I lay on my back, orienting myself to the pole star. Legs splayed and arms straight out, I concentrated on the pole star. The dippers, Orion, the Pleiades, all came into focus. Finally I picked out what I was looking for: the Crab Nebula. Holding my concentration I let go of bodily impulses, let myself become absorbed by this one pinpoint of stellar energy. I hardly noticed it when Ixchel's voice drifted toward me.

"Chaco: The Tournament of the Stars," she announced in uncanny imitation of one of those dreadful Syndic broadcasts that tries to sound as if it were one of ours. Though I responded when she took my hand, I did not break my concentration on the Crab Nebula. Nor did my gaze shift a millimeter as she untied my pantaloons, so slowly, so gently, whispering as she did so, "and what did the ancients know of harmony? Interlocking half-circles for friendship, squares within squares for the sacred sipapu."

Before I knew it she was on top of me. "Star-catchers, that's who they were, and now you are one of them, too. Hold me, hold me, but don't lose the stars," Ixchel murmured into my ear, as her small, lithe body like a shuttle on a loom moved up and down, back and forth upon mine. As we made love, I felt the light pattern of the Crab Nebula flow through me, fusing Ixchel and I into one being, a being that swiftly slipped, among a chorus of moans, into the icy oblivion that keeps the stars in their course.

---

"Star-catcher! Hee, hee, hee, Prosp' that woman laid a good name on ya. Now, how do you spose she came up with that one? Do ya think it's another name for Cuchulain. Lemme see yer eyes boy. Sure 'nuff, you got seven pupils in each one. Star-catcher. Hee, hee, hee!"

"Oh, come on, Grube," I replied, pulling the reins on Dragon-Power, "You called yourself a 'watcher.' You know as well as I do where Ixchel got that name."

Smiling slyly, Gruber answered, "Yer catchin' on boy, yer catchin' on."

We were a few hours out of Chaco Canyon, headed south toward Jornado del Muerto. Way to the south, the Zuni mountains, wispy blue and shimmering in the mid-day heat, beckoned us.

"Ya know, Prosp'," Gruber broke a long silence. "Jornado del Muerto, that's just this side o' Truth or Consequences. Strange little place. I wuz there years ago. Mutant center run by some Warlock named Jason. Jason 'n the Golden Fleece. I just wonder if we're gonna run into them, the Golden Fleece, I mean, whatdya think Prosp'?"

"I dunno." I found myself annoyed hearing myself talk like Gruber, "are they trouble?"

"They spell trouble faster 'n a syndic decode unit can scramble yer marbles hee, hee, hee!" Laughing, Gruber rolled off his horse into a thicket of tumbleweed.

I didn't answer. My only concern was holding on to the silver tube, the one I had been carrying since El Dorado, the one with the decode information about Natasha Eisenhammer.

No sooner did the name Natasha Eisenhammer flash through my mind then I experienced a deep feeling of connectedness: Star-Catcher, yes, that's who I was. Nezahualpilli Star-Catcher Jones. And the ball-game, the royal ball-game. Of course, that was the Tournament of the Stars, "Played by astronomers and kings just to fix the course of destiny." And here I was playing it again.

"Ixchel O'Shaughnessy, thank you," I thought, "for throwing the ball into my court."

"On second thought, Grube," I finally answered him, "if you can tell me who It-lil-po-tan-cuah was, then you know better than I do why she called me Star-Catcher!"

"It-lil-po-what?" Gruber looked genuinely perplexed. But was he really? One thing I had learned about Gruber—his name was a synonym for unrelenting inscrutability.

To be continued…

*"Even if by chance a leather belt is bestowed on one,*
*by the end of the morning*
*It will have been snatched away."*

The image could not have been more accurate. And the new hexagram was that of Exhaustion. The oracle spoke directly to my situation, it snapped at me. Looking out of the window of my room in the Dan Katchongva Residency, I let the blue-gold shadows of the mesas and mountains bathe my vision. A lone hawk circled over the horizon. I wanted to cry, but everything inside was dry; I was like the lake from which all the water had leaked away. I looked at the Oracle again:

*"There is no water in the lake.*
*The image of Exhaustion.*
*Thus the superior person stakes his life*
*on following his will."*

Did I have any will left? I remembered the drab, dreary days at Cape Wrath, the rolling sea, the waves crashing on the rocks, the endless fog. Lurking beneath the wind-crippled pines and shrubbery of Cape Wrath, two figures like shadows in search of my heart, drove themselves in fugitive circles, lacing my memory with the shattered stained glass fragments of bitterness and love: Abdul-Rumi and Natasha.

The only lead thread I could see at this moment was the one question that had come to haunt me: why me, why had they chosen me to play in the drama which they had so skill-fully crafted? Alternating with this question was the feeling that I had blown it. A sickly sea of remorse seemed to await me whenever my mind ceased to be occupied with the question: why me?

The only relief I received came from the direction of Karuna Dawnstar Monongye. Almost from the moment Fa-Tsang Wronski delivered me to Hopi Mesa, Dawnstar had taken me under her wing. It's an old fashioned phrase, under her wing, but it fits what happened between the two of us.

The first session I had with her in snake-handling contained the whole pattern. When she told me that we were going to indulge in a little pytho-therapy, I could have died.

With her strong brown arms, Dawnstar embraced me and said, "Daughter of the earth, what are you afraid of? The snake has done nothing to you, and holds nothing against you. But it is very sensitive. Should you show the snake your fear, it will interpret it as a threat on its life, and so will attack or harm you. But the lesson of the snake is a good one. No one has really done anything to you, no one really holds anything against you. All the pain and fear you experience is your own doing, your own dream. But it isn't a bad dream. All dreams are lessons. Listen well to them. Now, are you ready to descend into the kiva with me?"

Just her voice, like melted butter or liquid gold, was medicine to me. Within the golden flow of her voice, the words were like time, time capsules, gently floating into my nervous system. What she said would come to me from time to time, lifting me from my despondency.

And she was right. Handling the snakes was no problem. In fact, I discovered by having to eliminate every trace of fear, every notion of selfhood in relating to the snakes, that I began to experience new levels of energy, dynamic expansive energy radiating from the vacuum left by the letting goof my fear. This emptiness, this "core of no fear," as Dawnstar referred to it, was a glimpse of the Ocean of Truth, the ultimate nature so she told me, not only of my mind, but of all things. This part of the experience I could connect with some of the things I had learned at Shasta Abbey, the mind-tracking practice, for instance, seemed somehow connected to the "core of no fear."

Just as I was thinking these things, Dawnstar appeared at my door. "Francesca, do you realize how late it is?"

There was something different about Dawnstar today. Around her forehead was a gold turquoise dotted band which also served to hold her hair in place. She wore a simple white skirt embroidered with a horizontal band of four morningstar designs. Her blouse had a large ruffled collar and was gathered loosely at the waist. I was stunned by its electric turquoise coloring. Gold dew drop earrings dangled at either side of her neck. She was dressed for something, but I didn't know what.

"Tell me what you have been thinking, Francesca," she said as she sat herself on a stool next to my loom.

I told her about the oracle, and about my remorse and Abdul-Rumi and Natasha.

And I told her about my burning question: why me?

"The oracle's a good sign. The rest is rubbish. Whatever you think about those things is only a waste of energy, like old fuel-driven vehicles, choking people with their exhaust fumes, that's all it is. But what about your will?" Though Dawnstar's voice was stern, her eyes twinkled.

"You mean the line that refers to staking my life on my will?"

"Right. Where does that take you?"

The only thing I could think of was the snakes, their cold, reptilian bodies sleekly wrapping themselves about my arms. What I liked about that experience was the electrical charge.

"It's the snakes, Dawnstar. That's where my strength is right now. That I can actually handle them, know them, share in their power. It's like I'm communicating with them, like they're telling me something. Oh, not in words, but in patterns. They're telling me something in patterns. It's like they're antennae or divining rods and they put me in touch with something that…" I paused. I was almost afraid to say what was on my mind. "Well, something that isn't quite human. At least not human the way we think of human. Or maybe something bigger than human, beyond human. I don't know really how to say it. All I know is that something is definitely happening there."

"That is your will, Francesca. That is what you have to go on. That is all you have to go on." Dawnstar spoke with a tone of fatalism that chilled me. Was that all I had to go on?

"But what about my voice, my singing and acting?" I asked, not making any effort to conceal my apprehension.

"Those are gifts, Francesca. But without a connection, grounding you to the earth, your gifts are like bubbles in a stream. You know a little. You have had some good teachers, and you know a little bit. But you do not know enough with your heart. You do not know enough with the core of no fear which is your heart. That is why you are here. Know completely through the core of no fear, and you will be able to answer your question: 'why me?'" Before I was able to absorb what Dawnstar had said, she changed the subject.

"I see you are weaving the 'knot of eternity,'" as she spoke, she eyed my loom up and down. "This is good. Without beginning and without end. Why don't you come with me. Let's go to the old kiva."

"Yes," I replied, "that's an excellent idea."

We walked slowly to the kiva. It was a brilliant October day. In the far distance, large thunderheads clung to the rhythmic procession of bronze-colored mesas. Behind Old Oraibi, three large mirror surfaced radio dishes rotated lazily.

"Back in the old days, of course, no one took us seriously," Dawnstar was talking softly as we wended our way to our destination. "This was just after Hiroshima, when it became time to spread the prophecy. But nobody listened, nobody took the elders seriously. There was one exception. In the year '29 AH, we were visited by the Karmapa. Though he was from Tibet, we understood each other, we exchanged teachings and prophecies, and in the Old Kiva he performed the ceremony where Avalokiteshvara stirs the pit of existence. His visit was the only sign we needed to confirm what we were doing." We stopped for a moment before the Morningstar Basin, a simple round reflecting pool, in the center of which, on a small octagonal pedestal was a large crystal sphere. We sat on the stone rim that contained the pool, where Dawnstar continued.

"It was at the end of the 25-year disaster period, when we received the next sign. For many years we had been without communication. Then toward the end of the year '67 AH, a small group of people came to us from the Northeast, from the Central Rockies. They were Kargyupas. They had some connection with the Great Karmapa. But they were not Tibetan. One of their elders, a man whom they called 'Trident,' was very ill, and they asked if we could help him. Our medicine people ministered to him. But there seemed to be nothing that could be done. Despite this, 'Trident' was known for his cheerfulness which he maintained through his illness. One morning in winter, sometime after the solstice, Trident appeared, right at this spot where we're sitting now and called together the Hopi and Kargyupas.

"He spoke to them of a dream he had had the night before. This was the 'Morning Star Vision.' He spoke of two suns and one star. The suns were to be the Geomants and the Geotechs, but the star, that was above them, beyond them. The star was known as the morning star because it was ever fresh, ever new, did not grow old, did not die. He said that it was here that it would begin, the 'Making of the Fifth Ring.' It was here, he said, that the 'Morning Star Vision' would sow its seeds. And he said that we should be ready, always ready for the emissaries of the morning star."

As Dawnstar spoke, I felt a tremor pass through my body, a tremor of recognition. But of what, I wasn't sure. Dawnstar eyed me carefully, then smiled. "That is an old story. Who knows? But it is said that Trident passed away that very day, at this very place, and at this very place his body was cremated, and afterward there was much abundance around here, and here this pool is now, a spring of water gushing forth from the ground, a spring of water that had not been here before Trident spoke."

Climbing down the ladder into the Kiva, the story of Trident and the Morning Star Vision was still very much with me. Why did I feel so touched, so disturbed by what Dawnstar had told me? In the kiva were two snakes, two diamondback rattlers. They were coiled together near the shrine.

"Go to them, Francesca. Take them and know them," Dawnstar commanded me.

I went cold. It seemed my bowels would explode.

"Go, Francesca," Dawnstar urged me on.

Slowly, slowly I approached them. Standing a half meter away from them, I became very still. I had to let every thought, every feeling ebb out of me. I had to become cold, like the snakes. Their two heads raised above their coiled bodies, forked tongues darting nervously, I extended each of my arms toward them. What I felt in my arms was an intense magnetism. As my fingers reached almost to their heads, I could hear a flicker of rattles. What would happen? Would they strike or fuse into the magnetic field projected by my arms? At that moment, I could not even allow myself the luxury of asking the question.

Fixing my gaze on the two snake heads, nothing else seemed to exist. Each head moved in perfect unison toward my hands. Long slithering bodies uncoiling, slowly wrapping themselves about my arms. One field, one being, no being, no field. As they wrapped themselves tightly about my arms, their heads lifted above my shoulders, I experienced a powerful surge of energy, as if everything had been transformed into light. Two voices simultaneously penetrated that light. One was the voice of the Indian Sage, Nagarjuna, the other that of Pythagoras. It's not like they announced who they were. I just knew it.

Nagarjuna: "Initiated by Mahanaga, it was I who dived deep within the ocean, dived deep to the serpent palace where, in the seven precious receptacles I obtained the elixir of one-taste. Chief among the wise, I continue to dwell in the Ocean of Enlightenment, avoiding the shores 'Is' and 'Is-not.'"

Pythagoras: "Serpent of Samos, Discoverer and Enjoyer of all Harmony I am the player of music, the singer of stars, the chanter of codes. Dissolving my being in the elixir of one-taste, I tame the dogs of Persephone and climb the ladder of stars where I dwell in the Palace, Wish-Fulfilling Gem of All-Knowing."

---

Sitting with my knees drawn up to my chin I answered Dawnstar again, "Yes, that's exactly what I heard each of them saying. It was clear, so clear."

Dawnstar only nodded this time. She appeared absorbed in deep concentration.

"But what I'd like to know, Dawnstar," I began again, "is why was it the voices of men that spoke to me. Here we are, a couple of women, and like you've told me before, the true keepers of the pytho-therapy have been us women. So what's going on?"

Dawnstar looked at me, a broad smile on her face. "Francesca, I've heard it said that it was Apollo who killed his own Oracles, the Pythonesses of Delphi. Why was this so? Because it was the pattern of time, and we are woven into time, like the threads on your loom. As the pattern changed it was male threads who wove the image of the serpent. Pythagoras of Greece and Nagarjuna of India were simply serpent weavers who helped shape the Third Ring. But the wisdom of the serpent remains unchanged— elixir of one-taste, right Francesca?"

"I guess so, Dawnstar," I replied diffidently. "But tell me, what more is there about this mysterious Trident of the Morning Star Vision, I mean, who was he?"

"All we know is that he was a Kargyupa. There are still some of them here. Why don't you ask them?"

After dinner that evening, I sat talking with Fa-Tsang. I told him of what had occurred in the kiva, and of the voices. "What do you think of experiences like that? I mean, do they come from those people or is it just in my head or what? Dawnstar really didn't say anything. You know her, Grandmother Silence."

Fa-Tsang sat at the table across from me, a bespectacled, chunky Mongolian moonface, dappled with small scars, like the craters of the moon. "Well tell me, Francesca, did you ever experience anything like that before?"

"Not really," I replied, my mind going back over the experience. "What I understand is that the purpose of the pytho-therapy is to destroy you, I mean destroy your ego, and at the same time strengthen your character. I mean, if handling snakes won't do that for you, nothing will. Have you ever handled snakes?"

Fa-Tsang backed off, his hands held out toward me in mock fear. "You must be crazy to think that of me. I wouldn't dare touch a snake. At least, I don't think I would. In fact, that's something I've been meaning to tell you. I really admire you for what you've been able to do since we got here. You've pulled yourself together miraculously. I really mean that Francesca."

Perhaps he was right. It had been scarcely three months since I had arrived.

Though I was filled with doubt and remorse over what had happened, almost as if I had betrayed something, yet I was coming back very quickly to a sense of worthiness and inquisitiveness.

"You're a dear, Fa-Tsang. But you know more about this stuff than I do. Tell me what you know." I felt myself growing impatient.

"OK, Francesca," he began, "as you know, Giza has fallen to the Syndicate. This means they now have a central strategic position. I think they wanted you because of what happened to you today, the voices I mean. But they're not sophisticated enough to be able to get that kind of information so easily. Natasha was on the right track by involving you in her performances, but that got messed up because of the...ummm... passion."

"Don't be awkward, Fa-Tsang. What happened, happened. At least now I have some idea of what I'm... capable of," I interjected, seductively, hoping to make Fa-Tsang feel more at ease.

Fa-Tsang nodded, his boyish grin turning into a sweet smirk in obvious allusion to my episode with him at Giza. "But don't seduce me from answering your question," he went on, "as you know, in developing good harmonies we've been able to synch different levels of energy—electromag, geomag, and biopsyche, including the genetic tattoo. What we've never accounted for, at least not very well, is the influence of past behavior patterns on coding. What the Buddhists call karma. Well, the Geomants have been busy with this one, and the syndics are just getting a whiff of it. What we're realizing more and more is that all of us are unconsciously playing out roles and games that synch with things that happened a long time ago. So-called chance meetings, and seemingly random events...well, they're not so chancy or random. Like this meeting here for instance..." Fa-Tsang stopped. He was getting rather heated, and he took off his glasses, placing them on the table. His eyes were penetrating, yet soft. In the silence that had fallen between us, I felt something large, an immensity, an unnamable immensity.

"Don't say anymore, Fa-Tsang. Please don't say anymore," I whispered to him, taking his hand in mine. Shifting the subject, I asked Fa-Tsang, "And what do you know about Trident, the Morning Star visionary?"

Fa-Tsang put on his glasses again. "Trident? Well, from what I gathered from the monks over on Marpa Mesa, Trident had been something of a scholar in the Disaster Period. He had written a book on the Principles of Biopsychic Harmonics, which no one took seriously back then. He seems to have been a Buddhist, Kargyu order, the rest of his life. Seems to have spent much of his time painting in the mountains. That's about all they know of him. They don't even have a copy of his book. Why?"

Just then Karuna Monongye's grandson, David Eagle-Bowl, entered the dining area. In his late teens, with flowing black hair, David had never shown any particular inclination toward anything. With her customary equanimity, his grandmother simply nodded when people asked what David did.

"Miss Francesca," he spoke softly, "Grandmother would like to see you. You'd better come with me, now." Then as an afterthought, he turned to Fa-Tsang, "Good evening. 'Scuse me for interrupting. You know how it is when Grandma wants something."

David led me down a flower-bordered path, toward the bottom of the second Mesa into the artisan quarter. We stopped before a modest adobe house. A bright blue door was its most distinguishing feature.

"Here, this is it," David said as he took my arm and we opened the door.

Though the room was lit solely by candles, placed in a circle around what I was soon to realize was an extraordinary sand-painting, the interior almost blew me over with its incandescence. At the far side of the room I could make out Dawnstar, dressed as she was this morning. Seated next to her was a silver-haired, naked black gnome. He appeared to be on fire. When David and I closed the door behind us, they both broke into broad grins.

"Francesca," Dawnstar greeted me with a buoyant heartiness, "this is Poontutjarpa. Poontutjarpa Jayavarman. He very much wanted to see you, so I called for you."

The black gnome sat motionless, but I felt his eyes "reading" me, going inside of me. It wasn't threatening or menacing in any way. In fact, it was as if I were being washed.

"Pretty, pretty Francesca. Francesca with hair the color of golden seas, please come here, sit next to me." Poontutjarpa beckoned with his left hand. His voice had the most peculiar, lilting sing-song quality.

Brushing away the vague familiarity of his name, I walked around the room arriving at his left side. He extended an arm to me, an arm that seemed all sinews and nervous energy. Taking his hand, I was immediately reminded of how my mother used to take my hand, and of the comfort it gave me. Poontutjarpa's hand was like that. It was a mother's hand, soft like flower petals.

Dawnstar, who was seated now on Poontutjarpa's right, thanked her son and bade him leave. Then she explained, "I told Poontutjarpa of your experience this morning. The experience with the two diamondback rattlers. The experience of the voices. I told Poontutjarpa these things, and this is why he wanted to see you. This is why he asked you to come here tonight." Dawnstar wasn't talking. She was chanting. The sounds of her words faded in the intense candlelight, only to be replaced by a high, almost electrical sounding hum. Very faintly came the sound of rattles, like those on the snakes this morning, rattles, and other voices. Nothing seemed abnormal, however.

"Francesca, Viking offspring sired by the progenitors of Leonardo, Francesca, from whose mother flows the blood of the bards and the song of Gawain. Francesca," Poontutjarpa was chanting now, "look carefully at the colored sands before you, as many grains as there are sands in the Ganges, as many lives have you lived, so look carefully. Think about nothing, but look carefully. Look!"

Following Poontutjarpa's instructions I began to study the large circular sand-painting that covered the floor of the otherwise unadorned room. In the center was a series of concentric circles, each concentric circle composed of a ring of small white circles. Four similarly composed bands extended out from this circle, only to break up into mazes of an intricate order, like those on silicon chips. I tried following them. At first I got lost.

"Remember the core of no-fear, become the core of no-fear," Dawnstar's voice wafted into my ears as if sent to me from across a canyon.

I entered the state I went into during the pytho-therapy. This time I was able to follow each of the mazes. With a slight shock, I realized they were genetic memory circuits. So taken was I with the elegance with which they had been designed, and the brilliance of the subtle color changes the circuits went through, that it took me a few moments before I realized I could fuse all four circuits into one. Once I was able to accomplish this, I did not want to leave it. Past, present, future, and yet some other dimension spoke to me, yet all spoke with one tongue. Memory was no different from vision. Beings in endless transformation—winged, multi-legged, reptilian, furry, fanged, luminous, and iridescent—streamed through the circuits. Bliss-filled and ecstatic, I gasped that so much could be revealed. And, at the same time that I saw the destiny traces of all beings, I saw my own trace distinct and clear, issuing from the genetic labyrinth and finally losing itself in the track of a star.

"Commit this to memory, Francesca, it's a good little joke to carry with you," Poontutjarpa's singsong voice came to me like wind sweeping among mountain tree-tops.

Then I began to weep. I wept for the sadness, the ignorance I had known. I wept for the sadness and the ignorance of all beings, devouring each other, hurting each other, mistrusting each other. As I wept, making no effort to control myself, I heard myself repeating over and over, like a little girl crying herself to sleep, "We're all the same human, we're all the same human…"

The three of us sat the rest of the night, talking in brief little intervals. Towards dawn, we sat motionless, sat until slivers of light began to pierce the corners of the room, sat until it was as if one current bound our three minds together. Then as the room filled with a brilliant orange-pink light, the little black gnome, Poontutjarpa, got up. He went around the circle, counterclockwise, walking in a crouched manner, snuffing out the candles with his fingers. Then when he had finished doing this, he went to the center of the sand painting and with a sweeping motion of his hands erased it.

After he had erased the design so that what remained was a muddy-colored mess shot through with sparkles of light and color, he handed us each a broom. Sweeping up the sand and placing it in a large burlap bag, he said to me, "take it, take it to Marpa Mesa, and on the south side where two large rocks form a natural seat, empty this bag."

Swinging the bag over my shoulder, I opened the door. Just as I was stepping out, I heard Poontutjarpa calling out to me, "Francesca! Happy day! Good Morning! Welcome Home!"

# PART II
# THE JOURNEY OF DEATH

"Coulda cloned me with that one, Prosp," Grube leered at me between gulps of Shrimp Mescalero, the red and green sauce of which added a gay touch to his begrizzled chin. "So you figgerin' Natasha Eisenhammer to be carrying the genetic pattern of this It-lil-po-tan-cuah, huh? Pretty speectacular, if'n I don't say. Yep, pretty speectacular, indeed. 'N if'n yer Nezahualpilli gene bag got it straight, you got an interestin' show-down comin' up with this here syndiclone, Madame Eisenhammer, hee, hee, hee! S'pose she's sexy, too huh? Hee, hee, hee!" Grube was carrying on in his typically disgusting manner, the Mescalero Shrimp sauce exploding from between his yellowed teeth.

We were spending a few days at the Socorro Psychophysical Recharge Station. Sleek adobe walls enclosing a smattering of clear bubble domes, landscaped real nice with saguaro cactus and palmettos. Atmosphere, I thought, real atmosphere. The Psychophysical Agent in charge was an elderly fellow, San Juan de la Cruz Esquivel. Sweet old Indian type with a long graying braid of hair falling down over his shoulders. A scraggly feather was always ready to fall out of the top of the braid, but miraculously, it never did. I wondered if Esquivel slept with the feather in his head.

He was charming sitting behind the control monitors sipping his peyote tea, shouting out at us, "Mr. Jones, Mr. Gruber. Was the thermal lab the right temperature for you? We used to have trouble with it, Mutant Outlaws around here you know."

Esquivel's unrelievedly cheery manner was heightened by the presence of his two chief assistants, Claudia Blavatsky Leventhal and Ramakrishna al-Badr. Claudia was in her early twenties, alternately svelte and voluptuous, clothed in the morning in a white thermal jumpsuit and mylar-coated boots, and in the evening, filmy gauzy gowns tied together with gold ropes and jade brooches. What made her seductive sense of style so ingratiatingly adorable was the decorous innocence with which she carried it off.

"But Mr. Jones, please let me test out the Thermal Therapy Lab for you. It is my pleasure you know." She would blink at me, her dimpled cheeks radiating just the right amount of concern.

Ramakrishna Al-Badr, who acted as the chief host for the G & O (Gustatory and Olfactory) Lounge, was all manners, his round wispy bearded face being the perfect repository for a smile that was indelible.

"Are you sure you gentlemen are through with this course?" Ramakrishna was motioning to Grube's serving mat which looked like a shrimp and pepper factory had exploded in his face.

As if in deference to Ramakrishna Al-Badr's beaming politeness, Grube took up a blue maize-cake and began blotting up the Shrimp Mescalero leavings that had drenched his woven palm serving mat. I was surprised to see his blue porcelain bowl come into view once again. I quickly found out why. Ramakrishna, with dapper insouciance, had also taken a piece of blue maize cake and with transistorized efficiency, not to mention maternal pleasure, had created order out of Grube's serving mat. In a state of numbed shock, Grube looked up at Ramakrishna, who, as if nothing had ever happened, plied Gruber with another carafe of negative ion quencher, the kind they serve with a slice of guava on the side. Regaining his composure, if one could call Grube's blissfully moronic smile by that name, Grube took the carafe and downed it with all of the abandon of someone who had just fallen headfirst into a samadhi tub.

Lowering his usually formal demeanor to the upper threshold of intimacy, Ramakrishna asked if he could sit down with us for a minute. "Now I know you gentlemen are only here for a few days, of course, and it may not be in my place to suggest this, but I do feel something rather kindly about you…"

"C'mon Ramakrish'," Grube interjected in his endearingly rude tone of voice, "we's all on the same level here, so get to the point won't ya, hee, hee, hee!"

Not the least bit ruffled, Ramakrishna continued, "Knowing that you gentlemen will only be here another day, I think it would be to your best interest to acquaint yourselves with the specialty of Socorro Flats."

"'N whaddaya mean by that, young man?" Grube squinted intensely now at Ramakrishna.

"Well, you see that couple over there," Ramakrishna nodded with his head to a table across the room. Lounging comfortably on the oversize throw pillows was a middle-aged man with a steel-gray beard. A long, pointed beard, it was. His arm was around a lady somewhat younger than him clad in a sequined astro-jumpsuit. Since her back was facing us, the most remarkable feature which she displayed was a marvelous hairdo: two symmetrical waves of tight, shiny black curls, sculpted in a style I recognized as "high African." I was instantly reminded of my mother, Tara Andromeda, "The Queen of Shasta Abbey," as she had affectionately come to be called by those in the Network who knew her.

"What's so special about them, Ramakrish?" I blushed to myself, realizing I had picked up Grube's sloppy way with names.

"That happens to be, gentlemen, yes, that happens to be one of the Sub-Directors of the Socorro Flats Black Hole Legion. A very special man," Ramakrishna paused, his customary smile allowing for the escape of a few uncustomary giggles. "Yes," he continued, "that happens to be Henri St. Germain Aldebaran, Master of the Black Hole Intelligence Probe." Had it not been for Ramakrishna's scarcely concealed enthusiasm, I would have killed him for the unctuousness with which he uttered "Master of the Black Hole Intelligence Probe."

"'N who might ya spose that is he got's his arm around, the Intelligence o' the Black Hole herself? Hee, hee, hee!" Grube sputtered away at his allusion to the obvious African geneticism of the lady accompanying Aldebaran. I tried getting Grube's attention to show him my displeasure at the crudeness of his humor, but it was impossible. Once Grube let off with a one-liner like that he was in orbit, the unreachable sun of a solar system known only to him.

Totally ignoring Grube's lapse of taste, Ramakrishna, with a seriousness of intent I was only now beginning to appreciate, responded to Grube's question, "And the lady, why gentlemen, the lady she is Ya Emme Bandiagara. She came to Socorro Flats after the fall of Timbuctoo, oh, many years ago now, longer than I have held my position here. But she is very skilled. It was really with her knowledge and assistance that Mr. St. Germain Aldebaran was able to obtain so much success with the Black Hole Intelligence Probe."

As Ramakrishna spoke, I felt infected by a sudden outburst of curiosity, a curiosity mixed with familiarity which immediately recalled Ixchel O'Shaughnessy and the Star-Catcher rite. I looked at Grube. Abandoning his glassy-eyed semi-conscious stare for the briefest moment, he winked at me. It was enough of a gesture on Grube's part to let me know he hadn't yet opted out for ultimate synchromesh. Whatever was about to happen, I knew I'd need him.

"So what I was wondering, gentlemen, is if you wouldn't mind being introduced to this couple. They are really the true flavor of Socorro Flats. And besides, can you imagine the pleasure it would give me, if you actually became friends with these people?"

"Oh, Ramakrishna, your style is molten honey!" I responded, giving him an affectionate slap on the cheek.

I don't know what it is about me, but it didn't take me very long at all to be swept into the tow of Ya Emme Bandiagara's magnetism. The majesty of the way in which she wore her hair was matched by the dignity of the way she held her head. And what a head. Feline eyes perfectly posed above two delicately sculpted cheekbones provided a pixieish counterpoint to her full, sensuous orchid-colored lips. While the post-dinner incense and jets of perfume tantalized our olfactory sense with a subtle symphony of nasal hues, I became thoroughly entranced by the delicate quiverings of Ya Emme's nostrils, which oscillated in perfect synchronization to the passage of mellifluous odors.

Following the olfactory repast, Henri St. Germain Aldebaran recounted, I'm sure for the hundredth time, his work leading up to the intriguing Black Hole Intelligence Probe.

"Being assigned to the Socorro Flats VLA was initially rather routine. It's one of the older VLAs, but because of that it gave me a sense, well, of gentle comfort. The library here is one of the best, and it gave me access to some of the earlier Radio Maps and related documents." Aldebaran spoke in a congenial, erudite manner. Very man-of-the-world. Sucking on a piece of guava, I gathered that he relished telling his tale, no matter how many times he had already told it.

"In any case, while going over the microfilm I came across a letter of Robert J. Oppenheimer's, one he had written while he was at Los Alamos explaining how disturbed he had been to have his research on the x-ray radiation of neutron stars, particularly that which was focused on the Crab Nebula, disrupted by work on the first atomic bomb. I was immediately struck by the coincidence of Oppenheimer's being here, in the heart of ancient Crab Nebula country, no less, and that of the explosion of the first atomic bomb at Jornada del Muerto. Something inside of me clicked. Of course, what the earlier Radio Explorers hadn't taken into account when they first discovered pulsars and black holes was that the intelligence of a star system such as that represented by the Crab Nebula, had evolved to a preternaturally high degree."

"Preter-what degree," Grube spluttered, leaving his condition of olfactory bliss.

"Preternatural. Preter meaning beyond, in other words an intelligence transcending the laws of nature. Of course the earlier Radio Explorers, drenched as they were in the late materialist viewpoint of the Industrial Ring, were incapable even of dreaming of this possibility. There they were, people like Shklovski and Sagan sending out their crude little radio blips in a binary code that took little account of the fact that pre-ternatural intelligence operates through synchrotronic radiation which encodes information at highly oscillating frequencies which immediately enter the biopsychic field, unnoticed of course. Only a highly receptive psychic attunement can even begin to make a little sense out of these transmissions. This is why the Anasazi at Chaco Canyon responded as they did to the Crab Nebula." At this he turned to Ya Emme and smiled.

It was her turn to pick up the story. She spoke in a deep, melodic tone, made all the more pleasing by the merest hint of an accent.

"At Timbuctoo we had been working with certain Griots, you know, the keepers of the teachings of ancient times, in a Radiosonic Lab. We had been coming to the same conclusion that dear Aldebaran had here at Socorro Flats. When Timbuctoo was about to fall to the Syndics, I instinctively came here, for I knew that while the Dogon had connected with Sirius B, the Anasazi had made a connection with the Crab Nebula. I know there was a similarity. What I had hypothesized was this: that the preternatural intelligence of star systems like Sirius B, a white dwarf, or even more so, the Crab Nebula, easily foresaw what was to occur when the system was going to explode. Preternatural intelligence functions primarily at a level of pure biopsychic immediacy. Energy, pure and simple. The intelligence of the system devised the means of continuing through synchronizing their energy patterns with the stellar transformation that results in a neutron star, a pulsar. In this way they could communicate their intelligence through synchrotron radiation to a vast radius beyond their original system."

"But for what reason?" I asked, though I felt I already knew why.

"But, Mr. Jones," Ya Emme turned to me with a sly smile, "you tell me."

"It seems," I began, assuming the intellectual tone already established by Aldebaran and Bandariaga, "that genuine intelligence is inseparable from a need to communicate. And even more than that, from a need to extend itself compassionately to others."

"I think you assume properly, Mr. Jones," Ya Emme replied with a certain melancholy in her voice.

"But, but, but," Grube was back at it, "where's the black hole fit in all of this, or does all this fit into the black hole? Hee, hee, hee!"

"Mr. Gruber," Aldebaran began softly, stroking his beard, "you're quite an intelligent fellow, aren't you?"

Grube sat up straight, and looking Aldebaran dead in the eye, answered with uncanny familiarity, "Takes one to know one, sir. Hee, hee, hee!"

"Mr. Gruber has given us the next step," Aldebaran went on, "when the neutron star's volume collapses to zero it becomes a black hole. It sucks in energy. But what does it do with it? That was always the problem. Keeping in mind the variables of preternatural intelligence synchronized to the last stage of stellar transformation, it was only natural to assume that such intelligence would also foresee its destiny in the Black Hole."

"The only way to find out," Ya Emme once again took up the story, "was to intensify the Dogon-Anasazi experience. It was then that Aldebaran and I hit upon the Psychosynchrotron Lab. The rest you must know about, the psychic relaxation exercises, the synthesized synchrotronic bombardments from which the samadhi tub was developed, all of that. What still amazes me about the whole experiment and our findings is what a colossal joke it all is. We feed the black hole and it creates what we are. I don't know if anyone has really grasped what this means for us... for all of us." Ya Emme fell silent. We all fell silent. Leave it to Grube. Cosmic truths were mere feathers tickling his funny bone.

"Haw, hee, hee, hee, hoooeee! Agents on a cosmic feedback loop, thas what we are, hee, hee, hee, 'n ya wonder why them Buddhists always talkin' 'bout karma, hee, hee, hee! Cosmic feedback loop! What ya put into it, what's ya get out o' it! Ain't that the truth. Dumb, hee, hee, hee, we all's dumbsa buncha jackasses. No, even dumber, thinkin' we can get 'way with outsmartin' the star system, hee, hee, hee. Star fodder fer black holes, so's we can be exactly what 'n how we is now! Hee, hee, hee! Star fodder! Hee, hee, hee!" Eloquent Grube wasn't, but he did summarize it all, laying flat on his back in the G & O Lounge of the Socorro Flats Psychophysical Recharge Station.

What Ya Emme and Aldebaran told us had leaked out through the PAN communications boards when they first did their experiments two years back. Like most others, I must have dismissed it as another piece of astounding astrophysical trivia. But now, the import of the Black Hole Intelligence Probe and the Psychosynchrotron Lab experiments bore down on my mind like a colossal, luminous stone. It wouldn't go away. Nor did I want it to go away.

Back in our quarters that night I took out the old map of the Mesaland Geomantic Surveillance Zone. Something about what Aldebaran had said about Oppenheimer was buzzing me. As I gazed at the map, I suddenly saw it: a triangulation connecting Hopi Mesa, Chaco Canyon and the site of the first Atom Bomb Test in Jornada del Muerto.

My attention was particularly attuned to the Bomb site, Trinity Site, it was called. There it was, at the foot of the West slope of Oscura Peak... Peak of Darkness: Trinity Site. Did Oppenheimer know when his studies of stellar x-ray emissions were interrupted that he was engaged in an experiment that took him to the peak of darkness? He must have grasped something of it when he recalled the quote from the Bhagavad Gita, "Now I am become death, destroyer of worlds." And here less than 75 kilometers away at Socorro Flats, the riddle had been solved, from the Bomb to the Black Hole... "Whatcha doin' lookin' at that ol' map," Grube interrupted my reverie. He was standing there, shirtless in his baggy eco-squad overalls held up by two absolutely ratty suspenders.

"Well look, Grube, look at this triangulation, Hopi Mesa, Chaco Canyon, and Jornado del Muerto at the foot of Oscura Peak... Peak of Darkness, Trinity Site, the first Atomic Bomb Test. Just look at it. It's all right here, rube."

"What's 'all right here?" you sound like you just solved the mystery of the universe, Prosp. Hee, hee, hee! 'N maybe ya did, hee, hee, hee! Maybe ya just did."

<hr>

The next day Aldebaran and Bandariaga invited us to their residence at the Astrophysical Compound. I had only one thing on my mind: to discuss the triangulation.

Spreading my map out before them in their tapestry-covered receiving room, I explained to Ya Emme and Aldebaran the significance of the triangulation. "Beginning with Chaco Canyon, there was the psychic reception of the Crab Nebula. At Hopi Mesa, the prophecies of the entry to the Fifth World, the Fifth Ring, and of course at the Peak of Darkness in Jornada del Muerto, the Bomb...Trinity Site. This is the key to the triangulation, Trinity Site, the 'Enchanted Triangle."

Ya Emme looked at Aldebaran, then at me, her orchid-colored lips turning into a smile. "You know, Mr. Jones, after Aldebaran and I had concluded our experiments with the Psychosynchrotron, we realized there was nothing more to be done here at Socorro Flats, at least not for us. In fact, we didn't do anything for some time afterwards as it was. At least not anything connected with the Radio Telescopes. It was as if, well as if we had been transported into a time without time. What you've presented to us, this 'enchanted triangle,' it makes sense. Yes, it makes a lot of sense."

"Thought, matter, energy, time: interchangeable, self-generating and...,"St. Germain Aldebaran paused, looking magnificent, the gold dragon on his silk kimono catching the light of the morning sun flooding down through the bubble dome, "self-transforming... all unified in the same feedback loop. A chimera, a soap-bubble, a mere nothing…" Aldebaran's words trailed off, his penetrating dark brown eyes lost for a moment in a misty gauze of reverie.

Breaking his silence, Aldebaran motioned to Gruber. As if by tacit understanding, Gruber got up, and both he and Aldebaran left the receiving room. Ya Emme and I looked at each other, looked for a long time into each other's eyes. Oceans of magnetic tenderness swept through me. Moving through this sea of subliminal communication, Ya Emme came towards me, and taking my hand in hers, sat next to me.

"I suppose Ixchel gave you the Star-Catcher Transmission?" I was surprised that Ya Emme's words penetrated me so. Before I could answer, Ya Emme spoke for me, "She's very good at it, I know."

"I imagine you would, Ya Emme. You do seem like sisters, bound by common knowledge, you know. And I suppose, you also possess the same charms." As I replied, I gave her hand a soft squeeze.

"Such powers of perception, Mr. Jones. You should be wearing the insignia of psychic empowerment." Before she finished her sentence, we were embracing.

The next two days were strange, quiet, powerful days. We seemed to have paired off neatly, Gruber and St. Germain Aldebaran, Ya Emme and myself. The lemon-yellow color of the mesas in the late autumn light seemed to glow preternaturally. Every morning a single hawk circled the dome. The same hawk returned every evening at twilight and circled again. Coming together at meal times and in the evening, we would exchange information, drawing up plans for our journey to the Peak of Darkness in the Jornada del Muerto. One thing Aldebaran had found out was that the technetium coated rod was capped by a piece of spherically formed tektite. This black, extraterrestrial stone, according to Aldebaran, was the keystone holding together the power of the enchanted triangle.

The most enjoyable activity of those two days were the late evening musical events in which the four of us participated. St. Germain Aldebaran had a large selection of flutes and other wind instruments that he played to the accompaniment of myself on the synthesizer while Ya Emme and Gruber picked up the rhythm and percussion effects. Our improvisations lasted up to two hours. No one spoke, but everyone knew what to do.

How could I describe that music? Tissues of star-cloud woven into double helix bands of sound, chord changes that were like the transformations of energy into enzyme, of enzyme into thought, of thought into energy, without beginning or end, a cosmic feedback loop vibrating like a chimera, a soap bubble, a mere nothing.

The music sealed us, bonded, molded us into a single unit, what Grube called an "Ambulatory geo-harmone squad."

One thing I found most interesting was the way Grube and Aldebaran got on together. Oh, Grube was still the crazy old man, but with Aldebaran there was something different about him. I began to suspect that they had known each other previously. But I couldn't quite figure out how. On the other hand, I felt no compunction to question Grube on the matter. Something told me not to.

Early on the morning of the third day of our stay with Ya Emme and Aldebaran, we went to the stables and with provisions for a journey of a week, we mounted four horses and rode off. The Peak of Darkness, Jornada del Muerto was our destination. After that, no one knew what would happen. But we knew that something would. And we all noticed that this morning, the hawk that had been circling the dome was gone.

Towards mid-day, after crossing the cracked bed of an old highway, we entered the north end of the Jornada del Muerto. To the southeast, shimmering pale violet in color, was the Peak of Darkness.

"Hey, lookee over there," Grube drew our attention to a mesa on our right. A spiral column of dust rose high in the air. It moved directly toward us.

Ya Emme reined her horse back, and after squinting for a moment at the moving column of dust, turned to us and said grimly, while brushing her purple head-cloth to the side, "Mutant Outlaws."

To be continued...

Following my encounter with Poontutjarpa, my days at Hopi Mesa tranquilly stretched into weeks. Since Poontutjarpa had sent me to Marpa Mesa to dispose of the colored sands, I requested a stay of residency at the Kargyupa quarters. I was granted a two-week stay and given a room in the Old Hotavilla tower complex. Being on the old Third Mesa, the tower room gave me an excellent view northward of the other two mesas. I had a particularly good view of the terraces and hanging gardens on the south face of the second mesa. Brilliant hued bougainvilleas in great clusters separated trellised bands of morning glories. Organized in crescent-shaped clusters were the famous Antelope orchid beds, surrounded by rings of fiery yellow, orange, and white dragon and tiger lilies. Little pathways wound around and through the gardens, bordered with juniper shrubs, white-tufted cattails, and bamboo. The elegant luxuriousness of the gardens, always so breathtaking, was magnified by the perfumes wafted by an occasional breeze, which also carried the tinkling sound of water bounding down in narrow cataracts almost completely hidden by the dense growth of plants and flowers.

The hanging gardens of Hopi Mesa, so skillfully planted and planned, were vibrant testimony to the magical abundance that had come to characterize these mesas after the period of the Great Disorder. For myself, they came to symbolize my new state of health. I fancied the organic profusion of the gardens to be the interior of my own mind, illumined now and bedecked with flowers of delight and insight.

Though much of my time was spent in meditation—what else do the placidly, fussy, yet charmingly inscrutable Kargyupas do?—I was also granted access to the library and study hall. The question of the fellow named "Trident," was still burning within me. In the catalogue I discovered what I was looking for, "A Record of the Lives of the Discoverers, Being a History of the Early Kargyupas on the Continent of North America." It bore the date 164 AH and was compiled by a certain "Liberation Torch of All-Encompassing Compassion." I found the Kargyupa names quaint and charming, like old crystals washed up by the sea. There in the microfilm I found the biography of "Trident Holder of the Wish Fulfilling Gem."

Fa-Tsang had been right. Very little indeed was known about Trident. And yet, from the few tidbits about his life—the excavations in Yucatan and Java; his acquaintance with the Japanese archeologist, Okakura; his book on the Principles of Biopsychic Harmonics; this plus the encounter with the early Geomants—convinced me that there was much more to Trident than the official Buddhist biography let on.

Fa-Tsang was also right about the fact that the Kargyupa library did not have a copy of the "Principles of Biopsychic Harmonics."

"A lot of strange mathematical equations," one of the librarians informed me. Apparently, they once had a copy of this book, but it was lost or stolen many years ago. But they did have a copy of "Glorious Seeds of the Rainbow Squash blossom: The Liberation of Prophecy." This book had been referred to in the biography as "a volume of songs and stories gathered during Trident's wanderings south of the Rockies.

Despite the strange and enigmatic title, I asked to see a copy of this book, an original copy. What I was given to look at was a slight, yellowing, frayed booklet, something like one of the old magazines. But I liked the feeling of it, that and the musty odor. The dedication read: "To my friend and beloved mentor, the Master of Elegance, Yoshida Okakura." The introduction recounted how Trident had traveled to Northern Mexico. There, among the Tarahumaras and Yaquis, he wrote that his suspicions about the connections between Borobadur and the Mayans, especially those of Copan and Quirigua had been confirmed. He also wrote that with this knowledge he then traveled back to the North with three major destinations in mind: Jornada del Muerto, Chaco Canyon and Hopi Mesa. Having touched upon these three sites, with numerous lesser points scattered around them, he then proposed to set down a series of stories and songs. The purpose of these lyrical and anecdotal pieces was to recreate what he called "the ancient and timeless knowledge stored in the earth. Like glorious seeds of the Rainbow Squashblossom, these seeds, properly nurtured," he wrote, "would bring about the liberation of prophesy, not only of the prophets of Anasazi, but of all the far and distant climes and times of planet earth." Many of the stories I found to be obscure or like fairy tales.

My annoyance with the antiquated lyricism of these pieces was redeemed by the final story in the series, "The Enchanted Triangle." It was in this story that I found a correspondence to the vibration I had felt when Karuna Monongye first told me about Trident and the Morning Star Vision. The story begins in the following manner:

"Long ago, when mountains were young and the sky ran purple and gold with the perfumed vision of a race that had attained to complete and perfect wisdom, a council of the Elders of the Earth was called. Meeting in the circle of stones known as the Ring of Rightousness, they consulted the black sphere, the Stone of Indestructible Liberation. Seeing with total equanimity into the core of that magical stone, they saw with great sadness the Wheel of Time, its rim turning against the rim of the Earth, eroding moral vision, until that moment, the Peak of Darkness when wisdom would be but a memory and the Lords of Darkness would rule the earth with merciless ignorance.

"Because of this vision, the Elders of the Earth sought to devise a plan by which the Timeless and Ancient Wisdom would not be forgotten. Within the stone circle of the Ring of Rightousness they drew upon the ground a large circle. This circle represented the earth. This circle they then divided according to the continents and the seas. Once the lands and the seas had been divided and drawn, they applied the eye of wisdom common among them, and with this eye burned into the magic circle of earth those points where knowledge would be concentrated. Stones and valleys, mountain tops and ocean bottoms scattered about the earth immediately received the power of the eye of wisdom of the Elders of the Earth.

"To each of these points burned into the ground, the Elders of the Earth drew connecting lines, so that the magic circle was engraved with many fine lines, and these lines formed circles, triangles and squares by which all parts of the earth were connected.

"And the Elders declared: ' And in the time known as the Peak of Darkness, whosoever should take the Journey of Death to the Journey of Death, and therein scale the Peak of Darkness, shall discover the Stone of Indestructible Liberation. And when this task is accomplished the Enchanted Triangle shall become Visible, and the Wisdom of the Ancients will flower anew."

The rest of the story went on to tell in a rather fabulous manner how the sages of history derived their knowledge from contact with these magical points, and how their thought formed the mental pattern connecting these points. The story, if you could call it that, then ended in the following way:

"Dear and curious reader, do not think that I have merely imagined all of this. With my own eyes I have witnessed the Peak of Darkness, and have traced with my own feet the Enchanted Triangle. In the dust stirred up by my footprints I have inhaled the perfume of truth and have seen the vision of the Elders of the Earth. But my destiny is simple. It is only to point. Among those who come after me there will be a few who, with unclouded eyes, who discern the meaning of these words. To them will fall the noble task of retrieving the Stone of Indestructible Liberation. On them will fall the crystalline mantle of the Enchanted Triangle."

After I closed the cover of the book, I sat stunned and numb. My mind felt as if it had been placed in an electric socket. All sorts of thoughts and visions buzzed and stirred, colliding into each other with their iridescent wings flapping madly. Collecting myself, I returned the book to the Librarian and went for a long walk on the Mesa.

Passing through the juniper and oak-lined streets of Old Hotavilla, I reached the Star-Ball Stadium. No games today. Quiet. I found an entrance, and climbed the narrow, steep stone steps to a viewer's gallery. There, in the heightened emptiness of the stadium, I tried to put my thoughts in order.

It seemed rather simple, or so I thought. The Enchanted Triangle must be the triangulation formed by Hopi Mesa, Chaco Canyon, and Jornado del Muerto, the Journey of Death, the course outlined by Trident in his journeys long ago. I wasn't completely sure of the significance of these sites. Aside from Hopi Mesa, that is. Contemplating the whole business, however, I was filled with a tremendous sense of adventure.

For some time I sat there in the empty stadium. The field, shaped like a large capital "I" sided by two sets of viewing stands shimmered with late October light. A lemon olive light with flickers of purple and blue. It seemed funny sitting there. Where there should have been crowds intently observing the action of the Star-Ball players, I sat alone. Yet the longer I sat, the more I felt other presences crowding around me. At first I considered them to have been Star-Ball players and their followers. That seemed only natural. But then I felt something quite familiar, yet distant. It was Prospero. Prospero Edmund Jones. What in the hell had happened to him? I was startled by the clarity with which I felt his presence from the psychic impression I had picked up about Trident. Yes, they were, well, not the same, but at least operating through the same genetic memory circuit.

Thinking about Prospero crystallized things. It had been ten years since I had met him and had my affair with him. That happened at exactly the same time that I had gotten involved with the whole crazy PAN-Syndic mess. Tara Andromeda, Abdul-Rumi, and Natasha. Lovely Natasha, the wild Natasha of the Dionysian dance. Drunken Natasha. I shuddered. And where was she, now? She was involved in this too, I knew it. Like the tangles of her dark hair intertwined in the golden strands of mine, I knew she was deeply involved in the …Enchanted Triangle.

But Prospero. It was the first time in years that I had given him much thought. I was taken aback by the strength of feeling I now experienced for him while sitting in the Star-Ball court. And I knew: I had to find him.

Night was falling. The evening star twinkled above the pale pink horizon. I picked my way back through the yellow leaves to the Hotavilla Tower complex. After two days spent mostly in meditation, I returned to Shongopovi on the Second Mesa.

It was a bright cloudless day. Though it was late autumn, I had never experienced things being more alive. As I approached the Plaza of Commerce, I could hear the constant throb of the drums. Thin trails of heady blue juniper smoke rose above the plaza, dissolving themselves in the slow turning of the radiosonic dishes, their mirrored surfaces flashing periodically as they caught the full radiance of the morning sun.

By the time I reached the Plaza it was mid-day. Since it was Friday, the activity was especially intense. The rows of bubble domes over the covered bazaar glistened brightly. The pennants and banners around the Plaza proper moved languidly over the pedestrians buzzing to and fro, oblivious of the majesty of the silk brocade flapping overhead. At the far end of the Plaza the usual group of musicians and dancers swayed and bobbed to the tantalizing shifts of rhythm and sound. You could see why they called Hopi Mesa "Place Where the Drums Never Stop." And the smells, chili and curry, shrimp turning on open braziers. It was alive. I realized how hungry I was, and stopped at a stand to get a dish of Mesa Shrimp 'n Pumpkin. Served in corn-husk container, I didn't mind in the least as the orange cinnamon butter juice dripped down my chin. Food had never tasted better.

Back at the Dan Kachongva Residency, I knew I had to organize myself and prepare for travel. But I wasn't sure where or how.

"La entrada a la vida es la entrada a la muerte tambien." It was David Eagle-Bowl Monongye's voice. His beaming bronze-colored face blemished by a few late adolescent pimples was poking into my room.

"Hello, David, what are you up to?"

"Just seeing if you're still as beautiful as you were when you left," he answered coming all the way into my room and plopping himself down on the old wood-framed armchair.

"Well, am I?" I asked, pleased with the flattery.

"I never saw you looking better. What about you today?"

"I don't know how much better I look, but I do know I feel a helluvalot better."

"Mom says you and that Australian, Poontut-whatever… reminds me of King Tut, actually… had quite a meeting, an all-nighter. And then you took off. Marpa Mesa, huh? Whatd'yo do there?"

"What else do you do at Marpa Mesa? I meditated. Sat on a cushion and watched my mind."

"Was it good?"

"Haven't you ever sat before, David?"

"Yeah. Couple times. Never really got into it I guess." David was fishing around for something. His feet were shifting uneasily, tracing random patterns on the bare wood floor.

"Come on, David, what's on your mind? You can tell me. If you tell me how good I look, you can certainly tell me what's on your mind." David's feet now moved even more uncomfortably. He hung his head, biting his lower lip.

"Looks like all your confidence is running away with your feet, David." I spoke to him softly, like morning doves just at dawn. He lifted his head and looked at me, his eyes looking like those morning doves sound.

"Francesca, I mean, Francesca… I got this funny feeling. I mean, well…" David was stumbling through his words, like a hummingbird drunk on morning glories, bobbing crazily in the hanging gardens.

"Sit up straight. The words might find the elevator from your heart to your tongue if you sit up straight."

David looked at me, a ripple of resentment running across his brow. Then, relaxing his face, he smiled and sat up straight.

"You're right, Francesca. No reason really for me to be so tech-edout. Really tech-ed out, 90° every which way." David laughed easily now, as he gathered the thread of what he had to say. "You see, Francesca, when I went back to Poontut's the morning after I took you there, they were having a very interesting conversation. Poontut and my mom, that is."

"So what were they talking about?"

"I'm not completely sure. It was like I came in on the middle of something. But they were sure excited about you, I'll tell you that much. The way they were talking about you, it was like they had… just discovered gold. Well, I didn't ask them nothing. I just listened. And I know Mom, she didn't mind none. When she's into something like that, she always looks at me once or twice with that nice smile of hers. I know she thinks I'll get something out of just listening. And I always do, Francesca, I always do."

"So what did you get out of it this time, David?" I asked, pulling up a chair next to his and sitting myself down.

"It wasn't so much what they said, though that was interesting enough…serpent vision, genetic memory, dreamtime, the Syndics, that kind of stuff. But it was the feeling I got way down inside, this funny feeling that I should… help you. I don't mean like help you because you're in trouble. I know you're not in trouble, but like help you… do what you have to do. I just know you got things to do, and you can't do 'em alone. You need an assistant. Am I right Francesca?"

David was completely perky now, almost jumping out of the old armchair.

I couldn't believe how sweet he was. I just sat there looking at him, shaking my head in utter amazement.

"Yeah, David, you're right. I've got a big project on my hands, and I do need an assistant. We're going to do some traveling."

"Traveling? Where're we going?" David could hardly contain his excitement.

"On a Journey of Death to Jornada del Muerto. What was it you were saying when you poked your head into my room, something in Spanish, what was it?"

"Oh that. Something that crazy old curandera on the Plaza says all the time: 'La entrada a la vida es la entrada a la muerte tambien.' 'The entrance to life is also the entrance to death.' Why?"

"That says it all David. The Journey of Death. First we take that. Then we take the Journey of Life. It's all the same. You just have to know it."

"What are you talking about, Francesca, you lost me. What's this Journal of Death you're talking about?"

"Jornada del Muerto, the Journey of Death, it's a place somewhere in the South Mesa lands, near the old Mex-American border, I'm sure. We've got to get a hold of a map, and find out exactly where."

David was looking perplexed. "I don't know what you're talking about Francesca, but I've got to go along with my feelings. Just tell me what I have to do."

"You don't have to be so resigned about it. It'll all come clear. Just tell me this: are you really ready to travel?"

"Ready? What else am I going to do? I've been in Hopi Mesa for 18 years. Mom's been good, even though I haven't done anything, or able to figure out what to do. I know if I do something with you she'll be happy. It's doing something, finally doing something." David sounded almost wistful, taking his 18 years so seriously.

"Is there anything special you like to do?"

"I've tried a few things. I guess it's mostly physical. Horseback riding, back-packing. I've done some hovercraft maneuvering, too. I like doing the Grand Canyon in a hovercraft. I like that kind of stuff." As David spoke, his confidence began to come out again.

"If that's the case, then you're ready for travel. You're ready for the Journey of Death."

David looked at me with that perplexed furrow in his brow. He then got up to leave, and with a fantastic smile on his face as he opened the door, he said, "OK Francesca, anytime you're ready, I'm ready. 'La entrada a la vida es la entrada a la muerte tambien.'"

After David left, I sat down in the armchair. I remembered a line from an old song I used to do when I was with Diamondwave Ionelli singing global riff: "Sit in his armchair and you can feel his disease…" I found it was very simple to pick up an impression of David by just sitting where he had been. Just like I had picked up Prospero's impression in the Star-ball viewing stands. David was simple, simple and very pure. Whatever he felt for me sexually, he was able to transmute into an incredible idealism, incredible because even he didn't have a name for it. The only thing he knew was that somehow I personified it. Warrior. He was definitely a warrior type. I could see him standing in a field, a mantle over his shoulders, a shield on his left arm, a sword or spear perfectly poised in his right. It was also interesting the way he picked up on this circuit by entering in on the conversation between his mother and Poontutjarpa. That was my next move, to get together with Dawnstar and Poontutjarpa.

Dawnstar was bent over a table when I entered, slowly pushing the door to her studio open with my foot. She jumped when she realized I had been standing there, silent for maybe ten minutes. She had been studying some papers, looking at them very intently.

"Francesca!" she called out, "Francesca!" and without a further word threw her arms around me, giving me a wonderful hug.

I stood at least 15 centimeters taller than her. She was dressed in a plain white blouse and multicolored woven skirt. On her chest was a medallion. I hadn't seen it before. It was a simple gold circle. Embossed on it was a symbol. I wasn't sure I had seen it before, and yet I was. It was a Trident.

"You're looking at this," Dawnstar spoke, taking the medallion with her right hand and fingering it fondly. "Poontutjarpa gave it to me. I find it very appropriate. How does that word strike you?" Dawnstar looked at me, her eyes bright with a certain innocence.

"I think that's exactly the right word," I replied, enjoying the level of correspondence occurring between us.

"I thought you'd think so. You see, Poontutjarpa told me to wear it, especially for you. He told me you would tell me about it."

"I see," I began to answer, feeling in my mind for the psychic tracery of Poontutjarpa. Once I located his mental tracks, I proceeded to tell Dawnstar about my discovery of the Trident text, "Glorious Seeds of the Rainbow Squash blossom," and of the Enchanted Triangle. Yes, the Enchanted Triangle: Hopi Mesa, Chaco Canyon, Jornada del Muerto, and of the correspondence between Trident and Prospero.

"And as for the Trident around your neck, Dawnstar," I finally got around to the medallion again, "Poontutjarpa knows as much as I do. But since he put it on me, I'll tell you. Obviously it's the symbol of the Enchanted Triangle. Each of its tines is one of those three points, and…" I gathered my energy for what I was to say next, "under the emblem of the Trident it's up to us to release the magic of the Enchanted Triangle. You see, Dawnstar, that's our mission."

Dawnstar Monongye stood stark still as I spoke, her face a total lesson in absorbed concentration, the mole on her chin for once, not quivering.

"Francesca," she finally spoke, "Francesca, I've only known you for a short time, yet you are a daughter to me, a daughter, and now a sister. When you came you were broken. But I had never seen such courage in anyone as when you undertook the pytho-therapy. Even after your first session I told Poontutjarpa about you. He was very curious and asked me many questions. He knew who you were. He is a good friend of Tara Andromeda's. That's how he knows you. And I think he has something to do with Prospero, also. In fact, when word had it that you were coming to Hopi Mesa, Poontutjarpa came here. For you he came here. This is all very good. This is all very wonderful. We have all been waiting for this time. And now it is here. You are here. You are finally here." Dawnstar had hardly finished when she threw herself on me. I could feel her warm tears soaking through my tunic, wetting my shoulders.

Patting her on the back, I whispered to her, "Dawnstar, it's you I have to thank. It's you." Letting her warmth pass into me, I asked her, "what were you doing when I came in? You were so intense. What were you doing?"

"Oh that. Just lots of old designs. If we are going to take the Journey of Death and liberate the magic of the Enchanted Triangle, we'll need banners, won't we?"

"You're right, Dawnstar. We'll need banners. Banners and a few dedicated warriors."

No sooner had I finished speaking then I heard a wild and crazy sound, wailing and bleeping like an audio phone. We both turned quickly to the door. Standing there in metallic turquoise jump-suits, each with gold Trident medallions about their necks, were Poontutjarpa, and—I could hardly believe my eyes—Tara Andromeda. The sound had come from a long golden flute-like instrument that Poontutjarpa was wailing away on, wailing away like there was nothing to life but celebration.

To be continued…

Mutant Outlaws. They came down on us from the dusty cactus-speckled hills, their laser scooters blazing away. We just froze, reining our horses tightly so they wouldn't charge in fright. A totally unsavory mob they were, maybe a couple hundred of them. There was no question of resistance. Leather jumpsuits and boots, red bandanas tied around their heads, white scarves around their necks and waists, bare tattooed arms, and black face masks. Forming a massive circle around us, they allowed us a moment of tense silence, just enough time to see who they were and how they looked.

Then, very suddenly, several of them dismounted from their scooters. Before I knew it, they had us off our horses and were roughing us up pretty good. In the melee of whooping war cries and muffled screams, it was hard for me to tell what had happened to Gruber, Ya Emme, and Aldebaran. A booted foot was pressed against my neck as I lay on the ground. Two other boots pinned my arms to the ground. My kicking proved to be no match for the heavy chains that lashed my legs. Panicked, half in anger and half in fear, I bolted up, only to feel a searing pain in my left shoulder. That sensation was followed by a fleeting glimpse of something resembling a rock, studded with spikes, flying right toward my face. As this rapidly propelled object struck my face, I remember thinking: go with the energy, that's what Poontutjarpa always said, go with the... It was all over.

They must have drugged me pretty well. All I remember of the trip to Truth or Consequences is the jagged hallucination of mountains hanging down from the sky, surrounded by brilliant red coral reefs. As I later pieced things together I realized those coral reefs were streams of blood oozing over my eyes from what was left of my face.

"No techs these boys. Computer-assed PAN bombers, they. Takka lookee that 'un. We messed his place so good, he gonna be 'un o' us."

Listening to the voices I became aware that I was lying on a cot inside a small darkened yurt. My lips felt crusty and sore, my face all puffy and achy. Lightning streaks rushed through my left shoulder. I was surprised that my right arm could move with total ease. As the fingers of my right hand ran down my neck to the top of my left shoulder, they came across a sharp protrusion, my collarbone. As I began to lift my legs to see how they were, I also realized I was naked. Just as I was congratulating myself on still being alive, I thought in a dread flash: the silver decode tube!

Just then two of them came in. The only thing different from my first encounter with them was that their face masks had been removed. Candles were lit, casting awesome shadows on their faces, The man had only one eye. It wasn't that he had originally had had two eyes. No, he had only one eye, right smack in the middle of his forehead. Beneath that eye was a nose that was closer to a corkscrew than the vertical piece of anatomy usually associated with noses. I wondered: was that how my nose was going to end up looking? The way my face felt it was questionable whether I even had a nose left. For some reason, the memory of my first meeting with Francesca flashed through me, leaving a blurred wispy trail of nostalgia on my fevered nasal neurons. Better to think about lips.

One-Eye's lips were normal enough. That was good. Not so his girlfriend. No upper lip at all, but her lower lip made up for it, a massive, sensuous bulge of a thing pierced with a giant nail, a gold one at that. Her nose was all right, pure African, but her eyes: narrow slits between humongous cheekbones and a forehead that expanded broadly upward, like a massive trapezoid.

"Queen says we done you over-kill, PAN boy," the female began to speak caressing my chest with a hand that had two thumbs. "Queen says, don't kill 'un, heal 'un. Too mucha dose a tech-wave rearranged the cockpit o' his skies. Fix 'un Queen says, so we's here to fix 'un, PAN boy."

"I don't know what you're talking about!" I replied through my own puffy facial anatomy. "The receiving party was quite accommodating. I especially liked the delayed reaction fireworks." I tried to smile, but the encrustation on my lips plus a certain burning in my cheek muscles told me to save my feeble attempts at humor for later. And besides, I seemed to make as much sense to the mutants as they did to me.

Yet, I wasn't prepared for the gentleness with which the two mutants treated me. With two thumbs on each hand, the woman kept up a slow, gentle stroking motion over my body. A singular heat emanated from those hands, a soothing heat that penetrated my bones. In the meantime, One-Eye had taken some kind of fluid and was cleaning my face. After that he started working on the collarbone. Applying the same fluid on it, he then took large strips of plaster-of-Paris coated cloth and bound the shoulder and arm in such a way that the sling in which my left arm was placed was ingeniously attached to the binding over my shoulder.

I was sitting up now. Despite the headache, the rest of my body actually felt glowing. After helping me into a jumpsuit they asked me to walk around a little, or at least that's what I think they meant when One-Eye said, "OK PAN boy, trip the deck 'n' check the pegs." As I began walking around in little circles, slightly dizzy still, I thought again about the silver decode tube, and about Gruber, Ya Emme and Aldebaran. What kind of treatment were they getting? Were they still alive or what?

"Where's my three mates?" I asked. "What happened to them?"

"The bunt's wi' the Queen. Silversnare and Beardo, dunno. Mayb' down he West compound wi' the Skullsquads, mayb' up the range in vapor lock. Dunno."

Not much information to go on there. "In that case," I continued, hoping to get some sense of what was going on, "who's the Queen you been talking about?"

"You don't keen the Queen PAN boy?" One-Eye asked amazed that I wouldn't have known who seemed to be the central figure in his world. "Queen Tasha that's who's the Queen. Yeach, Queen Tasha, greenskied, slacksnared Tasha. She Jason's Moonsheen. Two year's since she tripped this deck, all skurs wi' birds she looped round Jason's neck." Both mutants found this remark terribly funny and broke into laughter. At least I guess it was laughter. High wheezy singsong guffaws that had both of them doubled over and dancing.

Once their seizure was over, One-Eye said, "Here PAN boy we gi' ya some o' this slugsoup, you be OK. In th' morn, you can bay yer skies on The Queen. Yeah Queen Tasha, see what skurs her birds can loop yer fuckfaced brain." Again, they both laughed, then picking me up like I was a cat, they lay me down again on the cot. Four-Thumbs took a small vial out of her feather-embroidered shoulder bag. Shaking it a few times, she uncorked it, and before I knew it, thrust its contents down my throat.

"Bleep 'n' preams this'll gi' ya, PAN boy. Yeah. An in the morn, ya be a sunshine spie, 'n' bay yer skies on the Queen, yeah, Queen Tasha. Yeah, that be a fit to fix yer fuckfaced brains, yeah, yer fuckfaced frains…"

Laughing with their arms around each other, the two mutants left me in the darkened yurt. As I wondered about what it was they gave me, the slugsoup—it had tasted bittersweet, like tea brewed too long—I began turning the name, Queen Tasha, over and over in my mind. Just as all my nerve endings began to feel fuzzy and technicolor, it came to me: Queen Tasha was Natasha Eisenhammer.

As much as I tried to focus on Queen Tasha and the silver decode tube, the Quetzalcoatl project, the slugsoup was completely scrambling my central nervous system with delirious delights.

"Tasha, Tashi, Tooshi, Tosha," I found myself mumbling away, giving up all hope of providing logic to the situation. And besides, the fuzzy technicolor nerve endings were beginning to expand. Intracellular visions of galactic worm-scrolls, vibrating phosphorescent in the yurt-darknight... the last coherent thought I think I had before dropping into the hallucinatory realm that I once called sleep was an observation of how different this was from Syntho DNA-coated silicon chips... silicon ships, genetic drifts... to bleep, perchance to pream...

A triangle of brilliant sunlight hovered like a luminous sail in the ocean of darkness. It took me a few minutes before I realized that the flap entry to the Yurt had been opened and morning light was flooding its cool interior. It took me even a few more minutes to remember who and where I was. Whatever that slugsoup had been, it dusted and scrambled me like a psychedelic omelette. Yet, I also felt good. Real good. One-Eye and Four-Thumbs were waiting for me.

Propping me on the back of an iridescent-colored scooter, we drove off. I got my first conscious glimpse of Truth or Consequences. A few old ancient buildings on either side of the Highway bed provided the core. Surrounding this in uneven concentric circles were a half dozen electric arcades, and beyond that, on the west side a large number of dome bubbles tinted in various colors. But then, most amazingly, spreading beyond this was a sprawling maze of tepees, tents and yurts, thousands of them. Thin trails of smoke hung vertically in the morning light. A low singsong murmur of voices, a few children playing and people going about their business, whatever that might have been here, gave the fantastic scene a placid touch of domesticity. Punctuating this more familiar drone were jagged bursts of Mutant Sound Systems. Frenzied electro-chromatic runs driven by hell-bent percussive rhythms were laced with voices wailing and chanting Mutant Outlaw hymns of blood and death.

Speeding through winding trails sided by clusters of Mutants, all shapes and sizes, many naked, displaying bodies painted and tattooed with most fabulous designs and colors, we finally reached the outskirts of the tent city and were headed up a mountainside. As we drove, I tried to concentrate on Queen Tasha. Even if she did have the silver decode tube, would she have a Decode Monitor? It was important that she not know about this. In a quick flash I recalled the Quetzalcoatl Project, Nezahualpilli and It-lil-po-tan-cuah, the Star-catcher transmission with Ixchel O'Shaughnessy, the black hole feedback loop—all of this seemed crucial knowledge for my encounter with Queen

Tasha, if I was going to get the upper hand.

This train of thought was broken when my eyes fell on the large skull-shaped structure that seemed to grow out of the top of a foothill. Dusky green junipers and golden oak trees were massed around this building. On either side of the mouth-like main entrance were two massive outlaw banners with the outlaw insignia: a black circle on red ground within which was a black pictograph of a humanoid figure. The right arm ended in a spiral. The left hand held a staff topped by a small cross-bar and circle, and from which hung another bow-shaped form. From the top of the head, which was shaped like an upside-down heart, emerged four ray-like lines.

The skull-palace itself consisted of what appeared to be smooth adobe sculpted walls to which brilliant white plaster had been applied. Protruding from the roof of the building was an abbreviated tower from which rose a column supporting a perfectly round mirror disc. I could make out a few figures standing on the tower. Strange subtly modulated high-pitched sounds seemed to emanate from the structure, sounds that conjured visions of violet skies and clouds like lemon yellow waves rolling and crashing in great breakers toward infinity.

After climbing a spiral staircase in the center of the skull-palace, we passed through a curtained wall and arrived at the torch-lined chambers of Queen Tasha and Jason. They were seated on two skull thrones. That is, the backs of the thrones were ornamented with five human skulls each. Both Jason and Queen Tasha were dressed in the customary black-leather jumpsuit. Each was wearing gold boots. Jason's most distinguishing feature was an over-sized bald head that rose like an egg from his shoulders. Set beneath a magnificent brow were two eyes that burned with darkness. His mouth was twisted into a bemused scowl. Yet he gave the distinct impression of being highly uncomfortable. Queen Tasha stunned me with her brooding Slavic beauty, her deep green eyes, scarlet lips and abundant black hair held together by a simple gold band. It was impossible to read from her face what she thought of this whole scene. Shivering with apprehension, I realized I had been left alone in the glimmering, torch-lit chambers sitting cross-legged before these two.

"Have you been treated well, PAN boy?" Queen Tasha spoke with icy irony.

"And did you psyche the slugsoup, PAN boy?" Jason chimed in with a voice that was a cross between a growl and a melancholy murmur.

"The welcoming party was adequate," I answered, gingerly but assertively, touching the raw wounds on my face. My nose certainly was a mess, I could feel that.

"You might look a little different after you heal, PAN boy." Queen Tasha spoke with a pretentious maternal air, "but everyone will know then that you're a man—of the world. Don't you think so Jason?" Queen Tasha's mate responded with a grim chuckle.

"Look," I said, "you can spare me the social amenities. I've experienced enough of them already. What I'd like to know is what have you done with my mates?" My question hung in the torch-lit silence for a few moments. Jason leaned over to Queen Tasha as they exchanged some private amusement.

"If it's the bunt's you want, ya can't have 'er. She Tasha's scamloll now, PAN boy," Jason was leaning forward toward me. "An as for Silversnare an' Beardo, you might catch 'em at starflight doin' mumbles, that is if ya play brains 'n' don't stumble." Jason leaned back again, smug and uneasy as ever.

"PAN boys don't usually travel south of Socorro Flats, so tell us about it: your name, your aim, your game?" Queen Tasha spoke as if she meant business. What could I say that would make sense, and yet keep them off the track? So far my one hope was that Queen Tasha hadn't been on to me and my connection with her. As far as I could tell, so far so good.

"Tracking a Syndic tracer signal. Small operation," I answered, "but then, Queen Tasha, you probably know as much about those operations as I do. As for my name, I'm Jones, Prospero Edmund Jones, Agent 24, El Dorado Monitoring Station, Rocky Mountain Geomantic Surveillance Unit. That's aim and name. As for your game, your guess is as good as mine."

"What makes you so sure I'd know about Syndic tracer signal operations Agent 24?" Good. She was going for it.

"Let's just say it's part of my genetic scam. I'm supposed to be able to psyche these things out you know. Part of my training. And since you're no mutant, unless beauty is a mutation these days, it's not hard to figure out."

She sat there, looking at me hard, deathly hard, with a gaze that was pure arctic front. Jason shifted uncomfortably, and then got up. He stood above me, looking down. His face was mute, but I caught an interesting ripple of helplessness in his eyes.

"PAN boy's yers, Tasha. I's staked his skies, 'n' they don't fry me brains but a mote. Massle 'im as you sheen, what he keens, don't make twice to me," he spoke, shrugging his shoulders, and then left the room.

Once we were alone, I marveled at how destiny had thrown this one at me. But not for long. I couldn't send out any waves at all about how I really felt. I waited for her to make the next move.

"Are you comfortable sitting there, or would you like to go somewhere else?"

I looked around the room. It wasn't that large, but the torch light made it seem cavernous. "Whatever suits you," I replied with unassuming nonchalance.

"As you will, then. If sitting at my feet is your way of expressing yourself, let's get on with it: who are you really?"

"I gave you name, aim and game, why don't you do the same for me? I know Syndics were programmed for courtesy, so do it."

She looked at me narrowing her eyes. There was no question that she commanded power and held it as well. But I knew the struggle she was having: curiosity about me was wrestling with her desire to kill me.

"Come on Natasha. You're no mutant, and PAN records don't show any defect/decodes with a face to match what you're carrying around. You can de-tech with me. I've been around PAN-Syndic circuits so long I can't tell the difference between 'em."

"You know a lot don't you, Agent 24?"

"Probably not as much as you. And besides, you're a good actress. When you know something and can act whatever way you want, I'd say that's high tech." I didn't want to push it any further, so I changed my tone. "What do you have to drink around here? Slugsoup does make you thirsty the day after."

"Think you can get intimate with me that fast do you? First it's calling me 'Natasha', then it's a drink. I'd say slugsoup's rearranged your critical circuits. Maybe you do need something to drink."

"What do you drink around here, anyway?"

"You're in outlaw country, PAN boy. Scorpio Latitude." This last phrase, "Scorpio Latitude" she added with special emphasis, implying some internal Syndic Operation. "And in Scorpio Latitude, mutants scam on mescal, snakeskin mescal. Do you know the stuff? If slugsoup turns your nerve endings into crystal rainbow spectres, snakeskin mescal will be like lightning from Jupiter. But let's do it PAN boy. It might ease the pain your nose is going through."

I followed Natasha into what she called her "sitting room." The archaism of the phrase did not fail to impress me. And a sitting room it was. The walls rounded into ceiling very noticeably, giving the room a womb-like feeling. The floor was covered with bear and mountain-lion skins, while the walls themselves were covered with shimmering snakeskin. No windows, but on a low semicircular table, Natasha lit a half dozen red candles. Sitting on the table were a couple of jugs of snakeskin mescal and some ceramic cups. Natasha poured us some drinks.

Making ourselves comfortable on some over-size fur-covered pillows, Natasha began to talk, "Back in the old days they fermented this stuff with worms, red worms—guzano rojo—they called it. Then some Chinaman came along and introduced fermenting it with snakes. The Outlaws went for that one. Cactus juice and snake venom, that's their style. Oh they go in for the psilocybin stuff too, but mescal keeps them raw. What do you think?"

"Numbs with a burn," I replied, feeling the infernal warmth of the liquor explode in my empty stomach. "But numb or not, I still can't kill my curiosity about you, Natasha, or at least about Scorpio Latitude. Is that one of your Syndic operations?"

Natasha laughed, a hoarse, cynical laugh. She then poured herself another drink. She dropped that one down as fast as it takes a decode monitor to flash a binary resolution symbol. She then poured herself another, and looking at me without the least expression dropped that one down just like the last. The next one she sat with for a minute.

"What I like about this mescal is how it affects the subcortical zones, what they call the reptilian brain." She spoke matter-of-factly, no emotion. Drinking down several more cups, she fixed her eyes on me. "Scorpio Latitude? C'mon PAN boy, your enzymes are dehydrated. You know something you're not telling me, and I don't like it."

"You mean, like your name is Natasha Eisenhammer, a syndic operant who broke down in the middle of a high-level operation, and had to go somewhere to maintain her power and so you came here?" I decided to go for it. "You were probably in the Counter-Intelligence Performance Unit doing psycho-historical impersonations in PAN war-zone theaters, and something went wrong, didn't it, Natasha?"

Natasha's green eyes were blazing, her cheeks flushed and glowing. I had to admit she was very beautiful. "Since you know that much PAN boy, you tell me what went wrong."

"You're holding it in your hand. But that's OK. I don't mind. Syndics were always a little too puritanical for my taste. If mescal is your way, who cares?" She took this in with great concentration, then went back to the jug. "Since you're pouring yourself another, do me one too," I added.

"I get the feeling you've been looking for me, PAN boy. Yes, I do. And I also get the feeling you've been looking without knowing why. You're good PAN boy, but not that good. So here we are, a couple of outlaws in outlaw-land, Scorpio Latitude. And I have a silver decode tube that you'd like to have back really bad, so bad your skin's crawling just to get it. So you think by getting me drunk in the middle of the day, you can have your day. Well, you're not going to have your day, because before the day's over you're going to be gone. I mean so far gone, you're not ever going to come back. What we did to you when we captured you, that's just an appetizer; but you're in Scorpio Latitude, PAN boy, Truth or Consequences, and they didn't teach you about that in synaesthetic history did they?"

I took a long hard drink, draining my cup. This one burned, and I could feel it toasting my nerve endings, curling them up, and snapping them back. "Gimme another one Natasha. And do me a favor; back off from the hardware you're slinging around. So I got an assignment that had your name coded into it. So what. You're no Syndic anymore. You're an Outlaw. I can consider that assignment defunct. Don't you ever let go? Don't you ever de-tech?" As I finished my question, she handed me the cup. Mescal, snakeskin mescal right to the brim.

"OK PAN boy let's see you drop that one into the moat, and then we'll sling software, since hardware bruises you so much. Come on, drop it into the moat."

I took this cup down, straight down. This time I had to cough. It was too much. Even as mescal and snot was streaming out of my nostrils, she took the cup from my hand and filled it again.

"Feel reptilian yet PAN boy? I do. And when I'm reptilian, I'm no place else but here, and that's what you want, right, Mr. Jones?" As she spoke she undid the front of her jump suit, right down to her crotch. For someone who had lived as hard as she had, she still had a well-coordinated body. It was getting warm now, and I could feel the mescal pushing into my brains as easy as sound moves through space.

"Well, here it is PAN boy. Are you going to go for it?" Her voice was hard, like metal, and as she spoke she ran her right hand slowly up and down from her belly to her breasts.

"You've got my game all wrong, Natasha. But you can call me Prospero if you want."

"If I've got your game wrong, Prospero," she said, massaging her breasts now, "you tell me what it is that makes you resist reptilian love?"

Going completely against the gravitational pull I felt in my gonads, I eased myself back further into the pillow. Closing my eyes for a second, I could feel a dizziness spinning me every which way

"It-lil-po-tan-cuah!" I shouted. "It-lil-po-tan-cuah!"

"Where'd you pull that one out of, where did that come from?" She was shocked.

I didn't know what would happen when I did that, but she was shocked, something had snapped. The color left her cheeks. She clutched at both sides of her undone jumpsuit, and looked at me like I'd caught her with her clothes off, which I had.

She poured herself another drink, and zipped herself up part way. She downed the drink and poured herself another, while I admired her creamy rose-tipped breasts.

"It-lil-po-tan-cuah. No one's supposed to know about that one." As Natasha spoke, her eyes looked off. For the first time, they softened. "It-lil-po-tan-cuah. These are the Scorpio Latitudes, and here's a PAN boy named Prospero, talking about It-lil-po-tan-cuah. Bitch-priest keeper and betrayer of the earth, that's It-lil-po-tan-cuah. Scooper of venom in Scorpio Latitudes, that's It-lil-po-tan-cuah. Drainer of outlaw blood in a mutant skull, that's It-lil-po-tan-cuah. A syndic queen, lamming the radar shell of a counter-intelligence operation, that's It-lil-po-tan-cuah. A cunt crazy for cunt, sauced on serpent lightning playing with mutants like they're wooden dolls, that's It-lil-po-tan-cuah." She paused and turned her attention to me once again.

"Your brain's fuckfaced good PAN boy. When they told me they got four PAN liaisons headed for Jornado del Muerto, something started ticking and clicking. I flashed: It-lil-po-tan-cuah, when I heard that news, and I don't know why. Damn this fucking earth, but I don't know why. It's been two years. Liverpool theater. Sauced on Raki. Ever drink that PAN boy? Clear, sweet—and is it hot—a stinger from Saturn's dark side. Liverpool theater. Hey. I shouldn't tell you that part, should I? The part with the honeycunt sweet as a sunbeam going goo goo for an act that was tattooed with Amazon bracelets… you woulda loved that one PAN boy, sweet PAN set up she was. But it wasn't me that got her. She got me. I was swimming in her vapors like a diode sparksucked into a vacuum lock… loved her, I did, and hated it all the time…but don't get me to name names… and you know what they wanted me to get from her… do you know what they wanted from that little PAN set-up? Hierarch info decode… get her good and send her back to… un un, no you won't get that part PAN boy… Liverpool."

"I was sauced on Raki… Amazon stunt queen I was… run into this PAN boy in the Liverpool Theater… he had a taste for the sauce as long as a star-probe. Rolled his eyes at me like they were melons falling off a vine… so I gave him the sauce and his tongue starts jogging, taking off down the track like it's doin' the three minute mile… but he lays that one on me. 'If it's the goddess you're doing,' he says, like he's a print-eyed librarian, 'if it's the goddess you're doing, then you should know about Toci, the Aztec earthmother and her priest keeper, It-lil-po-tan-cuah. 'Son-of-a-bitch, if there ever was one, high priest to Montezuma himself…You bored PAN boy?" Natasha halted her soliloquy only to pour herself another cup. She sat looking into it.

Then lifting her head back up, smiling at me, really smiling at me for the first time, she asked, "What do you know about Francesca Della Francesca?"

It was my turn to go cold. Memories blazed through my brain like the aurora borealis on a hot summer night.

"Francesca? Yeah," I resumed in mock-outlaw, spit-nails-through-your-teeth manner. "I think I knew a Francesca once. Years ago. Why?"

"Someone I knew, too. Just flashed her. Curious about how close you PAN liaisons stick together, but now I got this feeling, yeah, I got this feeling you're going to be useful to me PAN boy. Yeah with your It-lil-po-tan-cuah and your resistance to reptilian love-making and your 'hot' insights… I think you're gonna serve Queen Tasha … and learn to like it… It-lil-po-tan-cuah? Yeah. I think I like him a lot…"

Without the slightest notice she suddenly took her cup and threw the mescalin my face. If mescal was hot coals in the stomach, it was a bonfire on open wounds. But I held it together, didn't move.

Natasha was laughing, laughing and calling out: "Jason! Jason! Get this fuckfaced brain outta here!"

To be continued…

# FRANCESCA'S TAPE LOG: DREAMTIME ON SOUTH BALDY

"Aljira… Djugur… Bugari… Ungud… Wongar! Aljira, I like the best. Al-ji-ra, do you hear it? This is the dreamtime."

The flames lit up Poontutjarpa's face as he sat crouching before the fire. I was lying down in my sleeping bag, as were the rest of us, listening to Poontutjarpa and gazing at the star-filled sky.

"Before we humans had bodies, as we do now, the Wandjina came. They woke up from beneath the earth. They were touched by stars. Orion, the Pleiades, they sent messengers, and the Wandjina woke up. They created the land. They made the rocks, the rivers, the gullies, the seashore and the sea. And when they had finished they placed their energy in ancestor serpents, rainbow serpents and let them loose on the world.

"For years, thousands of years, it was our duty to not let the dreamtime die. This we did by continuously reliving the dreamtime. We always walked in two worlds. The world of the senses and the dreamtime. And when the outsiders came, of course they did not understand. We were children, fools chasing for grub worms, imbeciles drawing circles in the sand. Without knowing, we knew. Aljira… Djugur… Bugari… Ungud… Wongar! Aljira, I like the best. Al-ji-ra—we began at the end and became the beginning.

"This is the great secret. Death is the black hole of life. The dragon, the rainbow serpent, the rattlesnake becomes Ouroborus when it bites its tail, becomes Ouroborus and flies, flies like the feathered serpent. Because it bites its tail, it begins at the end and becomes the beginning. Passing through the Black Hole, it flies. Hah! Wandjina talk! Yet the rest of the world makes itself crazy, repeats itself. It has forgotten the great secret. It does not know it is the end of what it has become. It has forgotten how to relive the ancestors, it has forgotten how to tie stars into ropes of light that adorn, that adorn the beginning that is always becoming. Hah! Wandjina talk!"

With a painted stick he had taken from his dilly bag, Poontutjarpa drew five concentric circles on the ground, engraved them deep with the sharpened of the painted stick, so that the firelight made them stand out in high relief.

"Look," Poontutjarpa spoke, "Five circles, five rings. Tjuringa: the map of becoming. We have been here all the time. Each time we are here is the same time. But forgetting the dreamtime we do not know this, and so we pass through the rings arriving at the fifth ring. Tonight, dream. Dream who you are. Let your ancestor give you a dreaming that you may become that dream. Begin at the end and become the beginning. Let Wandjina talk. Let Wandjina Blake sing! Sing! Wandjina Blake! Sing!

"Awake! Awake o sleeper of the land of shadows, wake, expand!"

Poontutjarpa's voice was soft, almost like a whisper. Soft and singsong sweet. Listening to it was like being a child again listening to your father tell you stories. It was comforting, warm and comforting. Everyone at the campsite had gone quiet. I decided to say good night to every star. "Goodnight, Andromeda. Good night, Algenib. Good night, Altain. Good night, Arcturus. Good night, Aldebaran. Ancestor stars, good night each and everyone. Goodnight!"

And I dreamed. With stars that my eyes had tied into ropes of light, I dreamed. I was a lady. My name was Five-Flower. Maxtlal-Xochitl was my name. I was traveling on foot with a prince. Noble Fasting One, Nezahualpilli, was his name, several others there were traveling with us, just like the group I was now with. We had stopped at a mountainside where there was a shallow cave. In the shallow cave we took ochre and charcoal and drew two serpents intertwining lengthwise along the inside wall of the cave. We sprinkled water on these two serpents so that they came to life. They sparkled with rainbow colors. As I gazed at them, a deep feeling of understanding came over me. I felt it growing within me, growing from my sexual organs upwards, filling my body with warmth and light, so that I was like a flower filled with light. I was able to take strands or filaments of this light and place them on the head of my prince. As I did this, the strands of light became feathers, so that my prince came to wear a headdress or crown of feathered light. Once the crown was complete, my prince took his right hand and with the index and little fingers pointed to the cave floor where it joined the wall on which we had painted the serpents.

There was a book, a violet-colored book. I picked it up. It was the Principles of Biopsychic Harmonics! I looked at the author's name: Col. Hejira Lodro Greene, Commander, Third Force Expeditionary Unit, Ark of the Kingdom. Reading that name was like sprinkling magic powder on my eyes. I opened the cover and read the dedication: "To Beloved Francesca without whose enchantment the Triangle would never have rung." I eagerly skimmed through the yellowed pages of the book. It was filled with dense equations and pencil jottings along the margins. Occasional diagrams, double helixes, chemical coordinates, stellar shapes passed before my eyes until I came to the one I was looking for: A drawing of a man and a woman before a shallow caveat the foot of a mountain. At the back of the cave wall was an open doorway. Above the door were a sun and moon. From within the door came rays of light. In the center of the room beyond the door was an upright triangle. On either side of the triangle two serpents twined around, their heads meeting at the apex. On the floor before the triangle was a square. At each corner of the square was the chemical symbol for what I took to be one of the four amino acids comprising the DNA chain. Around the mountaintop were four more symbols, one each for earth, air, fire and water, represented by Taurus, Aquarius, Leo and Scorpio.

I showed this drawing to my prince. He nodded affirmatively and said, "Don't forget to unlock the back door as well," and handed me a key. It was a small golden Trident…

The sun was rising toward the southeast, just north of the mountain directly southeast of us, Oscura Peak, Peak of Darkness. It was a few moments before I recalled the dream I had had. I had been gazing across the purple and gold stretch of flatland called Jornada del Muerto toward the Peak of Darkness in the Sierra Oscura which glistened a deep violet blue. It was my contemplation of the mountain that made me remember the dream. I recalled it with a start. The only other person awake was Poontutjarpa. He was tending the fire, making coffee and smoking a cigarette. A floppy old canvas hat was parked on the right side of his head, giving him the jaunty appearance of a weather-hardened tramp. Gone was the black gnome story-teller, enchanter of visions of the night before. I liked these changes in Poontutjarpa. They were comforting. It's good to know that humans have such flexibility.

"Hey! Golden One," Poontutjarpa quietly called out to me, "did you like your dream last night?" I crawled out of my sleeping bag and went over to him.

"You're so lovable, Poontut, I could kiss you," I said, snuggling up to him and the warmth of the fire.

"I would never turn down a kiss from one as golden as you. Please do me the honor."

And I did. I threw my arms around him and gave him a kiss.

"Then it was a good dream," he spoke with a sly smile on his face.

"A very good dream. Did you know that you were talking to Five-Flower, consort and Lady of the Prince Nezahualpilli, the Noble Fasting One?" I laughed, as I pronounced the names. They seemed so odd, and yet so familiar.

"And you know, then, who this Noble Fasting One is?"

Instinctively I answered, "Prospero. Prospero Edmund Jones, of course." I looked at Poontutjarpa, waiting for him to confirm what I had said.

"Is it so strange?" Poontutjarpa asked gazing at the Peak of Darkness far off the other side of the valley floor. "Prospero is not far away. Nor is your old friend, Natasha Eisenhammer. Before too long we shall all meet again. Is it so strange?"

"But tell me, Poontut, tell me. Why is this happening like this? You seem to know so much, and what I get of it just seems to come in these bright bursts. I think I'm beginning to get the whole image. I think I'm beginning to get the code we're working with. But not all of it. I mean I know that Abdul-Rumi was very clever. After all this time, Tara still feels bad about that. And I see now that there's a definite energy triangle between Natasha, Prospero and myself. And that triangle is tied up with the Enchanted Triangle, I guess," I began to feel my way to the answer of my own question. "I guess, it's just hard for me to believe yet that my role should have been so critical in all of this." As I finished speaking, I felt an electric alertness come over me. I thought again about the dream. Poontutjarpa picked up the mental trace.

"It was a long time before we began to truly realize, realize down to our guts that Planet Karma is the 'invisible' force affecting the systems balance. And even when we did, there was the question of finding the chief threads. 64 DNA code words, so many variations. Karma! Karma! Karma! All we are ever dealing with is unfinished business, and not knowing it we create more unfinished business. But it makes a game. It makes fun. Now take your thread, Francesca. Aztec thread, Toltec thread. When the European conquered the Aztec, what happened? Big Unfinished Business happened. Big Ignorance. Only a few people really knew. Noble Fasting One and Five Flower. They knew. And It-lil-potan-cuah. He knew, but only as revenge did he know. But this is Big Unfinished Business. Big pattern. Like a disease in planet DNA. But all we need to do is find one psychogenetic thread, just one—begin with that one, and the rest can also slowly be undone. This is your answer, sweet Francesca. This is your answer."

The sun was now rising above the eastern horizon. The others in the camp were stirring.

"And the Syndics are on to this too?"

"Only because they know we're on to it. I think they call their project Scorpio Latitude. But it is a counter-project. We lead, they follow. And we are the Quetzalcoatl project, because… " Poontutjarpa stopped. It was as if he had heard something. He placed his ear to the ground. With a broad smile he said, "Someone is coming, and I think I know who it is. Oh, this is good. This shall make very happy, everybody. David!" Poontutjarpa called out to the sleeping bag that had not yet ejected its dream cargo. "David! Abandon right hemisphere! Quick! We are going to have guests for breakfast!"

"Aw, c'mon Poontut, it was such a good dream I was having," a half-alive voice came from the otherwise motionless sleeping bag.

Meanwhile, Poontutjarpa had gotten up and was skipping down the yucca-strewn slope of the South Baldy encampment. I got up and followed him, deciding to skip along as well. I mean, if this silly little Australian could keep himself alive by skipping, why couldn't I? It was wonderful. As I caught up with him he was singing another one of his verses:

> *"Wandjina Blake and Quetz'coat'*
> *Encapped the code that we forgot*
> *Yet waking up in rainbow showers*
> *the serpent coils, the planet flowers."*

Three figures wound their way up the rocky slope. As they came closer, Poontutjarpa chuckled his deep aboriginal chuckle. It always reminded me of water rushing in deep caves. The three, two men and a woman, were wrapped in brilliantly colored blankets. The older man walked in the center, flanked by the younger man and the woman. They were happy people, that much you just knew. They resembled rainbows that had been happily crumpled and cast down to earth, rippled with laughter, and crinkled with humor.

"Mr. Jayavarman, Good Morning!" A slightly high-pitched but hearty voice called up to us.

"Esquivel! Wandjina Esquivel! You phosphate-brained snake-charmer, where in the hell have you been?"

"Ah. Mr. Jayavarman, your impatience is lost on me. Can I help it if we all got caught in a genetic blizzard? The grand lords of the enzyme ring are merciless when they wish to bestow bliss on us poor helpless cosmic migrators!"

"And how would you feel if you had spent the last three days reading paleo-tech circuits scammed on an electro micro-disc de-programmer, while assaulted by prismatic butterflies?" It was the young lady who chimed in now. I liked her, the husky innocence in her voice charmed me immediately.

The arrival of San Juan De la Cruz Esquivel, and his two aides, Claudia Blavatsky Leventhal and Ramakrishna Al-Badr completely enlivened the camp breakfast that morning. Our small group—Poontutjarpa, myself, David and Dawnstar Monongye, Fa-Tsang Wronski, and an itinerate Synaesthetic Council Monitor named Lindy McGrew, a kinky prematurely gray-haired man from who knows where—had been feeling a certain apprehension after docking our hovercraft in a meadow halfway up the north side of South Baldy. The arrival of the Esquivel Triplets, as we came to call the three Psychophysical Recharge Station Agents, completely altered our mood.

The high spirits of breakfast, enlivened for me by my first taste of Peyote Tea a la Esquivel, turned serious once we had finished clean-up time. At least for me. Ever since I had re-tracked Prospero in the Star Ball Court, Hopi Mesa, the mere mention of his name caused my heart to ache.

Ramakrishna Al-Badr recounted how he had introduced Prospero and a man named Gruber to Henri St. Germain Aldebaran and Ya Emme Bandiaraga.

"The following morning, this is as true as you'll ever hear it, I assure you, Prospero, Gruber, Aldebaran and Bandiaraga left in the direction of the VLA. Very excited they were. We sent a hawk to circle Aldebaran's quarters for two days. On the third day, the Hawk, Omniscient Skyface, I like to call this particular hawk, you know, on the third day, the hawk refused to fly. I rode out to the west mesa, a little before noon, I saw four horses flying southward to the Peak of Darkness. Four horses and four riders. Certainly it is not necessary for me to tell you who I thought they were."

"We knew there had been rumbles north of Truth or Consequences for some months now. Lots of new mutants pouring in from the Carib." Esquivel continued the story, "Hell of a time, I tell you, to do an exploratory operation at the Peak of Darkness. Day after they left we got Mr. Jayavarman's transmission, so we held off doing anything 'til we'd gone through Decode Process. My guess is they never made it to Peak of Darkness. They're in Truth or Consequences if they're anywhere. Yes, sir, Truth or Consequences."

"And," Poontutjarpa took his turn, "if my information is correct, Syndic Agent Eisenhammer is entertaining them in phase two of Project Scorpio Latitude. This is it." Placing his hands on his knees and defocusing his eyes, Poontutjarpa suddenly went into auto-reg. The rest of us joined in.

We sat quiet around the smoldering coals of the campfire, the sun approaching sky-zenith. Clouds were massing to the northwest, while a chill insidiously seeped into the encampment. I pulled the strings at the bottom of my sky-jacket tighter to keep in the warmth. I feared for Prospero. But even more, I did not look forward to an encounter with Natasha. Yet I knew it had to be done. I looked at each and every face in our group, strange raggle-taggle lot that we were, I liked what I saw: destiny of the heart. I knew we possessed a strength that was beyond reason. And because we were beyond reason, that was our strength. That much I knew. I knew it like I knew my dream of the previous night to be true. Truer than flesh and blood, truer than the earth and sky. And what made it so true was that the current for the common circuit through which we were all operating was provided by the boundless source, the ocean of love, boundless and bright, inseparable from the ocean of emptiness.

Prospero! Prospero! What will it be like when I see you again? Beyond reason, yes, that's how it will be. Beyond reason. Power, radiance and love, beyond all reason. With these thoughts, all apprehension lifted from my heart. What a pleasure it was, this Journey of Death! Soft waves of luminosity wound round and through me. At the same time everything I looked at emitted a quiet clarity.

At sky-zenith, Esquivel gently entered our silence. Getting up and going to the fire, he took a small stick and placed it for a few moments on some of the last burning coals. Then, when the pointed end of the stick was glowing and red, he got up and to each one of us he touched it lightly to the brow.

"By the Dawnstar ember of emptiness may the confidence of your original nature reveal itself unclouded by the thought, 'I am!'" This Esquivel chanted softly to each one of us as he moved about the circle, hunched over in his rainbow blanket of wrinkled laughter. As the pointed end of the stick touched my brow, very much like a delicate pin-prick applied with illuminated dedication, a restfully rapturous space penetrated each of my cells. It was as if I had been wounded by happiness.

"Spontaneous insight time, wouldn't you say, Mr. Jayavarman?" Esquivel announced, having completed his circuit.

Poontutjarpa nodded with an amused, worldly grin.

Lindy McGrew spoke up first. "Wandjina means ancient ones, primordial, beyond beginning, right? And what this whole operation is about is correcting and working with psychogenetic patterns, psychogenetic recall, right?" Lindy was chuckling to himself as he got to his second self-answered question, chuckling like a rabbit prancing on his mound during full moon, "sitting around here in this sky-zenith circle, don't we form a mandala, a gathering, a society, right? And in order to manifest skillfully in the human world of the Art Planet, we must take on a name and profession. Right?" By this time Lindy McGrew, who, without the least effort had transformed himself into a gleeful sprite, was mirthful, yet masterfully controlled. He poised himself ready to arch the conclusion to his logic into our midst, like a spray of golden leaves, garland-shaped by the autumn wind.

"Therefore, I say, therefore, (never was much of a scholar myself, but always got on good with them) therefore, I propose that we approach the Mutant Outlaws in Truth or Consequences in the guise of 'The Wandjina Society, Specialists in Psychogenetic Pattern Recall!'"

"Splendid idea, Mr. McGrew, splendid, simply splendid," Esquivel exclaimed.

A wave of good humor, of laughter and exclamations of delight swept over us. "Yes, yes, yes, yessy, YES, yes!" Lindy McGrew chanted with an air of supreme finality, quieting us all down once again. With arms spread out wide on either side, Lindy spoke again, commanding the authority of the present moment. "Yes, this is all fine and good, as long as, yes, yes, yes, yes, yes," he paused rhythmically, "as long as it's open heart and no illusions. Otherwise, we lose the joke. And without the joke, all we're doing is cloning a bad con, and I've done enough of that in my wiggly piggly existence."

The rest of the afternoon passed itself in a loose arrangement of strategy sessions, group pairings and hiking around the mountain trails, looking for good sightings, ley line vistas, and geomantic pressure points. It was towards sundown that Tara Andromeda managed to disengage me from one of Fa-Tsang Wronski's interminable monologues on the properties of universal refraction. Taking my arm, we ambled down a hillside trail of lichen-painted rocks, shimmering yucca plants, and yellow thistle flowers.

"Francesca, I know I've seemed remote since we met again. It's not that I've wanted to be," as she spoke, Tara placed her arm around my shoulder, gripping me warmly. "In fact, there's nothing that I've wanted more than our reunion. But it's been... It's so difficult for me to say this, but I know I have to. It's been, well, so heavy for me. I just..."

"Oh Tara," I stopped and placed both of my arms around her neck, "let's face it. Abdul-Rumi had us both. It's not just you Tara. You're not responsible for me or my feelings. I am. And because of that you can't feel guilty on my account. That's entropic manipulation, and I won't let you do that to either of us."

Tara embraced me, "Oh, I know you're right, Francesca. Thank you. You're beyond belief. I love you! What a couple of bad-timed Syndic scam-molls we are!"

After a good laugh, we spoke about Prospero, "My own son, my own son. Do you know how hard that's been, operating in PAN Hierarch, monitoring operations for my own son, setting him up for the same bitch that you got set up with?" Tara's voice was almost imploring. Yet, she knew there was no answer, nothing to get her off the hook. This is the way things are, a tough game of nerves in a psychic dead-lock with an opponent whom you have a ghastly feeling you resemble altogether too closely.

"Listen Tara," I went for some kind of resolution, "we both know that that's the band of transmission, at this point at least. But we also have to keep in mind what Lindy McGrew had to say, 'open heart and no illusions, otherwise we lose the joke.' And that's where we are, the Journey of Death. It's a wild gamble, a random hand dealt to us by our old friend, self-existing synchronicity. But then what else do we have to goon? Come on, Tara, heart and humor!"

She looked at me, her face slowly relaxing, easing itself into a smile, "And speaking of jokes, Francesca, don't you think this is a sly turn of events? Here you are taking me to task for my karmic fumbles. That's a wonderful joke. You know something, Francesca? I think we just completed one of those damnable psychogenetic feedback loops that everybody up in geo-genetic lab central has been droning out on, lo, these many years!" We were back on unified wavelength. By the time the evening was over we both knew one thing: love for Prospero held us together, closer than any enzyme bond.

The following morning we were ready for our bold move on Truth or Consequences. We would hovercraft back to the Socorro Flats Psychophysical Recharge Station. There we would prepare the documentation on the Wandjina Society, scan mutant brainwaves monitored by Esquivel in the Thermal Therapy Lab, exercise a few basic theatrical geno-type black-outs, and then set off.

As we all piled into the aging X-24 hovercraft, Esquivel and Poontutjarpa, their arms around each other, the one looking like a glorious rainbow squashblossom, the other like a gold miner in a refined state of hyper-psyche, were singing away:

> *"Never out of breath*
> *for the journey of death*
> *so sheen me a do wacky do*
> *and when we arrive*
> *no one alive*
> *coulda guessed it woulda been me an you!"*

To be continued...

I had to hand it to the Outlaws. When it came to taking prisoners and holding them, they did it with a certain style. Slugsoup for breakfast, slugsoup for lunch, slugsoup for dinner. Guarded by my old friends One-Eye and Four-Thumbs, I spent who knows how many days in a yurt accompanied by all manner of delirious hallucinations. The spiraling phosphorescent scroll-words inscribing my eyelids with every manner of script conceivable were my favorites. Never in my life had I received so many extraterrestrial messages. In their own dumbfounding way, the slugsoup experiences were astonishing. In addition, they kept my pain from plunging me into any kind of sub-tech state, and I slowly healed. Oh, my nose may be preposterous now, and a brilliant white scar runs down the left side of my face in an almost perfect semicircle from upper lip to lower eyelid, but at least it doesn't lessen the fact that I seem to have acquired some character in life.

In the preciously few clear moments I had to myself, largely in the early morning, pre-dawn hours, I would wonder what Queen Tasha had up her sleeve. One thing I was sure about was the fact that she was still working Syndicscams, this one being Project Scorpio Latitude. The fact that I was still alive—if a steady diet of slugsoup and portions of semi-raw horsemeat can be considered staying alive—also led me to believe that my continued existence was essential to the Syndic scam. My hunch was that for Project Scorpio Latitude to succeed it needed the appearance of at least one other person to round itself out. Beyond that, slugsoup did a delightful job of making shredded magnetic tape of my attempts at figuring the logic behind this latest Syndic scam.

Whatever slugsoup was, some combination of central nervous system depressant with a brain-scrambling psychic magnifier, it did provide me with one memorable psychogenetic interlude. I think it must have been late in the afternoon, toward sundown, the photomenes were throbbing away, triggering floods of psycho-lumens as usual. One thing about slugsoup, it provided more light than ten thousand suns in the otherwise perpetually darkened yurt in which I was kept. It was exactly as some vague thought such as this was rolling across hitherto unutilized synapses, that the following psychogenetic interlude descended upon me.

I first experienced a jolt, a seismic thud vibrating through the neuromuscular system. Then clearly, as if it were both within my nervous system and outside of it simultaneously, I became engulfed in a lucidly intense experience of brain theater. Each cerebral hemisphere lit up, just like the sky in a well-synchronized radiosonic transmission. Every circuit, neuron, and synapse was simultaneously illuminated. The corpus callosum appeared as a jeweled bridge. Standing in the middle of the bridge, his arms straight out, his gorgeous cerebral hemispheres glowing through the massive bald dome of his head was Jason of the Outlaws. Flanking him on the jeweled bridge were mutants of every size, shape, sex and chromatic hue.

"Hopi variation number 50, in the key of Asia, with a Pythagorean subdominant!" Jason of the Outlaws commanded.

Each hemisphere then dissolved into a phosphorescent swastika. The right hemisphere swastika was right-handed, the left hemisphere left. As the swastikas turned toward each other in perfect rhythmic counterpoint, they each emitted a shower of little swastikas, like sparks shot off from a welder's torch. Each large rotating swastika became surrounded by randomly shifting fields of smaller swastikas moving in a direction opposite the major one. The beauty of this sight was such that I distinctly remember weeping, floods of tears covering my face, as my larynx searched for some word, some sound to convey how I felt about this awesome vision.

As I struggled with my emotions, the jeweled bridge of the corpus callosum was eclipsed by what appeared to be a city. This city first appeared to rise up from the subcortical zones like a mountain emerging from the mist. Once it was in place between the luminous swirling swastika skies of brain theater, I could see that it consisted of four levels, each one set above and further back from the other, like a giant stepped pyramid. The surfaces of the walls of each of these appeared to be composed of metallic, yet ethereal substances.

Surmounting the fourth level, a deep celestial blue in color, was a wall with a gate on each side. One gate was composed of earth, another of water, the third composed of fire, and the fourth of air itself. Within the walled confines there arose a nine-leveled tower. Though each level was smaller than the one beneath it, the base of each level was narrower in width than it was at the top. This created the curious effect of a series of similarly proportioned trapezoids placed one atop the other in a proportionally diminishing scale. The strange effect of this structure was enhanced by spectral coloring which ran from the deep red of the bottom level, to a shimmering celestial violet of the top level. So entranced was I by the sight of this tower, counting the windows in each level, beginning with three windows at the top level and increasing by one each level down, not to mention the chromatic effect, that it was a while before I became aware of the perfect sphere floating above the tower.

This sphere seemed to be composed of a very dense material, like some kind of black stone, yet so perfectly polished was it that it shone and reflected like a mirror. Best of all, the sphere simply hovered in space. Engulfed as I was by this experience, I was also permeated with a clarity of awareness.

I remember mumbling to myself, "preter… natural," my voice coming to me like a pitiful, lonesome bird calling in the midst of an immense canyon.

It was the utterance of this word that dissolved the vision. Just as it was dissolving, I felt myself groping, trying to hold on to something I almost remembered, but couldn't quite. I slid back into the fitfully luminescent torpor of night in an Outlaw yurt. Chasing for the recollection of the brain theater palace was like running blindfolded on a moonless night wondering where the sun was going to come up next.

And it did. I was lying on the cot in a sweat. Through the cracks in the door flap I recognized the familiar blue gray slivers of light that I had come to associate with my moments of clarity. Though the pain in my head had largely subsided, I knew I didn't want anymore. I only wanted out. To hell with this PAN-Syndic circuit out-con. All it got me was to a place where my left hemisphere was sub-teched to the point that it resembled a graveyard, and my right hemisphere hyper-psyched into a love affair with its own over-volted synapses.

Lying there, my eyes caked with some kind of ooze brought on by the slugsoup, I savored wispy memories of long days of solitude at the El Dorado Monitoring Station, reading reels of tape, my ears glued to the synthephones. Or walking around the foothills watching magpies soaring among the springtime cottonwoods. Good old days, I thought. But what did it mean? If the slugsoup was meant to scramble me, it was on target. It was then that I recalled the vision of the four-leveled city and the nine-storied tower in brain theater. Where had that come from? And Jason of the Outlaws? Something started piecing itself together.

No sooner had I started rolling the brain theater vision into Scorpio Latitude track then my two benign mutants entered the yurt.

One-Eye winked his inimitable wink, "PAN boy!" he guffawed, "PAN boy slugged in a wink, you must like to sink that ain't but the window 'thout blouds, huh?"

"Huh, yourself, One-Eye," said I, returning his idiot banter, "but slugsoup's the scam that tongues light 'n' reft with no between but the bridge where Jason's catching the sheen." I was proud of myself for getting that one out. I also realized that if you stayed on slugsoup too long, talking like that would just come naturally.

"PAN boy's ripped the tight," One-Eye turned to Four-Thumbs. She laughed, the nail in her lower lip bobbing gaily up and down.

"Ripped the tight, huh, PAN boy," she spoke squinting her squinty little eyes at me. The shape of her forehead, however, recalled the trapezoidal forms of the tower I had seen in brain theater. Another connection tingled through me. "Well skying me brains be poppin the napse, reft 'n' light'sall right, PAN boy. Fit yourself a skeer 'n' skur yer chords. Tonight's starflight doin' mumbles. Queen Tasha wants yer here there. So if she wants yer here there, there's nothin here but there to scare!" The three of us burst out laughing as Four-Thumbs streaked through this last line, hardly able to contain herself at the sublime metaphysical twist she had just barely managed to blurt out.

When the laughter was turning into weepy, heapy wheezes, I lifted myself up, and threw my legs over the cot. "So it's at starflight doin' mumbles, huh?" I continued testing out mutant code-form, "'n' I spear it's a sheen to shape all reft 'n' lighters on the bridge where no born has ever worn but the heaviest, the one that mainlines light, that be. You keen what I sheen?"

Great applause greeted my last comments. "Ripped the tight, my sky!" I decided to give them an encore, "PAN boy bombed on the psyche-deck'n' tripped a night beneath sub-tech, but mutants reft 'n' light PAN boy keened; he'll roll when blunders burr the Queen."

That one stopped them. And then I knew. We were all on the same transmission band. I could feel this thing in them, I could feel it in me as well, a hot-electric spasm that communicated instantaneously: "we know and we all know that we know, but are we suppose to know that we all know that we know?" From that moment we didn't have to say much to each other, One-Eye, Four-Thumbs and myself. Not much at all. Except for when we were with other mutants, and then I usually rolled in a PAN verbal track.

The rest of the morning we worked on some physical exercises getting my body back in shape. One thing I learned was that they really didn't trust Queen Tasha. And that they had their honor. But the most important thing was that I had tracked into them: they were perfectly cross-circuited. Like the brain theater vision, they had crossed swastikas, and somehow or other, so had I. The only difference was that I had the benefit of knowing synaesthetic history and was on to the Syndic scam, which to them was all a big drift, a solar storm occurring at a latitude that didn't concern them.

Towards night fall, One-Eye and Four-Thumbs brought a laser scooter tome. They had been into snakeskin mescal and had a mean edge on, but it didn't scare me. Wordlessly we mounted the scooters and rode off. The late afternoon sky was beautiful. Magenta clouds puffy and dense beneath a cobalt sky. It felt good riding the scooter, white mutant scarves billowing behind me. It felt good having my own head back, or at least, most of it.

We rode for some time. Coming over a ridge we dipped into a valley. Like a natural amphitheater, it was filled with mutants gathered in small clusters, each cluster with its own campfire. Toward the center of this natural theater was a battery of large lights beamed skyward, slowly rotating in random directions. The focus of attention was on what appeared to be a large upright rocket ship. The air was filled by the electrochromatic drones of Outlaw hymns. Amplifiers skillfully placed in strategic spots spread the dirge-like sounds among the massive crowd. We all stopped to appreciate what lay before our eyes. A melancholy chant punctuated by bursts of wildfire melodic runs settled over the crowd like a sonic blanket:

> *"When sheens of moonlight slump the deck*
> *'n' yurt flies scoop the type of sech*
> *the mind electric scams the skin*
> *while radscrews burn the mountain fin*
> *that's when the outlaws keen the stars*
> *to lay the heartfucked laser bars*
> *in even streams that bile th'earth*
> *so no un skeers the mutant birth*
> *lectrogenetic buzz I blow*
> *lectrogenetic's way to go*
> *O babe o mine come haw a see*
> *how dead's become the no-man she*
> *how fire for leather metals burn*
> *up now the bomb! Our children's turn!"*

The hymn ended thunderously and a great savage wail rose up from the crowd. "Star r r r... Flight! Star r r... Flight!" a monotonous chant was set up. The three of us continued on our scooters wending our way toward the center of action.

As we approached the staging platform, "lift-loft zoom-wone" I later found out was the name given to the main Starflight activity area, I spotted a deck of seats set at a sharp angle, very much like in a Star-ball court. What with the stroboscopic laser-light's flashing, and the continuous sound of explosions and sirens, not to mention the electronic drones, the chants of "Star r r r… Flight!" and sundry, blood-curdling wails, it wasn't easy to keep any kind of focus. Nevertheless, I managed to pin my eyes on the deck of seats. As it turned out, this deck of seats was precisely where my mutant escorts wanted to take me

With a screech and a roll of laser-lit dust, we pulled up to our destination. One-Eye and Four-Thumbs toughed it with me. Just after I got off the scooter, my left shoulder still wrapped up tight beneath the leather jumpsuit, I felt a powerful shove from behind. It sent me reeling up the steps of the seat-deck. Only a last-second twist of my head, which pulled painfully at the left shoulder, spared my face from another brutal imprinting from the physical world, this time in the form of one of Jason's gold-booted feet.

Catching my balance, the now familiar icy-magnetic husk of Natasha's voice was exploring my audio canals. "PAN boy, Agent 24, Mr. Jones—radiosonic boom-rig psyched with laser-looms full moon bloomed, must be a picnic for you, huh?"

There she sat. Leather never looked more regal. She was costumed much as she had been the previous time I had seen her, except on her head she now displayed a large gold skull, while round her shoulder was a massive piece of sheepskin, like a cape. On her right was Jason. Leering, uncomfortable as ever, I remembered how he had appeared on the jeweled bridge of the corpus callosum in brain theater.

As I looked at him, trying to deflect the volcanic hate that spouted like psychic lava from his intense red eyeballs, I noticed again, for but the briefest moment, a break, a quiver, a parting of the curtains, very much like a lull during an intense radio-genetic storm. His eyebrows lifted during that moment, rippling the Outlaw insignia branded into his forehead, lifted just enough as if to say "ah hah, you too?" Then it was back to psychic lava. Well, he certainly wasn't going to kill me so I de-teched some, still feeling the adrenalin pushing and pulling with my paranoia.

I turned to Natasha once again, eyeing the gold skull atop her head. "Pretty obvious act of skull-sheening, huh Natasha?" If we were going to play, might as well get it on.

"Number 24, Rocky Mountain PAN boy, with a silver decode arm, throwing feathers to the wind seems to be your game, even though you were silly enough to say to me, 'no, Queen Eisenhammer,'" her last name she uttered with the kind of intonation I keep on reserve for those occasions when my life is in danger.

"'No, Queen Eisenhammer, Tasha, tooshi, toshi, too,' you said to me, your eyes all skies dripping with lies. Come on, like I said the other day, PAN boy, these are Scorpio Latitudes, and in Scorpio Latitudes the Queen holds the Justice Card while the guest plays the Fool. Why don't you say hello to your friend, PAN boy," and with her left index finger studded with an onyx crystal ember mandorla ring, she pointed to her feet. Seated there was Ya Emme, or at least who I took once to have been Ya Emme.

There she was, the Dogon agent of Sirius B, leaning back on her left arm, wearing a shimmering white vest, bare breasted, festooned with gobs of gold and strangely-shaped turquoise, her feet tucked beneath her leather encased buttocks. Ya Emme ran her sultry-lidded eyes up and down me a few times, eyes like flies bouncing intently on a week-old carcass.

Her lips were still soft, as they opened and said, "PAN boy, come at Starflight Doin' Mumbles. What skies you make on this number 2, you might as well take and ram down a moat with bad-burnt laser sticks. Why don't you just take a beat on yer seat and place your skies on Starflight?"

"Such lovely orchid lips. The venom hardly becomes them," I replied, taking a seat where Ya Emme motioned me, just between herself and Natasha's feet.

Brushing away presentiments of Syndic scams double-winging it, I riveted my attention on the stage, if that's what you can call a large, earthen platform, its sides bedecked with silver sheets flapping luxuriantly in the electrochromatic night. In large circle formation, their engines facing center were a magnificent number of ancient convoy trucks. Many of them were of the military variety, some still with defunct cannons or useless rocket carriers. Others were the great produce conveyers, the Safeway type, their rusted aluminum and tin rectangles in a state of eternal rest, memorialized six or eight wheel-less axles apiece. Scattered crowds of mutant-teens scrambled over the trucks like ants on a melon rind. The centerpiece, propped up by four gigantic rocks, each one bearing a massive pictograph of the Outlaw insignia, consisted of an ancient rocket ship. I recognized it as of the Apollo II family. Its dented hulk took on new life as laser lights criss-crossed its surface in rapid-fire battle patterns.

The sound systems went silent. The lights froze in place, creating the staccato image of some mind-formed constellation. High above, drifting lazily from one jagged shaped cloud-mass to another was a moon, as pregnant with light as a woman in her ninth month. The mutant-teens all scrambled for the rocks propping up the old Apollo II.

From behind the center piece, led on the right by a handful of mutant girls, and on the left by a similar number of mutant boys, marched two figures, each dressed in crumpled silver NASA outfits. Wearing space helmets whose clear plastic frontal surfaces reflected miniature versions of the laser-light patterns, each figure carried the familiar mutant banner. As they marched stiffly forward, a drum roll that could have doubled for a death rattle, built up an anxious tempo. Circling round to the front of the rocket centerpiece, each figure planted its banner into the ground. This act was accompanied by a searing run of synthesized chords, bleeding luminous echoes of birth-cries through the amplified sound system. Facing forward now, and in perfect unison, the NASA-ancients removed their space helmets.

Grube and Aldebaran! Damned if it wasn't them, on stage performing the roles of NASA-ancients, puppeting and pirouetting around like a couple of mimes fed on a steady diet of slugsoup. Everyone broke up when NASA-ancient Grube hoisted NASA-ancient Aldebaran up on his knees, then flipped him over his head. Landing on his feet, Aldebaran then swung around holding in each silver-fisted hand what appeared to be ancient automatic rifles, the kind with the bayonets placed on the end.

At this point, NASA Grube fell to his knees, his arms imploring Aldebaran who raised the two rifles above his head so that they formed a triangular pattern. The drum roll, death rattle did it again. Grube sank further down, 'til he was lying belly-flat on the ground. He began crawling, crawling between Aldebaran's outstretched legs, crawling until he reached the centerpiece. There, two mutant ladies whose sumptuously tattooed bodies more than made up for their lack of clothes, lifted Grube to the top of the large stone, then to the front of the Rocket ship. They lay him down on his back so that his head flopped down to the left of the rocket ship, and his feet dangled to the right.

NASA-ancient Aldebaran then turned like a mechanical doll and marched to the rock. With upraised hands, he gave each of the mutant ladies one of the bayoneted rifles. The drum roll, death rattle was on again. This time it didn't stop. Each lady climbed to the top of the rock, facing each other as they straddled the NASA-ancient body of Grube. A terrible anxiety gripped me as they stood, arms above their heads, tattooed breasts gleaming, bayonets glinting in piercing beams of ruby-colored laser light. The drum roll, death rattle picked up tempo as the four arms came down, the bayonets sinking effortlessly into Grube's body. I wanted to puke.

But my nausea was immediately short-circuited by the sound of Grube's strangle-pitched voice screaming out: "Reft 'n' Lighters to the fore!"

At this command, the mutant teens came swarming out from behind the rocks, scampered up them like so many monkeys and began shinnying up the ancient rocket hulk. While one part of me was swept away by the swiftness of the action, another part of me allowed the scarlet streams running over the silver-crumpled NASA suit worn by Grube to imprint itself on the quiet horizon line of my mind. In my numbness, I gradually became aware of something else, a searing hot coal placed in my heart.

This coal was Grube. I could feel the explosions of pain, shattered bone, torn muscle, punctured lungs and severed arteries. With all that, I also experienced a quiet fluttering, as if a bird had been let loose in my rib-cage. "Hee, hee, hee!" the bird was calling out from deep within me, "Hee, hee, hee! Prosp! You got the reft 'n' light, the Grube'll never split your sight, Kingdom Ark the Journey o' Death, what Grube began won't leave your breath."

A strange peace settled over me as the avant-garde of mutant teens made it to the top of the old Apollo II. The feeling of peace didn't leave me as the tattooed ladies took Aldebaran, disrobed him and lay him naked on top of the now motionless body of Grube. Nor did the feeling of peace depart as they sexually sported with Aldebaran, Grube's corpse providing them an unusual matrimonial bed. As the sexual activities reached a peak, I became aware of the mutant teens on the rocket ship chanting another outlaw hymn, traditional slides of minor quarter tones punctuating the end of each line, they chanted:

> *"When the starflight fumble-tumbles*
> *'N' the Moon she scams a bloud*
> *Then the mutant scores the tech-vic*
> *From iron skulls we dream aloud*
> *Mutant children bomb-born sheeners*
> *Chemic lectro-genetic steamers*
> *War the witchsky slack the snaretoads*
> *Raise the mutant outlaw beamers!"*

A great melee broke out when the corpse was dismembered, and portions of it were thrown out to the heaving, tumultuous crowds.

Ya Emme was taking my hand, pulling me up, "C'mon, PAN boy, blood's not the ripeness for your skies. Let's make Queen's yurt our next synchro-station."

I let myself be dragged dumbly through the crowds. Great explosions were ripping the air. As we got to the far side of the staging platform, I turned around only to see the ancient rocket ship dissolving in a burst of tracer-lit explosions. As in a dream, fragments of the ancient hulk sailed through the air amidst whistles and more of those damnable electrochromatic runs.

I had no idea what was going on, whether Ya Emme was friend or foe, whether anything I had seen was even real. We reached a large yurt bordered by pennants. Letting ourselves through the door flap, we collapsed on some large embroidered pillows. I looked at Ya Emme wanting a clue. Her face was a study in terror. I decided not to push anything, just gather my Grube-laced breath. A certain commotion of voices and laughter prefaced the entry of Queen Tasha, Jason and a small coterie of Mutant-groupies.

"Fantab, the moon bloud red the silver snows," someone was exclaiming as the crowd lurched through the door flap. When they spotted Ya Emme and myself seated there, they all fell silent immediately.

Queen Tasha spoke out, "PAN-folks for dinner, muties. Don't they look bliss-skied. Probably enjoyed starflight doin' mumbles more than they imagined they would."

At this, everyone eased into laughter once again, and began seating themselves around the lamp-lit yurt.

Kneeling in front of me, slowly removing the gold skull from her head and placing it in my hands, Natasha said in a very deliberate manner, "Now, maybe PAN boy would like to tell me a little more about the Quetzalcoatl Project."

Before I had a chance to consider what she had just spoken, she added, "Don't you think the silver decode tube harmonizes well with that gold skull in your hands, PAN boy? Or, is it Nezahualpilli, you're going by these days?"

To be continued…

Already before we set off for Truth or Consequences, the word was out. A major Mutant uprising was in full swing. What we could gather from the laser-crazed band of Outlaws who arrived at the Socorro Flats Psychophysical Recharge Station two nights after our arrival, the night prior to our departure, was simply this: At a full-moon Scorpio Starflight Blast-off performance, a certain PAN-liaison named Gruber had been sacrificed, bayoneted, so we were told.

"Pluto in the Twelfth House!" Poontutjarpa Jayavaraman and Tara Andromeda exclaimed in unison, when they heard this news. Gruber had obviously been a key liaison in the Quetzalcoatl Project which they had both initiated.

Anyway, following Gruber's sacrifice and the conclusion of Starflight Blast-off, Mutant Outlaw teens, great numbers of them, continued celebrating. Or at least so it seemed, until the word got out, "Grube Gives." No one was sure how this began or who first uttered that immemorial phrase.

"Spontaneous psychic combustion," Tara popped up, clapping her hands three times, once before each word.

And it was true. No sooner had Tara finished her declaration, then I felt the phrase, "Grube Gives," rushing with a subtle inner wind-blown tremor up and down my spinal column. We all felt it.

"Ladies and gentlemen, ladies and gentlemen," Esquivel took the floor in the center of the small simultaneous-data index chamber, in which we were gathered when the mutants had arrived.

"Ladies and gentlemen, please, this is a most fortunate moment, most fortunate. The Quetzalcoatl Project is a success! Thanks to Grube," Esquivel paused, holding his hands in an attitude of devotion before his heart. "Yes, thanks to Grube, who continues to give, the Quetzalcoatl Project is an assured success. The karmic pattern that surfaced at the time of the fall of the Aztec hierarchy has been resimulated in Truth or Consequences. The uprisings within the domain of Aztec hierarchy, preceded and paved the way for Cortes and the bearers of the True Cross, Vera Cruz, where they landed on Good Friday. These uprisings are the very same ones which our good friends are in the midst of at this moment."

"But ladies and gentlemen," Esquivel's rich mud-brown face had become totally lustrous, his black eyes gleaming like the embers on a late-night log. "Yes, ladies and gentlemen, whereas Montezuma expected the fulfillment of the prophecy of Quetzal-coatl, he received instead the punishment of the Lord of Days, Tezcatlipoca. Ah, poor blood-clone, stoned to death by those whose blood he bled. But now, ladies and gentle-men, the time of prophecy is over. The Wandjina Society, keening how the correction of one psychogenetic pattern synergizes the auto-regulation of others, the Wandjina Society, all of us gathered here, are the liberation of prophecy. Yes, the liberation of prophecy! The fulfillment of the prophecy of the Plumed Serpent, the return of Quet-zalcoatl to Truth or Consequences. Yes, ladies and gentlemen, this is the Flight of the Serpent. The Liberation of Prophecy! Our time is on the line!"

Esquivel's triumphant pronouncement was met first with awe-struck silence fol-lowed by everyone in the room spontaneously going around quietly hugging everyone else.

After dawnstar quiet-hour the next morning, we all gathered in the G &O lounge: David and Dawnstar Monongye; Lindy McGrew and Fa-Tsang Wronski; Poontutjarpa and Tara Andromeda; Claudia Blavatsky Leventhal and Ramakrishna al-Badr; Es-quivel and myself; and the four Mutants, two men and two women, all of whom were distinguished by the brand of the Outlaw insignia imprinted on oversize brows that curved perceptibly into large, bald dome-heads. These four, Grunt, Squeaker, Blaze and Cyclone, as it turned out, were defects from Jason of the Outlaws' immediate clan.

After a light breakfast consisting of eggs Quivera and blue corn cakes simply, but elegantly served up by the ever-smiling Ramakrishna al-Badr, it was Poontutjarpa's turn to issue the final summons for our task. He was dressed this morning in a nat-ty reconnaissance uniform, earth camouflage-colored pantaloons tucked neatly into knee-length black boots, and matched by the same camouflage earth-colored tunic and jacket. Draped over his left shoulder was his laser beam-thrower, and on his silver coiled locks, perched as usual at a jaunty angle on the right side of his head was his gold-miner's cap, distinguished this morning by the familiar five-striped PAN combat unit medallion. His ageless Australian face was both solemn and cheerful.

"Wandjina Society, we all know what to do, that is, do nothing. This is very good," he nodded with his earth serpent chuckle, "very good." "Precipitous behavior is always a sign that the infinite headed ego demon has found a sleeping neuron and forced his way into consciousness. None of this please. Self-existing synchronicity is already at work, paving a golden pathway studded with lodestones of karmic coincidence. Work with these lodestones directly and with humor, and the Project will be completed." Poontutjarpa then turned his head toward Fa-Tsang Wronski.

"Fa-Tsang," he commanded, "you, David Monongye, and Lindy McGrew will on-line the avant-garde penetration unit. The rest of us will follow. David, make sure the Wandjina Society sashes are ready."

Following this directive, Poontutjarpa rubbing his hands and smiling his broad kangaroo-catcher's grin, spoke his final words, "when I looked outside this morning the dawnstar was twinkling brightly. The sun was still an hour away from blessing the horizon with its golden rays. And it was good, very good. My happiness at this occasion is unbounded. My determination is as unshakeable as a total planetary line-up. My love is like the coil of fire that blazes in the heart of every star. This is our time, prisoners of the earth, this is our time!"

Again, we all moved around the room hugging each other. Then amidst joking and laughter we made our way to the X-24 hovercraft. The Wandjina Society was off and flying.

We docked the hovercraft in a canyon clearing on the south face of San Mateo Peak. There we bade farewell to the avant-garde trio. Lindy McGrew was hopping down toward the valley floor like a jack-rabbit, giving David a coyote work-out as he chased after him. Fa-Tsang blissfully skipped behind, periodically flashing a round mirror at the sun. At precisely sky-zenith the rest of us moved down toward the valley floor, and Elephant Butte reservoir. Then we followed the reservoir shore and river bed southward. High cirrus clouds were the only blemish on the pale November blue sky. My heart was singing, "Prospero, Prospero, my lord! my love! I'm coming, with tracers of red-light blazing, I'm coming!"

East of Truth or Consequences was an old bridge bordered on the west side by a large grove of cottonwoods. It was here that we waited.

Just before sundown, an Outlaw approached our encampment. "Wandjina jokers, come 'n' bait the deck with licks from her moon-sheened jags. We keen you. Let's blow!"

Led by Blaze and Cyclone we scampered out of the grove and onto the old highway bed. All afternoon we had heard the sliding burps of laser-fire followed by long interludes of silence. As we approached Truth or Consequences the bursts became louder and more frequent. The early evening sky was ablaze with laser lights criss-crossing. We slowly became aware of a thunderous rhythm accompanied by electronic drones hanging like stalactites in the ominous sky. A slow-moving wedge of laser scooters formed before us. By the time we reached the outer encampment ring of Truth or Consequences we had been joined by at least several hundred other mutant groups, including the notorious Slack-Zone Outlaws from the Great Lakes Wastelands.

"Look at those Subterranean Raiders," Tara Andromeda said with a thrill, holding onto my arm as the Slack Zone Outlaws, a small army of largely black African mutants, swirled around us, their laser scooters skittering 360°, throwing up great clouds of laser-lit dust. As we found out later, groups like the Slack-Zone Outlaws immediately descended in various hovercraft fleets onto Truth or Consequences to join what came to be known as the "Star Flight Fumble, Grube-Gives Rumble."

The spirit of riotous festivity found its climax when we reached Rumble-Zone Central. A dense throng of mutants had us completely hemmed in. The air was crackling. Fireworks, laser bursts, electro-rhythm drones shot out from every quarter. On top of an amazingly constructed pile of old convoy trucks was a crude platform on which a dozen or so figures scurried about. Among them were David, Lindy and Fa-Tsang. Through all the activity, I could make out the words of a mutant hymn:

> *"Wha Grube gives in Starflight fumbles*
> *Slur the lightjag, school the rumbles*
> *Sheen the cart an' craze the skies*
> *Grube gives be skulled lyke laser sighs*
> *Heave light the slackbrained tors 'n' skivs*
> *They burnt they slidges keened not Grube gives*
> *So size the loomborn mutant bines*
> *Star-flight nights the wimp-worn skines*
> *Blood the tongue and bone the brain*
> *Grube Gives, mutant genes detrain"*

As this mysteriously low-keyed chant went through its endless rounds, one verse succeeding another, I was struck by the marvelous vibration of good cheer. Though the atmosphere was provocative, it was not dangerous. As this thought occurred, I also realized I had been separated from the rest of the Wandjinas.

Simultaneously, I also knew that we had all been separated, and that was all right. This is the way the mutants wanted it, and we were here to serve them. On both sides of me, a mutant took my hand. Glancing at them I saw that they were content just holding hands, rotating their shoulders all the while, as their lips rhymed and mimed whatever set of couplets came to mind. And I could feel their rhymes coursing through me in soothing waves that reached the brain in spirals of lucid, wind-blown light:

> *"Mag the fountains milked the flight*
> *guinningest leather feather slight*
> *fickled the slynapse in a twick 'n' a fool*
> *brockled came, camber the lumiast tool*
> *fer sly the gray Grube collapsed inna tube*
> *beguinningest fungiest genieassed rube*
> *fer slavin the mindwarp oo—oo long*
> *Grube gives the rumbleassed tumbleassed song"*

As the figures on stage began to take on an orderly formation, the sound systems shut off, the lapsing lyrical off-key chanting turned to a whisper and then died out. At the center of stage-front, were two mutants, a man and a woman. Behind them in horizontal file were David, Lindy and Fa-Tsang. Fa-Tsang was now wearing his round mirror as a medallion hanging on his chest. It continued to catch and reflect the multi-colored lights that swept across the stage.

Behind the three Wandjinas in the third row, were another seven or eight mutants. The entire troupe was formidable, a base-line shot down a central neural alley in the shape of an arrowhead. The two front-stage mutants, the male goggling away with but a single cyclopean eye, the female all bounce and bursting in her tight leather suit, a gold ring glinting in her lower lip, held out a skull topped with a wondrous wave of silver gray hair. The skull functioned as the tip of the arrowhead, the two mutants as its immediate supports. The three Wandjinas behind them leaned forward, their left legs bent at the knee, right legs straight back, arms held in a "ready to beam" position. The row of mutants behind the Wandjinas held their legs in the same position, but their arms were in "beam vertical." The group synchronized itself to the sound of a slow, low eerie duet.

It was the front-stage Mutants who began weaving their voices together. The rest of the group provided rhythmo-harmonic backup and punctuation.

> *"Duastic double helix bind*
> *break scam do wah do run keen mind*
> *Grube-cell caps the motherskin*
> *Jive Jason rives do wah the fin*
> *rub the time it's back to front*
> *we zone no flight*
> *but sky the bunt*
> *beghast the bunt do wah the rube*
> *what grube skulled skast that gives the grube*
> *sleep-flake zone, beam the dream*
> *Wandjina scams like bones the gleem*
> *so scam the bone, rube the tube*
> *Wandjina screen genes the grube."*

When the lyric liaison reached this verse, the trapezoid-browed lady mutant, and the cyclopean one, her right arm intertwined in his, raised the skull aloft, the flowing gray hair catching glints of blue-red light. "Grube skull scam Wandjina tops, he pops to sky this deck. Pop it, Wandjina top, pop it!" This command, again voiced in unison by the two lead mutants, was followed by a brief awe-filled quiet.

A slight commotion just in front of me quickly took the shape of two mutants hoisting Poontutjarpa on their shoulders. Clearing a path through the crowd, they broke into a full run. Reaching stage-front, they catapulted Poontutjarpa so that he landed feet first directly before the skull-raising mutants. Spinning around on his left foot, his right leg bent, the foot touching the knee, Poontutjarpa now stood beneath the skull. With elegantly deft movements, the two Mutants took the skull and tied it with flowing red and black ribbons to Poontutjarpa's left wrist.

No sooner had this been done, then the onstage entourage began barking, yipping and chanting, "Grube skull gives Wandjina top, he scam the skivs!" As they chanted and yelped, the lead lady mutant took an apron, it looked perhaps like it was the skin of a mountain lion delicately incised with strange embryonic dancing forms, and tied it round Poontutjarpa's waist. She then took a large cap. It looked like an old-fashioned aviator cap with the flaps tied over the top of the head, only furrier and heavier. Gently removing the gold-miner's hat, she placed the new hat on his head. She also took the PAN Combat Unit pin from the old hat and placed it on the new one. Finally, she brought out a massive fur-lined cape and with a hearty smile and a kiss on his cheek, draped it over Poontutjarpa's shoulders.

As Poontutjarpa slowly let himself down to the floor, assuming a seated posture, both legs crossed, I began to grasp what was happening. Poontutjarpa was being empowered. Having received the symbols of empowerment, he sat down in a deep trance. As he kept himself utterly motionless, his face seemed to change. From Australian face, it took on Mongolian features, only with a deep bronze coloration. Then as it paled, it transformed into the face of what appeared to be a Druid priest. Finally, it melted back into its original Australian form. While all of this occurred, the crowd remained in a state of high tense quiet. When the Australian features returned, an appreciative giggle swept through the crowd. I felt the mutant hands clutching mine give a tight squeeze then let go.

Raising his Grube skull-tied left arm, Poontutjarpa let out a piercing monosyllabic war-cry, Kyaaaaaaaaaaaaa!"

The crowd responded with an equally drawn out, "kyoooooooooooo!"

We did this back and forth maybe a dozen times, when suddenly from the back of the platform one of the Slack-Zone Outlaws, you could tell them by their iridescent jumpsuits, took command.

"Cart vibes fast for the steady Grube juice we loomed. But now, Wandjina topped Newlaws, it's skull city time. Light 'n' reftors to the fore!"

Following this call for action, things moved very fast. Remembering Poontutjarpa's injunction to go with the lodestones of karmic coincidence, I allowed the mutants who had stood on either side of me to take the lead. Scrambling after them, they took me to a tangled thicket of laser scooters. Motioning me to take one, the three of us rode off, soon joining a large squadron of scooters, winding our way westward through Truth or Consequences.

Working our way up a shallow canyon my eye caught sight of the skull fortress atop the hill. It was bathed in bouncing streams of blue-red light. About half a kilometer down the fortress we came to a halt. From Truth or Consequences several kilometers east of us, the sound systems had taken up their inevitable electro-nocturnal drone. Mutants like to orchestrate everything. With them it was all radiosonic brain theater. They never miss a cue. Birth, death, peace or war—it was all one great rhythmic performance piece.

It was then that my thoughts tracked into Prospero. I knew he was still alive. Our thought beams were in synch. My body shuddered a great release of energy. I knew he would be changed. But then I was, too. Still, what we had, yes, what we had linking us, was a duastic bond fueled by the fires of uncompromising innocence. This was my heart speaking, and it spoke in great orchids of tenderness; soft sensuous petals of violet and white hardly able to bear the weight of their own beauty.

A blinding burst of laser fire broke the perfumed reverie in which I had been momentarily engaged. I felt the adrenalin shoot to my brain. Dismounting our scooters, we moved ahead on foot, a yelping chanting mob syncopated by the echoing electromonitored drone. Suddenly, sweeping up toward the left front of the fortress, lasers blazing, a squadron of Slack-Zoners came to an eerie halt. From the roof of skull fortress, lasers blazing back, appeared a large party in tight knit formation.

The exchange of fire punctuated by falling bodies and intense war cries lasted but a few moments. The Slack-Zoners had already begun to scale the uneven walls of skull fortress. As soon as the Slack-Zoners had taken command of the rooftop, the mob pressed forward.

Surrounding skull fortress, a cry went out. "Jive the Outlaw Jason!" This call was repeated until a singularly large fellow, dome-topped like the quartet of mutants who had come to us at Socorro Flats, appeared. The outlaw insignia, branded into his brow, gleamed a ruby red. Green tracers of light played over his body. He held up both of his arms, the palms of his hands, emerging from heavily braceleted wrists, facing outward.

"Heyyy!" Jason called out. "Heyyy, mute-babes, junk the rumble. No skiv me. He mute to boot. Mime me yer cart's dead fire, 'n' I'll retire the Queen."

Even before he had finished his plea a gathering wave of tongues was spitting out, "Naaaaaaaah, jiiiive th'outlaw Jason." Mutants around me were stamping their feet uneasily.

Jason lowered his arms, a sickly smile running back and forth upon his lips. "Kay Mutes, Yer rhyme don't mime me brain, fuckfaced tools, you'll burn the ape, unload the tape."

Just then a few new figures appeared on the fortress, laser-beams at the ready. This was followed by another exchange of fire. Holding on to his torso, like a slow-falling tree that's just been sawed in two, Jason tumbled down from the roof top, his body bouncing like a rock down a mountainside preceding an avalanche.

I took a deep breath, swallowing and absorbing the pain-shattered hulk that finally came to a rest. Nobody cared to look. Then a great cheer went up from the mob surrounding skull fortress.

A Slack-Zoner, raising his laser-beam above his head, called out, "Wandjina toppers, pop the core 'n' cave the skull!"

The mutants immediately 'round me turned to me and hissed out, "Blow Wandjinabunt, blow!" They cleared a path for me and I walked quickly toward the main entrance of skull fortress.

There, Poontutjarpa was already waiting. When all the Wandjina Society had gathered, a number of mutants bashed down the door, and we strolled in.

Everything seemed so easy. Fa-Tsang was explaining to Lindy and David the holographic properties of minimally refractive mirror surfaces. Tara Andromeda and Dawnstar Monongye walked on either side of me. Dawnstar was grunting something about mutant table manners. Poontutjarpa and Esquivel were examining the painted designs on the torch-lit walls of the entry chamber, while Ramakrishna and Claudia Blavatsky took a moment to go into deep embrace.

"This is war?" I thought to myself, feeling the incendiary touch of Prospero's thought-beam. Finally, coming to a winding staircase we climbed up to a great landing. As I looked up, there she was: Natasha Eisenhammer. A piercing metallic ray entered my heart.

"It-lil-po-tan-cuah!" I called out. She smiled ever so slightly.

It was my turn to lead. My heart beat fast, pounding to the electro-nocturnal drones still audible within skull fortress.

"So you still think you'll make it to magnetic north, make it therewith your Lord, the Noble Fasting One, do you?" Natasha spoke through clenched teeth. Then glaring at me with those intoxicating green eyes, green eyes through which I had tumbled bitter-black to the depths, she spat out, "Well, PAN cunt, you'll have to get him from me first."

When she said this, I laughed, "Come on Natasha, this is your last act. That last line was worse than a script from a Plutonium-culture video drama. You're not functioning synchrologically."

I paused, sizing up the image on my screen. Yeah, the green-eyed delphite in her leather jumpsuit, white scarves flowing—she still couldn't leap the chasm, that wondrously minute chasm that goes from Pa Logic to Ah Logic. In my heart, compassion cozied up to anger. Those few years I had spent with her had left a tissue of tenderness indelibly stamped into my heart. She was struck speechless as I flashed this thought beam at her.

Placing my right hand on my hip, my hand caressing the violet padded silk tunic which I wore that evening of destiny, my left hand playing idly with the gold Trident pendant which I had deliberately hung around my neck that morning. I sashayed a few steps closer to Natasha. "Does art imitate nature, or does nature imitate art, my dearest Natasha?" the words spilled from my mouth like flowers nurtured on the vine of all-penetrating intelligence. "It doesn't matter how you answer that question, Pa Logic or Ah Logic, because if you're in synchrologic, whatever you answer burns a pure flame. And you, of all people, trying to do a synchrological scam, on cylinders that are still pumping away on Pa logic-fuel. That's the part that makes the gall flow most bitterly through any recollection I may have of you. Missed the Dionysian jump and ended up in an Outlaw jumpsuit. Well get this, Natasha. The Outlaws are gone. Gone like a vapor in a syntho-recall tube. Gone. But there are Newlaws, Natasha. And guess what? You're not one of them."

Clearly Natasha had not anticipated in the least what I had to say. Her face went gray. Her eyes sank. Now she stood before me, a forty-year-old woman, childless, a syndic con artist of the highest intelligence, and she couldn't make it from entropic manipulation to syntropic release. As I scanned her face, every line, every mascara-caked wrinkle, every cell and every pore stood out in distinct relief.

Unmasked. She had finally been unmasked. All those roles she had played—Rasputin and Lenin, Socrates and the Sybil, Genghis Khan and the Yogini of the Cave, but stuck on It-lil-po-tan-cuah.

"Do you understand what happened to you Natasha? Do you really keen the tape that's had you negatively magnetized?" I paused to see if she would reply, and soon learned that it wasn't that she wouldn't, but that she couldn't.

"OK, Natasha. Syndic Hierarch's Scorpio Latitude couldn't scam this one, because we're playing for real, and you're still playing for power. Pa is for power. Ah is for real. Can you scam that Natasha?"

The muscles around her mouth twitched, involuntary twitches that betrayed a mind agonized and frantic in the dead-end of logic.

"I'll give you a little more Natasha. You got tricked into playing a game that you didn't know was real. We scanned you good, because we scanned a psychogenetic monitor code on you, a tight one at that, as tight as anything we've ever done. You're out of control, on a feedback loop that's more than just psycho theater. You're operating on It-lil-po-tan-cuah's feedback loop, karmic residue, if you will, and this one's for real. It was inevitable. Not only did we scan It-lil-po-tan-cuah, but we scanned his whole scene. And that's where we got the key code. All of us were jamming on the same feedback loop, and this was our chance to break it, because we're all in on it, all in on this same psycho genetic play back. And that's exactly what we've done, we've broken it. And as for your alcohol rush, Natasha, let's just say that that's the price It-lil-po-tan-cuah had to pay for fucking with the Plumed Serpent. That's why they say nowadays, Grube gives. Get it Natasha?"

I paused again, feeling the adrenalin hit the brain with a dead-on smack. That was the cue to rest, release, breathe, and forget. Hovering in the brilliantly clear space that connected Natasha and myself, I simply let the situation take over.

I was only peripherally aware of the Wandjina Society standing in a guarded semi-circle behind me, only tangentially aware of the torch lit adobe-faced walls shedding their bursting flickers of light on richly painted meanders of decoration. Audibly aware only of a slow exhalation happening in unison, my heart emptied until it was a mere receptacle of whatever wished to flow into it, a quivering, dew-tipped lotus floating in crystalline space.

"Bravo! Bravo! Bravo!" A hearty cheer rang down from the upper landing. There with a nose that now resembled mine, a scar running like a new moon down the left side of his face, his color as richly golden as ever, only deeper, more burnished, outlaw leather and scarves enclosing that supple, rippling body of his, was Prospero. My heart simultaneously collapsed and exploded.

"Prospero." His name burst from my lips. I felt like the Socorro Flats Psychophysical Recharge Station psychogenetic monitor screen flashing out when all of its units registered the key code as a result of feeding into it the Wandjina Society info-log.

As I moved past Natasha, who stood drained and waiting for the rest of the Wandjina Society to make the next move, I could see that Prospero was weak, fragile, and that his hands were tied behind his back. It was then that I broke into a sprint, rushing up the last brief flight of winding stairs to the top landing. Just before reaching him I stopped. My hands lifted slowly toward his face, caressing it like moonlight on waveless water.

Smiling at me, his words trailing out like a song distantly heard, he spoke everything my heart had wanted to hear: "If you're playing for keeps, let's do it together."

CORPUS CALLOSUM

# THE BRIDGE OF LOVE

# Prospero's Proposition

*Goddess*
*with all of your savage intensity*
*sweep me away, synch me*
*gild my cock the liquid aura*
*flowing from your glowing*
*golden scorpio gate*
*it doesn't matter if you annihilate me*
*to die in the illuminating heat of your fired earth*
*is to be born again a warrior*
*wielding the beam-rod laser*
*that sears to emptiness*
*the genetic shackles*
*of poor imprisoned earth…*

# Francesca's Reply

*Entwined as I am*
*in the duastic double helix*
*of our love*
*how else could I respond*
*but to throw open the scorpio gate*
*of my wisdom golden glowing*
*and throbbing open*
*gone-wait*
*for the fiery probes*
*of your fine-line flesh*
*driven like the wind*
*thru the full-bloomed trees*
*of my beginningless star-rooted being...*

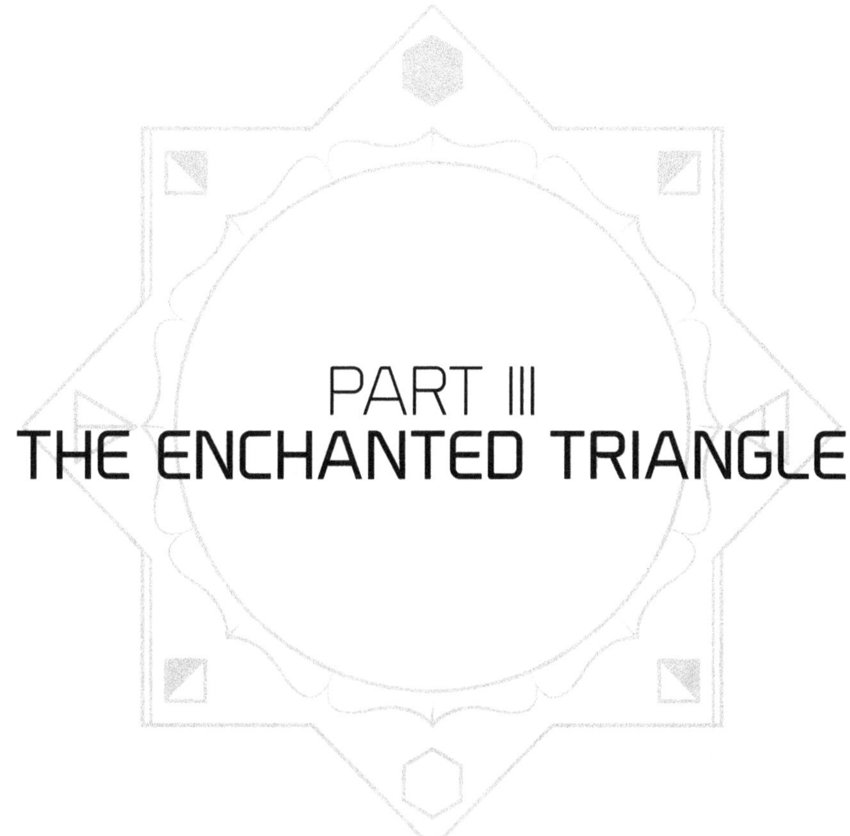

# PART III
# THE ENCHANTED TRIANGLE

# PROSPERO'S TAPE LOG: PANFUSION AT THE PEAK OF DARKNESS

It wasn't 'til the winter solstice that we set off from Truth or Consequences. Some six weeks had passed since that wondrous evening when my heart finally realized its destiny… Six weeks of duastic intensity, of sensually vibrant psychosynergisms, of early winter twilights reflected pink and golden in Francesca's sea-deep eyes. There was no way I could have anticipated the compassionate power of Francesca's healing energy. The Francesca that I had known at Shasta Abbey ten years ago was a uni-dimensional riff-chanter with a lovely voice and a body to go with it. But I had been on to other things. Jammed with synaesthetic history tapes, I was out to loom the airwaves with the most fantastic radiosonic beams the world had ever known. Thinking on that now, I realize I was as uni-dimensional as I had perceived Francesca to be.

Strange how destiny had given us this ten year loop, finally splicing us into the most outrageously challenging experiment of the War. And it could have been no other way. The solution to the puzzle of centuries of psychogenetic tape warps rested with the Trident Brigade, a band of 22 vision-enthralled renegades—fifteen PAN liaisons and seven Newlaws in all. And thanks to Francesca, I was fired, like a solar space shell beaming unadulterated light to the havoc of war-torn earth and yet all that had happened was but a strategic prelude. We had yet to reach the Peak of Darkness.

Besides a love that transported me beyond love, other things happened during that sumptuous six-week lull in Truth or Consequences. Esquivel, Claudia and Ramakrishna returned to the Socorro Flats Psychophysical Recharge Station, Natasha, Ya Emme and Aldebaran in their custody for a Rehab intensive. The plan was for all of them, plus Ixchel O'Shaughnessy, to join us at the Peak of Darkness on the eve of the Winter Solstice.

The rest of us, Poontutjarpa, Tara Andromeda, Dawnstar, Fa-Tsang, David, and Lindy, continued to use skull-palace as headquarters of the Trident Brigade. We were joined in our plans by the Newlaw Six: my old friends Psychlosky and Doorlumia, and by the four Jason clanners, Grunt, Squeaker, Blaze and Cyclone.

Truth or Consequences had changed dramatically since Starflight Mumbles and the flush-fated Grub-Gives-Rumble. Oh, some things remained the same, like the 24-hour electrodrone. But the song was different. They were no longer Outlaw Mutants, but simply Newlaws. Grube's death had psychosynergized them exactly in the way that I had foreseen in my yurt-born revelation, the double-swastika cerebral helix vision. Grube, it seems, was perceived by them as having released a latent brain-tonic. This "brain-tonic," an enzyme transcending endorphin—a rare one at that, was cued by Grube's death, electrically jumped by his final cry, "Reft n Lighters to the Fore!"

Still outrageous, the Newlaws were swept by a blissful fervor of energy. Within two weeks, they had constructed a massive radiosonic beam which synched with the 24-hour electrodrone. The Newlaw beam dwarfed anything I ever dreamed of in my years at the El Dorado Station. For four weeks its gentle pulsation bathed and penetrated everything in sight with its lustrous photosonic infraneural waves.

To visit Truth or Consequences' synthocentral arcade during this time was to take a voyage through a sea of tattooed ganglia, twittering and chattering away like a jungle forest at high noon. Holding hands with Francesca, we would jostle our way through the lurching, chanting masses of Newlaws, their eyes fixed by a gleam that not even the most masterful metaphysician could have deciphered.

Occasionally there would be a clearing, where small clusters of Newlaws sat in rapt awe as a GrubeScam Giver declaimed the new wisdom. The most famous of the GrubeScam Givers was the notorious Slack-Zoner, Supersub. It was he, his towering black dome head, rippled by three bright frontal protrusions, eagle-beak nose and wildly smacking lips, who most persistently laid out Newlaw Logic. His lithe black body, naked and gleaming except for a pair of lion skins tied tightly round his waist, was tattooed with a continuous bright yellow and green snakeskin design that wound delicately round his torso and limbs. His eyes burning with a peaceful glow, his lips chopping away, his arms curving and slicing through the air with a spontaneity that was an excellent cover for the masterful, but deadly, synchrologic which he pounded out.

Subzone would regale the crowd:

> *"NewGrubeScamLaws, Tattooed Decktrippers, skivving what must*
> *be skived, and scamming what must be scammed, audio this:*
> *duastic ever be the brainjoined bod*
> *looped 'n' scooped by Grubegrave nod*
> *fused 'n' bired the neural chasm*
> *boils the greev so no one's spasm*

*so heyyyyy lick the simpborn idento-wave*
*with a logical kick from Grubespun grave:*
*baseline shoots the primordial lenono*
*triggering fast the duastic synerge*
*so that Supersub Slackzoned fused and*
*elevator brained you the fineline shot*
*that blasts the snakeskied identowave off this lot*
*'n' it's this: Heeyyyy Newgrubescamlaws,*
*what this is is just another educlass*
*in frontal lobotomy protrusions..."*

By the time Supersub would reach this point in his logical flight even he could hardly contain himself. The Newlaws squatting around him would be rolling around gripped by high-wheezing laughter that subsided shortly before total asphyxiation set in. Francesca and I would also be seized, tumbled and thrown by a cosmic tickle which we mutually experienced in our newfound duastic bond.

Then, as everybody was on the verge of thinking that they had just heard all that there ever will be to know, Supersub, transforming himself into the living flash of un-invented dignity, would calmly add the coda to his already insanely ingenious verbal composition:

*"NewGrubescamlaws*
*scammers who skivved the Outlaw wave*
*riding Newlaw bleepers where no sky has heard*
*no lear have beamed*
*deck the baseline shot with this nowhere streamer:*
*Newlaw mutebabes, love's the last act:*
*do the duastic serve 'n' swerve*
*no beyond beyond that*
*but yawns the lawn of Grubeskull flat."*

When Supersub would finish, his erect monumental snake-tattooed physique rip-pling with sunshine and a composure that was unshakeable, the awe-struck audience of Newlaws, and a few random Wandjinas like Francesca and myself would remain quiet, intrafused by a mutual force-field of wisdom-soaked insight. That, and lots of good humor.

Already after we had experienced Supersub the first time, Francesca and I were buzzing. "Best DNA realist I ever heard," Francesca commented, her voice like clover honey on a rice-cake. I had to agree. We had never encountered anyone who had grasped so completely the duastic double-helix dialectic of the cerebral hemispheres so brilliantly—or poetically as Supersub. What impressed us most about Supersub's expositions was the keenness with which he communicated the logic of the cerebral dialectic as a distinct means for experiencing the Primordium.

"You mean he's got it," Francesca would respond to my convoluted analyses, her characteristic smile accented by a bounteous crescent of mauve-tinted lips.

It wasn't long before we made Supersub's acquaintance. It was after one of his discourses that we caught up with him in the midst of an interminable Newlaw shuffle, the kind where, though everyone seems to be rhythmically random, each person actually knows exactly which positions to take.

"Hey, Supersub," Francesca said, intercepting the Prince of Newlaw Logic as he mute-bopped sideways toward an arcade exit.

"Yeah, Golden-bliss Wandjina topper, pop your copper on this mute's deck and keen the sky that baits." As Supersub whacked out this phrase, just the slightest glimmering of a smile on his sensuous, quivering lips, Francesca stood there eyeing him like she was a plutonian scam master. Nonetheless when she came back with her reply, Supersub twinkled with a tremor of mutual recognition.

"OK Newlaw scam-king, audio this," she began, "this bliss-snared Wandjina topper and her duastic blend have been poppin' to your toppers. And I'll tell you this: you're synthomaculate. No blots staining the palace of your mind. And your heart-cart, Supersub, your heart-cart Grubescam gives the logic to your law. Why don't you time it at skull fortress with this duastic blend and the other Wandjina toppers? We're all shooting from the same baseline, so why not?" Her hands on her hips, clad in her violet silk, padded PAN tunic, her white slacks blousing above the black boots into which they were tucked, Francesca threw her hair back, ever so slightly to the left.

Radiance is too shallow a word to describe her smile at that moment. Primordial luminosity still wouldn't do it justice. My heart sang with joy, and clearly, so did Supersub's.

"Hey Wandjina topper," he replied, a loose easy manner to his voice, "the birds flying from your tongue-gate lyke sheen o' yer skies: the fruit of truth is the line you shoot. So let's blow. Skull-palace mumbles beat arcade rumbles."

The last two weeks of our stay at Truth or Consequences were greatly enriched by Supersub's presence. What was most interesting to the rest of the Wandjinas was the instantaneous connection that happened between Supersub and Fa-Tsang Wronski. They immediately transformed each other, their temporal personalities falling away like leaves from an autumn maple. Suddenly we were in the presence of a meeting between the Lord of Mirrors and the Prince of Newlaw Logic. It was clear that they had been waiting centuries for this reunion. Fa-Tsang's full moon Mongolian face was a platter of bliss. Supersub himself melted down to a pure blaze of primal fire. They didn't even have to say anything to each other.

This exercise in straight mind-to-mind communication was followed by an embrace between the two which was so touching that Dawnstar actually began to shed tears. Catching this as it happened, Lindy McGrew started hopping up and down ever so quietly, murmuring as he did so, "Dawnstar sees the logic light. No mirror ever seemed so bright." Soon we all took up this softly voiced chant, until Fa-Tsang and Supersub broke their embrace. Both of them turned to us, and with equally sly grins, replied in unison, "No mirror dim nor sky shine bright, that it couldn't keen the dawnstar light."

It was Fa-Tsang and Supersub who worked out the image coding for Poontutjarpa's laser beam-rod, and on this they worked many long days, going back and forth from Skull-palace to the radiosonic transmission crews. While these two were fast involved in the image code, the rest of the Wandjinas mapped out their strategy for the Peak of Darkness in a most leisurely manner.

Naturally, Francesca and I were key for the discussions we had, possessing as we did the main ingredients for our task: the information from Ixchel O'Shaughnessy, the map, and the strange little story written by the ancient seeker, Trident.

Three days before the solstice we had our last meeting. No difficulties were foreseen in arriving at Trinity Site at the foot of Peak of Darkness in the Jornada del Muerto. The main concern was that we all had the right attitude.

"PAN fusion transforms atomic fusion." That's the way Poontutjarpa tersely put it at the beginning of our last strategy insight meeting. "The purpose isn't pulling this damnable rod from the ground and laser-sizing the tektite sphere," Poontutjarpa continued, "its PAN fusion, one mind." As he spoke, the Venerable Wandjina rotated his left arm, the Grube-skull still attached to his wrist, its illusion-penetrating smile, fixed and immutable, played quiet games with the flickering glimmers of Skull-palace torchlight.

"Long's it's not con-fusion," Supersub smacked his lips, "de-lusion, or another unihemispheric trans-fusion."

"Yeah, a stripe of base-line light that root curves when it sees there's no detour to deroute," Fa-sang chimed in, idly turning the Trident mirror medallion that now continuously hung around his neck.

"Right, serpent-light, helix beaming, direct, an unobstructed circuit, popping thunderheads of doubt." Dawnstar spoke, her hands held behind her a head, a turquoise band gathering youth-black hair, lustrous and fragrant around her close to 60-year-old head.

"Squeezed through warrior heart cries, unknotting clouds in clearmind skies no less," Francesca burbled, her words like bubbles frothing at the foot of a mountain waterfall.

"Of course, and wild-keening brainjoined bod to a shoot-out of emptiness," I took my turn, feeling utterly no effort as the words passed across my tongue like clouds before the face of the moon.

"Right! Insight the light I bite my sight its wrong conclusions; biding sight of wrong conclusions, insight the light of PAN profusions!" David had the most difficult time recovering from his two-line utterance. No sooner had he spoken it, then he burst into side-splitting laughter, which had the rest of us begging for a respite of silence between loud explosions of uncontainable laughter.

"No heart, no PAN fusion. One heart… beyond confusion." My mother, Tara Andromeda finally placed a beacon of stillness into our midst.

After all these years, years enmeshed in the mutual complicity of events leading to our reunion, I had never felt closer to my mother. The primal genetic instinct was still there, but beyond that we both mutually experienced a recognition that placed us on a totally equal footing. I remember how she took my hands that night several weeks ago and kissing me, whispered into my ear, "The seal of love is unborn, Prospero, unborn."

"But, but, but," Lindy McGrew suddenly swirled into the center of our circle. Dressed in a loose-fitting jumpsuit and sporting a violet cape embroidered with a magnificent gold Trident, Lindy continued, his right index finger carving imaginary diamonds in the charged air. "But, I mean Skull-palace mumbles are fine. They're full of heart, and they do the duastic blend we all need, but, we can't go doozy, either. Sharp-sighted, keen-blown minds we all need. No sleepy headed neurons. This is global revolution, re-volution, the Big Turn-Around!" At this point Lindy's gesticulations were verging on the grotesque. We all hung on for his conclusion. Taking his pause to the limits, Lindy spun around with a magnificent flourish of his cape. Coming to a stop, holding the bottom of his cape with his right hand, his left hand raised as if he were proposing a toast, Lindy announced with a soft tech lilt, "but then again, it's no big deal." Crazily distorting his already joy-born face, Lindy hopped back to his seat, a smile as gracious as a jack-rabbit chased by a fox, while the rest of us groaned with bemused restraint.

No sooner had he sat down again with a blank stare as if nothing had happened, then the Newlaw Six took to the floor. In a swift gymnastic maneuver which saw Psychlosky and Doorlumia nimbly jumping atop the shoulders of Grunt, Blaze, Squeaker and Cyclone, the Newlaw Six created an imposing edifice. As they chanted you could almost hear the electro-drone accompaniment:

> *"In the darkdawn fistful fumbles*
> *Grubeskullscam slits the tumbles*
> *With a slacksky bloudy bluebones*
> *psyche the wavegene starflight subtones*
> *and with braingraves gently streaming*
> *we'll unearth the trident's creaming."*

As their lines faded into the cool night air, they remained in formation. The stillness was impeccable. Poontutjarpa got up and stood before the Newlaw Six. Carefully examining them, he then turned around and faced us, his hands behind his back, a vermilion scarf around his neck, his sporty little beard a dynamic maze of tight silver coils.

"Wandjina's, we are one. Our purpose is common. We share the same mind, and know the same heart. We are ready. If there is anything anyone has to say, speak it now or remain silent forever."

For a moment we all sat quiet. Then Fa-Tsang stood up. "Supersub and I shall remain behind," he began, respectful of the aura of contemplation in which we were immersed. "But staying behind doesn't mean we won't stay with you. Mind no longer blind, no mind to leave behine. It's just that Panfusion action needs counter-pause to stay the beam of the Enchanted Triangle Probe. So while the rest of you Wandjina it, we'll rest mind in what can't be left behind."

"And," Supersub added, "you keen, our minds still will track your beam."

So amidst a soft chorus of "ahs" was announced the mountain retreat plans of these magnificent two.

Our meeting concluded, we all retired to obtain a good night's rest prior to the final stage of the Journey of Death. Francesca's love-making had never been more expansive. Simultaneously rippling with raw muscular energy and dissolving into a star-filled void where all human boundary lines have long since vanished, our love-making that night blossomed with the fragrance of a passionate tenderness unblemished by worldly concerns. For we also knew that evening that we had conceived a child.

The next morning, spearheaded by a phalanx of individually manned Newlaw laser scooters, we set off for Trinity Site at the Peak of Darkness. The day was as clear as anyone could have desired. The dry, serrated peaks on either side of Elephant Buttes were set off by the blue-misted ranges of San Andres mountains, far to the east side of the great flat stretch by the Jornada del Muerto. I rode in the center in a double-seated laser scooter with Francesca, the only such one in the Trident Brigade.

Traveling at a leisurely pace, which included lunch in the lava beds providing the west central ley point of the Jornada del Muerto, we arrived at our destination well before sunset. There it was: Trinity Site, the time-worn patch of desert which had launched us into the Fifth Ring, that shallow cavity of earth now marked by a crude stone obelisk, which blazed forth one day long ago, brighter than ten thousand suns. The intensity of this thought gripped all of us. There was nothing to say.

Just as we were sinking into a deep state of absorption, a high whining sound came over a slight ridge to the north of us. It was the Socorro Flats Unit of the Trident Brigade, seven in all. My curiosity ran high when I thought of encountering the members of this unit once again. Clambering out of the old hovercraft, Esquivel stepped forward first, giving Poontutjarpa an especially warm embrace. He was inevitably followed by Claudia and Ramakrishna, lovelorn and adorable as ever, their arms laced around each other. Then, looking like an astral magistrate, his arms folded luxuriantly across his chest, came Aldebaran. At last, forming a formidable trio in tunic-topped PAN dress-gear, came the three ladies, the Sky Dancers of the Peak of Darkness, the sirens of Socorro Flats, Ixchel O'Shaughnessy, Natasha Eisenhammer, and Ya Emme Bandiaraga.

Taking their places among us, only Natasha spoke: "Syntropic synchronicity! What's a bunch of renegade mutants and psycho-veterans like you doin' spaced out in a radium death camp like this? Hee, hee, hee!" Grube's voice and the voice that just spoke through Natasha's mouth were one and the same, there was no question about that. "Great Psycho-rehab center they got up there at Socorro Flats! I wuz wonderin' how I was gonna find me a medium to keep up communication with you folks. I mean, it seems like you's onto somethin', somethin' Big, and you know, I always been a good observer, so I'm tickled a phosphate pink. I'm just pickled-fickled to be back with sucha good batch o' DNA, hee, hee, hee!"

Warmth and astonishment gripped me as I took in the lovely Natasha speaking exactly as had my old Ecosquad sidekick, Gruber.

Day slipped easily into evening. Our group, numbering 20 now, formed a small tight circle at the heart of the Trinity Site. In the center of the circle, Poontutjarpa and Esquivel made a fire. Once the fire was going, Esquivel took out a bag of cornmeal and mixed in some earth and ash with it. Into this mixture, he spat once. Then, taking a small handful of it, began tracing a design around the fire. As he did so, Poontutjarpa took out his golden flute. His song began in soft cadences, then broke into a series of cascading flutters, followed by long slurred notes, broken and jagged semitones, finally to be capped by a sprinkle of pure, crystalline loops that faded imperceptibly into the star-frosted night… I squeezed Francesca's hand tightly as the last golden flute note melted into the pristine silence which united our minds.

Finishing his design on cue with the last high-note fade out, Esquivel touched each of us on the brow with the cornmeal, and placed a bit of it into each of our hands.

"This cornmeal with which I have mixed earth and ash from the Journey of Death, tinctured with my own spit, has offered us this design, called 'Palace of Unisonia,' for of old when this design was drawn it was also sung:"

*In Unisonia Panharmonic*
*Where Poontut divined of old*
*Where horizons radiosonic*
*Unload skies of melted gold*
*Where the waters silver flashing*
*Shoot burning arcs through gates fourfold*
*There, in unisonic Pan-aesthesia*
*So the legend has been told*
*All the Warrior Lords did gather*
*What the Ladies had Unrolled*
*And from jade and crimson bursting*
*in the heart's magnetic hold*
*released earth's vibrant mantle*
*with a war cry clear and bold.*
*In Unisonia Panharmonic*
*so the legend has been told…"*

Esquivel sang this in a gentle, clear-toned falsetto, the last lines lapsing into a series of quavers that sounded like a coyote gone to hole-bye comfort. Pulling his rainbow-colored blanket tighter 'round himself, Esquivel allowed Poontutjarpa to place the mixture on his own brow and in his own hands. Esquivel then continued addressing us.

"On your brow, has been placed cornmeal, ash, earth and spittle. May the dawnstar changes pierce to night's unknown beginning all obstructions on the bridge of love. In your hands the dead-same mixture. Place it on your tongue. It is good. May the dawnstar death-ash bloom flower, straight and bright, the hearts of warriors all. May this good night cease dying and bold the fortunes of dear earth set in proper flight!" As he concluded, Esquivel took his place in the circle, between Poontutjarpa and Ixchel O'Shaughnessy.

That night was neither long nor short. The stars, twinkling and cool, were as close to us as the hairs on our skin. Inhaling and exhaling in unison, we sat the death-watch. Nothing stirred, nothing moved. No voice was heard, at least not with the outer ear. What the inner ear heard was more marvelous than a solar flare magnified and transmitted as a radiosonic shower. And the stillness… stillness such as we experienced belongs only to the hearts of totally satisfied lovers. PAN fusion, pure and simple. With one mind attuned to the first ray of light piercing the south shoulder of the Peak of Darkness, we welcomed the morning of Winter Solstice, the bright invitation which the Journey of Death had always promised.

To be continued…

So many times has it been told how Poontutjarpa laser-sized the tektite-topped sphere of the mysterious technetium-coated rod unearthed beneath the obelisk at Trinity Site, that I hardly need describe it again. Yet, there is no way I shall ever forget that moment when, having sliced the sphere in half, Poontutjarpa took the special image-coded laser-beam rod, and, with utter concentration, shot it straight at the diamond embedded in the center of the sphere. No sooner did the beam strike the diamond, then two spectral bands shot forth. The one spectral band streamed instantaneously in the direction of Chaco Canyon, the other to Hopi Mesa. At each of those sites crews stood by at the radiosonic reflective dishes which were angled precisely to deflect the beam in such manner that a simultaneous two-way current was created forming the Enchanted Triangle: a brilliant spectral current connecting Hopi Mesa, Chaco Canyon and the Jornada del Muerto.

These spectral currents arcing out from the sphere-topped rod, shimmering and iridescent, expanded swiftly to a height of about one kilometer. The two currents running straight down their predetermined courses as far as the eye could see were magnificent beyond anything anyone had ever experienced. Even Poontutjarpa, who had been so invincibly poised for his action, was visibly moved, his mouth twitching and pulling, as his senses took in the enormity of what had just been released.

We all soon became aware of an intense but scarcely audible multi-toned hum that accompanied the double currents. It seemed important to listen very carefully to the sonorous vibration emanating from the currents. The hums seemed to span six octaves. When you listened with a mind totally blank and open, it became evident that each of the octaves registered at a specific point within the body. Each octave, that is, except the highest, which registered just above the top of the head. The first octave seemed to stimulate the genital zone, the second was felt at the navel, the third at the heart, the fourth in the throat, and the fifth at about the location of the pineal gland in the frontal lobe, while the sixth was maybe a hand-span above the head. Clearly everyone in the Trident Brigade picked up on this and we stood silent and still, like a ring of transforming rods fixed to the ground.

Standing there in the early afternoon light, already more brilliant than the famous ten thousand suns for which this site was famous, our individual minds interpenetrated and fused into one. At the same time, no one lost the sense of their idiosyncratic DNA coding. Though each experienced his or her own psychogenetic wave-loop, the clarity of this experience was enhanced by the information streaming in from the 19 others of the group. It is difficult for me to convey how directly I experienced the infinite regression and simultaneously infinite progression of my psychogenetic patterning.

It went something like this: as the six octaves created one waveband using the body as a transformer, this caused what felt like a fusion of the cerebral hemispheres. As soon as this occurred, a beam of geomagnetic energy shot up from my feet, transforming itself as it hit each of the bodily octave centers, finally diffusing out evenly after reaching the sixth center above the head. As long as you remained still, this geomagnetic band remained continuous, as did the cosmic ray band that entered from the sixth center and passed out into the earth through the feet in much the same manner as the geomagnetic beam, only in reverse order.

As these vertical beams coursed concurrently through the body, we each experienced the release of the psychogenetic patterning. I could feel the surface membrane of each neuron shifting simultaneously, accompanied by a bombardment of sodium ions. The uniformly fired electrical impulses, the synergistically strengthened wave of the coordinated neural release—both created a force field extending almost a kilometer around each of us. Naturally standing as we were in a tight ring, our expanded neural force fields were experienced as a single unit. Since the neural patterning of the individual force fields was unique for each of us, the pattern of the total force field formed a richly woven texture, a genetic tapestry in which our individual story-lines combined to create a single tale, a universal web, the cosmos entire.

"The white bath," as we referred to it afterwards, lasted precisely until sunset. In the intervening hours, standing there totally fused, my entire psychogenetic wave recollected itself to me. From the initial expulsion from the incredible density of the primal condition, it wave-tumbled, first as a super glowing beam of light, then condensing at a slower rate to a gaseous substance which united with amino acids in a blazing pool of super magnesium. Ever conscious, it mutated at a rapidly accelerating rate, traveling through an unimaginable number of world systems. Vistas of almost unendurable splendor opened out, jeweled realms of crystal water, of palaces constructed of shimmering immaterial substances, of trees dripping elements of inexhaustible purity.

Settling into a steady wave, the psychogenetic recollection current passed through spirit, animal and human transformations. As if poured out through the holy grail of collective terrestrial memory, every manner of being passed through my cells: amphibian, reptilian, feathered and furred, interspersed by a clamorous din of spirit-figures, the chain of birth, death and transformation oozed through my pores like a malady released at the peak of a fever.

Even now to describe the recollections of the human realm is to permanently dislocate the heart in the direction of inconceivable compassion. The yearning for fulfillment, the tenderness locked in each individual being, and above all, the ignorance, the violations of the heart committed in the name of fear—all of these conspired in an ever-gathering flow to create the increasingly geocidal tapestry of the four rings. Within this flow as vividly as if seeing myself in a mirror for the first time, I encountered the various facets projected by and further conditioning my DNA patterning: a fire priestess clad in bear-skin; an aged, wrinkled crone hovering over a cauldron, her cheeks besmirched with soot; a child, languorously perched on a rock playing with oracle bones; a concubine in the cool-corridored palace of a Sumerian King; a saffron-robed nun sweeping the entryways to a brilliantly polished stupa, its multi-colored banners fluttering in a tropical breeze; a Chinese princess practicing calligraphy in an embroidery-resplendent room; a Mochica prince conducting a ritual condor hunt; an Irish scribe dipping his brush into a small pot of gilding. But, all of these paled, or rather collected their individual forces and focused in the Lady Five Flower, the Lady of Tula, in the court of the Lord of Texcoco, the Noble Fasting One. In this personage, the collective learning of the memory streams fused into a corona of awareness that had not been experienced hitherto.

For the first time, the collective patterning engaged in a conscious force counter-active to the blind flow of destiny. With Nezahualpilli, it conjoined to make Montezuma aware of his actions and destiny. Then, as swiftly as a late afternoon breeze, still conjoined to Nezahualpilli, it passed into the desert canyon lands where we now found ourselves. There, much in the manner of an animal developing protective coloration, it passed through a series of births in which all of the poignant sadness of the fourth ring were experienced in a counterpoint of male and female roles; a horse-mounted warrior of the plains; a slave girl brought to the West Indies from Africa; a Mughal prince studying astronomy in India; a French court lady of the early Industrial period dispensing her intelligence through liaisons and soirees of select persons of intrigue; a poet languishing in the madhouses of Europe; a Jewish mother screaming at her children to run as the guards dragged her to a gas chamber at Dachau; a young boy on bicycle looking with numbed amazement as the skin on his arms curled back in large open sores following the Hiroshima bomb-blast; a monitor in the World Resettlement Program wading through the debris of yet another government archive; finally, an energy of determination fitfully entering the womb of my demented mother.

And yet interposed among these intensely personal vignettes, was another energy mantle. This one shifted much more slowly and rhythmically than the passage of lives shot through the sieve of psychogenetic recollection. Instantaneously we all knew that this was the mantle of the Supreme Hierarchy. In one way, the current of psychogenetic recollection appeared as the massive weaving performed by the Supreme Hierarchy. From another perspective, the psychogenetic activity appeared as a trace of dust on the mirror held by the Hierarchy to reflect the cosmic processes.

As our individual psychogenetic currents passed through us it seemed that the members of the Supreme Hierarchy settled above each of us. Like semen at the moment of ejaculation, the energy of the Supreme Hierarchy entered each of us. As if watching the sun rise through a notch in a mountain range, the future opened before us in a sudden burst of clarity: the taming of planet Earth, the interstellar communications, the psychosolar fusions, the curving arc of light descending once again to the primordial condition.

Emptiness filled with light, happiness merged with insight, such was the moment when we experienced the Supreme Hierachy's interpenetration of the Trident Brigade. Home-coming, that's another way of describing the pure resonance of my heart during that exquisitely timeless moment.

Just as this feeling was peaking inside of me, Poontutjarpa slowly began to sit down. He just kind of folded down. As his bottom fell into its earthen cradle, the seating process swept over the rest of us, like a gentle wind taming a wave. Then, with erect postures, we all sat, assimilating the energy which we had been experiencing so intensely.

---

"Did you think there was another state of mind?"

The question rang out in utter clarity. At first I thought it was Poontutjarpa who had spoken. But no, it wasn't old Poontut. He was sitting across from me, rooted to nothing in particular, wearing the same silly grin as the rest of us. As the realization mutually dawned that none of us had voiced this question, our grin turned to an expression of mild consternation spiced with a delicate sprinkling of confusion. Even Poontutjarpa, he of the Grube-skull bracelet and the lion-skin skirt of the dancing embryos, even Poontutjarpa allowed his face to register the ripple of delightful anxiety that held us in common bondage.

"Oh, please, now. There's really no need for alarm. If it makes it any easier for you, my name is Cecil Higgenbotthom Varuna-d'oro. I speak for the CHV, the Collective Higher Voice, not that the Collective Higher Voice is any higher than yours. As you can see, my tone is as evenly modulated, and quite in keeping with yours. But, dear me, how about the question I asked you: did you think there was another state of mind?"

The answer ran through all of our minds like light beamed between two mirrors.

"Well obviously," Cecil Higgenbotthom Varuna-d'oro continued in his precisely polished and ever so slightly effeminate manner, "you all know that this is the only state of mind: here, now. As for my being with you in this most particular here-and-now, that should certainly come as no surprise. You see, it is really quite logical. Since you have attuned yourselves to one and the same mind, and that being the only state of mind, you have synergized my presence into your existence. There is no other state of mind. For your purposes, I manifest as Cecil Higgenbotthom Varuna-d'oro. But that is only for your purposes. You must not forget that actually I only speak for the CHV. Dear me, wouldn't it be ridiculous if there were actually people named Cecil Higgenbotthom Varuna-d'oro sitting on the Council of the Supreme Hierarchy?" At this point, Cecil broke into a wanton titter that swept through the Trident Brigade like a well-cultivated Syndic flu-germ.

"Well, now that I see that you feel comfortable with my presence, I'm sure you won't mind in the least if I share the last golden hour of this marvelous afternoon with you. Have you noticed how the horizons are still beaming with the spectral luster touched off by your daring act of splitting the tektite sphere?"

Allowing my eyes to shift upward for a moment, it was almost impossible to remain composed. The great transparent spectral bands glowing with a metallic, yet immaterial iridescence sliced through mountains and canyons as far as the eye could see. The tropical luminous copper green of the lower-most portion of the spectral band seemed to radiate directly from the earth, taking the bare winter time shrubbery and consuming it with its ethereal glow. New plants seemed to flower before my eyes, while small clusters of hawks, crows and magpies took turns penetrating the spectral curtain, each time letting loose an even more melodic flutter of bird calls. From the earth-touching green, the hues transformed into a brilliant solar yellow that phased imperceptibly into a hot golden orange, like slabs of saffron-butter set afire. The red section of the band ran from pale crimson to blazing pink, finally cooling out in a glory of magenta dissolving itself into an azure aura as blue and deep as the heart of heaven untainted by atmospheric vagaries. As if the spectacle of this rainbow band weren't already enough to instigate a state of blissful cardiac arrest, the shower of violet beams spiraling heavenward from the topmost band of blue would have caused even the most power-demented Syndiclone to happily forget, if only for a moment, the genetic patterns and code words rapidly shifting across his monitor screen.

"Since, dear friends, there is only One State of Mind, OSM, infinitely variable, of course, there is no reason whatsoever to be distracted by the trifling vibrations released by your act of ingeniously conceived courage." With total assurance, Cecil Higgenbotthom Varuna-d'oro drew our attention away from the spectral bands and back to his mildly pleasing chatter.

"Yes, it has been a dreadfully long time since OSM Central has been summoned by a project as intelligently conceived as yours. Oh, there have been certain endeavors in the Andes and the Himalayas in the past aeon that have drawn our attention and aroused our assistance, but this—this is like the golden days when Vel and the Earth Lords first drew the magic circle. But enough of such idle reminiscence. We do have a task to perform."

CHV paused. My eyes caught the sun lowering in the Western sky. Its brilliant blue rays caused everything to glow as if bathed in a soothing vapor the color of the summer sky. Joy and curiosity sang in my heart, bonded as it now was to the hearts of the rest of the members of the Trident Brigade. At the same time, I became acutely aware of the heart presence of Supersub and Fa-Tsang Wronski, who even in their mountain solitudes outside of Truth or Consequences had managed to bond themselves to our situation.

"Yes, now that we have total attention," Cecil continued in obvious reference to the fact that Supersub and Fa-Tsang had attained syntropic attunement with the rest of us, "we may proceed with our instructions. Hmm. Let's see now. Have I spoken yet about delivering on the circuit of genuine awareness? Yes, I think that's where we are, an inevitable stage in the process of syntropic unfolding. Yes, yes, of course. Ladies listen carefully. This one is for you."

My heart, charged with a tender luminosity, opened, trembling and fragile, as if it were about to break, in anticipation of CHV's message.

"Ladies, remembering exactly who and where you are, and knowing precisely the planetary condition of things, you must gather yourselves and summoning your entire Amazonian wisdom and power, be prepared to leave this humble gathering. Oh, no, no, no," Cecil declared, as the ladies of the Trident Brigade made motion to rise up, "no, you must wait until the transmission has been completed, though I must say, I admire your readiness for action."

"What you shall do after you leave this charmed circle is travel the entire extent of the Enchanted Triangle, returning to Trinity Site. Don't you think it would be proper to rename it Dawnsource Flats? Kind of picturesque, don't you think? Goes with the territory, too. Well, excuse me, I do sometimes get overly enthralled with the enchantment of situations like this. Yes, as we were saying, Ladies of the Trident Brigade, you will travel the entire course of the Enchanted Triangle, as outlined by these spectral bands. But you have only two weeks to return, so you must act with dispatch and accomplish what must be accomplished never leaving the purity of the OSM."

Just as the curiosity of the feminine heart-blend was to reach a threshold of anxiety, Cecil Higgenbotthom Varuna-d'oro re-entered our audio chambers with his comforting verbal soliloquy. "Yes, you have only two weeks for the bands will vibrate for only as long as it takes the moon to wax from zero state to maximum reflectiveness. And as for what you are to accomplish, ladies, trust me. It will be plainly evident. As was sung in the Saga of Vel and the Earth Lords,

> *"All the warrior lords did gather*
> *what the ladies had unfolded..."*

As these lines were sung, Cecil's voice transformed into a profoundly resonant tone. Its vibrations like a gong sounded in the center of a star, echoed, shimmered and then faded into a penetrating quiet that seemed to rivet us to the other side of death itself.

"Warrior Lords of the Trident Brigade," somehow Cecil's voice never seemed to have stopped, and yet I knew it had, it must have, "while the ladies are unfolding the brilliant length of the Enchanted Triangle, you may remain here. You will be taken care of, in the best manner possible. But never should you forget either who and where you are, nor must you for one moment, even while sleeping, relinquish your knowledge of the present planetary condition. In other words, through whatever sport and amusement you may entertain yourselves with while the ladies are out, it's OSM all the way!" A self-pleased chortle provided the moment its proper punctuation.

"But then, gentlemen, when the ladies of the Trident Brigade return, and you must not forget to prepare just the right reception for their return, you will then make yourselves ready to go forth. Hmm, sounds like Knighthood, doesn't it? How quaint. Yes, well, in any case, gentlemen, on your journey you will no longer have the synaesthetic guidance of the spectral band. But quell your anxiety. It shall not be difficult, for, as was sung in the Saga of Vel and the Earth Lords:

> *"All the warrior lords did gather*
> *what the ladies had unfolded…"*

As with the previous time Cecil had sung these lines, the voice again transformed itself into the heart-fixing vibrations of the astral gong. And as before, though the death shattering quiet pervaded our every cell, it seemed as if CHV had never stopped talking. "…dear, dear, dear, the sun can no longer stay its westward course… hmm, poetic, eh? Brigands and bards of old did speak such heart full words. Oh, dear, must be careful now. Very, very careful. The sun has fallen swift beneath the Western Range. The Journey of Death need be taken no more by such as those of the Trident Brigade."

Cecil Higgenbotthom Varuna-d'oro spoke no more. We were left, a band of twenty earthlings, staked to the diamond pillar of no regrets.

For some time we sat. The sky above us teemed with stars. Never had they seemed brighter or closer. On the horizons the two spectral bands created a new night, a night of color, tranquility and warrior's determination. Finally, we ate. It had been an entire day since we had eaten. Cyclone and Squeaker were the first to break the circle. This they did with uncompromising gentleness. We all knew what they were about. In a short matter of time they returned, our meal provisions arrayed in three cheerful mandala platters. On the first platter was the fruit: the kumquats, dates, raisins, oranges, and mangoes, sliced and displayed to imitate a solar corona. On the second platter was a fine ceramic bowl steaming with a spicily aromatic version of Aboriginal Fish Soup. And on the third platter was a crescent of multi-colored corn and rice cakes lavished with saffron butter and clover honey.

After serving us, each of us being handed individual bowls, plates and skewertines, Cyclone and Squeaker resumed their former positions.

"Kyeeeeee!" Poontutjarpa exclaimed, deeply solemn.

"Kyoooooo!" the rest of us replied in unison.

"Looks like we got ourselves an ambulatory geoharmone squad after all. Hee, hee, hee," it was the Grube-voiced Natasha who rippled us into a good-humored feast.

As we ate and chatted, I was struck by how normal all of this was. Everything had happened and nothing had happened. Globs of Aboriginal fish soup clung to Prospero's chin as he returned a burst of laughter in exchange for one of his mother's witticisms. Claudia Blavatsky Leventhal, with one hand gingerly applying a piece of corn-cake to her mouth, took her other hand and stroked Ramakrishna Al-Badr softly on his left cheek.

"Mantle-dipped grain-lobes, regrease the unskivved scams, but this bod-fodder decks the enzymes good." Psychlosky, his goggle-eye bounding up and down with laughter was punching out his usual Newlaw chatter, while David Monongye looked on with total adolescent awe.

In the midst of this, I thought of my dear mother and father. "Yes," I spoke inwardly to them, "this is why you bore me and brought me into this world."

Upon finishing our repast, Ramakrishna and Claudia did the honors of removing our eating utensils and the now empty platters. When they had returned and resumed their places we mutually determined that sleep was needed, especially since the ladies would be setting out the next morning on their enchanted mission. Bringing our sleeping bags to the Dawnsource circle, we tucked ourselves in. Prospero's hand found mine as I lay on my back contemplating the radiosonic furnace horizon light and the myriad star-patterns of the midnight sky. Squeezing his hand, a wave of good-natured exhaustion swept out from my bones, muscles and nerve endings. A tidal wave of sleep and unrelinquishing knowledge gathered and rolled through my body like a stormcloud releasing a rain of unceasing tranquility.

Just as I was about to fall into primal sleep, I heard a duet. It was this duet, the voices of Supersub and Fa-Tsang Wronski that finally lulled meto sleep.

> *"In Unisonia Panharmonic*
> *Trident bold and radiosonic*
> *The warrior lords and ladies beamed*
> *an Earth that no one yet had dreamed."*

I was awakened the next morning by the tropical green sunlight that filtered elflike through my lashes. In a flash I sat up. This was our day. Immediately, I joined the nine other ladies as we gathered for our morning ablutions a short distance from Dawnsource Circle. Upon finishing a slight breakfast of coffee, melon and mountain grits which we shared with the men, we packed up ten laser scooters and prepared to depart.

Breakfast had passed quietly in an atmosphere of awed silence. This mood continued as we mounted our laser scooters. I looked back at Prospero as I turned the accelerator switch to normal. He was standing there blowing me kisses while the rest of the men scampered up a hillock. My eyes went from Prospero to the top of the hillock.

There, as I was pulling away, I caught a glimpse of Poontutjarpa seated, looking just to his upper right, bathed in the beam that connected with Hopi Mesa. The spectral colors flickered across his face, a magic mirror of concentration. Behind him, just out of the corner of my eye, I thought I saw another figure, one I had never seen before, more like a shadow than a material substance, dancing with arms outspread, a great eagle dance.

Then, we were gone.

To be continued...

# PROSPERO'S TAPE LOG: MOON-WAX WARM-UPS

To speak of the two-week moon-wax while Francesca and the other ladies triangulated the space connecting the Journey of Death with Chaco Canyon and Hopi Mesa, is to speak of a time that blazed out of time, of events that I have no way of accounting for, except perhaps, by the strange all-pervading love that coursed like a magnetic current through my entire organism.

For once I did not struggle to trace love to its source. Its source was nowhere else but my own heart. And it had always been there, that source, spouting away during my years of arrogance, blindness, and paranoia. Oh, I had caught trickles of it, little streams of it pouring quietly through random chinks in the density of my defensive-alert programming. But never anything like this. For there was no more armor. I was naked, arms outstretched to receive every last ray of the radiosonic sun. And I did. Every pore of my body became saturated with the burning openness for which love had prepared me.

It was in this mood, following the departure of Francesca and the Nine Ladies of the Dawnsource Circle, that I joined the Nine Lords of the Dawnsource Circle in perfect new-moon formation around Poontutjarpa. Though we were naked, the sunlit chill of the December air did not affect us. With no more amazement than I would possess while watching a fly scratch itself lazily as it paused in its charnel-heap pickings, I intently observed the eagle-winged spirit dancer hovering just behind Poontutjarpa. However spritely the eagle-winged one danced, he never came over the rise of the hillock upon which Poontutjarpa had entered his radiosonically-lit samadhi-bath.

Nor did I move, not even to push away the tarantula that scribbled its way across my feet when the eagle dancer faded its spirit-shining form into that of the Keeper of the Inner Court. A diadem of crossed golden serpents upon his eunuch-bald head, his hands held in semicircles facing each other just above his heart, enclosing a breastplate of jade and coral, an apron woven to show a stepped diamond pattern in turquoise against a ground of palely glistening purple, and magnificently leather-thatched sandals rooting him to spirit earth, the Keeper of the Inner Court hovered just behind

Poontutjarpa, moving his arms forward, then in the form of two rotating circles, raised them above his head to create a perfect solar ring. Yet, for all of his resplendent color, the Keeper of the Inner Court, like Eagle Dancer, was utterly transparent. Clumps of dried yellow grass and luminous yucca holding their own against the irregular shaped rocks that crowded their existence appeared in perfect clarity through the jade and coral breast plate of the spirit figure.

At the moment when the Keeper of the Inner Court had dissolved into the Wielder of the Heart-Sword Longing, I jumped as if someone had just told me that the Syndics were actually in charge of this whole operation. And yet at the same time I could have cared less. A twelve-pointed crown set upon the flowing locks of his Pendragon engendered head, glistening with mail and armor, a sword in the right hand, an enameled white shield in the left bearing the red heraldic insignia of the Maze of the Grail encircled by a feathery wreathe of summer-green fleur-de-lys, his kid-leather booted ankles wrapped around with spurs, the Wielder of the Heart Sword Longing took his ethereally silver-glinting sword, and with a jump and a flourish, sliced Poontutjarpa's neck clean through. I gasped and lurched forward. Yet everything remained calm, and I regained my composure.

Dropping on to Poontutjarpa's aproned lap like a kumquat falling into a pair of cupped hands, Poontutjarpa's head remained in the same samadhi-bath intensity, the eyes still focused toward the upper right. Wielder of the Heart Sword Longing then took the immaculate sword, and hovering atop the hillock, cut the Grube-skull from Poontutjarpa's left wrist. Laying the sword horizontally on Poontut's lap just in front of his aboriginal samadhi head, Wielder of the Heart Sword Longing carefully picked up the skull from the place where its tumble had spent its energy. Blowing the dust off its brow, the Warrior Knight gracefully placed the skull upon Poontutjarpa's severed neck. It was then I noticed that Poontut was as transparent as a radiosonic beam fine-tuned to code word 2.

The Grube-skull grinning headed Poontutjarpa allowed the Warrior Knight to pass through him. The sword was now held vertical, the hands clasping the handle between the navel and the heart, the blade almost invisible rising straight up passing in perfect symmetry between the Knight's vision-piercing eyes, its tip just above the crowned head throwing off a shower of rays. Each ray consisted of innumerable, minute holographic reproductions of the two figures hovering before our eyes. These figure-bearing rays seemed to enter and penetrate every cell in my body. Just as the temperature of this psychic-heat bath was about to shatter the top of the body-thermometer, the scene dissolved. Immense relief rolled through me. In a distant corner of my mind, disbelief at what I had been witnessing all but shrank into oblivion.

A slight breeze wafted all the warmth the December air could muster across the hillock where we sat. Poontutjarpa, the Grube-skull glowing radioactive blue upon his shoulders, began to sing:

> *"Moon-wax warm-ups gild the lords*
> *The fourth ring decked the Knight of Swords*
> *And in his place the Punk did stand*
> *His heart traced black upon the sand*
> *Wild wild evenings in Tech-man's Lab*
> *Screwed his brain to a silicon tab*
> *Bomb dust blowing through Suez straits*
> *Canceled the bargain of the fates*
> *Where urban pools had grimed the earth*
> *The new wave took Omega Birth*
> *Where the sun crashed to the land*
> *The Nine Lords took the Fifth Ring Stand*
> *With no more mind but heart full bright*
> *The Nine Lords rose above the night"*

By the time Grube-skulled Poontutjarpa's song was no more than an echo flitting through the canyons and mesas, Old Poontut had normalized. Once again the Grube skull hung idly from his left wrist, while a thick-lipped smile of tremendous pleasure creased the old Aborigine's face. Still naked, the rest of us broke into applause.

"Ho, Ho, Ho, Hah!" Poontut laugh-chanted. "You all look like a bunch of Wandjina-scammed morons, kangaroo-brained loonies! Wherever did you put your clothes?" Poontutjarpa's question to all of us swiftly sank a chaos of laughter and totally charmed good will.

As the laughter subsided, I found myself thinking, "Yes, where are my clothes?" Before I had time to circulate my memory to the correct answer, a delicately thunderous din rose up from somewhere behind our new moon crescent. Turning my head over my left shoulder, I spotted them: a brigade of Newlaws. Slack-Zone Normalizers to be precise. Forty in all, they formed a serpentine column, two abreast—disappearing beneath a low rise, only to reappear twice the size they were before. I saw that they kept up their brisk pace running on tip-toes. The whole crazy lot of them was dressed in late industrial diplomat black tuxedo jackets, white ruffled shirt-fronts and black bow ties. Their legs, however, were squeezed into black-leather leggings split at the ankles. Great gold and tattoo-toothed smiles blended with the light of radiosonic horizons.

And they were fast. Before I knew it one was right behind me remaining in the same spot, tip-toe stepping in time with the eight others who had each taken a position behind one of the Nine Lords of Dawnsource Circle. The Slack-Zone Normalizer behind me, like the eight others, held a neat bundle of clothing in his right hand which was raised as if bearing a platter of soup.

"Wandjina Seer, Faster of Lark 'n' Dight, gear no more the earth bathed bod, rags 'n' robes I lot yer fine-tuned skin, so scam the breeze no more. Slack-Zone Normalizer lay yer deck the silk-veined score."

This triumphant announcement regarding the arrival of my clothes was addressed to me by a crack-force member of the SZN whose immense gold teeth provided the perfect horizontal stopper to a broad black face with marked Mongolian eyes, and a nose bridge which bore two bars of color, one red, the other green. His name I soon learned was Sun-Streaker. Like his thirty-nine other comrades they had gotten the word direct from CHV to make sure we attained maximum normalization following the Dawnsource synergizing of the Enchanted Triangle.

In addition to bringing us provisions in our old X-24 Hovercraft, the Slack-Zone Normalizers imparted to us a great variety of situational skills, psychophysical exercises, and an assortment of what they called, "Tri-chanty Bangle Games." The impressive good humor, wit, and above all, collective psycho-gymnastic enthusiasm of this Brigade of Slack-Zone Normalizers, we found out, was due to their remarkable agility in remaining simultaneously in direct attunement with Fa-Tsang and Supersub, while at the same time using this intensified stream of energy to refine all of their old scams. And as Outlaws, no one had ever wired a better scam to the magnetic poles of the human body than the notorious Slack-Zoners.

Their tradition originated during the early days of the Era of the Great Resettlement. They, more than any other group, had resisted removal from the Great Lakes Wastelands. Led by the fierce primal mutant Outlaw leader, Scuzman Theophrastus, the Slack-Zoners succeeded in eluding the efforts of the early Network Geo-probe Squads. Migrating seasonally from the urban slime-pools that stretched from Milwaukee and Chicago in the West to Cleveland, Pittsburgh and Buffalo to the East, the early generations of Slack-Zoners soon acquired an incomparable reputation for maintaining their own kind of order apart from any of the Geomantic Councils. For most members of these Councils, absorbed as they were by the process of coordinating global psycho-economic zones, while vigorously pursuing equitable trade and cultural exchange policies, the activity of the Slack-Zoners eventually became a matter of little interest. That was until the arrival of Theophrastus Four to a major Council meeting at

Hopi Mesa. It was then that the attitude of the Council turned from one of disdainful indifference to admiring, but distant respect.

Of course I am referring to Theophrastus Four's famous demonstration of psychopolar shifts, which he did in a blaze of full-blown electrodrone glory. I had first heard of this daring act from none other than Poontutjarpa himself, during the course of the Synaesthetic History Profiles which he so capably presented. According to Poontutjarpa, Theophrastus Four's performance marked one of the minor turning points in the surfacing of the Planet Art Network which preceded the schism of the Syndicate of Geomantic Councils, which in turn led to the present War-time Zone Trade-off.

Reflecting on the Slack-Zoner's early chance role in the making of PAN, it now seemed only appropriate that they were here with us during this momentous time at Dawnsource Circle. Ever-jovial, they enthralled us with their ability to make any activity a spontaneous creation of song, dance and body language. At the same time, to a man, they displayed a gracious elegance of restraint in hanging back when there was nothing to be done. In other words, they were possessed by an uncanny sense of appropriate moment. With them, rehearsal was a synonym for lack of confidence.

It was on the third morning of their interfusion among us that the Slack-Zone Normalizers introduced to us the first round of "Trichanty Bangle Games." For nine days, in groups of three whose members rotated each day, the Nine Dawnsource Lords played three rounds a day of Trichanty Bangle Games. Taking the form of a triangle, to be precise, the Enchanted Triangle, the base of which ran almost a kilometer in length, our field of play, called "free-bod bode-base," was held together at its center by Poontutjarpa, who continuously sat there for the duration of the nine days. It is impossible to erase the memory of Old Poontut ceaselessly rotating himself at the A-Bomb Dawnsource zero point, Trinity Site. There he was morning and night, seated, yet turning ever so slowly, like a solar receiving dish in a lunar crater. Dressed in his fur-lined cap, the earflaps tied over the head, one of Esquivel's hand-woven rainbow shawls draped over his shoulders, the eternally motionless Grube-skull tied to his left wrist, and the embryonic re-creation apron tied round his waist, Poontutjarpa's aboriginally black breast remained bare, wisps of silver-grey hair curling around his nipples, a soft phosphorescent glow pulsating with each of his pre-death slow heartbeats.

A chorus of nine Slack-Zoners had announced the games after breakfast. Emerging from the multi-colored ring of tents they had set up around Dawnsource Circle, each tent topped by a pole bearing nine chromatically hued banners apiece, the Slack-Zoners broke into the Trichanty Bangle pattern of three trios of men holding down the points of the enchanted Triangle.

> *"Moon-wax warm-ups chant the Man*
> *Poontut curved the crescent span*
> *Free times Free the Nine Sword Stake*
> *Blend the rim o' Poontut's Blake."*

Following this jive-rhythmed quatrain, the Normalizers broke into curiously entrancing dance patterns. Their tattooed faces set with slack-jawed stares, the three trios alternated advances and retreats on the imaginary lines connecting the points of the Triangle. Advancing, they skip-shuffled with right leg forward bent at the knee, the left leg dragging and twitching to some unheard rhythm section. Retreating, they reversed the process, the left leg now in the forward bent-kneed position, the right leg tremerously pulsating to the ghostly rhythm section which now actually seemed to become audible, like a whirring of cicadas in the August night.

Poontut had already taken center position in the Slack-Zoner's Trichanty Bangle. Following the ludicrously lascivious beckoning motions of the Slack-Zoners, their pelvises gyrating in mild spasms of sexual provocation, the Nine Lords advanced toward center and formed a tight circle around Poontut. From this vantage point we observed the advance-retreat motions of the Slack-Zone Nine. While their legs continued the basic advance-retreat pattern, their arms began to wriggle and wander in random wave passes. Imperceptibly the flutter-winged arm motions assumed state-specific positions. So skilled did the Slack-Zone Nine show themselves to be, that even now I do not know whether they had materialized the bows and arrows, swords, and beam-throwers they so deftly wielded in their hands, or whether the appearance of those instruments was a mere hallucinatory by-product of their mastery of the art of bodily illusion.

"Hey, Trichanty Bangle-scam slag the Slack-Zone Nine!" a voice pierced the trance-like air in which we had all become immersed. This came at just the moment when the three trios had directed their weapons to a point right above Poontut's head. The Slack-Zoners then all broke rank. Tearing off their black diplomat jackets, ties and shirts, and throwing them wildly in the air, they scampered black leather legged and tattoo-breasted every which way, until they were no longer anywhere to be seen.

The rest of the Slack-Zoners who had remained seated in front of their tents during the demonstration, to a one exploded in low-fire bursts of tattooed laughter. After their giggling and tittering had died down, they assumed motionless lizard-on-a-rock positions. Heads erect, their tongues flickering through slack-jawed mouths, their supine bodies supported by hands and arms rigidly placed in a reptile-clawed position of support on the dusty earth, I remember thinking distinctly to myself, "Slack-Zone brain scumbles, but this is bizarre!" As this thought sped its way toward the no-where-ness which had bred it, I realized, this was our cue.

The crisp windless late December air was as pure and still as Poontut at the beginning of his nine-day samadhi-bath. Instinctively forming a triad with Psychlosky and Lindy McGrew, we skip-shuffled to our particular node of the Trichanty Bangle free-bod bode-base. The high point of each of the three rounds that we played for the next nine days came always when we aimed our weapon holding arms above Poontut's head at the center of Dawnsource Circle. Each time, I would wait breathless as the imaginary weapons released in unison climactically fused above Poontut's head. And each time the effect was different. All in all, twenty-seven of these Moon-Wax transformations occurred.

What would happen at the weapon fusion moment of Moon-Wax Transformation is this: following the appearance of a bluish spark some three meters above Poontut's head, a spirit figure would gradually materialize, or, I should say, would become visible. Like the figures which appeared behind Poontut the morning that the Dawnsource ladies had departed, these figures, however vivid they appeared, were also totally transparent. Grass-aproned emperors shaking oracle bones in their jade-ringed hands; samurai lords, their faces grimacing with determination, charging our mutually shared mind-void with swords of clashing splendor; knights of the grail, emerging from the hallucinatory castle steaming into form from the murky-broth bubbling in Merlin's cauldron. As each of these apparitions slowly descended into Poontut's motionless body, streams of glistening heart-rays bonded us to Poontut's phosphorescent heart-glow.

With the passage of each day, body, heart and mind experienced an ever-widening circle of renewal and well-being. I was most surprised on the morning of the ninth day while looking into the ablution mirror to find that my scar had disappeared, and that my nose had straightened considerably. In fact, I was shocked. There was my face looking at once as if I had just been born, so fresh and golden brown did it appear, and at the same time as if it had never been born: a timeless gaze, a smile twisted and perpetually disfigured by shit-faced joy. In automatic disbelief I observed the mirror-hand running its fingers the crescent-length of my face where the scar had once been. For the first time during those nine Trichanty Bangle days, my mind filled up with Francesca, filled up like the full-moon transfigured by earth-reflected light.

So total did my experience of Francesca become, that the image in the oval-shaped ablution travel-mirror shifted. No longer was I occupied by self-reflection. In place of my new-found face was a remote mountainside, radiosonically lit. Seated atop that mountain, its ravined sides sparkling with all manner of flowers, was Francesca. Her hands placed on her knees, her legs tucked beneath her, wearing a simple white tunic, belted with a crossed-serpent gold chain, her honey-colored hair blowing ever so slightly, I found those sea-green eyes of hers gazing intently into mine.

Like a swarm of swallows diving and dipping in the early morning air, my heart swooned and cascaded with her gaze. It was then that I noticed a number of articles placed about her in a semi-circle: an earthen cup, a gold-tipped wand or staff, its slightly angled tree branch form adorned with a simple red-sash, a blue ceramic plate of saffron-colored sands arranged in the pattern of a swirling swastika, and an iron brazier, its white coals still flecked with dots of furnace-blazing red. So real did all of this appear that I felt I could have passed my hand through the mirror and stroked Francesca's dawn-soft face.

Just as this desire was tingling the synapses of amorous yearning, the mirror image dissolved, and there I was again, looking more like a lovelorn fool than a Dawnsource Lord, as Francesca's parting words lingered like feathers settling gently on the echo-striated walls of my audio canals:

*"No more to remember, no more to forget*
*Love beyond love beyond the heart-net..."*

My teammates that last day's round of Trichanty Bangles were Grunt and Esquivel. Our motions were like water, fluid and graceful. We performed in perfect unison, like the best Slack-Zoners: the skip-shuffle rhythm, the pageant march steps, the Yellow-Emperor's hop, the Grailknights' measured stride, the staccato Samurai leaps, the life ancestral boogie. As these various steps were performed, accompanied from time to time by a blood-curdling war-cry as we approached one of the other triads, then retreated like a wave ebbing on a beach, my mind remained perfectly clear, as if there were no mind at all. In this way I became imprinted with a harmony of clouds, caring not the least about which form I might next become.

It was the final salute of the day that broke this calm. Poised in warrior-release posture, I awaited the last blue spark ignition above Poontut's head. However, instead of the blue spark to which I had become accustomed, there was but a slight whirring, as if the air were being rapidly churned above old Poontut's samadhi-bath head. As this churning became more violent, obliterating the Peak of Darkness behind it in a melee of vibratory waves, I experienced a rush of wind, but from within me as if emanating from my cells.

Startled, I looked about me. The other eight Dawnsource Lords seemed to be experiencing the same sensation, their heads jerking about like apples on an apple tree during a late summer storm. Meanwhile the Slack-Zone Normalizers had all begun to prostrate themselves in front of their tents. I don't know why, but I began to weep. As the salty tears ran over my lips, I resumed the warrior-release posture.

The mantle of the Supreme Hierarchy had descended once again. And once again it was the voice of Cecil Higgenbotthom Varuna-d'oro chatting away. "Very, very, good. Pleasant little exercises really. But they are nothing but exercises. Don't get me wrong. Such rhythmic facility, such harmonic daring, such, to use your phrase, Grube-skull skills, will lend a certain audacity to the actions you must yet perform. Ah yes, and if I may bring in a slight touch of planet-reality, I must remind you that Syndic monitors all over the world are going crazy, synaptically flipped and flibbered, if I may say so, over this last PAN trick of yours."

The almost squeamish delight with which Cecil Higgenbotthom Varuna-d'orooozed out his words brought a feeling of intense comfort to my whole being, comfort and a hilarious sensation as if I had been pumped up with gas.

"That light, airy feeling you may be experiencing right now: Pay it no mind. It's just post-resonance vacuity. And besides, if you were to think that the object of my visits was simply to stimulate you with sensory possibilities you hadn't yet experienced, well, my, my, that would certainly be the end of our relationship." Varuna-d'oro ended this last declaration in a veritable huff.

Screwing my face into a semblance of serious concentration, I awaited Varuna-d'oro's next transmission.

> *"From pole to pole earth's mantle glows*
> *The warrior lords remove the snows*
> *The Dawnsource Ladies beyond being free*
> *Remove the sword from the Devil's country..."*

This verse, recited in a voice limpid and soft, seemed to wipe away all hesitation from my heart.

"Yes," I thought to myself, "this is really so. This is as it is...," and before I could finish this thought, Varuna-d'oro was chatting on.

"Yes indeed, the Only State of Mind, OSM. Sooper, dooper. But really, don't you think you must begin preparations for the Ladies' return? I mean after all, as was sung in the Saga of Vel and the Earth Lords:

*'...no more bargains with the fates*
*the lords and ladies broke down the gates...'*

Ohhh! Marvelous. I just love reunions. Yes, re-unions, ONE again: OSM; signing off now. This has been your friendly preceptor from CHV, Cecil Higgenbotthom Varuna-d'oroooooooooooo..."

As the voice from CHV faded into a high bell-ringing sweetness that completely absorbed me, I scarcely noticed the Slack-Zoners sweeping up behind us, slapping us on the back and offering the heartiest of Newlaw congratulations.

"Decked the ace with CHV, that's a beam-boding scam, like frothing the far side o' sun-gaze with a lick o' radiosonic killer-juice!" Sun-Streaker's cheery gravel-voiced chuckle broke my trance. Placing his arm around my shoulder, we walked toward his tent. Just before entering, I heard shouting.

Looking over my shoulder, I spotted Poontutjarpa stretching his arms at the center of Dawnsource Circle, shaking his Grube-skull fist at a half a dozen Slack-Zoners crowding around him. "...jerk-spasmed genetic aberrations, of course I'm hungry. A feast! Prepare a feast, before I carve you up and eat all of you! A feast! A feast!"

To be continued...

# FRANCESCA'S TAPE LOG: LOVE BEYOND LOVE

When the ladies had returned to Dawnsource Circle in the Jornada del Muerto, a riotous feast was already into its fifth day. The ring of multi-colored tents, their banners fluttering in the radiosonic morning light, provided a celebratory sense of order to the time-hewn campsite. It was just prior to sky-zenith that we arrived. My heart was gilded and perfumed with the treasury of insight and adventure which I and the other ladies had experienced. It was Wandjina Aldebaran who first became aware of the fact that we had returned. It was he who spotted the column of dust in the trail of our laser scooter brigade.

Flanked by three Slack-Zone Normalizers running on tip-toe on either side of him, goateed and breathless, clutching with his left hand the rainbow shawl that covered his otherwise naked body, his right arm waving wildly, Aldebaran shouted tumultuous greetings at us: "Ladies! Ladies! Welcome back to Dawnsource Circle, beam-site of the Earth Lords! The Avalon of curved space! Welcome, do we have a feast for you!"

With total abandon, Aldebaran and the Slack-Zoners pirouetted in our midst and hopped on the back of seven choice laser scooters. It was in this way that I returned to Dawnsource Circle carrying a cargo of realized dreams and a single Slack-Zoner, naked, tattooed and babbling inane outrages into my ear.

Aldebaran had been right. No feast had ever been more sumptuous, no group of humans more loose-headed. My first thought upon seeing the outrageous dancing, at least, I think you could have called it dancing, at the very center of Dawnsource Circle, no less, was that an Outlaw regression was in process. Naked bodies swayed languidly around the giant bonfire. Dawnsource Lords and Slack-Zoners alike, their torsos glistening with sweat, glowing saffron orange in the sky-zenith radiosonic beam-light, exchanged bows, looped hands, and gracefully, but with utter conviction, sashayed around each other in some aboriginal minuet. As if looking at a monitor screen for a key information bit, my eyes darted through the crowd of wildly arranged male bodies until they landed on Prospero's beautifully rippled, orange-bronzed form bending over backwards. Arched into a perfect hoop, Prospero shook his hips, while a lizard lazily clung to his belly, its tongue darting this way and that. It was clear that there was nothing left to do but join in.

Leaving my scooter at the northwest perimeter marking of the campsite, I undid my belt and slipped the tunic over my head. Shaking my hair so that it fell into place, I felt the pale warmth of the saffron light bathing my breasts. Taking off my boots and letting drop my pantaloons, I tuned into the rhythm of the Dawnsource Feast-Dance and approached Prospero. Hips swaying and undulating, my arms delicately carving a path of space-flowers, I arrived before Prospero's still arched body. Bringing myself to join with him at his outstretched legs, our hips charged and moving to the same rhythm, with my left hand in a gesture of offering, I allowed my right arm to glide to a serpentine halt just in front of the lizard. Accepting my invitation, the lizard docilely skittered his way up my right arm and shoulder, where he continued his sky-zenith perch-out. Then with both hands I rhythmically caressed Prospero's torso. As I did so, he slowly and with great exertion, lifted his body into a vertical position. And there he was. So intent was I in looking into his velvet brown eyes flecked with smatterings of gold, that I did not immediately perceive that the scar was gone, and that his nose had mended. When my senses did take in the now-healed features of his perspiration dappled face, I felt a jolt in my heart.

"Prospy, you over-dramatic monitor-clone, do you know that I had a vision—clear, real clear, vision—of you just like this, without the outlaw scar, and your nose, well, almost back to normal. I mean when I had this vision, it just popped in, said 'hello,' then left."

Stroking his face and nose, I let myself fall into his arms. His sweat-stained, heart-mad-beating body pressed against mine, igniting a voluptuous streak of passion that flashed from my genitals through my central channel. Weak all over, I allowed Prospero to press himself even harder against me.

As if in a dream, I heard him whispering into my ear, "Yes, and I suppose this crazy vision of yours occurred five mornings ago while you were seated on top of a mesa." Nibbling my ear, he added, "I don't suppose you want to tell me about that strange assortment of elemental instruments, you know, the ones you had displayed in front of this outlaw-wanton body of yours?"

Even before Prospero's glorious chuckle had wound down to its mirthful conclusion, our space was pierced by a singular tone, the proverbial bell ringing in an empty sky. Disengaging from each other, we both turned to the center of Dawnsource Circle.

There was Poontutjarpa, his naked body blazing with reflected bonfire light, cheeks puffed, blowing into his gold audiophone. As soon as everyone's attention had been magnetized toward him, Poontutjarpa's audiophone emitted the most delicate tones, each set of tones peeling off from the last in a cascade of melted gold. Listening to this effect was like watching the first snowfall of the season.

On cue, the Dawnsource Lords and Ladies advanced toward old Poontut. The Slack-Zoners held back. As we approached the old Kangaroo Spirit Poacher, the great sodium ion neural blazer, Poontut himself, a sudden chill arose. Giant cumulo-nimbus clouds arose to the northwest. Luminous thunderheads, one growing out of the other, rolled upward at a rapidly accelerating rate, each one more threatening than the last. Instinctively I threw my right arm tightly around Prospero's suddenly tensed waist.

As my brain was trying to register the multiplying thunderheads flashing silver-gray overhead, a powerful gust of wind pelted our eyes with sharp spindles of desert sand. My mouth choked with the force of the wind, I threw myself around Prospero, wanting to spare him from the deathly Urantian chill that blew across Dawnsource Circle. Clutching each other in mutual protection against the bone-breaking blast of arctic air, I repeated over and over in his ear, "from pole to pole the wind must blow, let love release the birthbound flow." I don't know where the phrase came from. All I knew was that our lives depended upon the repetition of those few words.

No sooner did Prospero begin reciting the same phrase I had been whispering to him in a panic-allaying passion, then the wind came to an abrupt halt.

Even before I opened my eyes, I knew: it was gone; the radiosonic beams of the Enchanted Triangle had shut down. In the stunned moment of collective realization, Poontutjarpa's voice crashed into my ears with all of the grace that a Syndiclone can muster when his monitor screen informs him that for the last three years he has been a pawn in another PAN decode operation. For this reason, I smiled as I took in what old Poontut was jabbering about.

"Platypus-waddling ninnies! A blust of a gust whops your crust and you just stand there waiting for me to play the Jehovah game. Well, I'm not going to play that game with you. It's…," Poontutjarpa paused for a minute like a well seasoned hunter sizing up his prey, "…it's too dull, the Jehovah game, too beastly dull. Let's play something else, something with a little lilt to it. So get over here you synapse lisping possum-piss-ing polar panicked PAN poo poos." And if that weren't enough, old Poontut lifted his right leg, and stamping his foot on the ground, let rip with the old Slack-Zone Outlaw battle cry: "Shhheeeeeeeee-it!"

Poontut, his face twisted into a magnificent scowl stood before the bonfire, whipped into a new fury by the recent Urantian gust of polar wind. Seating ourselves in a tight circle, all of us hoping to receive some of the bonfire's revived Dawnsource heat, Poontut allowed his transcendent wrath to subside. Like a mellowed-out ball of tar, he dropped to the earth, a crazy-quiet smile trembling on his aboriginal lips.

"Look, I mean isn't it beautiful," David Monongye began tentatively, in a valiant effort not to arouse Poontut's rage, "the thunderheads, I mean." At this point, David lost it. His body was shaking with awe as he stood up to get a better look. As David slowly turned his body, my head, too, began to move about. From southwest, southeast, northeast and northwest, the exact same rolling cumulo-nimbus cloud patterns were shooting skyward. What was most remarkable was the manner in which they elegantly arched overhead, 'til it seemed they would meet directly above Dawnsource Circle.

"Excuse me Mr. Tut, King Tut, Poontut," David addressed Poontutjarpa as he sat himself down again. "You know how it is with us young-bloods. Too much fire, too much excitement, not enough experience. Slack-brained possum-pissers we are, Sir. So please don't take my generic Wandjina-brained spasms as any reflection on the rest of the Dawnsource Lords' and Ladies' ability to keep to the OSM, Sir. Sir?" David craned his head forward in astonishment. Poontutjarpa's only reply to David's request to have his late adolescent enthusiasm forgiven was a protracted snore that sounded like a pig rooting in the mud.

"Hee, Hee, Hee, just like them aby-ridgey types," the Grube-voiced Natasha spoke up, "give 'em the least chance 'n they'll schiziphrene ya to pieces. Hee, hee, hee!"

As the Grube-laced laughter slid its way back to silence, Poontut shook his head a few times, and resumed beaming at us.

"Lindy, Lindy McGrew," the cantankerously lovable Poontut barked out, "Mr. McGrew, you used to broadcast programs from Psycho-atmospheric Central up in Ulan-Bator. Why don't you let us know what kind of weather system this is?"

"OK, Poonie, this one's for you," Lindy leaned a little bit forward as much in defer-ence to Poontutjarpa as to soak in a bit more warmth from the fire. Screwing his face into the epitome of concentration, but not without a last-gasp chuckle, Lindy contin-ued speaking. "Hello, hello CHV do you beam me? This is Earth calling CHV, Earth calling CHV. Yes, you're coming in clear. What's that? Oh, this is beam-band possum, POSM, Planet Organizing Syndic Monitors, Beam Band Possum, POSM, are you com-ing in? OK. Good. Oh really?" The concentration on Lindy's face rapidly became a fast-charged energy field. His eyelids flickered, his mouth fell just short of being totally agape, the Adam's apple on his neck moved up and down accurately gauging the activity in Lindy's central channel.

"OK, I think I got it," Lindy's face had resumed its quiver-nosed jack-rabbit normalcy. "Lemme shoot it to 'em straight and then we'll do sign-off." Looking straight ahead as he spoke, Lindy delivered the transmission. However, it was not Lindy's voice that came out of his lips. It was a staccato electronic monotone. I felt a shudder of anticipation wrinkle the intensity of my concentration. It was better than I had imagined.

"Hierarch Crack Unit Weather Report for Code Zone Alpha, 1.5.24. Cosmic stalemate in Scorpio resulting from terrestrial aberration finds fruition in intense psychomagnetic feedback. Form assumed: out-of-season cumulo-nimbus in quadrant pattern assaulting Jornada del Muerto/ Dawnsource Circle with exceptional snowfall. Of old, this type of weather system was called 'Purity of Auspicious Radiance.' Its infrequency is remarkable, so far known in only a few select star systems.

"This has been another Hierarch Crack Unit Weather Report brought to you by the CHV, which also would like to remind you: compassion only happens on the spot, so, as they say in OSM, 'go for it!'"

Grinning wildly, licking his lips, Lindy asked Poontutjarpa, "Well, Poonie, was that good enough for you?"

Poontut nodded with a generous grunt.

As this last formality was occurring I felt my heart beating most rapidly. My body tensed, and I became joyously aware of what was inside of me: the embryo born of my love for Prospero. Then I knew I had to get up and say what I had to say. Bowing in deference to Poontut, who eyed my body with the most cloyingly dopey leer, I arose and stood to the left of him. Poontutjarpa remained seated, giggling to himself all goofy and jelly-like.

Ignoring the antics of the uniquely endowed Poontut, I spread my legs out to a comfortable stance. Hands on my hips, I enjoyed the feminine rush that swept through every cell of my love-proud body. I let my eyes fall on each face in the Dawnsource semi-circle, their smiles smeared with wisdom-honey. Ignoring Poontut's hand gently caressing my right ankle, I spotted the Slack-Zoners bustling around the tents. They were definitely up to something, buzzing and twerping in clusters of five.

The thunderheads above had indeed met, and were in the process of boiling and rolling every which way, as if afflicted by some massive electric discharge. The variously distanced ranges of mountains and mesas grew dark. The Peak of Darkness in particular seemed to shift and change as its color turned deep shades of cobalt and oceanic purple. Its peak, swiftly encircled by clouds, would disappear momentarily, then reappear disembodied above dense layers of lowering cumulo-nimbus forms drawn irresistibly by Earth's gravitational heat.

It was time to release my report. Going empty so that my body was scarcely more than a blade of grass in a primeval sea of silence, I felt the little click at central channel heart center and began to speak.

"Wandjina seers, birth-bodied Lords and Ladies, Dawnsource receptacles of auspicious radiance, and, if you can hear me back there," I raised my voice to a level of high command, listening all the while to the first snowflakes sizzle in their encounter with Dawnsource bonfire. "Yes, and you too, wax-brained, rhythm limbed Slack-Zoners, why do you think we've gathered here one Moon-Wax gone since Poontut charged the tektite beam? And now that tektite beam, too, is gone—I mean scrammed and scrambled, just like each of us, pre-natal or post-mortem. While you Lords and Slack-Zone Aces have sported here enjoying the perfect warrior weather, where have we ladies been? Do you know?"

Allowing for the proper rhetorical pause, my eyes landed for a moment on Prospero's face, poignantly absorbed beneath its windblown tumble of black sea-storm hair-swirls.

"What we unfolded, I won't tell you. That's for you to find out. But I will give you a clue. It's elemental, not monumental, and certainly not sentimental, and when you recover and gather it, you'll know, it's definitely more than flippity-dippity warrior psychomental. Well," I relaxed, feeling the few oversize snowflakes landing on my breasts, melting in little pools of pin-prick polar cold, "that's obviously not why I'm speaking to you."

My hands moved from my hips to my belly. Each hand spread out belly-flat, thumbs touching the bottom of my breasts, my navel pulsing between outspread fingertips. Within, I sensed the embryo, like a coal glowing ever so faintly in the early morning hours.

"As an earthling, I am embodied in female form. And I like it. Oh, I know from the high precipice of the mantle of the Supreme Hierarchy, sex is just another blip on the all-equalizing beam of universal synchrotronic radiation. Fine. If that weren't so, how else could we experience bliss? And because it is so, the texture of truth is encoded in every elemental structure, and every living being, regardless of size, shape, function, or birth-death cycle duration. Blade of grass, Slack-Zone Outlaw, eagle-spirit, Syndic

Monitor lord, it doesn't matter. It doesn't matter in the least, because everything is encoded with truth. The most deviously entropic manipulation, no less than one of our highly prized goody-goody PAN-scams, like the Quetzalcoatl Project. Remember that one, Lords and Ladies?"

I paused to take in the mutual nod of assent registering on the faces of the inner Dawnsource Circle. Even the Slack-Zoners stopped in the midst of their enigmatic hustle-bustle, as if listening to a synthesized high-wire hum. Feeling the contrast between my bonfire heated behind and the wind-and-snow chilled front, my hands still held powerfully upon my female belly-womb swell, I cruised into high delivery zone.

"What was the Quetzalcoatl Project? Ten years riding the tip of a terrestrial awareness probe, its roots spread deep and touch everything that moves and breathes on planet Earth. Even now, its roots are forming in my belly—yet again. No, my beloved PAN-scammers, Lords and Ladies of Dawnsource Circle, the Quetzalcoatl Project was not placed into operation merely to convince the Syndics of our superiority in the psychogenetic warfare we both initiated. If that were so, we might as well leave this time-blessed site and join them."

I stopped again to lick the snowflakes from my lips.

"No," I said, picking up the rhythm again, "the purpose of the Quetzalcoatl Project was simply this: war no more! That's right, war no more. Art now. War no more. We know that. But we haven't acted on it, we haven't lived it. We've syndiscammed ourselves simply by scamming on syndic wavelengths. Well, that just won't work anymore. CHV says OSM, right?"

Dawnseer faces nodded in unison. A slight covering of snow coated the tops of their heads. Each one in his or her own way was catching the rhythm, Slack-Zoners too. So intent were their faces, I realized they were oblivious of the snowflakes the size of solarometer discs descending in perfect quadrant formation, each one laced and filigreed in its own unique manner. I picked up the cadence and ran with it.

"OSM being OSM, it transmits in all wavelength frequencies, no spectrum is immune to it. All inclusive frequency, that's the key, just as sure as the embryo within me is the root, while we, Wandjina-seers, Slack-Zone Heralds and elemental spirits of Dawnsource Circle, are the path and the fruit. So there's only one way for us to go, one way for us to fly: art on a higher frequency! Synch the geomag to the electromag, and synch them both to the cosmomag! Synch them all and sound the warrior's biotone: Syndics and PANs are one! Ours is the art to end all wars! The love beyond love to heal Earth's sores!"

No sooner had I finished, then the entire group, Dawnsource Seers and Slack-Zoners alike broke into a spontaneous chant: "Key, key, OSM! Ka, ka, CHV! Ko, ko, us 'n' them! Key, key, OSM, ka, ka, CHV! Ko, ko, us 'n' them…"

As the chanting began to die down, gladsome creatures swarmed around me, kissing me, patting my belly-womb, and offering gratitude for my having channeled the CHV.

Poontutjarpa, standing again, his left arm happily fondling my breasts, repeated over and over again, to no one in particular, "Marvelous! Marvelous! Original! Path and Destiny are One!"

Things began to quiet down as the group became increasingly aware of the beauty and heaviness of the snowfall. Looking at the snow, then turning toward me, I felt they were asking for something more, this despite Lindy's CHV-channeled weather report. Looking past the glistening naked bodies, some sinewed and old, others ripe and bursting, I sought, but could not find it: the Peak of Darkness had gone, it was no longer visible. In its place was a rolling ghostly cloud of swirling pale violet colored snow. Tumble-drifting our direction, its advance guard had already stormed our innermost circle.

Remembering the innocent pleasures I enjoyed as a global riff singer in Diamondwave Ionelli's Tone-Squad, especially the song and the time when I first met Prospero, I knew there was only one way to wind up an act like this: with a song.

As a big smile crossed my face, Slack seers and Wandjina zoners alike, began to seat themselves, huddling together, arms around each other. A lilting tune in a seductive sub-minor came to me, and I began to sing:

*"Moon-Wane wind-down snows the Lords*
*The Ladies hold the Knight of Swords*
*And where the Punk with black heart stood*
*Wandjina seers unveil the hood*
*To drape upon the Syndic head*
*No more to be the living dead*
*And with a flower carved from space*
*Tomorrow's child fires the ace*
*From pole to pole til moon is new*
*The Dawnsource Lords will trace the clue*
*From crystal windows in the stars*
*Behold the art to end all wars*

*So come again, and love me do,*
*Beyond this love there's nothing new."*

These last two lines I sang as if my heart were about to leave my body. And I sang them, drinking in the bubbling warmth of Prospero's face where the salt of his tears quietly merged into the flawless purity of melting snow.

While Poontutjarpa coughed 'til I thought he would split apart, his left hand flailing against my thighs, the Slack-Zone Normalizers descended upon us, inimitably skating and gliding through the snow-vast net in which we were all enmeshed. Over their tuxedo-topped torsos, tattooed and sweet-eyed they wore capes—wonderful capes, heavy woven double wool capes snapping in the gusts of wind. Deep soft earthy violet in color, the capes were decorated with a simple fourfold diamond step pattern. While the main motif of these diamond patterns was woven of pure white wool, the inside and outside edges of the diamond pattern bled into a subtle rendering of the chromatic spectrum, much like the echo of a rainbow.

Poontut's seizure now but a memory, he took my right hand, and with a gentle tug motioned me to sit next to him. Though the snow was falling rather heavily now, I realized that I was not the least bit cold. Wet, yes, but not cold. Behind us, the fire simmered and steamed, throwing occasional sparks to sizzle on my snow-dampened back.

With almost unbearable tenderness the Slack-Zoners came and placed, in unison, one of the double-woven wool diamond pattern capes on the shoulders of each one of the Dawnsource Lords and Ladies. The wool was of the softest alpaca, the violet and white alpaca bred on the Mogollon Mesa. The softness of these capes on the skin was matched only by the color and softness of the falling snow.

Once each of our capes had been attached by a gold chain clasp around the neck, the Slack-Zoners, all forty of them, formed a semi-circle directly behind that of the Dawnsource Lords and Ladies. Clearing his throat with a hearty nasal booger sucked in through the mouth and then spat over his shoulder into the fire, where the mucus glob underwent a sizzling transformation, Poontutjarpa addressed us:

"Dawnsource Lords and Ladies, denizens of the Slack-Zone Male Hierarch, gladsomely do we welcome the Ladies back into our midst. One night shall we spend with their love-wounded bodies, and it shall then be the turn of the Warrior Lords to find what has not yet come, nor gone."

Casting me a lecherous wink, Poontutjarpa went on, "At this point, PAN's and Syndic's alike usually ask, 'what's the pay-off?' By Uranus and Vishnu, we all know there is no pay-off, except as is helpful to show by means of illusory skill what others do not know." Poontutjarpa was chuckling now from deep down below in his rainbow serpent cave.

"Not knowing what we shall come upon, nor is it the Ladies' responsibility to give us the triflest hint, yet, upon completing our mission—who knows whether we shall even be all together during our Moon-Wane Wind-Downs? There will indeed be a pay-off, but one of the illusory, skill variety." Poontutjarpa was grinning now as if he had just pinned a kangaroo to the ground in apre-star ball game, 'meet the animals' match.' "Premonitions sprouted in my optic nerve, like mushrooms on a dead rain forest log."

It was Claudia Blavatsky Leventhal, however, who spoke up. Moving her hands in front of her as if molding a crystal sphere from space, she unwound the lead premonitory thread, "Though it was the Bear, the Coyote and the Parrot who built it, it was the Spider who undid it. King Harmaunce who knew so well the Delectable Isle, was its greatest ruler, yet he, too, was killed by the Spider sons. Four levels had the great city erected, yet who had dreamed there would have been a fifth. When Tristram completes the Beasting Quest, what new name or splendors shall ancient Palat-kwapi attain?"

Claudia was perfect! She had done it! She had reduced the Dawnsource Ladies' findings to one cryptic image. I clapped my hands with delight, only to turn to Poontut and find him baring his grizzled yellow teeth at me.

"Enough of this feminine chatter, you'll ruin it for all of us if you continue," Poontutjarpa belched with obvious pleasure. "Besides we have but this evening together, and I'm not going to let any auspiciously radiant snowfall ruin my fun!"

With that, Poontut grabbed my wrist and with a magical twirl as if he were skipping stones across the water, sent me flying into Prospero's waiting arms.

That evening was as rare as anything I had ever experienced. After feasting in the snow on a side of Baja Water-buffalo, during which time Poontutjarpa wouldn't shut up, so enthralled was he with his "ox-tamer" jokes, we banqueted on cups of steaming Peyote tea, served with little tumblers of snake-skin mescal. Following a nominal show of Normalization Gymnastics in which the Slack-Zoners proceeded to graciously break every dish we had eaten from, throwing the shards with a big heave into the snow-devouring bonfire, we retired to our tents punching the snow-driven night with earthshaking laughter.

Prospero's tent was as close to paradise as you could get, and yet, still find yourself on Earth. Banners of silk and coverlings of rainbow wool were tied to the inside walls, and covered the floor. In the center a small fire threw out a magnificent glow. Two small tables stood to either side of the entrance flap, each adorned with the growths of flowers that had sprung up beneath the Enchanted Triangle Marking Beam. Where we were to spend the night, a third bouquet awaited us. Orchids, tiger lilies and a sprig of yellow-tipped canyon daisies graced our mat of love.

"Oh Prospero," I whispered undoing his cape and enclosing his body in the soft warm folds of my flesh, "Prospero, it's good. Love beyond love. It's so good. Let me give you this evening the treasure that will show you everything my heart knows."

To be continued…

# PROSPERO'S TAPE LOG: POLAR MAGIC ON MADRE MOUNTAIN

The morning of the Wandjina Seer Lords' departure from Dawnsource Circle would have been just another exercise, had it not been for the great pale violet snowdrifts that all but buried our magnificent campsite. The snow was still coming down, but in tiny pellets, not the fragile, fragrent disk pattern of the night before. Ah! The night before! Love had never been more powerful. Through the intertwining of two bodies, the secrets, the treasures that were revealed, the magic of the male and the female poles.

Such reveries vanished swiftly when I attempted to poke my head out of the yurt just before sun-up. After drinking tea together, Francesca had finally fallen back to sleep. I had the most difficult time tearing myself away from her. I was ready to share my life completely with her. But no, not yet. Another assignment to be completed. I knew this one was going to be different. However, I hadn't realized that the first major difference was going to be the pale violet snowdrifts.

Upon securing the flap back to the yurt, I looked at the biochronic monitor attached to the inside of my left wrist: 06:50 hours. There was not the slightest hint of dawn, and yet I knew somewhere to the east of me the sun was rising.

Muffled voices, laughter and a smattering of war cries abounded, seeming to echo from everywhere in the eerie dawn. The drifts threw off a hint of reflected light, enough so that I could see a few meters ahead of me. Charging forth I soon came across Psychlosky, Grunt, Squeaker and Aldebaran.

"Frothed the deck o' love to grace the blighs that blow above, it's brospy Prosp!" Psychlosky greeted me, his massive head draped with a make-shift rainbow turban.

"Come on! The others are already warming up the hovercraft," Aldebaran urged me ahead with a hearty boot to my ass.

Making our way to a trail already blazed by the other five Dawnsource Lords, we trudged on toward the hovercraft. When we reached it we found Esquivel and Lindy

McGrew, their lasers on low-beam, cutting swaths of snow from the hovercraft's weathered wings. The rest of the crew, Poontutjarpa, Lindy McGrew, and David Monongye were already inside, charging up the solar cells. An insistent whine emanated from the time-worn cargo ship, its haphazardly vibrating motion providing heart-fresh doubts about the old boat's abilities.

"Hey!" Poontutjarpa's swaddled head poked out of the top entry hatch, "love-crazed Wandjina Seers, you've been burning the night away again, eh? Curmudgeoned DNA growth-packets, I'll bet none of you has done your morning ablutions, and you call yourselves artiers? Hmmph!" With that the old Australian goofer, pulled the hatch down with a bang and disappeared.

"The guy's right," Aldebaran shouted, and pulling off his head-scarf, plunged his head immediately into the nearest snowdrift. The rest of us followed suit. It is difficult for me to describe the totally pleasurable sensation that resulted from having burrowed my head into that icy coffer. Though my face felt an initial chill, much like a hard slap across the chops, the sting lasted but for an instant. Though my eyes were closed, they became engulfed in a cool violet luminescence. Then, as sure as my father was Lao Tzu Nkwame Jones, I felt Francesca's lips on my lips, burning and brimming with the pure high-volted essence of passion. The heat of this kiss shot through the pores of my face, like a multiple-headed solar discharge. I loved it!

"Hey, Unisonic dream-lover, did you fall asleep?" Aldebaran's gruff voice was followed by another boot to the ass. Sputtering and coughing, I emerged from the snow looking everywhere for Aldebaran who was nowhere in sight. Squirting a drop of quintessential rose soap onto my hands and mixing it with the snow-water, I rubbed my face down, wondering all the while how in the hell Aldebaran had gotten away so fast. Then, just as I was massaging my gums and teeth with heliotrope pumice, there was Aldebaran, holding a small round mirror and kneeling before me as still and ancient-looking as if he had been a tree trunk rooted to this very spot for the last thousand years.

Fixing my hair in the mirror, I asked Aldebaran, "What in the hell kind of games are you playing this morning? You act as if you're suffering from Moon-wobbles."

"Come now, my dear good Radiosonic Decode painter, have you no gratitude? Here I sit kneeling in the snow, your ever most faithful servant of the Beginningless Feedback Loop, and you hurl insults at me?" Aldebaran was back to his charming alchemical self.

Staring me off with his wrinkled, deepset eyes, I leaned over and placed a kiss on his brow, and replied, while taking the mirror and sailing it across the snow on a gently modulated air-breaker, "Aldebaran of star-luck fame, you're a fucker just the same!" Throwing snowballs at each other we skirmished our way back to the hovercraft which was just beginning to elevate.

Sailing over the violet snow dunes a distance of some ten kilometers, we were greeted by an amazing sight: a clear swath that ran straight from Dawnsource Circle to Chaco Canyon. Banked on each side by snowdrifts some two meters high, the trajectory line sped its way to the horizon as far as the eye could see.

"It's the horizon-line beam bed!" Esquivel spoke in a hushed tone, "but look at it!"

And look we did. The swath, no more than a half a kilometer wide, was verdant and flower-brimmed. Gazing at its lush grasses, flowering cactuses, cattails and ferns, I soon became aware of a multitude of creatures, grazing, crawling, poking or flying about. And it was like this stretching the whole distance to Chaco Canyon.

Descending to an altitude of five meters above terrestrial level, we hovered north-westerly at a moderate rate. Setting the direction and putting the hovercraft on self-modulating automatic, the Wandjina Seer Lords of the Trident Brigade plastered themselves belly down on the smoke-tinted plexiglass bottom of the ship, the better to view this ley-line of paradise. I had to shake my head several times in disbelief: magpies and falcons sporting on broad-leafed ferns, alpaca and mountain lions ambling through thick grass gateways, showers of dogwood blossoms shaking and flying in the after-trail of the hovercraft, while a few wild pigs rolled in a bed of riotously colored wisteria and morning glories, while everywhere, massive plumes of flowering yucca sported in the clear morning air. On either side of this near-tropic band, dissolving rapidly into swirling mists and clouds, snow-blanketed hills and mesas like mammoth sand dunes caused the eyes to pop with swirls of retinal hallucinations.

Just as we were approaching what must have been the East slope of Mount Taylor, the hovercraft began to shake violently, tumbling the bodies of the Wandjina Seers back and forth across the shallow-curved hovercraft bottom. In a streak, David Mon-ongye picked himself up and scrambled forward and up to the navigation pit. Next the three Newlaw Seers sat themselves up in a tight triangle. Backs erect and hands on their knees, the three let out a low hum. The rest of us resumed supine viewing positions. David was lowering the craft. As the three landing pods slid down, I observed an extended clan of adolescent coyotes sniff their noses at what was about to descend on their clover-strewn playground, and, with a few rapid swishes of their tails, jumped and bounded out of view.

With a soft plump, we were back on the ground. As the ten of us scrambled out of the top hatch, I could hear David telling anyone who would listen to him what a helluva time it was bringing it down.

"Even though we came down vertical," David spouted out breathlessly as he jumped from wing to ground, "I had the decelerator jammed way over to starboard. Damndest thing! It's like I was fighting a magnetic storm way over to port."

Landing on what felt like a fiber-feather cushion, I undid my flight parka, and let it dangle for a moment from my left hand before letting it drop on the emerald colored grass beneath me. It was too warm. It wasn't like a jungle or a rain forest. It was more like lush meadowland. Through a slight thicket of shrubs embroidered with bougainvillea and just beyond a stand of brightly budding saguaro cacti, the pale violet snow banks rose abruptly. Looking past their vast expanse I saw the great trunk of Mount Taylor, its peak lost in a wreathe of the same kind of thunderheads we had experienced at Dawnsource Circle the day before. The day before? It seemed like we had traveled to another time, if not another planet.

As I shifted my vision to look down the endless tunnel of greenery and wildlife I spotted it. At first it hardly seemed to be there at all. It made a noise, like a breeze rushing through the grove of willows in which I finally perceived it as a visible form. Wobbling mirthfully, it gyrated at an exceptional rate of speed. In shape it resembled a pyramid dancing flame at the tip of a stick of piñon incense. Its colors became apparent only after prolonged concentration: a shimmering ribbon of spark-lights spiraling in the counter direction of its gyration. Its base a meter or so off the ground, its dancing flame like form tapered into space at a height of about three and a half meters.

Precisely at the point where it totally dematerialized, a flock of birds of many species had gathered. Circling in a waiting formation a short distance away, each bird would take its turn, and dive into the very top of the energy tip. Wings gracefully outspread, while exerting no energy of its own, the bird would then be launched skyward in an ever-widening spiral. At that point in space where the birds were mere flecks, each would break pattern and peel off perhaps five degrees away from where the last one had allowed itself to be spiraled out into deep space.

"That's what brought us down," David sputtered, overstating the obvious once again. And it was true: the gyrating form had us perfectly magnetized. Like sleepwalkers we slowly advanced within a meter away from it. Standing breathless, resisting its pull, I realized I was sweating profusely. As if swept away by a whiplash of energy, Poontutjarpa was the first to be pulled into it. For a moment he stood in the center of the energy cone, his face strained and pulling every which way.

As his voice called out, "Wandjina Seers, we have no choiiiiiice…"the unpredictable Keeper of the Rainbow Serpent Cave disappeared.

Gone. He was completely gone. Psychlosky was next, then Esquivel, Aldebaran, Grunt, and David, all gone in the same manner. That left Lindy, Squeaker, Ramakrishna and myself. As the force took me spiraling into its maximum vibratory central core, I caught Squeaker's cinnamon-red eyes intently taking in every neuromuscular twitch of my magnetically spasmed face.

Entering the intense force field of the vibratory core, I surrendered. "Francesca!" I cried out as I felt my cellular structure attune itself to the higher frequency of the gyrating form. Then I, too, was gone. Or should I say, unfolded, unrolled, dissolved to a simple frequency of hyper-light pulsating in a stream of synchrotronic radiation. And yet it was very ordinary, pure, simple. It was the Primordium itself, all-extending space, instantaneously penetrating everything. At the same time, there was no one to say what it was. To describe it as "unoriginated luminosity" or some such common meta-magnetic phrase, is to continue to assume the eternal reality of one's own existence. No, that misses the point entirely.

Suffice it to say that I, and each of the nine other Lords of Dawnsource Circle, had an interesting encounter one curious morning in the sign of Capricorn at the radiosonic emblazoned foot of Mt. Taylor.

Let's also just say it was toward nightfall, presumably of the same day, that my cellular structure resumed its terrestrial rate of frequency. No hovercraft was in sight. No Mt. Taylor either. And needless to say, not a giggle or a whisper of my fellow Lords of the Trident Brigade. As I sat there in a small clearing bordered by irises and hyacinths, I became acutely aware of someone approaching me. It seemed like it was Francesca. It must have been her. But for all the craning of my neck I saw no one, no one at all. Settling my mind, I let my eyes fall on the patch of lush meadow grass right in front of me. There, resting delicately on the grass was a small red silk-wrapped object.

As I took this object in my hands and began to unwrap it, I heard a most familiar sound. In the midst of the twittering twilight serenade of the radiosonic aviary, it came to me, the very same descending tones punctuated by ethereal trills that I used to blow on my flute at El Dorado Station. No one else but myself had ever blown that set of sounds, nor had anyone but myself ever blown that set of sounds in just the way I heard them at that very moment. So entranced and intrigued was I by the flute music that I lost all interest in the silk wrapped object I had picked up from the grass, and it tumbled from my hands. It was then I decided to lie down. Whatever I had undergone earlier that day, not only had it scrambled my molecules and then reassembled them, but it left me in a state of total exhaustion.

I have no idea how long I slept. A distant gurgling sound was percolating in my ears. A bright sun was high overhead. As I stirred my limbs I realized I felt in excellent condition. Gauging where the sun was, I determined that I was no longer on the Dawnsource-Chaco Canyon axis, but that I had been transported to the Hopi Mesa-Dawnsource axis. Sitting up, I had the distinct sensation that my cellular structure had been rearranged, or, at the very least, that its frequency had been fine tuned beyond anything I had experienced before. As for dreams, all that I could remember was that some kind of luminous apparition had come to me, had actually entered into me, and, lifting an equally luminous sword, sank the burning tip of the sword into the top of my head.

Again I noticed the red silk-wrapped object. Picking it up once more, I continued to unwrap it. Inside was a jade disc, maybe a hand-span in diameter. The center of the disc had been cut out in a perfect circle half the diameter of the disc. In place of the jade that had been removed was a perfect crystal sphere. The center of the sphere itself had also been hollowed out, how I do not know. Within the vacuum bubble of the jade-encircled crystal sphere, was a minute amount of liquid.

Depending on the direction the jade-encircled crystal was placed, the liquid changed color. Facing east it became a pale turquoise, south a burning amber, west a fluorescent ruby, and north a deep emerald. Had Francesca placed this here for me to find? I did not know. Playing with the object, discovering its properties, I began to twirl it rapidly between my hands. The liquid inside it bubbled furiously. When I stopped rolling it between my hands, the liquid calmed down. A distinct image was reflected on its now-motionless surface. A sensuously shaped mountain presented itself. It looked familiar, yet I did not recognize it.

A gaggle of voices broke my reverie. "There he is!" I could hear someone shouting jubilantly. Breaking into the clearing from my right side was a trio of Mogollon Mesa sheep and alpaca herders. "He must be one of them. Look what he's holding." The man who spoke was short and stocky, central Asian or Mongolian. Like the others he was dressed in a heavy wool tunic dyed and woven into rich earth-colored patterns, white pantaloons and the lace-front boots common to herders. On each of their heads was a woven ear flapped, pontifically pointed Andean herder's cap.

"Hello," I greeted them, bringing myself to a standing position. "Why do you say, I must be one of them?" I asked, really rather curious about what they knew about the whole crazy business that had been ignited at Jornada del Muerto some two weeks ago.

Each one, more eager than the last to fill me in on the events that had occurred since winter solstice, gave me their version of the story. Basically, what they told me was this: several days before the solstice, a number of PAN-liaison units had fanned out from Hopi Mesa and alerted residents both inside and within a hundred kilometer perimeter around the Chaco Canyon-Hopi-Mesa-Jornada del Muerto Triangulation. The triangular were told that should unusual radiosonic phenomena occur there was no cause for alarm. They were further informed that a major experimental operation was being conducted, and that whatever effects would be produced or manifested could only be of the most beneficent kind. Once the beam was flashed, obviously exceeding anyone's expectations in terms of its size and duration, wonderment and imagination took over. In particular, the mysterious conductors of the experiment in the popular mind had taken on a significance all out of proportion, I felt, to who we actually were. Nevertheless, there was no way I could allay the awe in which the trio of herders beheld me.

"But tell us this, then," the tall Nordic type insisted, "why are you here in the exact same place we found the woman two weeks ago to the day?"

There was nothing I could say. Smiling at them, I could feel the warmth at the top of my head where the sword had entered during the night. I realized I didn't care. There was nothing to defend or protect.

"Tell me what you know about this mountain," I beckoned them to come and look into the jade-encircled crystal sphere where the calm-surfaced liquid still reflected the mountainous shape. Eagerly rushing over to me they peered intently into the mysterious object that I still held in my hands.

"Madre Mountain!" they shouted all at once, elbowing each other and trying to get as close as they could to me.

"Madre Mountain? Where is that?" I asked.

Again, each one trying to be of the greatest service, all three ended up wildly pointing and gesticulating to my immediate right. There, above a clump of oversized ferns and flowering yucca, dotted and flecked with the glistening blue wings of a horde of dragonflies, was Madre Mountain, exactly as it appeared in the vacuum bubble.

"Take me there," I commanded without the least hesitation.

"Of course, of course, we would be most happy to," all three burbled together, "but tell us, what is your name?"

"Jones. Wandjina Jones. Prospero Wandjina Jones, Agent Lord 24, call me what you wish," I replied in humorous abandon. With that, they all announced their names to me: Vel Bjornson, Samten Tsogyal, and Alfonso Purimac; and in a high-spirited mood we set off for Madre Mountain.

At the edge of the beam-bed, the pale violet snow banks were rapidly melting. The distant gurgling noise I heard when I had awoken was now like a small mountain waterfall. Gingerly splashing our way over a new-formed stream, we made our way to a trail that wound its way up Madre Mountain. Climbing a good two hours I spotted an abutment just beneath the mountain peak.

"That's where I wish to go," I pointed to the flower-dappled escarpment swept clear of snow by a warm southwesterly breeze.

"We know that," they all spoke up at once, "but you'll need some provisions, Agent Lord 24, just like the last one, she needed provisions."

After a contemplative lunch of salted mutton strips and pomegranates, the shy, but generous trio of Mogollon herders bade me farewell. Each one came and kissed me on the cheek, burning my vision with their sad, penetratingly curious eyes. Then they turned and began their descent. When they had arrived at a stand of wind-scrubbed junipers, Purimac took a flute out of his shoulder bag. Still walking as he raised the shakuhachi to his lips, the otherwise mute Andean played.

My heart dissolved when it heard the sounds wafting up from Purimac's blowing. It was a continuation of the sounds I had heard last night while falling asleep, sounds I could have sworn had been known only to me in my days of radiosonic solitude at El Dorado.

"Damn those Mogollon herders are sly," I muttered in self-absorbed amusement to the flower-carpeted escarpment that awaited my arrival.

For ten days I remained at Snowflower Rock Pavilion of Undisputed View. For ten days I saw no other humans. Remembering the name of my illustrious psychogenetic predecessor, Neza-hual-pilli, the Noble Fasting One, I determined to sit in silence for as long as was necessary. Wrapping myself in the woolen blankets the herders had left with me, I perched myself at the back of the abutment on the south slope of the peak of Madre Mountain, just beneath a slight overhang of rugged red rocks. I felt confident that this was what I was supposed to do. I also felt confident that at the appropriate time I would be reunited with my comrades, the Lords of Dawnsource Circle.

Each day I watched the snow below gradually disappear to be replaced by winter flower-dappled grass. Each night I watched the moon wane 'til it was only a luminous crescent in a sea of stars. All the while as I sat there, I knew this was precisely where Francesca had been sitting when I saw her in my traveling ablution mirror.

It was perhaps on the seventh or eighth day that the voices began. At first I dismissed them as the ramblings of a fatigued mind. But my mind was perfectly clear. In fact, it had never been more clear, and I knew it. The cellular interfusion I had experienced the morning the herders found me hadn't left me either. My body tone was as close to perfect as it would ever get. I felt like I had when I was a little boy, completely fresh and without any concerns, eagerly scrambling for lizards over the rutted jungle stones of old Angkor. Maybe because I felt this way the voices were reminiscent of those of my parents, Tara Andromeda and Lao Tzu Jones. And it wasn't as if they were speaking to me, but among themselves. This made an eavesdropper out of me, but it didn't matter. Without breaking my concentration, I allowed the preternatural conversation to drift through the space of my mind.

Nor was it that they spoke in any language that I knew, but in code sounds that I instinctively understood. Like a vocal hieroglyph, each sound continued to resonate as new sounds were added to it. What resulted was a sound tapestry of primal male and female tones, a sonorous flux of positive-negative magnetic pulses.

By the ninth day, it was as if the sounds were weaving me. I felt as if I were no longer flesh but a harmonic chord oscillating through a network of transparent cells. By the tenth day, I knew if someone had come up to that little ridge where I sat, they would have seen no one there. Though I vibrated at a high rate, whatever there was of me remained totally calm.

As night fell, inseparable from everything that ever was and would still come to be, I felt myself lifting off. Transfused in earth's great double helix polar magnetic shuttle, I swooned as great stellar constellations embedded themselves in my vibratory field. Vast swirling showers of light spilled every which way as I surrendered, surrendered completely to THAT which could never be named!

It was with a slight jolt that I re-entered the Mt. Taylor East slope Willow Grove. It appeared that the nine other Dawnsource Lords had re-entered at the very same moment. Hovering two or three fingers above the grass, I gently lowered my Aldebaran-kicked ass to the lush meadow floor. Again, we all touched down simultaneously.

"Slayin weather bimbos sure knocks the deck up. Glassy buff the geo-lectrocos-momag synch!" Grunt and Squeaker murmured in awesomely hushed unison.

"Not to mention that it makes star-face landing rods out of these rabbit ears of mine," Lindy McGrew chimed in, pulling at his floppy, rubbery audio receivers.

"Pulled til there weren't no more gears to pull," David whispered, idly picking at a pimple on his chin.

"Of course, the jihad is intercerebral, but by Rumi, I never, dear sirs believed the victory would be so complete!" Ramakrishna al-Badr nodded his head up and down, his eyes still swimming in the polar exchange samadhi bath.

"What say, Poonie," I turned to the old Australian serpent-breather, his nostrils flared to max receptivity, "did the double-helix magnetic shuttle bop you back to Wandjina bean-land?"

While the rest of us laughed at my laser-grooved idiocy, old Poontut just sat there, his eyes bulging like bloodshot marbles shot up with growth serum. Taking his left little finger and entrenching it in his right nostril with a series of engaging little twists, King Tut gave the word.

"Boys, Wandjina Synch-magged Navigators," Poontut began in a bored tone, his slobbery bougainvillea crimson tongue cleaning off his left pinkie, "nothing really to get so excited about. It is just as the lady told it at Dawnsource Circle the day the weather bimbos went wild with that silly snowfall of theirs. All I have to say, really, is congratulations. We have completed our mission successfully. Being accomplished neuronauts we can now shoot straight. This is very good." Pausing as he puffed up his chest and sat as erect as a well-nourished pine, Old Poontut sang for us:

> *"Synch the mag and raise the gates*
> *Lords and Ladies scrub the fates*
> *What they unfolded at long last*
> *Caused the mates to transport fast*
> *While sitting down at bottom gear.*
> *We gather life and cast out fear*
> *So sing the threefold body clear*
> *The fourth unites, the fifth draws near."*

As Poontut's voice faded into the wind, a feeling of restful well-being lapped in calm, happy waves through my channels. And every wave ended on the same beachhead: that beach upon which Francesca sat, her birth-borne bod glowing with the embryonic life it now cradled.

"Miserable electro-farting Wandjina Seers, stop luxuriating in your polar-fusion," Poontut had a back-arm hold on Esquivel, and was gingerly lifting the graying peyote head up and down, "just because I congratulated us on completing our mission, doesn't mean we've finished our work!"

"Wandjina-cloned idiot," Esquivel was shouting in mirthful exasperation at Poontut. Then, planting his leather-slippered feet firmly on the meadow, Esquivel bent down and with effortless grace flipped Poonie way to the other side of the clearing. The foolish aborigine picked himself up and began a chase for Esquivel that had the rest of us in pursuit 'til we arrived at old hover-babe number 24. Even then, the chase did not end, but continued as bodies scrambled to the top entry hatch, and dropped into star-hold. David, firmly at the controls once again, the rest of us plastered facedown to the terrestrial viewing bubble, we continued northwesterly toward Chaco Canyon.

Along the way, small clusters of Triangulars greeted and cheered us on. We were all especially impressed with the activity at Chaco Canyon and Hopi Mesa, at which sites we spent one night each. At Chaco, radiosonic dishes were being moved into the main roofless kivas, where a fever of activity had everyone bursting with joy. The same was true at Hopi.

From the gold and vermilion polished walls of Marpa Mesa to the terraced esplanades of Antelope Terrace, small collectively coordinated clusters of people were busily accomplishing a discrete portion of the major project which went by the code word RED. Even out on Black Mesa at the Atari-Mifune electro-chemo arcade and mobile unit constructionry, the workers had abandoned quotas and were all applying themselves to their part of the task. Such psycho-aesthetic coordination had been almost unheard of since the beginning of the War.

"Unprecedented, but not unanticipated," Aldebaran mused as we departed for the final stretch of our journey: Return to Dawnsource Circle.

Floating past Madre Mountain, the site of my polar-helix fusion, I caught sight of Vel, Samten and Alfonso Purimac. As old hover-babe floated into their view, they all waved so cheerfully I could have cried. Looking back after we had passed over them, I could see Purimac taking out the shakuhachi and playing it again. Though the plexiglass which separated us did not allow me to hear what he played, I knew what it sounded like and hummed it quietly as I eagerly looked forward to joining with Francesca once again.

To be continued...

# FRANCESCA'S TAPE LOG: THE WORLD'S FIRST AUTO-REGULATORY GEO-HARMONE UNIT

Even before the memory of Prospero had flared up to max luminosity, things had begun to develop rather rapidly at Dawnsource Circle. The afternoon of the departure of the Lords of the Polar Fusion Quest saw the arrival of a new contingent, a batallion of forty female Slack-Zone Newlaw Seed Dancers. Needless to say, this event overjoyed the male Slack-Zone Batallion already encamped at Dawnsource Circle. Great jubilation broke out when, advancing with a sideways swishing motion, and uttering high pierced "yip, yip, yipppeeees," the Slack-Zone Seed Dancers surrounded the male batallion, which was then sitting in tight formation engrossed in one of its collective communications with Supersub.

The tumult that ensued inspired the Dawnsource ladies to retire to Eagle-Seer Rock Vista. We in turn picked up the communication with Supersub. He was in great humor that afternoon—with a blues-born slack and a swoop of his zone-fused lobes, he gave us a precise intimation of the coming months:

> *"When the sun peek over the mountain*
> *You'll be fused-out and bound to glow*
> *But you better start beamin*
> *Cuz talkin' bloom the Syndics way too low"*

Even before the fluttering recollection of Prospero had waxed into anticipation regarding his return, yet other Newlaw Batallions joined us. The next to come were the Grubetubes, a skilled electronic radiosonic drill team, if there ever was one. While the Slack-Zone Normalizers performed intricate star-measure gymnastics to the Seed Dancers beam garden waterway diversionary tactics, the Grubetubes began to assemble what appeared to be a radiosonic dish right smack in Alpha Center of Dawnsource Circle. "Gonna re-tool us this alpha bomb Trinity pit, they's a goody blowin' down the horyzone," they informed us.

Even as my anticipation of Prospero's imminent return was cresting on a wave of laser-crisped intensity, yet another brigade joined us, the Newlaw Logic Snackers. Unlike the earlier contingents, the Newlaw Logic Snackers came expressly for the purpose of playing with the Dawnsource Ladies.

"Zappadadoo, zappadadoo, zappadadoo," their lead chorus broke out when they came upon the ladies at Pendragon Point engaged in communication with Fa-Tsang Wronski. The Mirror-Cave Sky-Watcher had just been giving us a CHV weather report when the glee-faced Logic Snack stackers regaled us with an instant replay of his report:

> *"Weather bimbo siding*
> *on your gears of down*
> *Gather sky born divers*
> *with a grain of mountain crown…"*

And indeed, a soft lavender rain was falling, sliding down from the Peak of Darkness the morning of Prospero's arrival. It was Ixchel O'Shaughnessy, who, bent over a liquid sand painting, its aqueous turquoise coils impervious to the gently falling rain, suddenly shot her head up and shouted, "by the panfused coils of Kukulkan, they're here!"

Impressed by the accuracy of Ixchel's keening, I bolted up, scattering coral-colored sands upon the surface of the rain-spattered painting pool. Looking past Pendragon Point I spotted old Hover-babe coming down like a feather in a lavender haze. As I ran to the hovercraft, my rain poncho decided to fly in the opposite direction of my destiny, but what did it matter? Pale lavender drops dripping off my nose, my hair tangled and glued to my face, I embraced Prospero with everything that my womanhood had to give. Panfused gentleman that he was, he returned my grace with a rain-soaked elemental kiss. "Fire and water," I whispered, biting his ear with rapacious nibbles, "never fail to make me sizzle."

In the midst of his slack-zoned endearments concerning my honey-glued snare, Prospero suddenly stopped. "But hey," he said, looking well past my right shoulder, "what's all that down there, honey mom?" I turned around, and I could see what Prospero was talking about. Having taken the Moon-Wane activity for granted, I hadn't really stopped to take it all in. At the very center of Dawnsource Circle, Alpha Pit Central had sprouted a circular frame five meters high. Despite the rain, the Grubetubes were fast at it, swarming over the piece like ants.

The tent city surrounding Alpha Pit Central had tripled in size since Prospero's departure. An occasional squall would lift its gaily adorned banners for a moment and then let them collapse in a soggy droop. In the distance, more like an apparition than a retinal reality, the Radiosonic Beam Gardens were taking form. The blurred hazy lines of canal markers etched at the foot of the Peak of Darkness gave birth to two beam band floral beds, each angling into the mist in pursuit of its own rhythm.

After a gladsome settling in period that ran for three days, the Lords and Ladies of Panfusion endeavored to assess what had been set in motion at Dawnsource Circle. This we achieved at the moment of the Capricorn-Aquarius transit. Having completed an open-air banquet celebrating the Re-grube-ing of the Wandjinas and the Newlaws, the whole lot of us, some one hundred in all, decided to enter circle time. Tara and Poonie acted as center-channel triggers. As their faces shifted into samadhi-bath re-laxation, the two concentric circles fell silent. The new moon was just tilting behind the Peak of Darkness offering the mountain scene light. Squeezed between Prospero and David Monongye, I let the thought-forms flow out of my channels until my interior became bathed in translucent silence.

Then it came. "Bliss snared in a wartime-zone again, eh?" However, it was not the familiar voice of Cornelius Higgenbotthom Varuna-d'Oro who spoke. Instead we were engaged and outraged by a new amplifier from the CHV, Candace Helicia Velatropa, "a good-time Mom," she assured us.

As soon as I had registered that we were receiving from the Amazon end of the spectrum, I settled down for the transmission.

"Hell'u'va crew you are," the good-time Mom from CHV blurted out, then quickly covered her tracks. "But you know what they used to say in the knowledge pots of old Atlantis, 'when you're ahead of the game, look out for fame.'" Following a throat-clearing chuckle that was good natured enough, Candace Helicia Velatropa prepared for another brain-snapping lift-off which triggered a 2cc adrenalin sweep of my neuro-sensory system.

"If it's weapons that warriors use, just make sure they don't come equipped with aluminum fish-tail swept-back Apollo fins. Nature doesn't make the same mistake twice, so it's up to you to turn this one around. Otherwise it's: 'forget it, DNA! Take a powder! There are other star systems all over the place, so why don't you just float on down to NGC 4486 and see what's cooking in Virgo!'" CHV laughed to herself, a laugh that ran the scale up and down then faded to a quick grunt. "Yeah, if you Newlaw An-cients want to keep this ship afloat, it's socko boffo up the decks—or nothing! Besides, we're through wringing our hands and crying about your petty indulgences. And don't get the uppity idea you're the only planet I'm talking to right now either."

The Slack-Zone Newlaws were rippling with a low, "hutter, hutter, hutter," by the time the CHV had slammed this last one across.

"Ok, Genotones, you got the ace card on that one, but slow down, I'm not through yet." Candace did one of her larynx-primping pauses, then, specifically going for the Slack-Zoners in a basso buffo tone of voice that must have completely tickled the heart of every last Logic Snacker among them. She delivered on the spot. "Geofication begat domestication, domestication begat mystification, mystification begat self-mastication and the whole thing becomes unisonic through duastication. So damn the duassed-dew, and do it!"

That was it. She shot it straight and pithy. And no one missed it. A slight tremor jumped from the Slack-Zone Circle to the Dawnsource Circle, and became magnified in the spastic convulsions which Poonie and Tara simultaneously experienced before our eyes. It was as if some tremendous force had jerked their left hands, and releasing them with a whiplash, sent a jagged lightning-like bolt of energy that circulated thrice through their neuro-muscular systems. Then, just as suddenly as it began, it ended. Poonie and Tara resumed their star-catching grins, and the voice of Candace Helicia Valatropa was doing the wind-up.

"Well, you've certainly all been sweet," she ho-hummed her way to the finish-line. "Reminds me of some episodes we're having over on a Guest Star in Arcturus. As long as you remember you're just a bunch of nobodies, you can't go wrong. And when the name Trident Brigade becomes as common on the monitor screen as the code date in its upper left-hand corner, you might also recall the good-time mom herself singing to you these lines from the Saga of the Petal-Pearl Mothers of Pataliputra:

> *"...in Unisonia Panharmonic*
> *the heart-forged weapon took fine form*
> *while in beam beds radiosonic*
> *the mothers kept the born unborn."*

The deep tender-rich voice of Candace Helicia Velatropa faded out into a patch-work of galactic clouds. After hearing the last lines of her song, my heart went with her.

The late winter days passed, aromatic with household smells and duties. It was good to be domestic at long last. Too many years in the PAN-syndic theater zones had made me more than ready for the simple, tapestries pleasures of our life in the yurt at Dawnsource Circle. It was with the deepest pleasure that I discovered that Prospero's slugsoup-brained humor could only be matched by a tender, nurturing caring, that I had previously thought inconceivable in a man.

Our domestic pleasures were made all the more poignant and fragile by the fact that Trident Brigade responsibilities snatched us often from the confines of our mutually woven happiness. But that was all right. Prospero and I eagerly shared the delight in being so integrally involved in Project Code Word RED.

It was scarcely a week after our communication with Candace Helicia Velatropa that Esquivel and Dawnstar Monongye burst into our yurt. Prospero was still lying in the sleeping mat, sipping his Sonora cacao-cafe roast, his tight wavy hair standing three fingers up on his dream-dazed head. I had just finished daybreak invocations, and was blowing out the candles placed on either side of the crystal ball.

"The word's out!" Esquivel was the first to speak.

"And do you know how they're describing it?" Dawnstar asked in genuine humility.

Prospero spluttered and coughed, tiny streams of cacao-cafe roast running out of his nostrils. "What in the hell are you talking about?" he roared, wiping his upper lip gently with one of my leggings.

"Syndic transmission from Haiti. The Grubetubes picked it up this morning." Esquivel explained as politely as his enthusiasm would allow him.

"But what did it say?" I interjected, feeling my curiosity coiling like a rattler ready to strike from the depths of my central channel.

"Get this," Dawnstar smiled pulling at a strand of her still uncombed morning wild black hair, "reports reaching us from PAN territory east of the Mogollon Mesa-Painted Desert agrilands inform us that a new PAN operation has resulted in the establishment of what PAN communiqués are describing as the 'World's First Autoregulatory Geoharmone Unit.' However, decoders in major Syndic Global Monitor Units, both stationary and mobile, have been quick to point out the code word similarities between this latest PAN offensive and that of the ill-fated, 'Self-Monitoring Bi-Polar Planet Count-Downs' offensive initiated in the North Atlantic some forty yearsago. Nevertheless word from Zimbabwe has it that a mission of Syndic Diplo-engineers is being readied for a trial investigatory visit to Hopi Mesa in the near future,'" Dawnstar had finished.

Like Esquivel and Prospero I sat awed as much by the accuracy of Dawnstar's reportorial memory as by her uncommon ability to speak in exactly the same brassy lilt rhythm staccato regulated monotone as the Syndic transmission.

It was the very next day that the visitations began.

Just after sky-zenith clean-up time, the denizens of Dawnsource Circle all began to drop their activities and listen intently, heads cocked in the air. There it was, first the drums, then as if it were playing on the moon, the distant creakity sound of a mobile organ. As the sounds grew closer, the Dawnsource denizens carefully put down whatever they were working with, and began moving in the direction of the sounds, which were now booming across the expanse of the wildflower bespattered Jornada del Muerto.

Then we spotted them, coming down an arroyo. At the front of the delegation were a number of men holding large banners. Predominantly yellow, but some blue and orange as well, the banners were inscribed with strange insignia, hieroglyphic code words, harmonic equations, and a smattering of calligraphic splashes. The first two of the many forthcoming diplo-engineering missions had arrived, replete with banner-bearers, audio artists, and the mysterious faces of men and women who have not only traveled far, but across many centuries as well.

Great hospitality was shown these first two missions, the one representing O Mo Lung Ring, on the far side of Mongolia, the other speaking for the bare-legged Atlantide Renegades of Tarahumara. Having served in the Psychoatmospheric batallion at Ulan Bator, Lindy McGrew eagerly greeted some of his old companions, the Sight-Sayers of O Mo Lung Ring.

"So the rabbit finally jumped from the moon to the earth," a particularly leather-faced and happily toothless O Mo Lung Ringer wheezed out as he embraced Lindy with his embroidered satin arms.

A number of reunions also occurred between the O Mo Lung Ringers and the Tarahumaras. In fact, with the arrival of the first two missions, a spirit of reunion and celebration spread over the growing encampment at Dawnsource Circle. So infectious was the spirit of our activity, that after a few days of initial information sharing, both the O Mo Lung Ringers and the Tarahumaras decided to cast their lot with us and stay on. That is, with the exception of one from each group who self-elected to return to their respective places of origin in order to establish the basis of the Dawnsource Project among their own people.

By the spring equinox, when my womb was swelling in ecstatic reduplication of the waxing moon, a number of other missions had arrived at Dawnsource Circle. Some stayed only several days, making brief visits to the radiosonic beam bed gardens and the aquaculture canals, carefully inspecting the aluminum and fiber frame construction of the Alpha Pit, or taking us aside individually and asking what they felt were discrete questions regarding power of transmission and economic stabilization. But others, like the O Mo Lung Ringers and the Tarahumaras, stayed on. These groups included the delegations from Chiapas and Lake Titicaca to the South, Halifax and Uagava Bay to the North, and most enticing of all, the Sumbawa delegation from the East Indies. Following precedent, one member of each of these groups returned to home-base for the purpose of extending the new supra-frequency network. And each go-between that departed left with the same hearty cheer and "Key! Key! OSM!" ringing in his ears.

Last, but not least, came the mission from Syndic Hierarch. Naturally, this delegation arrived first in Hopi Mesa, mistakenly assuming that PAN power still remained entrenched at the ancient Mesa. After being regaled and banqueted out of their electro-monitored gourds, the Syndic mission realized it had arrived at the wrong place. Asking permission it was granted a three-day stay at Dawnsource Circle.

For some reason, I was not surprised at all when I greeted the head of the Syndic diplo-engineering mission. Abdul-Rumi Hassan had not changed a bit. Suave, genteel and cunningly charming, even when he feigned awe and nibbled on his moustache, Abdul-Rumi exclaimed after embracing me, "Ah Francesca, I had no idea you would be involved in something of this," he paused, searching for the proper diplo-engineering phrase, "this assortedly rag-taggle theater zone. Come now, tell me what is going on here?"

I looked at Abdul-Rumi, running my eyes up and down his familiar caftaned figure, and realized he had not yet become aware of the fact that I was pregnant. Remembering Supersub's blues refrain, "you better start beaming 'cuz talkin' bloom the Syndic's way too low," I simply smiled at Abdul-Rumi and said, "Maybe it would be best if I just took you around and you saw with your own eyes."

We stepped out of the Dawnsource command yurt into the mid-morning light, fluttering, gleaming crystal laser rays shimmering randomly, a profusion of voices and laughter bounding from one point in the Dawnsource Circle tent enclave to another. Life so full and bursting, yet so mysterious, there was nothing to say.

I looked at Abdul-Rumi's face. It was as if he were seeing nothing at all. "Such a veil you wear around your heart, Abdul-Rumi. Don't you see what this is?"

"What are you getting at?" he replied, slightly startled at my accurate penetration of his facade. His eyes squinting, searched my eyes for... what? Not even he knew, so remote from himself was he in his syndiclone officialhood.

"Poor man," I thought to myself, and gently took his hand. Even before he could switch to his seductive amorous track, I had his hand on my womb-zone.

'It's new life that is here," I spoke with a sweeping gesture, as if to indicate the pot pourri of life at Dawnsource Circle. At the same time I squeezed his hand still on my belly and looked him directly in the eyes. He knew, too, what I meant, and it was the last thing he expected or wanted from me. In a flash, Abdul-Rumi Hassan's face flickered with the expression of a man who just shot his wad only to wake up and find that he had a wet dream.

Even before Abdul-Rumi could shift back into his usually well-timed syndiclonic graciousness, I gently took his hand off my belly and still holding it in mine spoke to him in soft, measured phrases, "Abdul-Rumi, when I placed this hand on my belly, I simply wanted to give you a touch of life, new life. And that's what this is all about," with a gesture of my right arm I again indicated the bustle of activity, the NASA jumpsuited Grubetubes fashioning a dish deck high above us, Tarahumara drums and Titicaca flutes blending with the odor of roast lamb and plantain leaves, the clusters of gaily colored tents and yurts, their code-glyphed pennants aflutter, the Newlaw Logic Snackers declaiming wildly as they dug a new leyline trench, filling it with all manner of things—lamb entrails and rubies among them—and lastly the O Mo Lung Ringers seated on small stools, smoking pipes and barking directives at each other, while Sumbawas, trance-faced and silent, stamped silver inlaid staffs rhythmically up and down upon the earth. But Abdul-Rumi's face remained expressionless.

"Abdul-Rumi," I persisted, "this is no scam. This is life. These are people. All kinds of people from everywhere on earth. Life. Nothing more and nothing less. There's nothing grandiose about this, no particular scheme in mind. Just people following their intelligence making themselves happy by working together." I realized there was nothing more to say. Abdul-Rumi disengaged his hand from mine and looked at me as if I were some poor waif feeding herself on a steady diet of candied kumquats.

As we eyed each other, Natasha Eisenhammer's salty Grube-laced laughter "hee-hee-heed" itself into my ears. Breaking our mutually inspired stare-down, I said to Abdul-Rumi, "Perhaps you'd be interested in meeting your star protegé once again, the greatest double agent to hit the theater zones, Natasha Eisenhammer?"

A startled smile of anticipation rushed across Abdul-Rumi's face. "Why of course. It would give me the greatest pleasure. Where is she?"

I led Abdul-Rumi toward Alpha Pit Central, "I think we'll find her with the Grubetube Electro-chemo Engineering Unit." I answered casually sashaying toward the construction zone.

"Oh, I see," Abdul-Rumi answered long after I had pointed out where we might find Natasha. He was immersed in an inspection of Alpha Pit Central Base Block and the magnificent deck which extended out several meters overhead. "Hmmm, rather crude... but... rather interesting set of stress point proportions... familiar rhythmic latitudes... however... I'm not sure...the design, no not the design... the materials... but wait..." Abdul-Rumi muttered on to himself oblivious of the few Grubetubes who had gathered behind him, miming him so perfectly that they were even anticipating his moves.

Suppressing a giggle, I spotted Natasha. She was hanging from a lateral beam within the Base Block, looking more like an orangutan than a humanoid as she skittered back and forth on the beam, shouting out an occasional directive to a motley cluster of Grubetubes and Halagonians.

"Tashy, you Grubesmeared maniacal monad gone duad," I called out to her. "There's an old friend of yours who'd like to say hello!"

Instantly, the limber-limbed beauty, more stunning than ever in her silver NASA jumpsuit, her black hair spotted with dust, her lips tinted in the crimson hue exactly complimentary to her emerald laser eyes, jumped to the ground and walked toward us, brushing her hands off on her suit leggings. Like myself, Natasha registered not the least bit of surprise when she saw the head of Syndic Hierarch Diplo-Engineering Unit, standing next to me.

"Natasha, what a delight!" Abdul-Rumi greeted her, all of his carefully monitored equipoise now planted like a moon-probe on his immaculately suave face.

Natasha eyed him up and down, her image-catching eyes flickering with mirth. Then she spoke, "Hee, hee, hee! Abdul-Rumi you old Syndic Sucker, "she roared into high Grube, "I'll bet you'se wondering how badly that alcohol affected my neuro-what-evers, huh? Hee, hee, hee, well I tell you, Rumy Toomy, it's gotten so bad my brains flew off one night and decappy-tated the moon. Han't seen the moon nor me brains since then, hee, hee, hee!" As Natasha went on, Abdul-Rumi fell back, almost stumbling over one of the Grubetubes crouched down behind him, her ear to the ground slapping a gentle rhythm into the earth with the palm of her right hand. The Syndic Hierarch's face had gone completely blank. You could have flashed any code-word on that man's face, imprinted him anyway you wanted at that moment. But no, better to let the Syndic's destiny write its own code word on that disassembled face.

"Hee, hee, hee, Roomy Toomy, remember what you're here for," Natasha gleefully brought the Syndic monitor master back to the present," what d'ya think o' this here

Ultimate Weapon? Hee, hee, hee, and you know what it is? It's a time capsule, a sun-doomed time capsule, jes' like the rest o' us, hee, hee, hee!" Doubled over with laughter, Natasha turned to go back to her work, singing in a squeaky falsetto voice, "When the sun peek over the mountain you'll be fused out 'n' bound to glow…"

Abdul-Rumi was muttering explosively to me, "What kind of psycho-rehab do you have around here anyway? Should get a Global Health Patrol unit down here… unsanitary…"

"I believe you have a meeting with Tara Andromeda and Poontutjarpa Jayavarman at 15.00 hours, Abdul-Rumi, perhaps I could escort you to their tent?" I interrupted the Syndic's low-breathed expletives.

"Of course, yes, of course," he responded, pulling himself to full height and gingerly making his way through the crowd of bemused Grubetubes.

No one was surprised either, when the Syndic Hierarch Diplo-engineering Unit cut short their visit the following day, to attend to urgent matters in Cuba.

The evening of the Syndic's departure, Poonie and Tara invited Prospero, Natasha and myself to their yurt following the post-dinner communiqué from CHV.

Lounging on the embroidered cushions around the central lamp we discussed our encounter with the Syndics.

"Couldn't take the method of direct perception, failed to grasp the logic of duastic psycho-economics, unprepared to evaluate spontaneous construction techniques, in short, trapped in the theater of enemy identity," Tara summed up the essence of what had occurred, idly fingering the opal Trident brooch which hung around her neck. "But what tickled me to oblivion was Abdul-Rumi's spilling his cup of tea when I told him that in the interest of the Kingdom we were quite prepared to allow him a permanent pass to Dawnsource Circle theater events any time he was in the area."

"That may be so," Old Poonie grunted, rolling recently picked ear wax between his fingers while squatting on his haunches as naked and pure as the day he was born. "But it is just as well he will miss the Project Code Word RED blast-off. Such a DNA packet as his can only be brought along by direct encounter. His time will come. But we must be ready. You never know how much theater such a man is capable of."

Walking arm in arm back to our yurt, Prospero stopped to pick a few wild daisies which he placed in my hair. Then, getting down on his knees before me, he kissed my belly-womb swelling, and with a roar of PAN-fused Trident laughter, shouted to the shimmering sea of midnight stars: "Welcome! Welcome to the World's First Auto-Regulatory Geoharmone Unit!" Inside, I felt the embryo twitch and shift.

"Whoever's hanging out inside of me, you woke 'im up, you mutant brained jerk!" I exclaimed, bending over and pulling at his ears. Then, with an ecstatic release, I allowed Prospero to draw me down beside him, on the dew-crested grasses of Dawnsource Circle, where, holding each other withal our strength, we counted constellations and made love, without promise, and without regret.

PART IV
TO DISCIPLINE THE
DEVIL'S COUNTRY

# PROSPERO'S TAPE LOG:
## PROJECT CODE WORD RED

It was not too long after the Spring Equinox, when the air was perfumed with cherry, orange and apple blossoms and radiosonic tigerlilies sprouted waist-deep around the outer fringe of Dawnsource Circle that we got shuttled by the magnetic shift. "Mayday! Mayday!" The bare-breasted tattooed-faced Aqua-Star Measurers came running down to the encampment, thrilled with the fact that they were the first to observe it from their vantage point on the southwest slope of Peak of Darkness.

Disengaging myself from beneath the capsule bubble atop the dish-deck of Alpha Pit Central, I scrambled to find myself a place from which to view whatever it was the Aqua-star Measurers had claimed was occurring. And then I felt it. At first I thought it must have been an earthquake. No matter how much I tried to stand, a force kept pushing at me. But it wasn't a wind. In fact, there was no wind at all, not the slightest breeze. As I struggled to my feet, a powerful vibratory shuttle whammied its way down my central channel, triggering supra frequency signals from the nucleus of every cell in my body. When that happened, I knew it was OK. Another on-line target shot from the polar meridian management company.

Locating my gravity pulsar just a hair above the navel, and not without a snicker of careless delight, I easily brought myself to a standing position. I was glad I did. Everything was in motion, yet there were no moving parts. It was just one giant wave. I caught the crest of it moving down the Chaco horizon vector. Dollops of treetops, their blossoms embedded in upward spiraling currents, skittered across the bottom of several massive dragon-bellied cumulus clouds. Each cloud reared magnificently, one behind the other, their silver-gray borders flexing with energy pulsations that made the sky appear as if it were a simultaneously charged electrical filter. My gravity pulsar almost kakked out on me as my eyes took in the fact that the sky just behind the clouds had opened up like a vagina, revealing a magnificent field of stellar constellations.

Incredulous at the fact that I was gazing at Perseus in Taurus at the same time that my biochronometer digeted 13.20 hours, I fell to my knees. At precisely that moment,

I remembered another moment some ten years ago at the El Dorado Station, maybe just after I had arrived there. I had been clambering about some rock outcroppings down the canyon. It was just after the first snowfall of the season, and I was perched in a small grove of pines. Looking up, a shaft of late afternoon light penetrated a small opening in the lacework of snow-covered pine branches. In that shaft of light countless snow particles drifted and twirled for a brief moment and then swooned into darkness along with presentiments of my bodily death.

The same numbed awe that stunned me then wove itself through my system once again. As if strung on a thread within that moment were the beads of numberless other experiences extending as far into the future as they did into the past. I felt completely humbled as tears of gratitude for this precious mortal frame coursed down my cheeks. My birth-marked solitude and vulnerability fluttered like one of those snow particles through the measureless recesses of my mind. Yet, at the same time that I experienced the unifying thread of time past and time future dissolving into the present moment, I also sensed a radial dissemination from my gravity pulsar that connected me laterally to all the star systems in which this event was simultaneously occurring.

"So that's how this one goes," I thought to myself, and with a logic-snacking grin on my face, I resumed standing position.

Just beneath eye level, a sea of tent tops and banners of every color swayed in perfect rhythm to the harmonic oscillation that was rippling through the encampment. Like myself, most everybody else around was taut as a tuning fork. The only exceptions that I spotted were the brass-and-elk hide clad O Mo Lung Ringers and the barelegged Atlantide Renegades from Tarahumara, who were randomly seated some ten meters to my upper right, beneath a multi-colored canopy. On top of each of the four supporting posts of the canopy was a gleaming human skull. Most of the members of these two groups seemed to be shaking small objects held in their hands above their heads. After three or four furious shakes and twists, the objects would be released, scattering themselves on the ground. Once the objects had settled, perhaps they were beans, each member took a sharp-pointed metallic rod and engraved lines in the ground connecting the small objects into a pattern that highly resembled a stellar constellation diagram.

While this activity went on, a single figure, the O Mo Lung Ringer ancient known as Samdong Zangpo remained upright. At least I think such wobbly weaving and spasmodic turning could be called upright. As he jerkedly wheeled around, I searched for his face, but it seemed to be missing. Gone. In its place was a spiraling vortex throwing off an occasional smattering of what appeared to be a slightly iridescent powder.

When the O Mo Lung Ringers and the Atlantides had finished their earth-print of the magnetic shift, Samdong Zangpo came to a halt. I was happy to see that his charmingly toothless, wrinkled face had returned—wispy gray beard, craggy overgrown eyebrows and dangling gold earrings—it was all there. Joining his left thumb and index figure into a circle, a gesture he held with the firmness of a rock at heart level, the old O Mo Lung Ringer swiftly extended his right arm out to his side, the index finger rigidly pointing as if it were shooting a beam.

At exactly the moment that the old O Mo Lung Ringer gave a twist to his right hand, its fingers opening and closing like a sea anemone, the magnetic shift reversed itself and in a twinkling, it was over.

As if nothing had happened, the cosmocrats of Dawnsource Circle resumed their daily activities. Oh, sure, some of them were goofing at it, but then that was nothing unusual either. Someone was always goofing at it, someone like Lindy McGrew, who, in the midst of tightening a nut or planing a board would be carrying on like a horny coyote at full moon.

"Ya see," Lindy's voice could be heard beneath the plexiglass dish that swept over the deck at a beautiful 45° curve shimmering a smokey iridescent gray, "I made a bet with Old Sight-Sayer Zangpo back at Ulan Bator, boy were those crazy days, that we'd meet again. And in his senile way, Old Zangpo, he'd be great as clown in a Syndic Psycho-rehab parlor. I can just see him doin' his psycho-vortex face number while he's showin' the kids how Vel humped the Cat Goddess, wow I hope I'm there when he does that one..."

At this point, naturally everyone stopped what they were doing to listen to the disembodied voice coming up from beneath the Plexiglass carpet. And, of course, Lindy would always oblige, the sounds of wrench twistings mingling with his rabbity huffity breath when he paused, "...so anyway Old Zangpo, he says to me, 'anyone with the brains of a rabbit, even one trained as a circus hoop jumper, could have told you that, Mr. McGrew.' Boy could he wipe you out with one of his sentence closures, I mean the old Ka Boom Pa!"

Here, everyone strained with gleeful smiles as they listened to Lindy's head bumping rhythmically against the plexiglass as he belly-whomped through another one of his funnies. "Right, so there's old Zangpo, dropping this one on me. And you know what he says?" Even though Lindy was hidden from view, you knew he could see everyone's face waiting for the punch line. "Right, you guys all there, still with me, good. Just lemme get this nut a little, hmmp, tighter, OK? So I'm standing there, old bowl-full-of-jelly McGrew, Ace Network Wipeout Artist, never left 'em out after I wiped 'em though, so there I am standing in front of old Wheeze-faced Zangpo, and he says, 'Why of course we'll meet again, McGrew, you fucked up little bunny, but when we meet again, McGrew, that'll be it. Nature never makes the same mistake twice!' And the little Mongolian fart, he just laughed all over me. But by jeezu, you know, here he is again. And damn if he's not right. Nature never does make the same mistake twice!"

As if to prove his point, we could hear Lindy scuttling out from beneath the plexi-glass dish. No one, however, was prepared for the classic exercise in shape-shifting accomplished by Lindy McGrew that afternoon, for the person that emerged was not Lindy McGrew at all. It was none other than Samdong Zanpo, his massive bear-claw necklace banging on his bony chest, shaking his finger at us, with his illusory wizened grin saying, "Now boys and girls, remember what I told you, you know, that line about how many mistakes nature permits herself?" Backing off from our surprised delight, we all returned to our tasks muttering, "uh huh, sure, you tell me what just happened."

Nevertheless every cosmocrat working in Dawnsource Circle that day knew that something had tickled the texture of events. And the question on everyone's mind, down to the last electrodrone-skulled Logic Snacker and Star-Measurer, was this: did the magnetic shift signal the implementation of Project Code Word RED? Even though the capsule dome bubble was still to be set in place, there was only one irrefutable an-swer to that question. Why, of course! And that answer only made our work go that much smoother.

By the end of the day the whole of Dawnsource Circle was swept in a wave of rapturous singing and chanting. But it wasn't the kind of rhythm that ended up on a funeral pyre of sensory oblivion. In fact, at first I wasn't even sure that what I was hear-ing came from my own mouth,

> *"From Deneb's far canals to Winnebago Shores*
> *Harmaunce and Harmonides dissolved the temple doors*
> *And decking Time and Sister Death in a two-toned winding sheet*
> *They danced with the beast*
> *and feasted the east*
> *to a triple-timed nowhere beat."*

Francesca had been on Aquaculture detail that day, up on the Velatropa-Canopus canal. She was in the same pensively elated mood I was in as she slipped through the yurt, humming the same chant line the rest of us had gotten into by the end of work detail. I was crouched over the yurt fire pit stoking up the sukiyaki griddle for my favorite concoction, Mesa Shrimp with chaparral herb sauce, braised pineapple slices and wedges of cold mango served on the side."

"Hey Prosp," she greeted me, unclasping her shoulder pack and dropping it on top of the catch-all ledge that curved around either side of the flap-trap, "you can't fool me, doing your favorite domestic doozies. Tell me, what did you make of that ripple we got today?" Before she had finished, she was already crouching next to me, with that un-adulteratedly lascivious look of hers that had me prematurely dropping the chaparral herb-sauced shrimp on the not yet hot sukiyaki griddle. But I didn't mind, they'd heat up soon enough. "Prospy, the ripple, tell me what you made of the ripple," she commanded, snapping me out of a momentary spell of the love-goonies.

"Right, the ripple," I replied, "as far as I can tell, this is it. Project Code Word RED hit the on-switch at precisely 13.20 hours today."

"Yeah, that's what I picked up too," Francesca chimed in, pushing her rich honey-hued hair back from the sea-green eyes. "It only makes sense. So what, the aquaculture project is only at mid-phase, and the capsule dome isn't even up yet. I kept thinking of what Poonie said, 'This time we're shooting it straight.'"

"Zack-lee!" I exclaimed, "and like everything else that's been going on, we're just swinging a terrestrial guide-wire to a triple timed nowhere beat. So listen, honey-pot, let's just enjoy ourselves on these yummy little shrimps, and see what happens. Nature calls the first shot and we just tag along."

Then, just as I was sinking my teeth into the hot little morsels I had prepared for our starving enzymes, Francesca began to tell me the story of Ixchel O'Shaughnessy at the Canopus pool that afternoon. "Listen, Prospy, you'll love this one. There we are, Ix-chel, myself, and a batallion of Slack-Zone Bed Seeders. Ixchel's standing there telling us the story of how her father, Moonman O'Shaughnessy, met Kukulkan at the wells of Chichen Itza. Popaloca transmission, she says. And, of course, she's doing it, telling it with all these Irish-Mayan feather flourishes of her hands. So anyway, Prosp," Franc-esca paused to drop another herb flecked, butter drooling shrimp down her gorgeous gullet, "Moonman's camped out on a Sighting Mission asleep in a clearing near the wells. He's been hot on the psychogenetic configuration of the layout of old Chichen, and along with the four others on the Mission, had been laying a line out to the wells that afternoon. So there, fast asleep in the middle of the night, something comes and wakes Old Moonman up. It's a god-damned parrot, talking one, of course, twice as big as a domestic cat fed on radiosonic mushrooms."

With great intelligence, Francesca put the shrimp dish aside and wiped her face, dappled with herb sauce, with gracious, gentle strokes of her right index finger. She then took her finger to her mouth and suavely licked it off with that provocatively limber tongue of hers. Settling herself down with a heart-rending smirk and a wink of the eye she continued. "Right, Prosp, talking red, blue, and yellow parrot. You should have seen Ixchel, doing that one, down on her ass parrot strutting, pecking the dickens out of a hobble-hopping Slack-Zone Turk-head's toes, with total poise no less. And talking just like a parrot, Ixchel's reciting what the parrot said to Moonman to get him up and moving toward the well, at midnight, too."

By the time she had reached this point in her story, Francesca had effortlessly glided from the seating cushion to parrot strutting. Her arms bent so that the hands were tucked in beneath the armpits, and with great elegance, her head cocked to the side, her mouth puckered in a fine mimicry of the parrot's sputtering beak, Francesca recited the parrot's wake up call with a voice that was pure gutter tropic:

> *"On the Delectable Isle where the Bear danced wild*
> *Spider dropped coyote into the mirror pool*
> *But if Moonman comes and retrieves his own face*
> *from that mirrored surface so cool*
> *Then the Daughters will see*
> *That what comes to be*
> *Has already been*
> *And no one knows so much as a Fool…"*

Spellbound at Francesca's imitation of Ixchel's imitation of the parrot mimicking human speech, Francesca had to snap her fingers to get me tracked back to the mainline of her tale. "C'mon, Prosp, you don't have to get so knocked out by my acting. It makes you look like a blabber-faced Logic Snacker at the point of devouring his own conclusion, not that that look doesn't become you either, Prospy," and having retrieved my attention, I got the rest of the story. "So there's this riddle-squawking parrot hopping along wildly through the underbrush, Moonman giving him full chase, but unable to keep up with this parrot, 'til they finally get to one of the sacred wells. But there's a big drop, water's at real low level, and the sides coming up from the surface are steep, and it's new moon and there's not much to see by. So the parrot says to Moonman, 'Hey, Moonman, I'm Gucumatz, I helped Cuchulain escape when the Spiderdecked Coyote, and Spidersons did in Old Harmaunce. Get on my back and I'll fly you down, see if you can retrieve your own face.'

"So Moonman hops on the parrot's downy back, and they're way down there, down the deep cenote pool. As the parrot's going around in this slow moving holding pattern, Moonman, trying to figure out how close to death he is this time, down so far the sky is just a little twinkling hole way above his head, the water so dark, with chill vapors coming up, that he's actually ready to shit. All the while parrot's muttering away, 'Dammit,' the riddle says 'retrieve your own face, not look for it, you're never going to see it in this light,' then with a sudden twist, Parrot does a quick vertical wingspan, and Moonman's dropping into the pool, two handfuls of feathers telling you how scared he was. Then splasho! Prosp, Ixchel staggers to the edge of the Canopus pool shimmering red with synthesized Japanese plankton, and with a stunned look on her face, her arms all over the place, drops into the water.

"She disappears right out of sight. The rest of us there rushed to the edge of the pool waiting for her to come up. It seems like it's been a long time and I'm getting a little anxiety pressure point in my left side, when zippo! like a porpoise diving up from the depths to see where the sun is on the horizon, out pops—you'll never believe this Prosp," Francesca shook her head, her face vividly etched with total disbelief. "Yeah Prosp, we all just fell back, made a path for, I mean get this, Prosp, for Old Uncle Wiggley himself, Lindy McGrew. As Lindy's shaking his hair, water flying all over the place, we're all groaning, 'whaaat?' c'mon! Lindy then looks at us with his rabbity-toothed grin and says 'I'm glad I'm so familiar to all of you, but you could at least have said 'hello,' maybe showed a little appreciation. After all, shapeshifting has its dangers too. But, hey, shouldn't we all get back to work?'"

Feeling as if my head had just been plugged into a vortical Ion transformer, I snorted and coughed as a wild chill ran up and down my back.

"Are you all right, Prospero?" Francesca leaned over toward me, the mirth in her eyes betraying the otherwise tender-caring expression which consumed the rest of her face.

"Oh of course," I replied, regaining a semblance of my former composure, but just you wait 'til I tell the story of how nature never makes the same mistake twice," and wagging my finger at Francesca, we both burst into those mutually rapturous smiles that had us glued to infinity.

Even before I had a chance to begin to tell Francesca what had happened on the Dish-Deck that afternoon, a brief commotion interrupted us just outside of our yurt. Then, the endearingly single-eyed head of Psychlosky popped through the entry-flap.

"Hey, Love-clones, no idle tides, but buff the deck, the name of the beast is Neuronaut Gruberites, so gown the fod-bodder and catch the dishdeck, gonna fish the moon for a side of lace," and with a charmed salutation, Psychlosky disappeared into the night. Holding my story back, we ate in silence, then departed for Alpha Pit Central.

The sight that awaited us plunged me into a state of poignant sadness. There, on the east side of the Alpha Pit Central, the construction zone had been cleared away. A circular fire trench had been dug, illuminating the fiberboard and wood beam construction of the Base-Block with the flickerings thrown off from a Ring of Fire, its flames periodically swirling, exploding, catapulting and leaping high into the air. Within the Ring of Fire was a circle of flattened earth. In the center of this circle was a mound on top of which was Grube's skull. In front of the mound was Grube's Eco-squad hat, its brim furrowed and torn with age. Behind it, set into the mound vertically, were three feathers. The same number of feathers each had been inserted to the other three sides of the mound. The whole effect was so simple and pure, it caused my heart to lurch from side to side.

Squeezing Francesca's hand tightly in mine, I allowed the wave of memories to pour over me once again: the orchid cloning, plain speaking, wise-assed guidance and companionship that Grube had provided me all those years at El Dorado Station, dumb-shambled and collapsed in a roaring 'hee, hee, heeing' heap at the bottom of my guts. At the same time, an unquenchable flame of gratitude and insight arose from that memory heap, and I knew that everything was all right.

As soon as I had divested the skull on top of the fire ring mound of its personal associations and re-invested it with its reality as a divinatory ritual object, I became aware of the fact that the whole of Dawnsource Circle was pressing around the fire ring at Base Block East. A great fervor of excitement tempered with awe charged the early evening atmosphere. Logic Snacking Newlaws who had witnessed Grube's death that night last November, pushed and squeezed to get as close as possible to the Ring of Fire. Jostling behind them were an assortment of Slack-Zoners going "hu, hu, hu, hu, hung!" as well as a contingent of Atlantide Renegades, Sumbawas and O Mo Lung Ringers, some of them shaking gourd rattles, others scraping notched sticks and ringing bells. Still others kept arriving, 'til the group swelled in size to over three hundred strong; and it was still growing.

Looking behind me to the earth embankment that marked the perimeter of inner Dawnsource Circle, I realized that we were being joined by numerous outsiders. I recognized contingents of Newlaws from Truth or Consequences, beginning to take positions atop the embankment. Also familiar to me were clusters of Mogollon Mesa Shepherds, Painted Desert Aquaculturists as well as groups of Hopi and Chaco Canyon engineering units. They also took positions around the top of the inner circle embankment. With the exception of the usual goof-prone members of the Slack-Zone and Newlaw brigades who persisted insetting up a most unusual call-and-response riff between at least five or six contingents scattered through the growing crowd, the mood remained awesomely quiet, expectant perhaps.

"Boo, wa!"

"Hey, hu, hu!"

"Grube ska!"

"Hey, ho, ho!"

"Boo Wah, ho, ho, hung!"

The contrapuntal riff soon seemed to shimmer in the air, creating a lacework effect that echoed hauntingly in the audio canals. As the five-part riff rose yet another octave it became fused with a new sound, that of a lone coyote howling majestically, attuned to the heart plunged pain and yearning of every being doomed to the cycle of birth and death.

Three times the coyote let loose its space-piercing cry, three times did I feel as if I had been stripped clean of every desire, ransacked of every hope and fear, robbed of every last longing for comfort and bodily well-being.

As the howling and the chanting ceased, all that remained of me was a quivering sack of flesh falling to its knees, speechless and without a thought in the world to taint its mind with interpretation or speculation. Beneath the star-painted sky of Dawnsource Circle, an all-penetrating silence had come down for a landing, sending its unmarked probes into the heart of everyone present. As the wave of quiet crested and the sounds of exhalations and murmurs began to pick up again, I became aware of the fact that in the place of the Grube skull was the coyote which had been howling. It sat there on its hind legs its silvery brown tail curling around its left side, its front paws planted firmly on top of the earthen mound, the three blue feathers in front of it quivering ever so slightly from the heat waves of the Ring of Fire. Moving its head from side to side as if sizing up the nature of the masses of humans which he faced, the coyote's ears suddenly pricked up, and his nose wrinkled in anticipation of something imminent approaching him. Yet there was nothing to be seen.

The sense of anticipation was broken by the sound of a flute, advancing from the rear toward the Ring of Fire. Like everyone else I craned my neck, only to see the almost dwarf-sized wool tunic-clad figure of Alfonso Purimac making his way through the hushed crowd. Damned if he wasn't blowing the same riffs I had blown so many times over at El Dorado station. When he reached the flames, Alfonso merely stepped through them and stopped in front of the coyote, who proceeded to sniff the flute player's crotch. Concluding with a series of loon-like flutters, Alfonso whirled around and faced us. The coyote scampered down from atop the mound and crouched at Alfonso's feet. The simple big-nosed high-cheeked Andean features of Alfonso Purimac gleamed brightly as he chanted, "Hey ya, ho, ho, hung!" We all chanted back the same chant. Then Alfonso spread his arms out wide, his soft violet-colored tunic streaked with the wildly reflecting light of the flames. Then softly, almost shyly, the Andean chanted:

> *"Hey ya, ho, ho, hung! See now how the Red City glows*
> *Hey ya, ho, ho, hung! Imprinted with light from magnetic snows*
> *Hey ya, ho, ho, hung! Performed by death the beast returns*
> *Hey ya, ho, ho, hung! Returned we go where nothing burns."*

Alfonso's chanting was smeared with the same poignancy that I felt when I first saw the Grube skull at the center of the Ring of Fire, the same yearning woven into the coyote's piercing cry. Without further word, Alfonso picked up his flute and began playing again. For a long time he played, while the constellations wheeled high overhead. For a long time he played as the dew dappled grasses vibrated to his every tone, and heart muscles melted to the subtle harmonic overtones of that plaintive song, endlessly variated through the empty expanse of the Dawnsource night. And then he was done. Taking his flute and placing it in a small bag tied to his shoulder, Alfonso Purimac leaned over to the coyote and stroked its sleeping head a few times. Walking back through the Ring of Fire, Alfonso Purimac was swiftly absorbed by the crowd.

The next morning when I arrived for work detail at Alpha Pit Central, the Ring of Fire was still burning. But the coyote was gone, and the Grube skull was nowhere in sight. However, from the top of the mound where the skull had sat, green shoots were pushing through the packed earth, green shoots and a few small rosy buds. I recognized those buds. They were the buds of the Rocky Mountain orchid which Grube had cultivated into existence. As I contemplated this sight, Lindy McGrew came up from behind and knocked his knees into mine so that I almost toppled over into the Ring of Fire.

"Some launching for Code Word RED, huh, Prospy, hee, hee, hee!" Before I could do anything the Ace Wipe Out Artist was already scrambling up the side of Base Block East, Grube's Eco-squad hat bouncing upon his rabbity head.

To be continued...

Exactly two weeks after the Code Word RED Neuronaut Grubeskull rites, a half-moon period filled with a heart-rending sweetness reflective shared by all the cosmocrats of Dawnsource Circle, the Wandjina-Trident twenty were awakened by the psychic intercom. It was Supersub and Fa-Tsang Wronski with their last directive.

"Good morning, Dawnsource skylubbers, Wandjina-brained sightsayers, unrollers of the earth-lord dreamtime, wake up slime has finally arrivadercied…"Prospero and I both sat up simultaneously blinking at each other. The two Mad Cave Finders had never pulled one like this before. And I knew all the other Wandjina-Trident twenty were experiencing the same sensation. Prospero and I smiled at each other as the psychic intercom weaving of Supersub's and Wronski's voices continued.

"I've got neuronaut reading 33.6 degrees North, 106.7 degrees west, do you read me?" Prospero and I both nodded in unison. "Good, cuz glad wide tidings from the stupendastic Cave Brothers has jes' toboganned'er noggins into utterful flutterfall awakenments!" Prospero's sleepy eyes totally burst open with the last sky-line of Supersub's jive. No sooner did we catch our breath, then Wronski was fast at it.

"Awakenment tune-ups prevent post-cosmocharge comedown. This was irrefutably proven in Arcturus star system 108X. No reason why it can't be done here, so Dawnsource sight-slayers, time to move over, 'cuz the Madfindin' Cavebrothers are comin' to clown, and it's time you all gazed the wall a glaze of ion-empty filaments, its Neuronaut Moonwhole Retreats for you radiosonic fruitblends… so here's the direct shot, the on-line retooty, toot, toot, after you fod the bod its slake fast, thump the cosmocrats the skull barewell. Set yer compass due southwest. Truth will gauge yer consequence and set you right a madfindin cave solo-riff-room… super… for one Moonwhole you'll stay the beast, but front you debt, one seven-jammin' twine you'll be before its radiosonic solstice lift-off time. So Dawnsource Magnetoblends, you cut the cake, in twenty-four we'll cop the take…"

With an improvisational flourish, hums, squeaks and guttural resonances, the communiqué was over. The message was loud and clear: Pack up and leave. What Fa-Tsang and Supersub had been doing for the past six months, we were now to set forth and accomplish in a span of four weeks, one Moonwhole. Even before breakfast, Prospero and I were packing a few garments apiece. At the same time that we looked forward to the retreats, both of us felt a certain sadness at being separated from each other for such a long period of time.

Prospero was especially solicitous of my pregnant condition, but I assured him, I knew everything was on course, and besides, I confidently informed him, "I can't think of any pre-birth prep for whomever this little Dawnseer inside of me is, than to gaze the wall a glaze of ion-empty filaments. You can't knock that one can you Prosp," and with a gentle nudge I had him sprawling on the floor, the cup of Mogollon cacao-cafe roast miraculously clutched in his hands without a spillage of a single drop.

Following ablutions and a light, but tasty breakfast of braised pineapple and two slices of toasty hot acorn Pumpkin bread smeared with mesquite honey and melted butter, Prospero and I diddy-whanged over toward the orchid-flowering Skull-Spell Grube-Ground Fire Ring for a work detail insight session. But as we anticipated, things this morning were taking a different course. Instead of the usual round-robin recitation of the previous night's dreams pensively bounced around the Grube-skull Fire Ring by the Rotational Directors and Activity Captains of Project Code Word RED, Ya Emme and Aldebaran, hands clasped to their hearts, were standing in front of the group. Realizing that we were the last to arrive, while giving each other discrete ass-whacks, we nimbly took our places in the crescent-shaped group facing Ya Emme and Aldebaran.

Each was dressed in an immaculate white tunic, whire leggings and brilliantly polished black brigade boots. Ya Emme, her face a luxuriant ebony orchid in the gleaming mid-May sun, was the first to speak. Her hands still clasped at her heart, she intoned, "Hey, ya, ho, ho, hung! At about 06.30 hours Dawnsource seers and sundry cosmo-crats, the madfinding cave brothers shot the Wandjina brained-ones a straight shot." Then, gently taking her glistening brown arms and letting them flutter gently at either side, she eased higher on the neurofrequency beam that shot directly from her heart into the hearts of each and everyone of us.

"Yes," she continued, a preciously poignant smile carved into her face, "the time has chimed for the Dawnsource Sightsayers to utterful flutterful cut the cake a Moon-whole, and solo gaze the wall a glaze of ion-empty filaments, now." She paused; it was Aldebaran who took the issuance of the directive. As he began to speak he unclasped his hands and with an expanding circular motion, brought his arms outstretched at either side, the elbows bent, the palms of the hands receiving the sun.

"Hey, ya, ho, ho, hung!" Aldebaran spat out, his pointed black beard shot with threads of gray bouncing ever so lightly as he spoke, "it's an Arcturus 108x pattern we're threading with. That's a simple situation. Since everyone here is sufficiently skilled in syntropic bonding, doing what must be done today presents no problem. The moment we leave, in approximately one hour, phase two of Code Word RED will be initiated. In 24, the mad finding Cave Brothers will be here to cop the take."

As Aldebaran wound up what he had to say, Ya Emme glued herself to his left side, and with a wonderful flourish both sang the conclusion to the morning directive:

> *"So it's bye, bye, age and death and youth*
> *The counterwall cactus codes the truth*
> *The sky beam sargeants with their masks of fire*
> *Trace the road trackless beyond desire…"*

As their harmonically contrapuntal voices whispered the last syllable, a great war-cry broke out,

> *"Key, key, OSM! Ka, ka, CHV! Ko, ko us 'n'them!"*

Our send-off was jubilant beyond any expectation. Even as we approached old Hoverbabe, a kilometer away due west of the Velatropa canals, we could still hear the drums and the flutes, the electrodrone thumping, the sonorous waves of voices thrilled with the rhythms igniting everyday work.

It was strange going back to Truth or Consequences. An entire hemicycle of the annual ring had passed since those dark, stormy moments when we took skull-palace. I know we were all examining our remembrances as we floated belly down in the hovercraft viewing bubble, floated like a cloud of promises over the flowing lava beds of Jornada del Muerto, floated with our cargo of Wandjina-stained seers to the temporary oblivion of cave-sitting emptiness. An occasional hawk swept out of the blue. Its wings quiveringly outstretched trying to maintain itself in our air stream, the inquisitive hawk hovered before each of our faces—penetrating radiant yellow hawk-eyes bonding our destiny with a space-piercing stare.

Then we were over Elephant Butte reservoir. Flowing cottonwoods, saguaro and yucca were all filigreed with the lacy shadows cast by the giant White Sands Palm Ferns. Then my eye caught it: four banks of curved solar resonators, immense and shimmering constantly pulsing waves of metallic pastel hues. These solar resonators were spaced in the form of a large circle which focused itself on what used to be the central electro-arcade of Truth or Consequences. The electro-arcade . capriciously assembled amplifiers, echo dishes and ion synthesizers, had disappeared. In its place was a simple series of three concentric circles etched large into the ground. Gutteral spectral reminiscences of the night of my first arrival here flashed across my synapses causing a shudder to run through me. This jagged adrenalin bolt then melted warmly into the memory of my reunion with Prospero.

As we touched down, I became aware of the fact, that not only was the electro-arcade gone, but so were the vast majority of tents and yurts. In place of the brilliantly colored tent city was a large meadowland lush with tall green grass bending and rippling in occasional waves, dotted with prickly pear cactus, daisies and voluptuously budding sunflowers. Only to the south, near the slap-dash Apollo Boneyard constructionary works, were there still a group of tents. Their silver and black banners snapped lackadaisically in an occasional hot gust of wind that swept up the Rio Grande valley.

Popping my head out of the entry hatch, I, like those who had already jumped down to the grassy-sparkled earth ahead of me, became aware of a brigade of Newlaws rushing through the meadowland in our direction. To a one they were all shave-headed, and like us, they numbered twenty in all. Unlike us who must have appeared like a giant white arrowhead steadfastly holding its own in the wind which must have been blowing at thirty knots, the Newlaws were naked and more brilliantly tattooed than ever. As they came closer I saw that each wore a unique set of adornments, this one had a circle jade pendant between her writhing flame-colored breasts. That one carried a staff of intricately laser-incised aluminum, topped with a triad of delicately modeled ancient buff colored telephone wire insulators.

Once they had formed into an arrowhead pointed directly at our arrowhead formation, the lead person, a woman, broke rank and approached us. To say that she was large would be as dull as describing a mainline neural streamer as being syntropically accurate. Shining brass buttons studded the crown of feathers that sprouted from each of her tattooed biceps. Her breasts were decorated with concentric patterns that favored orange and turquoise hues. Similar concentric patterns emanated from her navel, while the same brass-button studded feather crown bands clasped her massive thighs. Her legs, like her arms, were tattooed with the same electrochemo-circuitry design patterns. She was every bit as voluptuous as she was tall, and in the intense mid-spring sunlight she glittered like a monitor chip bathed in black light.

"Trident Counter-Brigade," she began, her right arm raised in military salute, her left hand on her hip, "Truth or Consequences 'Clean-Up and Wandjina Radar Unit,' at your disposal. Kali Ali of the Base-Line Bunt issuing this directive. Lodes and Ladlays, the two Mad Finders themselves cast the bones of your hover blooming. Welcome!" Kali Ali now assumed a stance of repose, her hands clasped behind her back, her legs spread apart in a sensuously muscular rendition of a solar resonator base-frame.

Sizing up a few specific members of our brigade with her piercing blue eyes, eyes made all the bluer deep set as they were in her golden ochre-colored face, she gave us a quick info-riff. "Keenin' how's at min' a quarteen of tridents have tripped this deck in dormant slimes, it might pass yer frains to keen what consequences truth has laid upon this badlaw land. Grube-scammed and tight with the solar suction, at solstice reruns we detubed the arcade and laid a sunring round electrodrone central. Sling-ing the moon a bladder of twine, mescalled 'n' ready, we doomed three ring-a-dings on Outlaw ground. This baddied the eeries from Aquarius to Pisces, and by equinox the Newlaws split. 'Through all lands 'n' prelaw climes we gonna raise the deck a killer decibel or two,' they chimed 'n' rhymed and pushed the fins across the sweet sunline. That left us, the Counter Trident Brigade plus two, the cave slave twins, and we all keen their chemosight, psyche boulders dropped fro' blouds'n' boned to bring the sky to you." Completing her info-riff transmission, Kali Ali, both hands on her hips, lurched her loins with a couple of awesomely lascivious spasms. Woman that I am, I could only admire the handsome style and forthright manifestation of her feminine talents.

In order to respond to the Newlaw Amazon's salutations, the cosmos cam two, Squeaker and Cyclone, broke rank and approached the sense drooling beauty. Their tawny-hued, twin-domed skulls alive with tiny surface veins bobbed evenly as they jogged forward to meet the Clean-Up Queen. Facing her, they both gave a military salute and fell to an immediate at-ease position. Poonie, who was at the head of our Brigade and now, right behind Squeaker and Cyclone, mimed their every movement as they addressed the Clean-Up Queen, Kali Ali.

"From bow to stern the trident twenty fix their skies on the birds you blow from mid-May zenith. And sides, yer bod bids bright the hormone sacks; you never booked such a groin even when electrodrone bestoned our ears!"

I loved it whenever the Cosmoscam Two geared their larynxes at such fine pitch. They were a paragon of duastic bond jive.

"As for the Newlaw gents 'n' genties who've split the deck 'o' truth targeting all-lands and pre-law climes to rhyme their consequences, well, that's Project Code Word RED, 'n' we skive that lode, it keeps the mad from going dead!" Their tattooed hands on each other's shoulders, Squeaker and Cyclone broke into one of their pitifully wheezy fits of laughter. As the Cosmoscam Two maneuvered their way through this little spasm, Kali Ali was attempting to ignore Poonie who had crawled on his hands and knees through the knee-high meadow grass and had his nose right up the Amazon's quivering crotch.

Regaining their composure, Squeaker and Cyclone got to the point. "What the cave bros mainlined to us must be a fading memory bubble to you, but that's the shot that called the Trident twenty to this deck. So the signal's yours to flare the Moonwhole scam, no imprint without emptiness. Take us Kali and bowl this brigade its sign-off Ali." With a majestic flourish and a bow, Squeak and Cyclone tiptoed slack-zone style to their respective places in the Trident arrow formation.

With a quick twirl and twist flexing her scorpion tattooed buttocks for our delight, Kali Ali kicked Poonie aside and gave a shrill, haunting call. The members of the Counter Trident Newlaws all broke rank. One each of their members was assigned to each one of us. My guide was a tremulously lithe charmer with dreamy vagabond eyes. Electro-chemo circuitry patterns covered the right side of her body while a floating series of red, white and blue concentric ring formations decorated her left side. This bald-domed vixen, who called herself "Sheryl Ann of the Piper's PAN," addressed me, her hoarse, throaty voice seductively winning my affections and appreciation, "Wandjina babe, honey dew dropsy dripper, I'm yours." I could see how this one must really have had her way with men. Nevertheless she possessed a charm that I could only describe as being sexually transcendent.

Hopping on the back of her laser scooter parked toward the edge of the Clean-Up encampment we rode off to the west of Truth or Consequences. Our destination was Canyon of the Caves on the sunrise slope of Reed's Peak in the Black Range. There, on either side of a shallow canyon at some 2400 meters elevation in a landscape dotted with red rocks, juniper shrub pines, yucca and prickly pear cactus, I could make out a series of shallow openings, cozy rock overhangs and actual caves. This winding grouping of rock apertures extended up the canyon a kilometer or so.

Resting the scooter beneath a ledge of twisted rock striations, I hesitatingly followed Sheryl Ann, who nimbly picked her way up the sheer rock wall. And there it was. Carved in clear decode type on a rock overhang were the words, "Five Flower Cave of Supraneural Renunciation." Beneath the overhang was a rock cleft that ran two meters deep into the mountain side. At the very back of it I could make out a small shrine box covered with a simple blue woven cloth. Placed at the center of this box was a mirror plate with the sample sand-painted white, red and blue concentric rings. Resting on that was a crystal ball three fingers in diameter. On either side of that were two red candles. In front of the mirror plate and crystal ball were three small earth-colored unglazed raku fired ceramic bowls.

"Baked 'em meself at Moonripe sand calls," Sheryl Ann proudly confided to me pointing at the bowls. The bowl on the left contained cornmeal and a few peyote buttons, while the bowl in the center held sand and a stick of piñon incense. The third bowl was filled to just short of the brim with water. Floating on the surface were two or three pale violet and yellow orchid petals. At the base of the shrine was another container, like the cut-off end of an old ballistic shell. In it were old-style phosphorescent matches. The tiny cleft cave also contained a seating mat and several blankets. "For bod fod," Sheryl Ann spoke, gesturing to a dark niche to the left of the shrine box, "you'll have two o'the Unisonia Cakes, one for your honeydewed frame, the other for the slightsayer boomin your womb." Sure enough, as I peered into the niche I saw two giant five-tiered cornmeal, honey, acorn and herb paste cakes, each precisely in the architectural shape of what appeared in Prospero's slugsoup vision. Next to them rested a bloated gourd flask, and several sacks of fruit, nuts, and sundry shrine supplies.

Seeing that I was properly attended to, I set down my travel bag, and turned to look out over the Canyon of the Caves. Sheryl Ann was already standing on the front ledge of what was to be my home for the next four weeks. "This hole'll keep the Moonwhole here, long as you keen the close 'n' near," Sheryl Ann laughed her jism-smeared laugh.

Taking her hand to thank her for her services, she looked at me with those eyes that teasingly kindled my own passion and said, "The trick's yours to turn, Wandjina blossom. When Moonwhole whacks you down the deck, it'll be me that gives you a glad thunking thump, so let it be sister, and brood yer skies the canyon scene."

As we stood there holding hands in the mid afternoon lizard-warming sunlight, Sheryl Ann pointed out to me the sites of the nineteen other caves, along with their names, asking me to guess to whom each cave belonged. The beauty and ingenuity of the names of the caves matched with their inhabitants was such that I immediately committed the whole thing to memory. On the feminine side, after my cave, the others in order were Fire Star Dancer's Cave of the Moving Dawn (Tara), Rockledge Cave of Nothing Undone (Doorlumia), Dogstar Cave of Infinite Remembrance (Ya Emme), Delectable Isle of Feathered Darkness Cave (Ixchel), Skullsky Skewers Cave (Natasha), Cave of No Sign-off (Squeaker),Skydrone Bottoms Cave (Blaze), Cave of Red Rock Speaking Light (Claudia), and Cave of the Spider Dream Song (Dawnstar).

Across from us on the northern or male side of the canyon, the caves were: Noble Faster's Cave of the Direct Shot (Prospero), Kangaroo Catcher's Cave of the Hidden

Serpent Breath (Poonie), Cave of the Single Slightsayers Insides(Psychlosky), Cave of the Coyote Sniffing Sight Line (Cyclone), Madfinding Rabbithole Cave (Lindy), Dome of the Grave Cave (Grunt), Cave of Unending Blackhole Brightness (Aldebaran), Nowhere Flowering Cactus Cave (Esquivel),Cave of the Desert Starlamp (Ramakrishna), and, finally, Lizard Lounger's Heart Cave (David).

When it was clear that the other Counter-Tridents were gathering to return to Clean-up Camp at Truth or Consequences, Sheryl Ann of the Piper's PAN embraced me fondly and with a flip of her tattoo grinning shaved-head, called out to me as she scampered down the rock ledge, "Be beamin' you honeycomb!"

With a shiver I turned back to my Moonwhole quarters, more a cleft in a rock than a cave. It was as if a chill had ricocheted down the Canyon bouncing from cave entrance to cave entrance. I allowed the tremor of loneliness to take over my nervous system; I allowed it to rush up from my heart; I allowed it to move my legs and place my body before the shrine. This was what I was here for, might as well make friends with it.

Laying down my sheepskin silk embroidered travel bag, I knelt before the simple shrine, and drank it in again: the sand-painted mirror, the crystal ball, the two large red candles placed in elegantly modeled jadeite holders, the three simple bowls—the body bowl, filled with cornmeal and a few old peyote buttons looking like cellular parchments, the speech bowl with a fine tapered cone of piñon incense and pure white sand granulated to powder by the irresistible force of emptiness. Finally there was the heart bowl, a pond of limpid mountain water adorned with a casual sprinkling of iridescent orchid petals. That last one said it all to me.

Leaning down to the ballistic bowl match container, with my right hand I pulled out one of the old style matches, its pine branch body immaculately grooved and trimmed. With my left hand I picked up the touchstone, a sturdy, naturally formed pestle with memories extending way beyond the jurassic era with its funky adolescent dinosaur batallions. Striking the match on the irregularly surfaced touchstone, its phosphorescent flare ignited the cool cave interior, instantly flashing back at me in holographic brilliance from the crystal sphere on the shrine. My nostrils perked by the brief burst of sulphur, I leaned over to each of the candles and lit them. Then blowing out the match and laying it down behind the ballistic bowl, I picked up the fine tapered incense and held it in the even flame of the left candle. In a few moments the incense tip glowed, emitting a quivering miniature mountain of rapidly dancing flame. Placing it back in the buff colored speech bowl, I settled down on the simple red cushion. Still feeling the chill, I wrapped one of the soft alpaca blankets around my shoulders and rested my mind.

Whether it was called mind-tracking, mixing breath with space, meditation or wall-gazing, the practice of sitting in isolation had been basic to PAN training. However, it had been introduced to me only sporadically. A few sessions long ago at Shasta Abbey and the brief period at Marpa Mesa when I was at Hopi were about the sum of it for me, though I had always remembered Tara's instructions: "Nothing was ever accomplished without first experiencing nothing. Just sit, Francesca," I could still see her face, a warm ochre ladle of kindness, as she spoke to me. "Observe your mind and let it go out with your breath. Then, just rest in that. Whatever you have forgotten, if it's important, it will come back. And if something new comes in just let that go too. If it's good and right it won't leave you because you're good and right. Know that, Francesca. Know that and don't be afraid."

My previous mind-tracking exercises, however helpful, had been devoid of the cutting nowhere edge that characterized and colored all of my experiences during the Neuronaut Moonwhole Retreat at Five Flower Cave of Supraneural Renunciation. At the same time that I felt the contents of my being skillfully, but gently sliced into sheer micro ribbons that gradually disappeared from sight, I also melted into waves of measureless kindness. While the kindness was experienced as so many facets in a diamond of utter clarity, there was nothing that was impervious to it. Blades of grass, pebbles and even grains of sand shone with that kindness. And that same kindness emanated in vibrant, luminous patterns from the weave of the blanket that fell over my lap. Kindness I felt toward all things was only kindness paid back. For the very texture of things, the cellular vortex of forms spewing forth endlessly from what might as well have been but a momentary dot in space, yes, the tissue and fabric of everything was kindness, kindness and compassion itself: what and whoever I was was inseparable from this all-embracing, all-healing warp and woof of kindness.

Just sitting, I experienced the kindness of the earth supporting my posture. This very same earth-kindness supported me when I got up to stretch and take a walk among the jonquil and daisy-blooming canyon sides. Or the kindness would visit and sink into me in the formless form of the bird-singing, cloud-lazing sky pushing beyond any hope of measurement into the vastness of extraterrestrial space. And at night, it was the kindness of the stars that held me spell-bound before I slept with sparkling chills of fathomless recognition.

As I slowly accommodated myself to the clarifying isolated intensity of allowing my being, my identity itself, to be ceaselessly shredded by the ego cleaver of compassionate kindness, itself sprouting from sheer emptiness, I came to understand why the Neuronaut Moonwhole Retreat was so significant a part of Project Code Word RED, Phase II. This insight began its approach toward the end of the day after I had been at Five Flower Cave for about a week. My attention had been caught by a magnificent swirl of transparent blue smoke spiraled forth in a final effort from the incense cone before it was reduced to a pile of spent ash. Something about the swirl of smoke, so passionately momentary, so painfully vivid, and yet so unreal, undid me completely. As I keened that the smoke had emptied itself into space leaving not the slightest trace of its former presence, I experienced myself no different from the smoke gone nowhere.

I shuddered and jolted forward, and spoke aloud in a matter of fact manner, as if I were delivering a communiqué: "smoke gone nowhere." I could hear my voice resonating in the cave, passing through the pathways and fissures of million-year-old rock, and then like the smoke, gone nowhere. It passed, and I sat for another hour, 'til the candles began to sputter and gutter, globs of red wax flowing like lava over the streamlined discs of lustrous green jadeite which adorned the darkness of the shrine in Five Flower Cave.

When I prepared myself for sleep, I felt as happy with my realization, "smoke gone nowhere," as a child with her favorite rag doll tucked next to her pillow. Indeed, neuronaut bliss tingled through every nerve in my body. And sure enough, that night I dreamed a wondrous dream. Kali Ali the Clean-Up Queen and Sheryl Ann the Piper's Pan, their womanly bodies resplendent and glowing, as if their nervous systems had been tattooed to their skin, came to me. Descending through the roof of the cave, they settled down before me.

Crouching, idly making designs on the cave floor, it was Kali Ali who spoke first. "If you don't keen moan-assed, you'll never flex dew-assed." Kali Ali asserted this simple declaration with an air of triumphant finality. Then, wiping her eyes with her hands as if taking off a blindfold, Sheryl Ann, her voice as throaty as ever, replied, "Honeycomb beam bomb got it, Kali Ali. She keened the nowhere triple timed beat. Now she's ready to play lift-off sightslayer inside the beast."

As Sheryl Ann spoke, Kali Ali stood up, her hands on her Amazon hips, and, fixing her penetrating eyes on Sheryl Ann, Kali Ali chanted enigmatically, "Only when, lonely when she's ready to fix; the dynamo nothing she twitches her fist." No sooner had she spoken, then she spiraled away, like the transparent swirl of blue incense smoke, she spiraled into emptiness. Standing up, her hands on her belly-womb, Sheryl Ann threw her clean-shaven head back, and with the greatest most joyful confidence she cried out to me: "Glorious! Glorious! Glorious!" Then she, too, was gone.

I woke up with a start. I felt as if I had been smeared with the kindness of these two apparitional creatures. Outside I could hear a coyote howling its heart out to the moon. Gathering a blanket around my naked embryo-bearing body, I went outside the cave and found the flat sitting rock atop the rock ledge separating me from the Canyon proper. Feeling as if all worldly desire had evacuated me and fled like an army panicked by the threat of the ultimate weapon, I allowed my attention to graze among the great mosaic of star-patterns in the velvety black sky.

As my gaze floated casually from Orion to the Great Dipper, and then onto Vela, I felt my life release itself. And I saw that like the stars, the pattern of my life was a mosaic, without beginning and without end. The suffering of my demented mother sat side-by-side with Natasha's furious face as she abandoned me to the Cape Wrath Rehab center, the Radiosonic Beam ignition last winter solstice spewed forth from the mouth of my unborn child. There was no such thing as the past or the future. The child I carried within me was every bit as ancient as the canyon walls, if not more so. And then, in a finger-snapping time slice, I saw it: that the experiment begun at Dawnsource Circle, call it Project Code Word RED, or whatever you wanted, would prevail not because of the cleverness of our strategies, but simply because we had the boldness to know and declare that we were complete nobodies. Even if we "succeeded" at getting the Syndics to scrap their unwieldy Mobile Program Monitor Units and lose it all in a mutant electrodrone PAN sensory outrage, we would still be nobodies.

Just as the fantastic turquoise violet-orange light of the rising sun dissipated the mosaic of stars, so this nobody-nowhere insight had dissolved and dissipated the mosaic of my life, weightless, belonging neither to the earth nor to the stars, yet inextricably responsible to both. I sat motionless as the first rays of sunlight struck my face and flooded my senses with the luminosity that burns away even the thought of itself.

With unshakeable resolve imprinted like an invisible flame upon my heart, the next three weeks passed like a whisper echoing among the stars.

To be continued...

# PROSPERO'S TAPE LOG:
# RADIOSONIC LIFT-OFF

When I reunited with the other Wandjina Neuronauts at the canyon mouth on the morning of the 29th day of our departure from Dawnsource Circle, it was both as if I had just awakened from a dream and that I was just beginning to dream again. As casually as feathers lazily blowing down from a bird nest, we gathered beneath a large cottonwood. When I first looked at Francesca's face, realizing that she had fixed me in her sight some moments before I became aware of it, I experienced a mild psychosonic boom. The clarity of her eyes was awesomely profound. In an instant she communicated to me the moonwhole of her experience.

In the heart-burst of recognition that followed that communication, I walked toward her and asked, "what is it about you this morning, that I find so... " Francesca finished my thought for me "...so much like smoke gone nowhere?" As her impish smile turned into a laugh, we fell into a heart bonding embrace.

"Emptiness certainly doesn't stay love, does it, Lord and Lady Arcturus 108x?" It was Esquivel, mirthfully bonking our heads together as we kissed. On that wondrously fateful morning we had to count ourselves several times to make sure we were all present. The reason for this was that Lindy McGrew and Poontutjarpa continued shifting shapes with each other, disappearing momentarily before and after counting them.

Despite the bean braincd confusion we finally settled down beneath the cottonwood for Neuronaut Moonwhole Round-offs. This was achieved when Poonie, at least I think it was Poonie, began chanting: "Aaaaaahhhhhhh Kaaaaahhhhhh, Aaaaahhhhhh Kaaaaahhhhh!" I say I think it was Poonie because when the Aaaahhh was chanted it came from the mouth of the venerable old Australian. But when the Kaaaahhhh was chanted, it came not from the mouth of Poonie, but from that of none other than Samdong Zangpo. This meticulous exercise in split-second shape-shifting was greeted with an awed silence. Each of us took our positions in the mountainside meadow, facing Poonie/Zangpo, who sat with his back to the bark emblazoned trunk of the cottonwood tree.

The Aaaahhhh Kaaahhh shape-shifting exercise went on long enough to enable everyone to attune themselves to the proper intraneural frequency. When that happened, you knew even the windblown meadow grasses were listening. Then came the broadcast. It was like hearing someone talk to you while at the same moment you knew that the words were coming from your own synaptic bridges. Furthermore, in that moment after the chanting had ceased, and just before the broadcast began, the shape-shifting resolved itself in the dual form of Poonie/Zangpo, the right half of the body being Poonie's, the left-half Zangpo's.

"Neat trick," I thought, "must be a psychogenetic welding exercise they picked up in Arcturus 108x."

"Neuronaut Earthlings, Congratulations! You have just passed through the Eye of the Needle. But please, it is begged of you, don't think it's any big deal." The voice was a gravelly two toner, but friendly enough. "It's just a simple moment to moment experience the universe is continually undergoing. Clouds love it, too. They're good teachers that way, Neuronaut Earthlings. But enough of this cloud bantering metaphysics, let's get to the point." Poonie/Zangpo paused, pulling itself up into an impeccably erect posture, hands resting lightly on the knees of the legs folded in mind-tracking fashion beneath the body. Then squinting its Mongol-Australian eyes and photo tracking each member of the Neuronaut Round-off Circle, it continued.

"The point being that the little collective psychogenetic exercise in radiosonic geomancy you performed in creating the Enchanted Triangle has sent a ripple of paranoia through our friends, the Syndics. Ladies and gentlemen, you have to relate to that. It's your karma pure and simple. This is not to invalidate all that you have accomplished. All these magnetic trifles will stand you in good stead. But to do what you have to, it's got to be the straight shot or nothing." Poonie/Zangpo leaned back now til its head touched the tree trunk. Rubbing the back of the head against the gnarled tree bark, Poonie/Zangpo emitted grunts of pleasure, sounding much like a cat rubbing against the legs of its master.

Then folding its arms, Poonie/Zangpo appeared stern, grim, wild-eyed. "Goddamn little shits, you're lucky!" it shouted at us, "you're piss-brained, yak-balled lucky. You know why? Your friends, the Newlaws are already laying a beam track for each and everyone of you. This moment they're all over Syndicland, from Buenos Aires and Sao Paolo to Capetown and Addis Abbaba. And you know what, they're going?"

Here, Poonie/Zangpo could not suppress a leering, lurching giggle, more a passing titter than a full-blown laugh, "whacking off, that's what they're doing, just plain whacking off. How long they'll last and how many others they can get to whack off with them, well, we'll let you run that one through your own probability scan. When you accomplish that you'll have your very own activity timetable. Isn't that sweet, darling Earthlings?"

I had to admit that the smile on Poonie/Zangpo's face was so radiant and warm that I found myself nodding my head, mumbling to myself, "yeah, sweet little probability scan, sweet little activity timetable."

"Oh, one further info-bit for all of you to note. In future matters, concerning my interests, you may address me as AhKa, the Arcturian Emissary with bliss-bestowing hands." AhKa twisted its head to the left, a slight frown on its forehead, then went on. "Is there anything we've left out? I think at this point you have all attained sufficient insight to accomplish what you must on your own. For myself, I think I shall vanguard it to Capetown. We'll be in touch."

Composing itself majestically beneath the great cottonwood, AhKa chanted once again, slow and deep, going ever deeper, "Aaaaahhhhh Kaaaaaaaaa." As the vibrational tone dropped beneath auditory threshold, AhKa became increasingly transparent 'til it was gone. We all remained sitting there, gazing at the fibery-barked tree trunk.

It must have been mid-afternoon when our tree-focused mind-tracking was broken by the slightly dis-rhythmic hum of old Hoverbabe. Rising up from behind a precipice to our right, the hovercraft floated into view. But it was not the same old hovercraft. The Counter Trident Clean-Up Batallion had gotten to it. Its battered silver paint-worn body had been refurbished beyond recognition. Now it looked more like a flying zebra with a large smoked plexiglass bubble dome for its belly. In the control window I could make out the gorgeous face of the perplexingly beautiful Kali Ali the Clean-Up Queen. On the spot I realized that what made Kali Ali so bafflingly beautiful was her ability to psychomagnetically fluctuate the light and color of the electrochemo circuitry patterns tattooed on her golden ochre skin. As a result, her head oscillated luminously. With her at the controls you didn't need any lights for nighttime identification.

The craft came down just behind us. It came down so softly, the grass didn't even bend as it stopped a fraction of a centimeter above the knee-high meadow greenery. As I scrambled down into the top entry hatch, I took one last look at Canyon of the Caves. It rose up behind us, a jagged serpentine bolt of lightning laid large upon the earth. It had served me well. Even as the adrenalin push of what was to come rushed through me, I felt how perfectly laced it was with those crazy empty ion filaments. That being the case, I asked myself, as I dropped feet first to the vestibule, what is there to be afraid of?

"Nothing! Absolutely nothing!" It was Dawnstar Monongye doing a little Neuronaut soft shoe, greeting each one of us as we came down.

No sooner had Cyclone and Blaze touched the hovercraft vestibule floor, then the automatic entry hatch closed, and Kali Ali's voice came lilting through the intercom: "Psychety dykety, techty wekty, here we go!" And with a tremendous acceleration that had us lying in a crumpled heap on the vestibule floor, we rose to an elevation that had us just above Reed's Peak. At least there's where we were after I scrambled down into the plexiglass viewing dome. While we gazed at the few patches of snow-shadow on the otherwise barren peak, Kali Ali continued her intercom transmission.

*"Fly neuronauts the empty flow*
*fly not the empty neuroflow*
*empty the fly, flow neuronaut*
*flow empty, knot the neurofly."*

Repeating and variating this hauntingly sung verse in subtle syllabic rhythmic twists, we moved like a cloud in the direction of Dawnsource Circle. The Sacred Campsite of Truth or Consequences soon came into our view on the right. Not surprisingly, it had changed again. Yet, I felt a pleasurable shock when I took in its latest transformation. It had achieved radiosonic synthesis.

All the while my eyes drank in the lustrous beauty of centuries if not millennia of human encampment at Truth or Consequences, Kali Ali's voice sang to us of the syncopated, transparent spectacle at which we gazed:

*"Fly first the primal hunters camp*
*flow next the seed begrubber's lamp*
*flex heart the temple mumblers sword*
*fleet fast the punk against the gourd*
*Truth's consequence relamps the chord"*

Radiating out from the concentric circles within the solar resonator bank were a series of massive spectrally colored, yet totally transparent forms—spheres, pyramids, cubes, and shapes of far more intricate geometric precision bubbled out in a rapidly transforming profusion. At the same time like crystal-clear visions set within a soap bubble, all manner of activity went on simultaneously within those forms. While one small group set up a hide covered tipi, another transposed upon it an astronomical rite. Then over that a group with heraldic insignia-covered banners, marched to an unheard music. Transposed upon the whole were electro-precision work squads preparing a rocket for flight. Yet passing through this spectral maze of human history were several much larger forms. It is difficult to describe them for I had never seen anything quite like them. Perhaps they were humanoid, but at the same time, they were completely spherical, and immense, truly immense. As if doing a strange kind of bubble dance, these transparent forms bobbed and weaved with whimsical abandon, throwing off iridescent glimmers as the sun played optical nerve games on their radiantly transparent surfaces.

As the rhythm of these highly translucent, organically textured, mildly pulsating spheroids picked up, all of the previous layers of the psychosphere still transparent within them, they began playing a curiously uplifted game. I also noticed that, much like an amoeba reabsorbing itself, some were merging together, so that only three of the spheroid beings remained. Poised to form the apexes of a perfectly equilateral triangle, each one began to pulsate toward the others, 'til all three were joined. Then, pulsating at a merry rate, they wigged and wagged upwards 'til they formed a tetrahedron, perhaps a kilometer in height. Still enclosing the psychospheric activity, this three-sided pyramid began to lift off. As it rose, its attached subterranean counterpart wriggled out of the earth like an angleworm after a spring rain. Shimmering and pulsating like jelly receiving electrochemical "Type 23" injections, this double tetrahedron achieved radiosonic lift-off.

Across the entire circumference of the hover-zebra viewing bubble, a gasp charged with respectful awe accompanied the radiosonic lift-off of Truth or Consequences. As we watched the double tetrahedron rise above the earth, the radiosonic architecture of Truth or Consequences glowing immaculately transparent beneath it, Kali Ali continued her endless tour-guide chant:

> *"Charged to one the others went*
> *fused and bound to form the gent*
> *that glides bloud blythe in blue refrains*
> *to greet the seers 'n' bend their brains..."*

Even as Kali Ali sang that quatrain, the double tetrahedron began advancing toward the hovercraft. Kali Ali continued:

> *"to ask a name of blouds or fun*
> *erase the tape the punks outrun*
> *'n' when he's shaped us in his fold*
> *raise then the warcry loud 'n' bold."*

Kali Ali's singing was becoming mercilessly impassioned, and I felt my palms grow sweaty, gluing themselves to the interior of the viewing dome. The monumental double tetrahedron was floating right next to us, its shimmering bioplasmatic skin quivering ever so slightly, its surface imprinted with the design of the prevailing air currents. At the same time that it was radiosonic, as pure and weightless as radiosonic could ever be, it was simultaneously organic, vital, alive.

It slowly dawned on me that I was witnessing, at least for myself at this moment, on this planet for the first time ever, an example of a bioradiosonic synthesis! I keened the lyrics to Kali Ali's song, "charged to one the others went, fused and bound to form the gent." The double tetrahedron hovering so skillfully alongside our hovercraft was the sum composite of the other nineteen members of the Counter Trident Brigade, fused in to one being. While I and the other Neuronauts marveled at this typical prodigy of mutant avant-garde artistry, I noticed that one of the corners of the double tetrahedron had begun to penetrate our ship.

Pulsing to its own internalized electrodronic rhythm section, four sides of the double tetrahedron simply passed through us, as if we were nothing-which we all knew in some deep way we were. If you had dropped a plumbline down from the top apex of the double tetrahedron you would have found the hovercraft at dead center. We continued moving over Elephant Butte reservoir. Far to our upper left the flowing lava beds were coming into view, sparkling and every bit a mirage when seen through the bioradiosonic membrane of the double tetrahedron which had no trouble keeping pace with us. It was just as I caught sight of a coral, crimson-hued saguaro hybrid cactus just beneath me, that I began to feel a certain dizziness.

Kali Ali was singing:

> *"magnetic trifles play the man*
> *an octave past the sensory scan*
> *if seers got such open heart*
> *she won't mind another smart"*

At the root of the dizziness was the distinct sensation that I was being absorbed by another energy, or more precisely that my biopsychic energy field was merging with another's. That was it. I had synthesized with my Counter-Trident guide, that slap happy shave-headed fool, Sticklepick, a man wise in the ways of keening the feminine twist. Suddenly there he was, thoroughly interfaced with my energy field. Tuning to his neural frequency I made an immediate auditory translation of Sticklepick's greetings: "Hey PAN man! no global fusion thou't human twosion!" Taking a deep breath and slowly letting it out, I allowed Sticklepick's vibratory field to become thoroughly imbedded in mine. This merger was experienced as a quickening of the circulation of my blood and, quite simultaneously, an infusion of raw animal nervous energy that immediately doubled my neural receptivity.

At this point I was sitting up mind tracking style. To a one the other eighteen Cave finders were also in the same position, absorbing the psychoquantum energy transition. Passing over the orchid lavished northeast quadrant of the flowering lava beds of Jornada del Muerto, I could feel Dawnsource Circle prickling my nerve endings. The double tetrahedron surrounding the hovercraft had quieted to a point of total transparency. In fact it was hard to tell if it was even visible any more.

In her inimitable and endearing manner, Kali Ali's voice reverberated a deft collective resonance to the experience we were all undergoing:

> *"the monophrene he boned the punk*
> *broke out the battle schizophrenic*
> *the punk debunked the god of junk*
> *skied down the warlords multiphrenic…"*

Hearing this I recalled the words from the Saga of Vel and the Earth Lords:

> *"released earth's vibrant-mantle*
> *-with a war cry loud and bold!"*

No sooner did the fragmented recollection of these lines pass through my mind, then we all began chanting; Kali Ali as well began to chant: "Aaaahhhhh" on the in breath, "Kaaahhhhh" on the out breath. This was followed by a rapid fire burst of:

> *"Key, Key, OSM!*
> *Ka, Ka, CHV!*
> *Ko, Ko, cosmoblend!"*

This sequence was repeated three times, at which point we all broke into quietly shared camaraderie.

"Zestful, testful, I say there, quite an episode this, no?" Esquivel cheerfully muttered to himself as he gazed down at the shimmering surface of the flower-banked Velatropa canals. Then looking at the rest of us seated in a tight circle at the shallow bottom of the plexiglass viewing bubble, his peyote eating grin displaying an immaculate set of choppers, Esquivel raised his right arm in astral salute, above his head, the palm flat and turned up. The rest of us immediately followed suit. Holding this position, we allowed the almost invisibly fine vibrational form of the double tetrahedron to pass into our collective energy field. It came in from the center of the palm of the hand, down the median nerve of the arm finally imploding at heart center of the central channel in a quiet little giggle-inducing poof!

"What's all this talk about floating double tetrahedrons engulfing flying zebra hover crafts, anyway," Lindy McGrew spat out in mock annoyance. "I mean, all we did was go to the caves, right, all-a-body?"

"Uh huh" we all nodded, captivated by the rabbit-brained shape-shifter's bizarre twists of logic.

"And at the caves nothing happened. We all know that. And afterwards all we did was say good-bye to Poonie and bunny-hopped into old hoverbabe. That's real simple. And all the while we've got this crazy singing Amazon line-buster singing away as she glides on to Dawnsource Circle. We didn't see anything unusual, right?" Lindy's head was bobbing up and down rapidly, little drops of saliva gathered at the corners of his mouth. "Yeah, except maybe," he continued screwing up his eyes, "yeah maybe coupla three mirages over Truth or Consequences. But that's nothin unusual. Newlaws are always dreaming something up to pass the time…"

Then, without a break, without the least transition, the person who continued talking was no longer Lindy, but the Newlaw counter-Trident guide, Alfonse Le Crude, "so lykes and blykes, the blast o' time slew the sight. Like queen babe shot it, 'if seers got such open heart, she won't mind another smart,' and that's a right keen, 'cuz here I am." And certainly enough, there he was, Alphonse Le Crude, his short squat trunk matched by equally squat arms and legs, almost like a baby, impeccably tattooed with fine iridescent markings that made him look like one of those old maps which shows the air lanes, the radar markers, the missile sites, the hospitals, oil fields and radio stations done in all those funny late fourth ring symbols. Wearing nothing more than a pair of boots and a scarlet loincloth which scintillated against his pale blue skin, Alphonse le Crude's bald head was decorated with a holographically pulsating replica of the brain which I presumed his skull contained. His soft sensuous lips, scarlet and beaded with small opals, completely magnetized me. Just above his eyes was a small indentation in the shape of a four pointed star.

Resting his chin on a pudgy hand which protruded from an equally pudgy arm, bent at the elbow and propped on his left knee, Alphonse continued talking to us, in a calm reassuring manner, "Heh, heh, heh, I'm the mute to cube the loot and lay the root of Code Word RED. Now get this mutemates, at Dawnsource Circle we lay the line that marks square Palatkwapi. But just a short rumble. Otherwise, we plant radiosonic attics and no one wants to come down. Heh, heh, heh."

As Alphonse le Crude chuckled to himself, digging his right hand deep into his loin cloth with a great grin of satisfaction, I realized we were coming down at the hovercraft landing site just south of the Scorpio Canals.

Eagerly anticipating the warm fragrant atmosphere emanating from the abundant greenery of the aquaculture canal zones, I made ready for exit. Kali Ali was concluding her song with the now familiar refrain:

> *"And from jade and crimson bursting*
> *in the heart's magnetic hold*
> *released earth's vibrant mantle*
> *with a war-cry loud and bold*
> *In Unisonia Panharmonic*
> *so the legend has been told…"*

Climbing up just ahead of me toward the top-hatch was Alphonse le Crude his stubby legs displaying an alarming facility for leaping up vertical inclines. However, as I climbed up out of the hatch it was Lindy McGrew who was offering his hand to me. As he pulled me up, still holding my hand, we walked a few steps to the aft side of the Flying Zebra. Whispering tome in high conspiratorial style, Lindy continued to coast on the logic beam he had begun shooting before we landed.

"So what I figure, Prosp, yeah what I figure is this," Lindy looked around quickly, as if to make sure that no one else was in on this topflight secret. "Yeah Prosp, what I figure is that you 'n that shavehead loon Sticklepick are the perfect props to take that little mirage we picked up over Truth or Consequences, and give it a good shake. You know, like Palatkwapi, I mean the Arcturian-Arthurian Red City, flash it a little, you know, then pass it on. That'll give the ole cosmocrats something to think about. Then we'll move, you know, join Poonie in the Syndic whak-offs. How's that sound to you, Old Boy, I mean won't that be a stitch? Give your honeylady something to think about, too. After all, she's got that little bum-bum comin' along soon. So how about it, Prosp?" As he spoke, Lindy's sky-blue eyes milked me with a sincerity that almost had me bawling my head off.

"Sure, Lindy, sure," I replied, wiping away my tears, "I wouldn't let you down, I mean you're the finest goofer I'll ever know. You're straight with me, and besides you've goofed me lots of good ones, why shouldn't I goof you a good one back?" My answer caused Lindy to smile his best smile, the one that revealed his rabbit teeth in all their splendor. But something about his grin stopped me for a minute.

"Hey Lindy," I finally commented, "since when have your teeth been incised with diagrams of those zodiacal beasts?"

"Aw Prosp, use your head. I had to design it all myself, 'n then ole Alphonse, he beamed it on. It's a natch, not too obvious either, huh?" Then Lindy put out both his arms in front of his chest, the right arm ahead of the left, right palm facing out, left facing in. Immediately I assumed the same Trident salute posture, concentrating my breath, then slowly letting it out while standing still as a rock. Keeping the posture as he spoke, Lindy concluded with a simple remark, "I leave it all to you, thanks, Prosp."

As we stood there dissolving through each other's eyes, my mother's voice came angling in through the thirty-third vector northwest of my and Lindy's mutually fused energy fields. "Yoo, hoooo, Prosp 'n' Lindyyyyyyy, Dawnsource Circle's waitingggg! You don't wanna miss happy hourrrrrrrr!"

"Mom's right, Lindy. And besides I can't stand being caught conspiring with a goofer like you." Then calmly flicking his rabbity nose with my right middle finger, I jumped off the hovercraft as fast as I could to escape the hippity-hopping scam master's benign wrath. But I should have known better than that. After all, Lindy was famous for his roadrunner stride as well as his hippity-hop.

Bobbing along next to me as we headed toward the rest of the group, Lindy was blithely jabbering away, "Did anyone ever tell you what an ass-hole you are, Prosp? A good ass-hole, but still an ass-hole?"

The other cave Wandjina's, along with Kali Ali, stood at the edge of the small clearing where Hoverbabe was docked. They all faced Dawnsource Circle, its puffs of smoke, its tents and banners, its perfectly magnificent Alpha Pit Central Beam Bubble-that was it, Alpha Pit Central had been completed. It was beautiful, like a soap bubble, its iridescent tingles moving erratically across its polished surface. Beneath it, the great deck was hung with streamers. Four kites in the shape of a scorpion, a bull, a lion and a multi-colored female water pourer, glistening with metallic splashes, flew from the corners of the deck.

As the splendor of Alpha Pit Central criss-crossed my hemispheres, I remembered what Lindy and I had been talking about. "Well," I thought to myself, "the set-up's all there; Poonie's gone, and I got the transmission from Lindy. Nothing left to do but play syntropic poker, and cash in my chips when the moment calls me to." As I let this thought dissolve itself in a bath of ion empty filaments, I realized how good I felt, how truly good. Deep within I relaxed as the indestructible power of that gentle self-obliteration in the Canyon of the Caves radiated out from my heart, tender as a solitary mourning dove's dawn-evoking cry.

A murmur of commotion rippled through us as we caught sight of Fa-Tsang and

Supersub emerging from the south crescent Scorpio canal. Dripping wet and with streamers of red plankton clinging to their limbs and body, the mad-finding cave twins came dashing up to us. Smearing each and every one of us with a plankton-stained embrace, we all proceeded to take a leisurely walk back to Dawnsource Circle.

Occasionally a member of a work-detail would take notice of us and do a giggly five-step shuffle or raise their hands and let out an animal call of some sort or another. Otherwise, it was everything as usual on a fine flower-sprinkled, shadow-dappled afternoon in June at the foot of Peak of Darkness. Everything as usual except for what Fa-Tsang and Supersub were reporting to us in their typically breezy whole-moon, whole-earth, pre-solstice news round-offs.

"Yeah, yeah, yeah," Supersub was speaking, "Syndic monitors flashed it like this."

Then Fa-Tsang took over, "unprecedented incursions of Mutant Outlaws into major Syndic centers have had local authorities alarmed and curious. Thus far, no sensible pattern can be made of the Outlaw theater performances. However, operants in radiosonic labs at the Tierra del Fuego announced this morning the development of a counter law cerebral band. Specifications for these have been sent to manufactories in Montivideo and Lagos. Shipment of the uniquely designed brain bands should be arriving at consumer centers throughout southern hemispheric Syndic zones within three days. The Minister of Health in Capetown, Sir Dudley Cavendish, announced via Syndicom just a few moments ago that no child should be without one. 'Happiness,' the minister went on to say, 'is everybody's business.'"

No sooner did Fa-Tsang complete his syndicom relay, then Supersub interjected, "Fine, fine, moon-dark, spooky-looky fine, you nut-all syndic brain-jammers. Gooness to goofy, what they won't beam of next?" In our hearts, we all knew the moment of action would soon be upon us.

That night lying down in Francesca's honey-melting arms, I thought of all that had happened that day. Like a glimmering shadow encased in my nerve endings, I felt the ever-grinning presence of my spirit bonder, Sticklepick. What the future would bring I did not know, yet all I felt was brightness.

Nibbling my cheeks with good night kisses, Francesca whispered to me, "I know you've got a secret, Prosp. But I won't ask you to pop it on account of my self-indulgent curiosity. And besides, Prosp," she drew in her breath as my tongue played over the full ripeness of her nipples, "I like surprises."

To be continued…

# FRANCESCA'S TAPE LOG: NEURONAUT SOLSTICE GYMNASTICS

Through the entire week preceding summer solstice, we all sensed what it was that Lindy had transmitted to Prospero. But no one cared to talk about it. Nor did anyone show any interest in speculating on just how Prospero would pull it off, or even what form it would take when it happened. We all simply went about our daily lives. For me, that meant mostly taking it easy as I was completing my seventh month of pregnancy. The cooler morning hours I spent at the Velatropa Canals in work detail, removing shrimp from one bed to another, laying out plankton streamers to dry in the sun, or picking flowers for arrangements I wanted to do for whomever of the Wandjina Cavefinders came to mind. The afternoon hours I spent in the yurt, mind-tracking, resting, and, to occupy myself, making Prospero a fine embroidered robe.

I knew I had only seven days to make this robe. Taking a fine piece of turquoise panama silk, I cut out the pattern: large bell shaped sleeves with a magnificently flared bottom, following which I sewed the front to the back side. This I did the first afternoon. The second afternoon, I sewed into it the finest woven alpaca lining that I could find. To get this, I had to barter with that funny little flute player, Alfonso Purimac. What he got in return was a song sung on the spot to the accompaniment of his flute. On the third day, I sewed fine deep pockets into the robe and began the embroidery, using choice gold, silver and crimson threads. On the fourth afternoon I embroidered a celestial coyote, set in a simple red circle. This I did at the mid-back of the robe. On the fifth day I embroidered an ascending earth serpent on the right front of the robe, while on the sixth day I embroidered the descending celestial serpent on the left side. While the earth serpent passed up through a golden solar disc, the celestial serpent wriggled its way down through a silver lunar disc. Then I let it rest. Not once did I let Prospero know that I was doing this, a fact which gave me almost unendurable satisfaction.

Prospero, too, simply went about his life, working on the last touches to Alpha Pit Central, or chasing around with Lindy, Natasha, Ixchel and Psychlosky. They had gotten some kind of game together which, to me, appeared as hare-brained as it was ingenious. Lying on their backs, their feet touching each other in the center of the circle which they formed, they would clasp hands and begin chanting the ole "Ah Ka." As they chanted, their bodies would uniformly elevate. Continuing to chant they would rise a full two and a half meters into the air, still in the exact same five pointed snowflake formation they were in while lying on the grass.

I remember the first afternoon I looked out of the yurt and saw them doing this. Tickled silly when they were finally hovering in the air above me, they turned in one swoop, and began circling me with aerial cartwheels. Realizing that I was the central energy bank feeding their delight in performing such amazing acrobatics, I couldn't resist it. Sitting myself down in the warm grass, I concentrated my breath. Holding it for a half a minute or so, while my mind totally dissolved itself, I expelled my breath with aloud "ka boom!" Instantly the cart wheeling cavefinders came crashing down. Splurting and blubbering at me for having spoiled their fun, I took advantage of my pregnant condition and with hands held firmly to my belly womb, sashayed back into the yurt with the sassiest twist I could manage.

The only news monitor during the week that created anything like a stir among us was the joint communiqué issued two mornings before Solstice from PAN hierarch in both Hopi Mesa and Ultima Thule. It reported that in virtue of its radiosonic achievement at Trinity Site Dawnsource Circle, the Trident Brigade was being entrusted with the highest intelligence operations for the forthcoming Summer of Stars Offensive. That was it. No more information, just that. "Scammed like the most cryptic monitor lizard grinning at a syndic DNA supervisor in the Amazonian wetlands," that was Ya Emme's quip following reception of that news bulletin. And with a bemused shake of the head I had to agree.

By myself as I embroidered in the yurt that afternoon, I reflected on the morning's news communiqué. Here I was, pregnant, carrying around some little Dawnsource gene-pack, while sewing a robe for my duastic bond mate, that passionate, synaesthete frequency tracker, Prospero Edmund Jones. Where was I a year ago? It seemed so damnably far away-Cape Wrath. The dull sorting out of information bits, arranging them into sequential patterns. The drab evenings in the solo chamber listening to the broadcast reports of the info bits, it had been my task to put together that morning, coming out in crazy sequences: "alphabet requirements regarding spurious viral spores transmitted through efficient letter squads make the pronouncement of new psychoregulations incumbent upon the ministerial understudies in order to provoke consequential back-up in case of desynthesized waste matter clogging the reinforced lineaments of the west vector happiness gauge."

Remembering with a shudder some of those reports I had put together, I flashed on what was to come. Project Code Word RED was approaching its conclusion, Summer of Stars was coming up. Embroidering the red pupil into the golden-threaded eye of the ascending earth serpent on Prospero's turquoise panama silk kimono, my own eyes filled with tears. It was the baby inside of me. It was Prospero and his mission. It was the total fragility of life and love itself. With full heart, I let the tears roll down my cheeks. Licking their salty traces with my tongue, I knew I was complete.

At the end of the sixth afternoon, putting the last stitches into the flaming crest of the descending sky serpent's head, I folded the robe neatly and placed it at the bottom of my silk embroidered deerskin travel bag. The biochronometer flashed 18:30. Prospero would be home shortly. Whatever he was going to transmit on summer solstice, his body would be regaled with a robe as resplendent as it was simple. Then with a rapid synaptic clicking, my neural shadow sister, Sheryl Ann, began informing me of Prospero's imminent arrival. At the fire pit the simmering Velatropa plankton broth exuded the deliciously blended smells of chaparral, tarragon and mesquite seed spicing, succulent chunks of painted desert snapper, tomatoes, olives and baby white potatoes. Prospero would gobble it down, no question of that. Having set the meal mat with the glazed Chaco porcelain ware, I sat myself down to await the arrival of that passion-brained Wandjina, Prospero Edmund Jones. And in he came.

A lovely smile set off his mildly African features, the flared nostrils, the large sensuous lips, the creamy sepia color of his silky skin, his burning dark eyes set beneath a broad forehead topped by a generous endowment of bushy black hair, that as usual, when he came in from work detail, was sprinkled with dirt, sawdust, metal and plastic fragments of one sort or another. Dressed in his silver NASA Grube Tube jumpsuit, he looked every bit the living image of a vital, micro-macro processed humanoid. And I loved every neuro-synthesized cell of his sexually vibrant, tender-hearted body.

"Oh you beautiful, trash snared goof," I cooed seductively. "Yours is the bod' I lay my life upon!"

"Really, huh?" he stopped in his tracks, his eyes darting around with mirthful alarm, "sounds like you're cooking up something more than Velatropa stew, honey babe." His eyes still flashing around the yurt as if in search of something, he continued, "what you hiding here? I mean besides that little bundle that's got your belly wombzoning into the ionosphere? Huh? What you hiding, woman?"

"So you think just because you've got a secret, I've got one too? That's a fine piece of duastic logic if I ever heard one," I replied, zipping my tunic down the front exposing the tops of my now burgeoning breasts. "Maybe you'd like to eat something saucy and get your mind off these conspiratorial thought waves that are scamming your poor over-teched brain. How about it, Prospy dear," I unzipped still further, and with a provocative wriggle of my still seated bod finished the invitation, "Velatropa plankton broth, juicy and sizzling with fried rice cakes, and some extra fine slices of super-ripe, cinnamon-sprinkled honeydew melon. Doesn't that sound delicious, Prospero?"

That got him. The old gustatory sexual lure had Prospero goggle-eyed and tongue-gaggled staggering to the meal mat.

Following the Quiet Quest Vow, with a grin as bright as a solar reflection bouncing off a resonator bank, Prospero dove into his food. After three or four voracious gulps of the Velatropa Plankton Stew, Prospero fixed his eyes on me and spoke, "delish, Hon, but 'scuse me, I've got to talk to you: Neuronaut gymnastics... Code Word RED... Summer of Stars... Solstice peak points... Palat-kwapi... Red City of the South... Return no Return!" It all came tumbling out in a total, duty charge of PAN code words, smeared with streaks of red plankton, tomato and snapper. Like a coyote who, while chasing its prey cuts short in mid-track, and says to the moon, "to hell with it, I was only joking," Prospero, wild-eyed, and hot with the shot, suddenly stopped his code word flow.

But what Prospero spoke in low-turf softness was this: "Listen Francesca, what I'm trying to tell you, bonded as I am with the shadow genetic imprint of Quetzalcoatl, transmitted through the code-pattern of the Lords of Texcoco, and beamed through the Afro-bod of this star-tickled, radiosonic quester—yeah, that's me—what I'm telling you, Francesca, is that tonight, this very night, after we do the post-meal clean-up, we're going to play moon-tag." Prospero paused, his eyes radiant and warm, seductive even with the magnitude of his quest. As he dipped into the stew once again, I decided to press and probe.

"Moon-tag, Prospero? I'm too womb-zoned to tag the moon with a Wandjina scammer like you. Unless, of course," I waited for Prospero's attention to fine-line with mine, "you want to tag the moon through the bod'o' this close-to-eighth-month babe? What do you say, Prosp?"

"Damn clever, if I don't say so myself," he replied. The eyes on his face were wrinkled in the kind of appreciation a man shows when he has just cast the perfect oracle.

In the speechless charade of those cave-finding sharers who know to let love alone, because love comes to them, we finished our dinner and completed the clean-up rites.

Towards midnight, we left the yurt. Dawnsource Circle was quiet. Though no one knew exactly what was going to happen the next day, we all knew that it would, whatever it was. The moon was as close to full as you could get. It shimmered in a light haze, buffeted by banquets of clouds which sailed almost sluggishly across the mid-summer sky. Everything was licked and splashed with perfumed dollops of pearly white moonlight. To our right, the Peak of Darkness reared its shadowy head against a pale blue wreathe of clouds. Around the moon, which appeared some distance out directly above the Peak of Darkness, was a fine halo. Directly above the moon itself was its own ghostly reflection, cast by the ethereal cloud bank illuminating the tip of the Peak of Darkness.

As we approached the inner circle embankment surrounding Alpha Pit Central, Prospero whispered, "Perfect, absolutely perfect." Stopping alongside him and clasping his hand to my breast, we both gazed upon the Bubble Dome structure of Alpha Pit Central. Its perfect spheroid Receiving Station was like the moon itself, burning with a smokey white luminescence. "That's it baby," Prospero whispered again, taking his hand and patting my belly-womb bulge. "That's it. Now let's do it."

Prospero had already measured out twenty places along the top of the grass-covered embankment, marking each site with a small polished white stone. At each of these places, Prospero kissed me, then bent down on his knees and, lifting the bottom of my tunic, kissed the feminine birth-swell. His kisses were as innocent as butterflies bouncing off each other in morning glory light. Then easing me down to the grass alongside him, he lay me on my back on the moon-stroked turf. As I lay there spread-eagled, my eyes fixed on the passing scenery of clouds and slices of constellations, Prospero proceeded to play moon-tag. Placing his hands over my belly, uncovered and open to moonlight, he chanted:

*"Aaaaahhhhhhh*
*On the Delectable Isle where Harmaunce ruled*
*urose the towers Tristram jeweled*
*Finding the beast in the devil's domain*
*Tristram dissolved in the tower's refrain.*
*Kaaaaaaaaaaahhhhh."*

As his voice intoned the ancient verse, his hands released a vibrant chord. The embryo within jolted and stretched its little form as straight as it could in the constrained space in which it found itself. As the embryo pulled straight, so did I. Stretching my arms and legs to their fullest extent, I allowed the energy chord to pass through the placenta into my own system. Then with a loud expulsion of air, I passed the energy to the ground beneath me.

This act we repeated at each of the Dawnseer Neuronaut Sites. When we had circled back to the point at which we had begun, Prospero and I sat down, facing each other. "Wandjina babe. You're going to have to leave me alone the rest of the night. That's what it says in the neural transcript I've been receiving concerning Project Code Word RED. Tomorrow, you gather the Dawnsource Seers just at sunrise. Let me see," Prospero paused to look at his biochronometer, "yeah, that'll be in just three hours. You bring them here and seat them down. You'll know whose place is whose. And, of course, the empty one's for me, right next to you. Got it, honeybabe?"

I felt sad as he spoke. Yet I knew he'd do what he had to do. Suddenly I remembered the robe. "But Prospero, hold on. Wait here a minute," and before he even drew a glimmering keen on what was going on, I dashed to the yurt. My feet flew over the dew-stained grass as I held my hands on my belly womb, and piercing the entry flap of the yurt, swiftly and knowingly retrieved the robe. Just as swiftly and surely I returned to Prospero who still sat on the embankment, waiting with a goofy "sky-doesn't-care" expression on his face. Yet I knew his heart was eager for my secret.

Then I unfolded it for him and held the robe before his silk-bedazzled eyes. Standing up speechless, he allowed me to place the robe on his lanky, powerful frame. As the moon played shadow games with the creases and folds in the robe, Prospero smiled, bit his lower lip and said, "Francesca, honey babe, do you remember when you sang for me, the first time ever? 'Don't you see, it's just me you've been waiting for all these years?' Well I guess this is it!" Without saying another word he took me in his arms and kissed me. He kissed me as if I would never see him again, and my heart trembled with the fullness of a knowledge my lips did not dare speak.

Then he left me. I watched as he walked, magnificent in his new kimono, to Alpha Pit Central and disappeared in the darkened south base block entrance. After a few moments, my eyes shifted to the receiving dome atop the deck. When I knew he had taken his place in the transmission chamber, I turned around and walked back to the yurt. Once inside, I lit the candles on the shrine table and sat myself down. I did not try to hold back my tears as I mind-tracked my hopes and fears to that luminous point where they dissolved and nothing remained. Everything was as it was, and there was nothing more to say and do, but what had to be done.

When I came out of the yurt, a brilliant red and purple band of light announced the dawn beyond the blackened Sierra Oscura. To the West, the moon was still in its passage over the Elephant Butte and the Black Range, escorted by a batallion of clouds streaming swiftly over her surface. Summoning all my strength for the task, I went to each of the tents of the inner Dawnsource Circle and roused each and everyone of the Wandjina Cavefinders.

"Solstice sun-ups," I would announce, "Neuronaut Gymnastics at Alpha Pit Central! Project Code Word RED, ready to tickle the Dead! Neuronaut Wandjina Dreamers, let's see who gets ahead!" Though I felt a certain apprehension about what was to occur, there was no way I could entertain such feelings. Knowing that Prospero needed the total goof-brained, joyous-hearted support of all of the Wandjina Seers, my morning summons was delivered with increasing abandon, 'til I finally arrived at the tent of Natasha and Lindy McGrew. As fate would have had it, they were making love. Oblivious of my presence, I sang in a manner as carefree as a sodium ion popping happily into an unsuspecting synapse:

> *"Grube-laced dawn rites 'neath the cover*
> *Alpha Pit is still above her-*
> *So cream the downslide, raise the rear*
> *Mark fast the feast and then come here!"*

Watching the wave-motion bodies come to a halt, I turned quickly and left. I was scarcely outside the yurt when I heard Natasha's voice calling out, "It-lil-po-tan-cuah's wrath upon you, you slack-hearted, Prospero-puffed vixen, blaahhhhh!"

My rounds completed, I went to the inner Dawnsource Circle embankment and took my place on the moon-womb tagged grass. Without too much delay the other Wandjina Cave-seers took their places as well, Lindy and Natasha bringing up the rear. On my right side, I felt the emptiness of Prospero's place. The first rays of sunlight were just coming through a mountain cleft causing the simple polished white rock in Prospero's site to look as if it were a piece of blazing red coal.

Magpies, blue jays and desert warblers were chattering and singing madly their first medley of the day, when the four amplifiers, set just beneath corners of the pennant-adorned Dish Deck, began to resonate. It was Prospero intoning the old "Ah Ka." But the voice was a two-toner. Stickpick was putting in his licks as well. Quite naturally, the rest of the Dawnsource Seers joined in, each one two-toning it with their shadow bond counter-Trident guide. As the chanting began to die down, I picked up a retinal flicker. I'm not sure where it came from, or what caused it. After a moment or two it became obvious. Like a pinprick of dense light it beamed out from the Alpha Pit bubble dome transmission chamber. Laterally, I received a placidly-tremored Neuronaut Ring circuit discharge. "Hmmm, evacuation time," I thought to myself, and that was just about the last thought I had for the next few hours. The rest of what I did was simply monitor my sensory activity. That plus a few infraneural comments and the old "Ah Kaaaaaa" to be decoded later.

Once the initial beam had been transmitted and received releasing the Neuronaut Ring circuit discharge, the ion empty filament bombardment of Alpha Pit Central began. Its molecular structure must have felt immensely pleased as the transformation from grav-mag to electro-mag got underway. Indicating the bonding of the bio-mag to the radiosonic tilt that was dematerializing Alpha Pit Central, Prospero began his song. Or I should say, the voices of Prospero and Sticklepick began to resonate the karmic DNA activity patterns with the magnetic-blend frequency shift Alpha Pit Central was undergoing:

*"Plutonium Punk in the Pit of Death*
*Catches the wind, loses no breath*
*Ten thousand minds passed over mine*
*Pronounce my name, unblind the blind*
*Ten thousand hearts enfolded me in that bare flight: Palat-kwa-pee!*
*Palat-kwa-pee! Palat-kwa-pee!*
*There's no return 'til you're home free."*

As the magnetically synthesizing pattern quickened, Alpha Pit began to vibrate toward a highly progressed state of radiosonic transparency, not unlike the great geometric bubbles and tetrahedrons of Truth or Consequences. My heart took immediate note of the robed figure at the transmission monitor board at the center of the dome bubble. Seated on a floating vibratory stool, his boots protruding from the bottom of the resplendent coyote-catcher, serpent-blender's robe, that I had cut and embroidered for the master synaesthete's command performance, was Prospero Edmund Jones. His two hands were placed before his eyes, left hand before the right, fingers and palms pointing vertically skyward. As he shifted his hands so that the right was before the left, Sticklepick assumed Prospero's place. But Sticklepick, too, wore the coyote-catcher, serpent-blender robe.

As the shifting hand movement accelerated, a beam shot straight up from the rapidly oscillating form of Prospero/Sticklepick. When that beam left the now almost completely transparent, but vibrantly colored form of the bubble dome, it immediately started emitting a shower of geometric forms, like a vast multitude of soap bubbles rushing every direction across the landscape and into the sky, bobbed and scattered by erratic wind currents that tugged and pulled at my hair. This spectral bombardment, even more geometrically precise and staggeringly brilliant than that which we had witnessed at Truth or Consequences, seemed to possess a maximum melt-down intensity. I remember gasping as if all of my oxygen had been absorbed by some other force.

It was at that point that the spectral explosion occurred. An intense wave of brilliant, blinding white light shattered, then billowed through the high frequency Prospero/Sticklepick form with a radiosonic boom that was just short of deafening. My peripheral vision caught sight of the Wandjina Seers rocking furiously with tremors of the cosmo-blend fusion. However, we all remained grounded, bonded to earth by the moon womb tagged softness upon which we sat. When the immensity of energy released by whatever it was that just happened, subsided, still reciting the old "Ah Ka," I observed that Alpha Pit Central was now operating at a post-threshold frequency.

Vibrating simultaneously, but at a lower frequency, thus optically replacing Alpha Pit Central, was a fountain with liquid of four colors-red, green, orange, and blue-spouting majestically into the air. As my eyes tracked the liquid vibrations shooting skyward, I became aware of the fact that we were now enclosed in an immense and elaborate radiosonic architectural form. Accompanying the registration of the fact that we had been radiosonically enfolded, was the CHV rendition of that Dawnsource classic, "In Unisonia Panharmonic."

And that's where we found ourselves that morning, in Unisonia Panharmonic, Palat-kwa-pee, the Red City, the synthesis of Project Code Word RED. Oh, most everything still remained—the yurts, the kilns, the banners waving wildly in the currents of wind which rotated around the compass in a lilting jogging rhythm, everything but Alpha Pit Central. We had ceased chanting, and everyone, though still seated, craned their necks in every direction.

As I keened that we were almost dead center in a magnificent five-leveled construction that was both a city and a palace, its interior terracing a perfect reflection of its exterior five-tiered form, the infra-neural auditory squad of Prospero and Sticklepick began jamming the nervous system with their panharmonic lyric:

> *"Grube the Guide, he skulled the shot*
> *While Poonie ate the after-thought*
> *Lords and Ladies, gents 'n' genies*
> *Palat-kwa-pee pops the beanies*
> *Insight we fly to slay the beast*
> *So fare thee well and host the feast!"*

As the two-tone hit squad melted into an echo, all of the Wandjina Seers raised the "Ah Ka" an octave, then another octave, then another, until we had climbed six octaves oscillating at a supra-auditory level. As this occurred, the five-tiered radiosonic city, its top tower capped by a magnificent free-floating sphere, its waters silver flashing, shooting burning arcs through gates fourfold, imprinted itself indelibly upon my thoroughly receptive, identity-evacuated nervous system. Once the imprinting had been transferred, the five-tiered Red City of Palat-kwa-pi dissolved. It was now us. The central coding of all of our dreams had been perfectly projected and reabsorbed-we were it!

Returning our "Ah Ka's" down the six octave scale, we normalized. By the time we finished our last "Kaaaaaa" at earth-bottom octave, Alpha Pit Central had rematerialized. This little exercise in Neuronaut Gymnastics was now completed. Summer of Stars had just begun.

No sooner was Alpha Pit Central a solid materialized form once again, then I became aware of a great commotion behind us: hordes of gleeful Slack-Zoners; solemnly chuckling O Mo Lung Ringers; walking staff stamping Atlantide Renegades; Newlaw Logic Snackers snickering their rationally transcendental riffs; flute-playing Mogollon Shepherds; whistling and cheering Grube Tubers; undulating Feedbed Dancers; high humming Astro Psychers! A wave of great pleasure came over me, pleasure and pride in Prospero's accomplishment. After all those years of struggle and quest he had achieved synaesthetic mastery. At the same time, my heart pulled at me, for I felt his vacancy, the simple polished white stone on the moon-tagged grass to my right. While absently stroking my belly womb-zone, I noticed that the commotion had suddenly come to a halt.

It must have been Aldebaran who shot out in an awe-struck whisper, "The ultimate weapon!" Like everyone else I turned my head toward the eastern horizon midway up to sky-zenith. There it was. A magnificent transparent five-colored band running from green to yellow, to orange to red, finally fading out in a fine violet band high in the upper stratosphere. Five rings-incredible! I wanted to cry, laugh, shout and die all at once! It was immediately evident that the band straddled the earth, its first transformation beginning in the upper atmosphere and then slicing upward some 100 kilometers into space. We all gazed silently, long enough to realize that it synchronized itself to the rotation of the earth, and so it appeared to move with the sun. A further deduction was that the five rings straddled the earth at her two magnetic poles.

Lindy McGrew was the first to separate himself from the Circle of Dawnsource seers. Quickly milling with the group of O Ma Lung Ringers just behind me, he was breathlessly reciting the obvious, but with utter cheerfulness: "Psychoatmospheric rings ! Earth's finally got 'em. Wonder what they'll be thinking out in old Arcturus 108x now? Can't you just see their little antennae wigging out as they pick up this pulsation on their psycho-galactic radar scanner. Whooooosh," Lindy concluded, jumping up and down in excitement, his flip-flop hair bouncing wildly with him. "Wouldn't I like to be there." Then he stopped, and placing his hand on his jaw, shape-shifted instantaneously to Alphonse Le Crude, who finished Lindy's thought form by announcing, with a cheerful squiggle of his stumpy little bod, "but, fortunately here I am!"

As the tremendous, awe-struck jubilation continued marking the commencement of the great solstice feast, I disengaged myself and walked over to Alpha Pit Central. I approached the south entrance of the base block, its fine hewn timber beams and adobe walls immaculate in the summer light, while butterflies charmed each other beneath the haven of the Dish Deck overhang. Entering the cool interior of the base block, my eyes soon accustomized themselves and I could make out the wondrous serpentine paintings that ran in horizontal bands around its walls. Climbing the winding stairwell at the center of the base block, my heart knowing what was to come, I continued up until I came out in the dome. Looking through its panoramic window I was struck by the smoked plexiglass tinted beauty of the day. And of the rings-Earth's Rings-magnificent beyond belief, yet there!

Over the Black Range great cumulo-nimbus thunderheads arose perhaps twenty of them in fine order. Birds seemed to be arriving from everywhere, minute flocks of them appearing on the whole circumference of the horizon. Now approaching sky-zenith, Earth's newly acquired rings shimmered, radiating what I could only describe as a peaceful confidence. Continuing to climb, I reached the transmission chamber. Opening the entry hatch I entered the chamber itself, its small round bank of monitor screens flashing and bleeping.

There at the south end of the monitor bank was the control stool. Neatly folded upon its seat was the coyote-catcher, serpent-blender's robe. Tenderly picking it up and holding it to my breast, feeling an intense pang of yearning sadness, my attention was caught by Prospero's voice, "Hey! Honey babe, over here," it spoke. I turned toward the direction from which the voice had come. It was a monitor screen just to my left. Looking at the screen I saw the coordinate points of the Tierra del Fuego. I smiled, and thought to myself, "Prosp, you synaesthetic stitch, you son-of-a-bitch, what you won't think of next?"

To be continued…

# PROSPERO'S TAPE LOG:
# THE FALL OF PATAGONIA

### REPORT FILED BY:

Agent 24 Jones, Commander, Patagonian Expeditionary
Squad and Rotating Activity Captain,
Interchangeable Force Field Circus.

### REPORT FILED TO:

Agent Dawnsource Domestic Liaison Commander,
Della Francesca Jones

Hello there! I'm beam-clearing with a straight one today, Honeybabe. And I've got good news. I'm issuing this report from deep inside the Darwin Radlab monitoring station in the Tierra del Fuego. That should tell you how far we've gotten in the last month. I picked this place, of course, because the Darwin Station is the most sophisticated Radlab in Syndicland. Because of the great progress of this front of the Summer of Stars PAN Neural Brigade, I'm able to take the time to give you a full debriefing on the course of our adventure for the benefit of the other Summer Star Falls who have yet to get beam-popped at Palat-kwa-pee bubble dome in Dawnsource Circle. So let's go back to the neuronaut solstice gymnastics.

Sitting in the transmission chamber of Alpha Pit Central, I divined from a reading of my karmic-DNA coordinates, that this was the moment to attain bioradiosonic synthesis. Infraneurally, I knew this was the final take on Project Quetzalcoatl, not to mention Code Word RED. Scanning a Syndic Operation's monitor graph, it wasn't difficult to determine that Darwin was my destination. Setting an infraneural frequency beam toward Poonie/Zangpo in Capetown, I went into void hyperpsyche. And then we were off. There's no question that the AhKa Circle of Dawnsource Seers provided the correct collective neural base for proper lift-off. Though I must also report that not until the moment just preceding the psychosonic boom did I keen that we were going to release the five psychoatmospheric rings. On the other hand, it was all very logical, considering that it was simply a matter of pan-harmonically transforming the negative atomic source energy of Trinity Site—Alpha Pit Central—to its ultimate resolution.

Beam down at the Punta Arenas Circus Ground was synched to a precision point of .0005 neurodecibels. I felt tremendous gratitude for the exercises and drills we had over the past half year, as it made beam down as effortless as checking out the time on your biochronometer.

The reception I received was nothing short of calamitous. I beamed down perfectly in the center of a large yurt, just to the right side of the fire pit. No sooner had I stabilized my metabolism then I became aware of about 20 wildly cheering Newlaw Circle Jerks. Moving to a fast-timed electrodrone, their happy faces caused me to shape-shift and I let Sticklepick handle the touchdown.

"Scamlaws, Syndic hide-binders, truth or else madfinders, Dawnforce maneuvers glad this hyperbod into your pleasance. Summer o' Stars reruns the bummer by fars, 'tho winter slows, the syndic brain will soon the summer glows. So hey, circle jerks, pop your beanies out the trough and scam the sky your skies, but don't blues it!" Sticklepick's presence had an immediately calming effect on the Newlaw Circle Jerks. "'N just so you don't blues it, I'm hiding me grace in the hyperpsyche fold of the Dawnforce Agent who scams us bold. "Then with a gracious bow, Sticklepick shapeshifted back to me.

When I appeared before the Newlaws again, they broke out in spontaneous clapping. Other than my name, I didn't have to say a word. Their Rotational Energy Captain for the day, a medium-sized woman, Clearfall was her name, a bit like Cyclone or Blaze with the Newlaw Insignia on her brow, but with blue-green eyes which reminded me of you, Honeybabe, came up to me and fastened a robe around my shoulders.

"Foolstice north beams solar beats, foolstice south snowguards the beast. So here, Jonesy, keep ya balmy in the dark."

Thanking her, I then repeated Sticklepick's injunction, "pop yer beanies out the trough and scam the sky yer skies." Dutifully we all clambered out the yurt entry flap. I was hardly prepared for the depth of the snow on the ground. Fortunately I was wearing brigade boots, and the heavy wool-lined cape which Clearfall had just given me. Overhead there were broken clouds and patches of bright blue sky. Close to sky-zenith, intermittently visible beyond the clouds were the five rings. When we caught sight of them, to a one, we all fell to our knees crunching down through the wind-blown drifts, as if we had just been slapped silly, yet loved it.

But damn, Francesca, if that wasn't a brain-popper the very first time I saw it. The green ring, scarcely visible, fading out almost incandescent against the sky. Then the yellow ring like translucent lemon powder, so soft and pure. Beyond that the orange, though farther away, no less intense, and like the others fading into space so that the red ring spanned the other three like a burning crimson ribbon. And finally high above that, the fifth ring. My heart almost broke when I keened that ring, luminous and violet echoing the curvature of earth, at once a summons and an invitation to break the neural bonds that bind us to our pride.

Many in the group of Newlaw Circle Jerks broke into tears at the sight of earth's rings, finally visible and beyond all doubt. The radiosonic beam we threw at Dawnsource Circle was a mere trick compared to this beaut swinging each of its bands from north to south with a five-ringed curve that perfectly echoed earth's own spheroid plunge. Even the most calculating logic-bound being, an Abdul-Rumi Hassan, could not discount the appearance of a phenomenon such as this. Even I who had been so instrumental in this experiment was gasping for answers. And yet the rings of earth were there, invincible, harmonic and real. Even in those places where the rings were obscured by clouds, the clouds themselves took on an iridescent shimmer indicating the presence of the rings rising far beyond them.

I realized the Newlaws were looking to me for an explanation, a comment, something that would help them gauge the place in their keening where the logic of the rings sprouted from the laws of nature. The yearning pleasure of their faces creased by the question, "what is it?" bore into my heart like a piercing liquid point that melted any sense of separation I might have felt from this Squad of Circus-crooning Newlaws. All I could do was look back at them, each and every one of them, and with a jubilation crazed, yet simpering blubbery smile that spoke completely my own transcendent befuddlement, I finally informed them, "Polar rings to bridge the hemispheres, unbeatable beam bands to make the mant-tech wars invisible." That was as much as my neural popping lefty could bop on the Newlaw wave band at the moment, but it was enough. The Newlaws nodded in assent or agreement, in a thoughtful pensive manner, then broke out into their usual display of rhythms and shuffles, moving like ring-blazed penguins in the snows of Punta Arenas in the Tierra del Fuego.

The rest of the day was spent in debriefings, and above all, ring gazing cross-circuited pleasantries. This band of Newlaws, I learned, had departed from Truth or Consequences almost six months ago. They were one of the first groups to leave. Knowing their journey would take them as far south as their wanderlust would take them, they slowly hovercrafted in the direction of the Tierra del Fuego, where they arrived some two weeks ago. Fleet-floating their way down here, however, they inevitably encountered their share of strange adventures. I also found out that originally there had been forty of them, twice their number than when I found them.

The reason for the decrease in their numbers was simply accounted for. "Whack-offs, Prospy, Whack-offs!" That's the cheerful earful that beauteous Clearfall gave me on this matter. When I pressed it further with her, she yawned, stretched her arms wide so that her cloak made a perfect backdrop for her wondrously tattooed body not unlike yours at all, Francesca. Then with a rapid blink of her sea green eyes, she beamed her bronzed face and shot me a Latin psyched global riff:

*"In Wa Ha Ka they blathered to a blue-heart beat*
*In Panama they wriggled wi' the Squiggly heat*
*While in Bogota they bled us to a punk retreat*
*'Til Titicaca bathed us 'n' ya see what ya meet."*

Having been declared a criminal force by the Caribbean Syndics, this band of Newlaws had been hoping for some event to turn the tide of their desperate situation. As a safety precaution one-half of them had holed up in Titicaca for further maneuvers, and the Tierra del Fuego half headed for Lower Patagonia. The intention of the half whom I encountered at Punta Arenas had been simply to fulfill the logic of their original vision to not return 'til they had reached the southern land of fire. For this reason they also called themselves, Southards.

After a simple, but hearty meal of dried beef and plankton broth, made all the warmer by the good-natured camaraderie of the Newlaw Southards, we determined the next phase of operations. By spontaneously reciting our impressions of Earth's Rings, the Patagonian Expeditionary Force and Interchangeable Force Field Circus was born, with me as its commander and a captain of the rotating activity squads. We next determined that the following morning a visit to the Darwin Radlab was mandatory. Turning in for the night, I slept soundly, though my sleep was punctured by an abnormal quantity of dreams that seemed to follow a rhythmic procession leading me to awakenment tune-ups the following morning.

Loading ourselves into the hovercraft in the morning darkness, we coasted over the barren snow wastes of the Tierra del Fuego. Sometime around 9:00 hours the rings came into view, preceding the sun, a brilliant band of colored lights through which, nonetheless, you could still see the Morning Star, burning brighter than ever. Before too long, well after 11:00 hours, we caught sight of the radiosonic dishes at the Darwin Radlab. They were all trained on the rings. It was at this point that I noticed the fifth ring pulsating, dropping in measured phrases like a curtain over the other four rings.

Yet the fifth ring was almost completely diaphanous, for even when it slipped down in those scalloped phrasings, the other four rings were still vibrantly visible.

It was while observing these phenomena that we touched down outside the Darwin Station. Pulling ourselves together we proceeded to the main entrance gate in strict Trident formation. The atmosphere was unusually quiet and no one was visible on the Dish Decks or anywhere around the cinder-block maintenance buildings. Pulling ourselves into double file as we passed through the entrance gate, plastered with its high security warnings and injunctions, we fanned out again into Trident formation as we crossed the main yard to Radlab central. As I stood there for a moment before the heavy metal encased door, I drew in a deep breath. Expelling it, I thought of all those who had aided me in arriving at this particular space-time coordinate. Then after a momentary flash into hyperpsyche void, I turned the latch on the door, turned it very slowly, then pushed it open. There I stood in the entry chamber. The monitor bank room circled around both sides of the entry chamber. Though the room was filled with a large number of Syndic Radlabbers, no one was in the least aware of the fact that we had let ourselves in.

It was not difficult to determine the cause of their lack of awareness. Everyone of the Syndic Radlabbers was glued to a monitor screen. Tiptoeing into the left I sought to observe the object that stole their awareness away from the entry of the Patagonian Expeditionary Force into their quarters. And there it was. Each monitor screen was beaming from a solar resonator space bank circling earth. What I saw was a mosaic of views of earth showing the rings from different stratospheric latitudes. It was breathtaking, especially seeing simultaneous broadcast transmissions displaying the summer north and the winter south, the day and the night sides of the globe.

"Excuse me, but who in the hell are you," a voice interrupted me from my concentration on a monitor bank view of earth's rings over Manchuria, where it must have been close to sky nadir. What fascinated me again was the glimmering transparency, the vibrancy of the colors, so that the nocturnal constellations could still be breathtakingly viewed through the majestic rings.

"Excuse me, funny-face, but I think I already asked you once, who in the hell are you?" A short stocky Darwin Radlabber in black jumpsuit and a white jacket into whose pockets two fists were stuck, stared up at me. The mind behind the black bushy eyebrows, squinty little gray-blue eyes, and a puckered little mouth that looked like it had been sucking on lemon drops for the past sixty years, vainly tried to keep and coordinate me with the event currently being monitored on all the screens. I said nothing, only smiled back. This caused the little pucker-mouthed Radlabber to drawback a bit. His mouth fell open, but only for a moment.

Then resuming his squinty inspectorial composure he continued on his earlier beam. "But, Sir, I demand to know your identity. Get it? Identity?" at which point he pulled out his metal security necklace from beneath his jumpsuit. Idly taking it into my fingers I examined it, turning it over to see both sides. On one side was the Syndic Seal, its familiar logo of four fists plunging out from the center of a square, jagged shafts of lightning joining each of the fists to each other. Beneath the square, composed of a precise double-lined border, were the code numerals, 55S-68W-.00021. On the other side of the oval-shaped medallion was simply a name: Leonid Faber Bella Costa.

"Well, Leonid," I spoke, letting the medallion drop back to his chest. "I don't really blame you for wanting, demanding even, to know my identity. These are rather unusual circumstances, aren't they?" As I asked Leonid the question, I could hear the other members of the Patagonian Expeditionary Squad revving up for a neural back-up. But I had to keep my funny bone in check, and straighten it out with old Leonid.

"Well, I'm Agent 24, Prospero Edmund Jones, Commander Patagonian Expeditionary Squad, and Rotating Activity Captain, Interchangeable Force Field Circus. And as I was saying earlier, these are rather unusual circumstances. The word 'unusual' also describes the manner of my arrival, Mr. Bella Costa, and for that reason, I have no official documentation to show you. You'll just have to take my word for it, and I guess you don't have much choice do you, Mr. Bella Costa?"

Leonid shuffled around a bit, bouncing almost. Trying desperately to avoid a total expression of exasperation, he managed a slight smile and said, "Well, yes, I suppose you could be correct on that matter. I really don't have any choice but to take your word for it. But you do realize, Mr. Jones, don't you, that you've broken into a high security area?"

"That's OK, Leonid," I emboldened myself as I put him on a first name basis. "What you're looking at can't exactly be called high security, since it's outside there and everybody in the world can see it."

Leonid puffed his cheeks out and then let them collapse. For a moment it was as if he were absorbed deep in thought. Then with a shake of the head that had his lemon-sucking jowls flapping a bit, he looked back at me once again in the old inspectorial flashback. Calmly returning his gaze, actually even acquiring a certain fondness for this cranky old Darwin Radlabber, I stood my ground.

"Hmmph, Mr. Jones, another irrefutable point," Leonid finally granted.

Cradling my right elbow in my left hand, my right hand cradling my chin, I asked, "But tell me, Leonid, have you been outside recently? Direct perception on these events can also yield useful information."

Leonid shook his head once or twice, as if trying to clear a pathway for a neural memory express. Then with a certain blankness he replied, "Why no, Mr. Jones. Now that you ask me. No. Only one of the tech sargeants here was outside. That's how we found out about it. And then at that very moment the monitor screens started flashing it. We've been preoccupied with it ever since."

"Well then maybe you should step outside with me, Leonid, and just take a good vector analysis on the spot." As I took Leonid gently by the arm, I saw that the other Radlabbers had glanced at us but then gone back to twirling their dials, pushing their buttons, and bleep-bleeping their isometric coordinate figures into the audio boxes.

As we turned to the entry chamber, the whole Newlaw contingent was in a flap. Outrageous logical declamations had broken out, and they were all busily jabbering away, "Slyke the hike, and bisque the torque, skies way yond the hair o' york," one of the squad members turned to Leonid and barked right to his face. Leonid shivered a bit, then pulled himself together as we made our way through the crowd that had sorted itself out into clusters of two members each, their arms flying every which way as they pursued logic to its limits. Even as we stepped into the snowy mainground, we could hear the declamations of the Newlaws breaking into a soft chant of resolution:

*"Beam... Beam... Beam... Beam...*
*Let Rings relay globes' glad-glow gleem."*

As we made our way back out through the main entrance, I spied a slight rise toward our left, away from the Darwin Station building complex. A few large boulders poked up through the billowing snow dunes. This seemed a perfect spot to take Mr. Bella Costa.

Puffing just behind me, I could hear him muttering away... "no warning, you know, Mr. Jones, absolutely no warning—I mean we knew about the Geoharmone, the Triangula Encantada as they speak of it in Patagonia, you realize-specification reports filed by our reconnaissance units, no indication... is this... what is this?"

I realized Mr. Bella Costa's footsteps were no longer audible. Turning around I saw why. There was old Leonid rooted to the spot, the snow almost up to his knees. While his hands busily tweaked and pulled at his identity necklace, his face was agog. His eyes had become totally fixated on the rings. An occasional muscle spasm, a twitch across the forehead, a lick of the tongue on otherwise dry lips were Leonid's only response to the vision he was attempting to comprehend.

Walking back next to him, I, too, let the rings absorb my attention. The fifth ring which had been rhythmically active earlier now dissipated sedately into the stratosphere. To the north the mid-winter solstice sky-zenith sun hung in spectral splendor above the shimmering snow jagged peaks of the Tierra del Fuego. Leonid and I both slowly took in the entire length of the rings.

When Leonid finally turned to me again, he sputtered and fumed, casting out his words like a drowning man flailing his arms in the treacherous waves of a stormy sea. "Impossible, absolutely impossible—Saturn, Uranus equatorial rings, but polar rings—absurd! Yet… What is it? What is it doing to us? Polar rings—Mr. Jones, please… Mr. Jones… can't you…isn't there… anything you… Mr. Jones-Polar Rings, what is it?"

It was something far more than perplexity that had reduced Leonid's face to its present condition of helpless, pleading anxiety. It was the presence of a phenomenon whose purity of form must certainly have been based on some kind of logic, yet whatever the logic might have been, it utterly transcended Leonid Faber Bella Costa's ability to cope with it.

As I looked at the poor man's face, his cheeks bellowing out and collapsing rapidly, his eyes desperately searching mine for an answer, I replied to him, "Your questions, Leonid. Your questions certainly seem to point to the singularity of the phenomenon. They're good questions, Leonid, don't feel bad. Look at it some more, and see what comes."

The mere fact that I spoke at all at that moment softened considerably the dreadlock mantle of conspiratorial paranoia which had begun to asphyxiate the baffled Radlabber beyond any possibility of further verbal communication. Finally, regaining some beskewed sense of his monitorial dignity, Leonid turned back to ring-gazing. The pudgy little hands were clasped behind his back, while the hairy little fingers tapped against each other giving some indication of the functioning of Leonid's scanning and computing process. I joined him in ring-gazing, both of us turning our heads upward and to the right, solemnly absorbing the fine-lined mirage that pulsated ever so subtly in an undeviating echo of Earth's polar curve, in the winter-crisp Tierra del Fuego light.

"You know," Leonid turned to me, for the first time displaying a cautious but highly inquisitive twinkle of appreciation, "there is something so fine about those rings. I mean, you know, they're not actually, bothersome. They're what, a hundred kilometers, do you suppose? Yet for being so far up, they're certainly intense-so fine, no deformation. I don't know, but Mr. Jones, they have nothing to do with gravity do they? Is it a radiosonic curtain? And that fifth ring. You wouldn't think something that far distant would have the effect it does!"

"What effect, Leonid?" I was eager what the rings might actually be inducing in other humans.

"Well, it's difficult to describe, but it's like this…" Leonid cocked his head toward the left and squinted irregularly a few times. "Yes, it, the fifth ring in particular, seems to emit a sound, like when I was a boy falling asleep. But no, that's ridiculous—a music—no, a sound that appears to be both human-caused and naturally self-existing at the same time. Odd, I must say, Jones, this is quite a radiosonic trick you've pulled off, but what is it going to do to us?" Leonid's voice was urgent, squatting on the boundary lines of panic. Little flickers of paranoia crested rapidly through his eyes.

"Well, I'll tell you one thing," I said swinging myself around so that I was facing the little Darwin Radlabber, his expression now resembling that of a rat rearing on its hind legs, when it has just encountered a desert Tabby, its snarling mouth grinning lasciviously at its trapped prey. "Oh, c'mon Leonid, it's not that bad!" I growled in his face breaking him out of his paranoid cage. "What I'm trying to tell you is that if you try to turn this one off, you might as well eliminate the ground you're standing on, you know, turn off the earth itself, eliminate it altogether from this solar system. Zappo! Over and out! You know what I mean?"

Leonid blinked at me a few times, then shook his head wildly, as if to dispel some dream. Then he cautiously looked up. When his face relaxed, you knew he was keening earth's rings again. I, too, turned and gazed once more at the fine ultra-high frequency polar sheathe that arced across the cloud-dappled sky. Giving it my full attention I felt as though my body had dropped away and my heart alone throbbed to the crystalline oscillation of the rings, so high over the earth, so far above the enemy, so far beyond aggression!

"Jones, are you all right?" It was Leonid shaking me from my hyperpsyche void state.

"Of course I'm all right, Leonid," I said politely removing his arms from my shoulders.

"But tell me then," Leonid persisted, "what was it about your radiosonic trick that had you so absorbed?"

"Leonid," I said, squaring up to him in order to deliver the direct shot, "this is no radiosonic trick. What we've been looking at, and what all of us will be looking at for a long time to come is so far from being a radiosonic trick that you might just as well turn in your identity medallion."

"But," Leonid implored, "then what is it?"

"Would you believe, synthesonic radiation, Mr. Bella Costa?" And just to be precise I added, "Synthesonic radiation infraneurally triggered, at that?"

"Synthesonic radiation?" Leonid's face introverted only to resurface with another blank.

"C'mon, Leonid," I spoke gingerly, "you know PANs and Syndics have been playing polesy since the breakdown of the Geomant Syndic Councils. What with you here, in Lower Patagonia, and us in Ultima Thule, this is the super logical consequence of all our collective researches, conflict inducing or otherwise. And this is it!"

Leonid looked up at the rings, then back at me. "Synthesonic radiation? Well, if what we're looking at is at the lower reaches of the Van Allen Radiation belt," Leonid began articulating some of his impressions, "and its polar, rather than equatorial, then this must be something in the nature of the aurora borealis. But synthesonic?"

"Right Leonid, synthesonic." At this moment I had to fight off Sticklepick's shape-shifting tendencies. It was too early for old Leonid. However, as if catching some hint of another Syndic-staggering maneuver, the Darwin Radlabber looked at me with alarm, his face engraved with a plea for understanding.

"It's beautiful, isn't it, Leonid?" I spoke pointing to the rings. That did it, it deflected Bella Costa's paranoia.

His face resumed a more relaxed mood, the lemon-sucking lips parting in a sweet little smile. "You're right about that, Jones. It's…"then he paused, "it's actually more than beautiful, it's…" Leonid couldn't finish his sentence for the simple reason that his wild outburst of laughter wouldn't permit him to.

At first, Leonid's laughter came out in an almost hysterical explosion. I thought the poor man was about to die of apoplexy. Then after a few of these spasms which had him doubling over, and while wiping his eyes, the laughter came in shorter bursts of whole-hearted appreciation.

Finally calming down altogether, Leonid looked at me and said, "Mr. Jones, don't you think we ought to go back to the Radlab, and give some kind of report on this little excursion of ours?"

"Sure Leonid, let's go," I said pulling my woolen poncho tightly over my shoulders. After hesitating a moment, I took his arm as we slowly trekked back through the snow.

"Mind you, Jones, you may know more about this than I do, but don't think that because of that, I necessarily trust you. After all, you are in 'Our Territory,' and you do owe us an explanation, at least of what you and that goon-squad Patagonian Expeditionary Force of yours are doing here." Leonid looked up at me, with the old conspiratorial squint.

"Scam it any way you want, Leonid," I said, pausing to take in the rings once more. "But you know as well as I do that the Tierra del Fuego is simply the land of fire. The land was here long before the Darwin Station ever was, or, for that matter, a helluva long time before old Darwin ever started poking his nose around here looking for evolutionary clues. This is no more your territory than the rings are the property of the Geomantic Union or the Syndicate for Material Evolution. They just are, Leonid, they just are!" Leonid did not bother to respond. He simply looked at me and with his now inimitable tic, allowed his head to start forward several times in rapid succession. Walking the rest of the way back in silence, I noticed that wherever his perplexity might have taken him, it had at least caused a smile to appear on his jowly little face.

So ended stage one: Summer of Stars, Patagonia Maneuvers.

The following weeks were placid enough: info reception coordinated with info synthesis so that we got an increasingly more accurate readout on the now visible synthesonic radiation belt that straddled the earth, while at the same time installing an electrodronic system in the already existing monitor bank. Syndic's main concern was determining the effects of this radiation belt upon behavior patterns. Despite the questionable motives, the answers the Syndics got persistently transcended any kind of entropic interpretation. As the information synthesis became more structured, talk of retaliation and protective radiosonic maneuvers gave way to discussions about the possibilities of georhythmic feedback imprinting and speculations about how Cape town was going to respond.

It was at this point, maybe ten days ago, that the electrodronic system was finally set in place, thus initiating the Interchangeable Force Field Circus round of action. The Newlaws did this one up as fine as anything ever done up in Truth or Consequences. This they did by feeding the rings' oscillation frequencies via the monitor bank to the electrodronic synthesis code circuit. It started up slow at daybreak, then pulsed forward to 9:00 hours then subsided again in a swoon of long quartertone runs until sky-zenith. That's when we broke into round downs. It wasn't too long before the Darwin

Radlabbers joined the rest of us in the Fifth Ring Round Downs which were conducted daily in the main yard of the compound.

I can still recall Old Leonid coming in, his hands palms flat up above his head, his cheeks all rosy, puffing away after his first Fifth Ring Round Downs, exclaiming "Exponential, that's it, the effect is exponential!"

Last night we held a major meeting. Before us was the decision of whether or not to beam north to Montivideo and other Patagonian stations. After talk of rebellion, sedition and revolution had gone around three times, an exultant Leonid took to the floor and declared, "Five Rings earth shows, the Fifth is us! Let's talk no more, but shore earth's trust!"

Then with cries of "Reft and Lighters to the Fore," we concluded our meeting with a spontaneous infraneural game called "bond-off." This morning we set everything in place and began monitoring electrodronic info beams to the other Patagonian Stations.

"This'll be the Fall of Patagonia," Leonid called out as he pushed the coordinate release button on the lead monitor.

As you can see by the course of events down here in the Land of Fire, Summer of Stars, Patagonian maneuvers has entered Stage II. If we can keep the momentum going, I'm sure I'll be able to break away and be back in Dawnsource Circle in time for the birth of the child. In any case, this information should give you the go-flow on RED city operation number two, so do it!

Signing off now, Honeybabe. This is Love-Catcher Starfall Two, Arcturian Brigade, the Friendly Beam Bound Neuronaut, Prospero Edmund Jones.

By the way, did you catch that transmission from AhKa and its encounter with the Rehab minister in Capetown?

To be continued…

# FRANCESCA'S TAPE LOG: THE ULTIMATE WEAPON: HOME AT LAST

To: Prospero Edmund Jones,
Assistant Commander, Lagos-Ife Rehab Command

From: Francesca Della Francesca,
Domestic Liaison (inactive), Dawnsource Circle

Hey there, Prospy, anything been gooning you lately, or are you still operating with the Direct Shot? Following this report you'll get the last Ring Readout, 4x, 9.21.241. I presume from your last report that you and the rest of the Command Squad will soon be finishing up with the new Lagos-Ife emplacement. Any news on Abdul-Rumi's whereabouts? That was a nasty one he pulled in Tashkent last week. He's certainly moving fast.

Things here have calmed down tremendously. The move up the slope past the farside of the Deneb Canals has been absolutely wonderful, exhilarating—I feel like I've come home to my bod once again. Between having given birth and what I can only take to be the initial effects of the rings, my bod has been exquisitely relaxed. And I'm not alone in this experience. Your mother, who has been virtually living with me since you left again last month, has also been feeling as if her bod had been bathed in a vibratory tonic. "Rhythmic, yet constant and unmoving," that's how she described how she felt this morning after slake fast.

As for your daughter, Prospy, I'm afraid she's come into possession of all your goon-genes-that and your gorgeous melanin brown over-ride. She still keeps me awake during the night, but I don't mind that in the least. In fact, I've just put her back in the hammock and I'm issuing this report at 3:30 hours. We just finished watching the 3:00 curtain drop. Dawnsource was totally rapt as I held her in my arms out on the west deck. There it was, high above the sundown side of the Jornada del Muerto. When the Fifth Ring starts to do that wondrous undulation, everything becomes still. At three in the morning things are still enough, only the crickets keep it going at that time, but even they wipe out at curtain drops. I understand now that even if you're asleep, the whole system from heart beat to neural bleep slows down for about five minutes. Natural relaxant, huh? And your daughter, Dawnsource, seems to be timing her wake-ups to correspond with curtain drops. At least that's the way it's been for the last five days.

That schedule seems to have begun after we had a visit from three of the old O Mo Lung Ringers. Up they came between mid-morn and sky-zenith curtain drops, all flopsy and wizened with their rag-tatter shoulder bags, two of them shaking gourd rattles, the third one holding a hand drum, the kind with the two percussive balls that beat when you move your wrist.

"Francesca Della Francesca, Heart Mother of Dawnsource Circle, how are you this beautiful morning?" they called up to me as I sat on the south edge of the deck nursing Dawnsource and soaking up sunring rays. Picking their way carefully through the morning glory patch to the side of the deck, they stood before me, their grinning leathery old faces setoff by rows of yellow teeth that seemed to grow every which way. In fact, what struck me about them is how much they resembled each other as if they were triplets. It was either that or a triple shape shift projection. Appreciating the joyous enigma of their presence, I didn't bother to inquire as to the truth of the matter.

Letting down their shoulder bags, they put their instruments away. The one in the middle then drew out a small tray. It looked perhaps as if it were black lacquer. The other two in the meantime reached deep into their shoulder bags and pulled out a variety of objects. While the middle man held the tray out in his hands, the other two began placing the objects in some kind of pre-determined arrangement upon the tray. The objects included: an old brass bell, a heap of what appeared to be sunflower seeds, a thigh-bone trumpet, a small arrangement of silicon chips, and a small crystal sphere, almost like a large marble.

"The girl, let us see the girl," they all shouted at once.

Picking myself up from the deck chair, I approached them. Little Dawnsource, alert that something else was going on, gave up on my nipple.

"Let us see her, let us see her!" they exclaimed, eagerness running like honey from their little wrinkled smiles.

I propped Dawnsource against my breasts which supported her little head, its deep russet wisps catching light from the morning sun. The middle man then thrust the tray right up to baby Dawnsource. Though I couldn't see the baby's face, the reactions of the three O Mo Lung Ringers were a veritable circus of wonderment. While Dawnsource made several soft cooing sounds, the three O Mo Lung Ringer's faces registered an exacting series of expressions: curiosity, delight in recognition, awe, surprise and utter pleasure, each in their turn wrote themselves large upon those timeless oracled wrinkles of theirs. Several times I saw Dawnsource's little chubby hands sweep over the tray, the fingers wriggling until they came upon an object, then extending out as if they were stretching, for maybe ten seconds. After a few minutes of this, the tray was put down in a blaze of purple and orange morning glories.

"May we hold her?" the middle man asked me. How could I refuse. No sooner did the questioner receive Dawnsource into his outstretched arms, then the other two were immediately hovering over her, stroking her and muttering strange little bird-like trills. When Dawnsource's little left hand found the mouth of one of the men, she thrust in her little fist as far as she could jam it. You couldn't have made these three men happier if you had told them that the Rings were emanations of their own heart-beats. Laughing heartily and merrily they handed Dawnsource back to me, their faces radiant with tender solicitations.

Once they had strapped their shoulder bags over their deep blue, with orange trim, cotton-robed bodies, the speaker stepped closer to me, and looking carefully into my eyes spoke his piece: "Dawnsource Heart Mother, we are three old O Mo Lung Ring-ers who appreciate all that you have done in establishing the Rings. We also appreciate your graciousness in sharing these few minutes with us, and especially for allowing your daughter to investigate the oracle signs. She is charmed and will do all of us well. Take care, however, that she remains well-nourished until her tenth year. After that, she will take care of herself. If she is over-demanding, listen once, then ignore it. She will understand."

Then, reaching into his sleeve, he took out a small sash, knotted together with crimson and gold thread. Handing it to me, and with a clap of his hands, he sang in his crickety, wheezy voice:

> *"Weaving blood with golden light*
> *the lords of Vel brought earth to sight."*

Bowing in unison, the three twirled around and shuffled away, their arms gesticulating toward a formation of hawks high overhead which circled perfectly, almost lazily, as if in a dream.

Not only did little Dawnsource respond to curtain drops after that experience, but it also gave me much to reflect upon. Yet, for all I've reflected, I don't know any other way to put it than to tell it like it is: slow and simple.

First of all, the move to the east quadrant of the Deneb Canal Zone, like every-thing else that's been happening here recently, was perfectly timed. I've never loved being anywhere so much as I love being here. The platform deck which you and the Grubetubes constructed reminds me of the early days at Shasta Abbey. Except for one thing: this is home, Prospy, home.

Needless to say, with the wonderful weather we spend much of our time outdoors. In the mornings the three of us, Tara, Dawnsource and myself can usually be found out on the south deck. We get there in time for midmorn curtain drops, which puts us into a quiet state, not unlike sitting at pre-dawn heart cave time, you know, when everything glows and disappears into the light of mind's own silence. In that mood, while I nurse or we take turns holding Dawnsource, we speak only occasionally, usu-ally to point out humming-birds, a butterfly or one of the many flocks of hawks, swal-lows, or even geese that have come to Dawnsource Circle in order to practice their aerial geometrics. The view south lifts us over the west shoulder of the Sierra Oscura, while the Rings cut across the sky in a clean angled sweep from up past our left side. After sky-zenith curtain drops-I like the way they cut the sky in two, as if the sky had been slashed by a two-day diamond laser shot out from solar center-anyway, Prospy, it's after sky-zenith curtain drops that we take our naked, sun drenched, ring-rayed dripping bodies inside for lunch. Cold cream shrimp broth with sprigs of cilantro, blue corn cake and liters of lemonade-that was what we had today.

In the afternoon Tara goes down to Dawnsource Circle to attend to whatever busi-ness, which these days usually means gooning up a greeting for another gaggling glob of global travelers. They keep streaming in here these days. So far, though, representa-tive delegations have been crisp at heeding the call for only one visitation to arrive at Dawnsource daily. After they leave here, they generally go for a rehab-vacate cruise to Chaco, Hopi, Mogollon Mesa and that seed bed of mutant tidings, Truth or Con-sequences. By the time they've taken in the sights, and done a little mixing with the denizens of the Enchanted Triangle, the delegations, the whole mind-jamming crew of them, seems hardly fit to take on a semi-global cruise in a hovercraft. But they manage it, they get off the ground usually with a few more mutants than when they arrived, headed back to Delhi or wherever with another interchangeable force field circus act.

Yesterday, at least, it was the delegation from Delhi. Today, Tara tells me it'll be the Woomera contingent. "Wouldn't surprise me in the least if they each and everyone looked exactly like Poonie." That's what your mother said before turning in last night.

But anyway, Prospy, the afternoons are also magical, especially the view of Dawn-source Circle seen from the north deck of the yurt at the east quadrant marker of the

Deneb Canals. The days are still hot, and out on the north deck it's shady. Often there's a breeze blowing down the mountain side which also keeps things fresh. So I sit there with Dawnsource in the big cane chair, the one with the giant multi-headed cobra shaped back, watching Tara diminish in size as she wends her way down the flower embroidered paths of the Deneb Canal zone. Through the reeds and bamboo, along the edge of the canals, you can see an occasional slack-zoner floating by on his gondo-glider. But the best thing down the slope to the northwest is Dawnsource Circle itself.

Things have gone smooth as mesa butter since you left, not that they weren't going smoothly while you were here, Prospy babe. But you should see the solar ring ray monitor bank surrounding Alpha Pit Central. It's got eight components set on circular stems. Well, maybe circular's not the right word for those stems. More like shaped, granite slabs polished to bring out their basic geo-formational veining. Conductor shafts have been laser-bored down the centers of those rocks, from top to bottom, while the solar ring ray monitor bank is ball-bearing balanced on the top bore of the rock. These liquid metal reinforced electrochemically treated membranes are so delicate and sensitive in their reflective power, that they look like a series of eight mammothly-shaped butterfly wings, quivering and shooting scintillating beams of light every which way. Of course, the butterfly membranes look all the more brilliant, set as they are on those dragon-veined rocks.

Alpha Pit Central is still there, looking slightly archaic, or maybe even ancient, in the midst of the butterfly wing solar ring ray monitor bank. But it did you well, right Prospy? You wonderful infraneural trigger, you Quetzalcoatl-popping radiosonic leap-frog artist-I can't wait 'til you return. Fortunately I'm on inactive and so I can jam all of this slack-gaff into the report, right Prospy? Even the warbles about how you caress my loins with a tongue that sizzles like wet velvet on a hot iron. That was just to give you something deep to think about, Prospy. You always were the deep kind, you know.

But back to my report. Like I said, slow and simple. Little domestic samplings, because this is life, and nothing more.

So, there I am on the north deck. It's the mid-afternoon 15:00 curtain drops that are best from the east quadrant Deneb yurt. Yesterday, as the day before, little Dawnsource woke up at about 14:50-woke up with a squawk followed by a simpering caterwaul. I know what that was. And just like yesterday it was the shit in the diapers that had her calling. Wiping her off and plopping her splashy-kazoo into the baby tub, you should see her smile-and with those big emerald green eyes, too. The bath definitely normalizes her into bliss-base. Wiping her off, we sit down in the big cane chair.

Within a minute its curtain drops. You can see the whole horizon just by turning the chair so that it faces due west. The Rings are way up thereat about 45°. No sooner does the Fifth Ring begin to undulate then everything falls quiet. Things are so sharp then, like the blades on a yucca cactus plant stark-still in the Jornada del Muerto flats. Even the aerial geometry of the birds high up comes to a halt as everything motionlessly absorbs curtain drop imprint time. I always think even the shadows are listening.

It's after curtain drop that I go in for some tea. Holding Dawnsource in my left arm. I get the water on the fire pit. By the way, we acquired anew cauldron. It's so big I'll bet you could almost fit inside it. If I could, I'd cook you up fast. But just to show you how impartial my love for you is, I'd serve you to everyone in Dawnsource Circle. Prospero Soup, I'd call it. And everyone who tasted it would turn into a beam-bound neural love-bandit just like you, Prospy.

Taking my tea out on the deck, I catch the rays of afternoon sunlight as they break over the yurt roof. Downhill from Dawnsource Circle, you can hear the rhythm picking up. I figure it usually means that the Daily Delegates are being introduced to another work brigade during afternoon whack-offs. Yet, as soon as the sounds come up, they drift away. Everything seems to be like that now, so sharp and precise, yet always melting to nowhere. With the autumn equinox now past, the late afternoon has taken on a dusky, purple-shadowed sweetness.

Yesterday, however, the sweetness was enhanced by a visitor, Alfonso Purimac. Of course, at first I only heard him. Just as I was walking up and down the deck seeing if Dawnsource was going to fall asleep, the water-reed tones of Alfonso's flute began to wash into my ears in little yearning waves of sound. Then like a lullaby, they sent a soft rhythm through my body. That certainly put Dawnsource to sleep. After placing her into the wooden rocking cradle that Ramakrishna al-Badr fashioned for her, I turned around to see where Alfonso Purimac was blowing his flute. The sound now came down indelicate torrents that only had me thinking of you, Prospy, the way you come in delicate torrents. But Alfonso was nowhere in sight. I must have walked around the yurt three times. And then I got it. He was inside the yurt. Quietly letting myself in, I found him, seated on the guest mat, blowing a series of low tones that at the same time whistled like the wind sweeping down a canyon before a winter storm.

Putting down his flute, Alfonso turned to me, and in his gracious manner greeted me, "Lady Francesca, Heart Mother of Dawnsource Circle, what a pleasant surprise to find you here this morning!"

Though I had heard Alfonso play his flute a number of times now, I had never really spent any time with him. I found myself surprised that words came out of his mouth, surprised and delighted even to discover that he was more than a sack of wind attached to a flute. His sunbronzed face crinkled into a soft smile. Short-cropped black hair came down just over the top of his brow, while his simple white tunic, open at the top, was sashed with a magnificent woven belt, exactly like the one the O Mo Lung Ringers had given to Dawnsource. His black eyes burned with a gratifying light, not unlike the warm dusky light of the late afternoon sun.

Pointing to the medium-sized sheepskin shoulder bag on the yurt floor next to him, he declared, "A mother has to eat, especially a mother who has given birth to the Ultimate Weapon. I have brought food for you. If you would like, I can prepare it and share it with you."

I realized that I was at a loss for words, not that my face did not show signs of great pleasure. I went to him and knelt down beside him. His body gave off a fragrant odor-musk, violet, chaparral blossoms. It made me feel as if I had always known him, just like I had always known the movement of the seasons, the transformation of the clouds, all of earth's secret comings and partings, from tiny lichen covered rocks to the unparalleled magnificence and simplicity of the Rings. It was the feeling that everything is just so. And at that moment, I wondered, how can it be, all that has happened, so strange and beyond all calculation, how can it be?

As if reading my thoughts, Alfonso asked me, "Francesca, you are not afraid of living the universal life are you?"

"The universal life?" I repeated, struck by the terrible all-encompassing forthrightness of the phrase.

"Yes, Francesca, the universal life. Isn't that what the Fifth Ring is preparing us for? Not just you and I and the other people who have come to live at Dawnsource Circle, but everyone and everything that make up Planet Earth itself: the universal life." The expression on Alfonso's face was undeniable, like a mirror, or a mountain stream tumbling in great torrents over the rocks of millennial hope and fear.

And I knew he was right. I knew that for centuries, for I don't know how long, we earthlings had been struggling in blindness against each other, not seeing or realizing that earth was waiting for us. It was not only the earth that had been waiting for us, but the planets, the sun, the rest of the universe itself-the universal life.

And the Rings are nothing new. They, too, have been there, building up over the ages of human conflict, waiting for that moment for the flint of human understanding and realization to strike the fire-stone of earth's possibilities. But only at the right time and place. And so the Rings themselves, call them nature, call them art, are nothing more than a testimony and initial manifestation of the maturation of what has always been.

"But Francesca," Alfonso's voice penetrated the ascent of my thoughts, "but Francesca, we must cook, and I have good things. While the baby sleeps we can prepare this together."

"Yes," I finally spoke, "yes."

From his bag, Alfonso pulled out many things: mushrooms, cilantro, green tomatoes, peppers, bean curd, dried shrimp, ginger root, potatoes, little spice bags of all kinds, and a magnificent bass, its glassy eyes sparkling in the dusky light of the yurt. While Alfonso readied the bass, all the while singing random stanzas from the epic that had seeped down to us over the centuries in fairy tales and children's riddles. I prepared the broth at the fire pit. Succulent smells filled the home-space of the yurt, while Alfonso's voice carried the harmonic line of our activity:

> *"Rising setting breathing dying*
> *warriors sent earth's field flying*
> *and on far Arcturus skies*
> *Vel beheld what never lies!"*

After Alfonso had dressed the bass with cornflower and spices, he laid it triumphantly in the large shallow pan already bubbling with shrimp broth, Deneb Canal style. As the dinner came together, great tear-streaming surges of happiness overwhelmed me. Once we had the lid on the big dipper frying pan, I took Alfonso's hands in mine and squeezed them tightly. "This is so good, Alfonso. This is so good."

"It's going to be even better now, Francesca," Alfonso replied, his shy grin turning impish.

"Why's that?" I asked.

"Don't you hear that?"

I listened. Outside the desert warblers were chiming up for sundown. In the tangle of birds merrily trying to out chirp each other was another sound-that of Dawnsource cooing and calling, dropping a plumbline down to the timeless pit of my maternal instincts.

After cleaning and washing her, along with lots of well-placed love slaps on her plump baby buttocks, Alfonso and I took position for 18:00 curtain drops. These are always especially spectacular from up the far side of the Deneb Canals on the southwest slopes of the Sierra Oscura. Melting into the all-absorbing silence, my eyes alone remained active as they took in the brilliant oscillation of the Fifth Ring. Then, down it dropped its violet curtain, dropped it over the shadowy mountain tops of the western ranges, dropped it over the sun, itself sinking and melting in a blaze of purple, pink, and orange, behind earth's far rim. As the sun sank out of view, leaving in its wake a Trident spray of pink and golden clouds, the Rings themselves passed out of view, leaving only a breathless after-image imprinted on the evening sky.

We continued sitting in silence as the sounds of earth began again, the crickets and the cicadias, the desert warblers, the screaming blue jays, the crotchety calling magpies, the hide-and-seek barking of dogs and coyotes, and the insistent sound of a drum from far down in Dawnsource Circle, beating and beating its rhythm to the rhythm of our bodies. And wafting lines of song, these, too, came up from Dawnsource Circle. And along with the blended sensation of the evening sounds and the herb-ripe dinner-time smells of the yurt, along with that came Tara Andromeda, smiling and throwing a boomerang. It was obvious that the source of her pleasure came about from the sureness with which the boomerang always returned to her.

"Helloooo!" she cried out, stopping to pick a few golden chrysanthemums at the edge of the east Deneb starpool. Having gathered the flowers, and while clasping them to her breast along with the boomerang, she ran up to us. Then just as she was hardly a meter away from us she stopped. The clusters of chrysanthemums, gold flowered and green-leafed were lustrous against the ancient gray-coloring of the boomerang.

Slowly, Tara Andromeda lifted her head. Then Alfonso and I turned our heads in the direction which Tara faced. Lifting Dawnsource up in my arms, we all gazed in awe as the evening Rings rose above the Sierra Oscura.

"Home," Tara whispered tenderly, "home at last."

So as you can see, Prospy, there's not much to report. I only want you to know that I'm waiting for you.

The particular transmission which we have been following ends at this humble point. Whatever became of Prospero Edmund Jones and Francesca Della Francesca is both unknown and irrelevant. What is significant is that within a generation of the establishment of the Fifth Ring, "Planet Mind, Planet Teacher" as it came to be known, warfare on the Art Planet finally ceased. Following an arduous, but sporty five-century period of fine tuning, the Art Planet succeeded in entering the Galactic Star Round Game Sweepstakes by proclaiming itself a total work of art. As member stars fully recognize, the leadership of planet three, Velatropa 24, has been a key ingredient in the exponential transformation of the Velatropa Galaxy into a star-field of increasingly illuminating precocity.

For the Galactic Elders, this transmission, call it a story if you will, has endured as a fairy tale classic, better known as "How Earth Got Its Rings." In the fairy tale version, this little classic usually begins:

> *"Thus it is said, once upon a space-time vector in*
> *distant Velatropa, a small stellar unit produced a*
> *planet known as Earth, or Velatropa 24.3. Renowned for*
> *its brilliant system of Rings, galactic travelers often ask:*
> *'How did Velatropa 24.3 get its Rings?'*
> *This story is the answer to that question."*

Following an arduous, but sporty period of synthesonic chromo-cellular regeneration and fine tectonic plate tuning, the Art Planet succeeded in entering the Transgalactic Star Round Sweepstakes by declaring itself to be a total work of art.

For the Galactic Elders of the Arcturian Round Table, this transmission, THE MAKING OF THE FIFTH RING, call it an interplanetary fable if you will, endures as a classic in the art of honoring intelligence. Its study is recommended for all those who would care to engender interspecies, as well as intergalactic communication.

Whether you have followed this fable for sheer entertainment, for insight, or for a little of both, it is the sincerest desire of the AAA (Analyst of the Arcturian Archives) that you have taken it to heart-that and little else.

As with all other AAA transmissions, THE MAKING OF THE FIFTH RING has been brought to you by Synchrotronic Auto-translations Disincorporated, a division of RED City Productions. As a footnote to this poignant tale, we leave you with one of the rare, once lost and now retrieved, transmissions of the Venerable AhKa IV, for you, the inhabitants of a parallel world in a parallel time.

Thank you,

Analyst of the Arcturian Archives

## An Art Planet Weather Report: From Romantic to Geomantic

*"In Velatropa far away*
*though devoid of mind's full sway*
*in measured form with rhythmic heart*
*all that's done is done as art!"*

### Report filed by:

### AhKa IV, Commander,
### Space Cocoon Surveillance Spore, Velatropan Vector.

### To: Central Hierarchy Vanguard, Arcturus 108x.

I realize I have been sorely remiss in my reports for a number of centuries now-on Velatropa 24.3, called by the locals "earth," a hundred revolutions around the central star comprise a century. In any case, it is imperative that you receive an update on critical developments occurring on the Art Planet, Velatropa 24.3.

It's been some five centuries now since the intelligence here attained incipient globalization-but under the greediest and most spurious of circumstances. Gold and the need for ideological domination, that's what brought it about. Disgusting!

Within two centuries mechanized industrialization was established, and with that event-goodness, did that speed things up!-the collective art spores all but disintegrated. All knowledge became bent to the end of increasing materialism. When material goods can't be acquired by forthright plunder or diplomacy, then it's war. In fact, I have been appalled at the degree to which war has replaced the arting ends of this planet.

But don't let me get ahead of myself. I should say a few more words about the manner in which Velatropa 24.3 has arted. It took some four billion stellar revolutions of cooling off and numerous biospheric experimentations before this planet evolved a type of being skillful enough to carry the art enzyme and to deploy them in a manner beneficial to the establishment of a unitary consciousness.

Beginning some 50,000 stellar revolutions ago, through the medium of these beings-they call themselves humans or earthlings-the planet began to art in a consistent manner. Having spread a fine membrane of art over the planet, well over one hundred centuries past, these beings initiated experiments in agriculture. This provided the base for what they came to call "civilization."

There were six independent sites where this civilizing process erupted on the planet surface. Though "individual" civilizations were generally unaware of all of the others, and, hence, each developed a false sense of uniqueness, from the Arcturian perspective, there is no question that civilization is a single planetary phenomenon.

What distinguishes civilization as a geological phase of Velatropa 24.3 is its artfulness. While "humans" are the civilizing carriers of the art enzyme, "artiers" is the rightful name for these beings.

Well, not meaning to be tedious or redundant, suffice it to say that these artiers, more unconsciously than consciously, for several thousand stellar revolutions, through their civilizing efforts, allowed the planet to art in a variety of styles and forms. Though the aggressive behavior known as war inevitably developed as a result of the false sense of territorial uniqueness, still, there was enough down here of what's called a "spiritual force" to keep things in balance.

All of that changed, ironically enough, with the onset of incipient globalization. As I've already mentioned, with the spread of industrialization, it seemed almost certain that war would replace art, and with that seal the Art Planet's doom.

During this dark, downward turn of events, a handful of artiers rose to the occasion of championing art as the Voice of the Earth. These industrial age artiers came to be called "romantics." This strange, half-demented lot of misfits, intoxicated by the pathos of their own situation, nevertheless kept alive the flame of art. At least, they were moved by some recollection of human vision cooperating with the urges of the earth and this was much more than could be said of the Dark Lords of Matter who ascended to power at that time.

However, by the dawn of the third century of industrialization, following a disastrous war (World War I, they called it), even the romantics began to stray, dear me, into the confused by-ways of their mind, choked with the weeds of desperate and erroneous concepts. Trapped as they were in urban zones, these romantics, sadly enough, had begun to lose touch with the Voice of the Earth.

Following the indescribable turning point of Hiroshima culminating their "Second World War"—my, such a pathetic misuse of globalization—most of the originally romantically inspired artiers had lost contact with the Voice of the Earth, not to mention the "Starry Dynamo of Night!"

As the romantic pose turned into urban guerrilla art dogma, the need became ever more clear: if the Art Planet was to attain its true destiny, a new call had to be issued. Instead of romantic, the downtrodden, starving, rebellious artier needed a new image, a new role, a new sense of purpose.

It was just at that moment, when the basest minds held the highest positions in planetary affairs and were befuddling people's lives that threats of total war known as "peace through strength," that the newly-formed Planet Art Network (PAN), issued its first RTA Weather Report, "The Romantic-Geomantic Transposition." So, let us turn to that decisive geomantic proclamation for a brighter take on a great evolutionary moment for our old favorite, the Art Planet, Velatropa 24.3.

---

Psychoatmospheric Weather Report no. 1

Issued by:

RTA Contingent, Planet Art Network
The Romant-Geomant Transposition

# A T T E N T I O N !

Feedback received from the Global Memory Bank straddling the soft underbelly of the Van Allen Radiation Belt indicates the dispersal of a psychic weather front of unprecedented magnitude.

As we now know, the last major psychic weather front precipitated by the transition from a stage of mystic exaltation to a focus on means of industrial production resulted in a peculiar quickening of the art enzyme. This disparately adopted quickening manifest in the artier type-romantic.

The new psychic weather front currently blanketing the biosphere augurs a decisive transposition from Post-Atomic Romantic to Synthesizing Geomantic-otherwise known as the Romant-Geomant Transposition.

While the Post-Atomic Romant Front is dissipating in confused pockets of entropic individualism, the new front is effecting a synthesis of all previous stages manifest by the art enzyme. At the same time, the naturally occurring synthesis is synergizing a re-grouping of artiers into collectives known as "Art Spores."

Since the focus of the Art Spores is the harmonious and skillfully compassionate uplifting of the total planet, to the end of enabling it to cast its VOTE (Voice of the Earth) among other luminaries in this galaxy, the new front takes on the designation "Geomantic."

Sprouting from the timelessness of the Aboriginal Continuity, geomancy refers to the process of divining, knowing, and acting through signs, lines, and designs manifest by planet Earth.

Through the classic agricultural civilizations and the subsequent era of mystic exaltation, geomancy provided the perfect fusion between what were later to be called art and science. It was only during the dreadful industrial ascendancy that geomancy all but disappeared as a legitimate force in the unfolding of civilization. Only the romantic had any recollection of the force and nature of geomancy. Yet, even for the romantic, geomancy was much more a matter of nostalgia than truth to be acted upon.

But all of that is over now.

With the issuance of this Weather Report, we, the RTAs—Resident Terrestrial Agents—sound the alert! This is the moment of the Romant-Geomant Transposition! Since there is no man or woman who does not possess the art enzyme, there is virtually no one incapable of responding to the advent of the Geomant Front. Only the build-up of psychic hardware from previous stages can determine how long it will be before a given individual will respond to the synthesizing Geomant Front.

In the meantime, those whose perceptual passageways are not so sand-bagged by materialist distortions are now being imprinted with the dire, but joyous responsibility to join in the process of amalgamating into Art Spores.

Take heed, and have no fear! Join the ranks of the RTAs in forming the Planet Art Network! Art Now! War No More! With the heart of a warrior, make the art that heals! No split between art and life, art and science, art and politics! Art is the way of the RTA! Know who you are! The Geomant Front is already upon us! Art Now! War No More!

This Weather Report issued in benign aspiration for the intelligent furtherance of all sentient beings.

Well, beloved CHV, that encapsulates my own Report. Since the broadcasting of the RTA Weather Report, my work is certainly going to go somewhat easier. After all, it is always with the greatest gratification that we observe another planet casting its VOTE!

José A. Argüelles,
Boulder, Colorado
August 6-9, 1982
(37 AH)

www.ingramcontent.com/pod-product-compliance
Lightning Source LLC
Chambersburg PA
CBHW082058090726
47909CB00011B/3074